W9-CSN-097

RUIN

BY ISOBEL NOBLE

Isobel Noble

BOOK ONE: THE TENT CITY

COPYRIGHT © 2005

AN EARTHBOUND BOOK
PUBLISHED IN THE BERKSHIRES, MASSACHUSETTS

ISBN 0-9771818-0-4

PUBLISHED IN THE BERKSHIRES, MASSACHUSETTS
PRINTED BY THE STUDLEY PRESS, DALTON, MASSACHUSETTS

Cover by the Author

Lo! Death has reared himself a throne
In a strange city lying alone
Far down within the dim West,
Where the good and the bad and the worst and the best
Have gone to their eternal rest.
There, shrines and palaces and towers
(Time-eaten towers that tremble not)
Resemble nothing that is ours...

Edgar Allen Poe, "The City in the Sea"

PROLOGUE

His parents were fighting, again.

Behind the tapestry hanging that separated his sleeping area from the rest of his mother's tent, Deke Wolfson heard the blow, heard his mother's cry of shock and pain, heard his father curse her for a witch before storming from the graceful pavilion.

Slowly, he sank down on the lynx-pelt throw that covered his bed. The fights always began the same way, with his father accusing his mother of one infidelity or another perpetrated when he was away to war. His mother generally laughed and pointed out that Barr Wolfson, great leader of all the Wolf People, was known near and far for his appetite for young women.

This usually made Barr roar, for it enraged him to think his business was so well-known to his beautiful, wise, and thus far, completely unmanageable wife, Tilva.

The fact was, the boy mused, cupping his chin in one square, brown hand, his mother was chaste. He'd been into every bit of Wolf business since infancy, and would have known otherwise. In every way Tilva seemed to play the perfect wife, caring for him and his father meticulously.

Deke's red-gold curls fell unheeded over his face and his brilliant, blue eyes grew more intense. It must be that, he decided. It must be that his mother merely play-acted the role, for her own reasons. His father liked to own things, but he could not own Tilva. Tilva was the People's foremost witch woman, and such a one never could be tamed fully even by a chieftain.

I will never marry, Deke thought matter-of-factly.

He rose quickly, a lithe, well-coordinated youngster who moved with uncanny grace and fluidity. His skin was sun-bronzed even in early winter, a result of ultra-violet exposure caused by the war's depletion of the ozone layer. Many faint scars criss-crossed his flesh, the minor wounds of a healthy, active twelve-year-old, with the occasional deeper wound gotten during the rigorous weapons training a chieftain's son had to undergo each day of his life. He shook his gleaming hair from his forehead with a characteristic gesture, and checked to be sure he had his knife and slingshot in his carrying sack.

"Mother," he called. "I'm going out."

Tilva came from behind the hangings, his stoicism moving her as always. That tawny mask he wore would cripple him as it had crippled his father, as it crippled all the people of the Wolf. Tilva's people came from the south, almost at the edge of the world. Proximity to the ruins had taught them

5

that life could be short, therefore it was something to be nurtured. Wolf folk, on the other hand, were nomads, warlike and proud. They were hardier, more self-contained than southerners. Frequently Tilva could see these two sides battling within her son. Right now he was all Wolfson. She motioned him towards her and gave him a swift kiss, smoothing his hair with a gentle hand, noticing how tall and straight he had become.

"Off with you, then," she said, hiding her thoughts.

His eyes shifted to meet hers before moving away. "Everything will be all right," he muttered roughly, wishing he could say more. Then he sped from the tent.

Tilva looked after him, her throat aching. "No tears," she told herself sternly. She had given up crying long ago. Her people now lived peacefully to the south because seventeen years previously, at fifteen, she had been handed over by her father to the bearded chieftain of the barbaric wildmen who had swept down out of the north threatening to plunder everything of worth her people possessed. From the moment the horsemen thundered into her city, she had felt Barr Wolfson's eyes singling her out. Somehow she had known what he wanted, had understood the price he would demand for their survival.

Normally Tilva had few regrets. She'd always craved adventure, and in the early years of riding behind her husband had come to love the boisterous, colorful bandit, for she learned that within his own frame of reference, Barr was neither cruel nor unjust, merely absolute in his power and voracious in his appetites.

She sighed and twisted her dark hair into a knot on the back of her neck. It was freezing in the tent, and her breath made smoke in the air. She called for servants to bring a brazier, despising the cold. Spring will come soon, she told herself, rubbing her reddened fingers together briskly.

A shiver rippled through her as she contemplated the arrival of spring, and Deke's thirteenth birthday. Thirteen had its own meaning for boys. The rites of passage for young men were terrifying and barbaric, and Tilva wondered how her son, unusually intelligent and gifted with the *sensitivity*, would endure the trials of the Wolf.

She withdrew her forecasting tiles from their deerskin pouch and sat at a broad table set convenient to the kitchen area. She'd never dared look at the time of Deke's testing before, fearing she might betray an anxiety that would cripple her son and keep him from being able to outthink fate, karma, or whatever was necessary to survive. But now, filled with inexplicable foreboding, Tilva prepared her mind for casting the tiles. She had to know if her son was to fail this spring as did many youths, or whether he would succeed to become veritable king over a domain stretching three hundred miles in every direction, controlling more than half a million souls and a hundred communities, the largest area and population to be united under one ruler since the great war more than a millennium earlier.

Her hands barely quivered as she made her first cast, studying the position of each tile with accomplished skill. They hadn't fallen in any resolved patterns. Reluctantly, she gathered them up and threw once more. Again there was no discernible pattern. A small frown formed between her brows. Third time would tell the tale. With great care she picked up the tiles, and muttering a quick prayer to her personal spirit guide, let them fly. She stared disbelievingly at the table. The tiles still lay in random and meaningless heaps. There was nothing for her adept clairvoyance to *see*. This was very unusual, and meant her spirit guide didn't wish to divulge Deke's future to her.

Agitated, Tilva returned the tiles to their pouch. Later, when she was calmer, she would try again. In the meantime, she would meditate, for perhaps the fault lay with her own concentration.

Huddling deeper into her cloak, she looked up as servants brought the brazier of hot coals and set it nearby. She stretched her hands towards the heat thankfully, and cursed the cold anew. Nothing good could come of a people who loved ice and snow, she philosophized dourly, for they were the worshippers of death.

Light snow was falling as Deke made his way down the hill away from his mother's tent. He drew his heavy cloak closer about him and pulled the hood down across his eyes. His sheepskin boots made no sound in the two or three inches of new snow layering the ground, and all the noises of the community were muffled as people hurried to get under cover.

From his tent at the top of the hill, Barr Wolfson watched his son's progress through the snowstorm and marked his direction. Damn his eyes! Had the boy been in his mother's tent throughout that whole spat?

As usual, Barr's feelings were mixed. On the one hand, he knew the constant domestic battles were scarring his son, and this he would end if he could. But on the other hand, the boy had replaced the father in his wife's heart, and this rankled Barr, making him shout at Deke when really it wasn't the lad's fault Tilva was what she was. Aye, what wouldn't he give to see affection just once in his boy's eyes instead of the usual caution!

Barr scrubbed his red beard with both hands, his midnight-blue eyes narrowed to crevices. His broad, massive frame was powerful with no trace of fat along the ridged musculature. He was dressed in sheepskin and leather; sheepskin-lined leather boots, wool-lined doeskin trousers and parka, with a fur-trimmed winter cloak over all. He was better than six feet tall with authority ingrained into every inch of him. Barr Wolfson could wither a man with a stare and fell a steer with a blow of his fist. Yet for all his physical and intellectual force, he couldn't intimidate the witch or her witch's whelp. He didn't know what tricks she was teaching the boy, but he knew in his heart the boy was learning something. There were times when Deke's brilliant eyes seemed to travel all the way through him, and at those times Barr felt he had been assessed and found wanting. This infuriated him, for who was a child to judge a proven man? And why should the boy be so stiff-necked in his appraisals?

Barr's own great vitality protested his son's nature, because he sensed Deke didn't love life. This saddened him, for despite his tempers and tantrums, the chieftain celebrated each day with relish and gusto. If it weren't for Tilva's and Deke's strangeness, he would be content. Especially if Tilva would learn her place and stay in it.

A wry smile touched his lips. Not bloody likely, he thought with grim humor. She hadn't changed since the first day he had seen her and fallen wildly, obsessively, in love with her. Aye, what a woman she had been, even at fifteen. He'd had to have her for his wife, despite the warnings of advisors who predicted that southern ways were insidious, and treachery must be her only motive in agreeing to come along with him. Barr knew that might have been true in the beginning, but after a time her passion had rivaled his own. At least, he modified, until the day her love for him had died and become instead a studied and dutiful acquiescence. He frowned slightly, remembering that day, and wondered what madness had been upon him that he should have come to his young wife without first bathing the stench of that fort whore from his flesh.

A large, wolfish dog who until now had rested silently at his feet, stirred and stretched. Absently, Barr reached down to stroke the animal's head, and for a moment considered calling out to his son. Then, changing his mind, he wondered why he should. To apologize? To explain? What would be the point? So long as the boy lived with his mother, there would remain that distance between them.

Next year, Barr thought, when he's a man and has his own tent, then we'll see about mending things between us. After all, Deke was a boy any man should be proud to call son and heir: smart, sound, and with that special glow which won men's and women's hearts alike. The boy had charisma, Barr acknowledged honestly. If only he were a bit more...something, Barr didn't know what, couldn't quite put his finger on what it was that made Deke strange to his heart of hearts.

By the ruins, he loved the boy. If he also felt combative around him then it was his job as man and father to put those feelings aside. He nodded to himself and watched his son's back disappear beyond the edge of the Wolf encampment where the chieftain's horses were stabled.

A few moments later, Deke re-appeared astride his own horse, a fiery mare of about four years. He rode with only a hackamore, his seat impeccable.

He drummed his heels against the mare's flanks and she leaped forward. For a second Barr thought his son was riding to greet him, then a slow burn started in his temples as he realized the boy had seen him but had deliberately turned his horse away to disappear behind a line of tents belonging to the less high, the laborers and merchant classes.

Ah, my son, he thought, you will pay for that insolence with unpleasant chores which you hate. Maybe that will temper your arrogance a little. Barr turned and stalked into his tent, the dog following.

Deke called his mare Micmac after the people who had bred the sire and studded him to a Wolfson brood mare. In color she was grey, white, brown, and black, with the clear and flashy markings prized by the People. Within a thousand yards there wasn't a horse who could stay near her. She had been given to Deke for his twelfth birthday, and he had trained her himself.

The snow was flying thicker and faster, and there was a cold wind behind it promising twenty-four hours of foul weather. Deke squinted against the blowing flakes. Going back was unthinkable. Micmac pranced restlessly beneath him as he glanced indecisively from left to right. Then, making up his mind, he wheeled the mare west into the oncoming wall of snow, away from escarpments that stood like sentinels along the borders of the ruins.

Tilva paced her tent, every so often glancing at the spring-wound fort clock that adorned one corner. It had been built by folk who lived west of the People's wintering grounds, and taken during a raid of conquest. It was one of the first gifts Barr had given her, back in the days when their marriage was new and filled with the hopes of two cultures.

The boy had been gone too long. The wind howled outside, shaking the tent with its fury. The blizzard was worse than anyone had anticipated, and Tilva was beside herself with worry.

A sudden blast of icy air chilled her anew, and she turned to see Barr tying fast the door. Snow fell from his cloak and gathered about his boots. The wolfish dog settled near the brazier, black eyes gleaming in the lamplight.

"Call Deke out here," Barr growled.

"He's gone," Tilva said.

Barr's scowl deepened. "He was here before," he said accusingly. "Listening!"

"He lives here," Tilva stated curtly.

"Never mind. I saw him and that pony hightailing it. I thought sure he'd be back by now."

"You let him go in this weather?" Tilva's eyes began to burn and she took a step closer to her husband.

"He's nearly a man, or so he keeps telling me." The chieftain's expression was cold and his tone held a warning.

"He's a boy of twelve," Tilva spat. "Only a boy."

"And so you'd keep him, eh, woman?" Barr unfastened his cloak and threw back the hood.

"Don't get too comfortable," Tilva replied stiffly. "I intend sleeping alone tonight."

Barr's eyes stayed level. "Perhaps." He went to the table and poured wine. "He probably went to see Mastra." He turned the wine goblet in his hand, admiring it, recalling the village he had plundered to obtain it. "That's where he'll turn up."

Tilva shook her head. "No. He's in the storm."

"Despite your best efforts, the boy has sense enough to come in out of a blizzard!"

"Yes, my lord. But at this moment he is alone in the wilderness to the west."

Barr studied her. Her voice had the odd cadence it got when spirits spoke through her, and utterances made at these times were never in vain or casually stated. Barr didn't understand such matters very well, but he knew there were powers abroad in the world which acted whether a man understood them or not, believed in them or not. He was intimately acquainted with the power that moved within Tilva at certain moments, using her body as an instrument of expression. It was this entity that gave Tilva her abilities not only to heal and divine future events, but to *see* into human minds and hearts.

"What is he doing there?" he asked finally.

"He is meeting his greater Self."

A wave of superstitious fear washed through him. "Do you mean he's dying?"

The voice was Tilva's again. "No," she said. "But he will die if someone doesn't find him soon."

Barr's expression hardened and he went to the tent flap where he called for a servant. When a woman came, mufflered against the storm, he spoke tersely. She bobbed a curtsey to him, cast a worried glance at Tilva, and fled from the tent. Barr refastened his cloak, strode through the hangings into the boy's quarters and swept up a spare boot. "Canis!" he called, and the dog came to stand expectantly at his feet. "Mark it, Canis. Find Deke."

At the mention of the boy's name the dog pricked up his ears. He sniffed the boot deeply and barked, moving impatiently for the door.

Barr tossed the boot to Tilva, then threw open the door flaps. Canis bounded eagerly into the snow and Barr plodded after him, the storm making him a dark shadow before swallowing him from sight. Tilva came to the tent door and looked out with foreboding. The snowflakes were tiny and driven by a gale force wind. Already her husband's footprints were nearly obliterated. It would be a miracle if they found the boy, she thought. Even the dog wouldn't be able to catch a scent in such a storm. She drew down the flaps and looped them shut. Still the sound of the wind reached her, and on it she thought she heard the distant scream of a lion, though she couldn't be sure.

I've been here before, Deke thought numbly, feeling as if his essential self had drawn inward away from the lash of the storm, finding a quiet refuge where he could hear himself think. This place, this situation; I know it, I recognize it.

His mind was filled with unusual clarity. He felt that if he could only separate from his physical situation he would be able to *see* everything, and know what to do. Even now, a part of him was doing just that, and he sensed a wisp of emotion that had to be his mother's seeking out into the blizzard. It was easy for him to sidestep that probe. He had known for a long time that his own gift of sensitivity far outshone hers. He also knew one must want to be found before he could be found in fact.

He sensed the bearlike presence of his father riding behind Canis, and it was the dog who made him most wary. Canis was of the wild ruins breed, and possessed heightened sensitivity in those areas pertinent to his species' survival, particularly tracking prey. If anyone could find him against his will it would be the dog.

Micmac whinnied loudly as a particularly fierce blast of wind drove stinging particles of snow against her tender muzzle. The sound dragged Deke back to the frozen landscape and he examined his predicament with slowly accelerating panic. He could barely feel his extremities. His horse was moving uncertainly in a slow circle, unwilling or unable to proceed directly into the wind. When he looked around, he realized he had no idea where he was. Visibility was zero. His disorientation progressed, and with a cushioned thump, he landed on the ground at his horse's feet. With shocked surprise, he stumbled to his feet and clutched the mare's lead rope. Which way should he go?

As if in answer to his unspoken question, a heavily cloaked figure appeared at his side and silently lifted him onto Micmac's back. Taking the lead in one fur-mitted hand, the stranger set off into the snowstorm, leading horse and boy behind him.

Deke made no effort to struggle. Whether captor or rescuer, at this moment the stranger represented salvation, and Deke was too cold and confused to argue or worry about it.

Together they faded into the storm, and moments later, wind and snow erased their tracks completely.

Deke became aware of warmth and light, stony walls and leaping shadows; knew he lay on a fur-covered platform inside a cave. His ears told him Micmac and other horses were nearby, as well as a single person preparing food. His stomach gave a growl as he propped himself on an elbow.

A spare, doeskin-clad man knelt by a fireplace. He threw a pinch of something into the flames and the fire leapt up in a flurry of sparks and smoke.

Unexpectedly, Deke felt awe. It was something about the man's face.

Ancient, it was, criss-crossed with a thousand lines. His eyes were black and deeply set, and they, too, gave an impression of great age. The hair was silver and worn in long braids, contrasting sharply with the mahogany hue of his flesh.

Deke watched for a moment longer, registering him. "Who are you?"

Jet eyes regarded the boy penetratingly. "I am myself and selves," he said, his voice rich and crisp.

"I'm Deke Wolfson. Thank you for helping me." He gestured to the cave. "Do you live here?"

"Here, there, many places. For now, I am here."

"Where exactly is here?"

"Here is where we are." Humor twinkled briefly in the black eyes before he lowered his gaze to the fire once again, whether to hide laughter or watch the stewpot Deke couldn't be sure.

"What are you cooking?" He sniffed appreciatively.

The man ladled a generous portion into a wooden bowl and offered it with a spoon.

Deke climbed from the bed, relieved to find the cold had done him no lasting damage. He took the bowl, tasted the steaming mixture. A combination of meat and root vegetables thickened with grains and herbs, he noted. Delicious.

The man took a portion for himself and settled back on his haunches to eat. Until his bowl was clean, he said nothing further. Noticing the boy's bowl was empty, he gestured to the pot. Though he easily could have eaten more, Deke refused another helping. Winters were hard this far north, and it was possible the old man needed every bit of his rations.

"Your people are seeking you," the old man said, handing across a skin of drinking water.

A twinge of remorse passed through the boy as he quenched his thirst. He imagined his mother's desperation, and, if truth were to be told, his father's as well. "Aye," he replied. "But how would you know that? Does my father know you?"

"Our paths have crossed." The old man's eyes were shrewd as he watched Deke. "Come, I will show you a *brujo* secret, and then we will sleep until Mother Storm has passed." He withdrew a leather pouch from his belt and removed a carefully wrapped bundle. On a flat rock, he set an unusually carved wooden pipe and a box covered with bizarre symbols.

"Brujo?"

"First we will smoke," he said to the wide-eyed youngster. "This is an act designed to open the way."

"What way?" Deke asked, his trepidation overpowered by curiosity. He watched while his host opened the wooden box and took a generous pinch of the substance inside between his fingers. Rolling it into a ball, he dropped the stuff into the pipe bowl. Then he offered the pipe stem-first.

Deke admired the smooth, worn feel of the wood, appreciating the superior craftsmanship that had gone into its carving. Then he fumbled quickly in the fire and popped a small coal onto the smoking mixture, his fingers moving too swiftly to be burned. He looked up and met the dark gaze watching him. He felt something momentous was about to happen, and his eyes were alight with anticipation. Before he could lose his nerve, he put the stem to his lips and drew, filling his lungs with cold, aromatic smoke that expanded the longer it was inside him, until with a choking gasp, he exhaled in a strangled cough.

Lungs aching, he looked up to see the old man's silent scrutiny.

"Again," the old one said.

"Is this tobacco?" Deke asked hoarsely. He felt warm all over.

"No questions. Smoke."

Deciding the fellow hadn't rescued him merely to kill him in this weird way, Deke raised the pipe and inhaled strongly. Again he exploded with coughing, but this time the fit passed more quickly. When he had himself under control, he realized he was discovering things, things like the many-textured surfaces of the stones comprising this cave, surfaces that breathed. There was a pattern to the way the smoke curled upward from the fire, traveling along a thermal pathway into a crack in the rocky ceiling, and thence, Deke supposed, out of the cave and into the world. For an instant he felt himself following the smoke, as incorporeal as it was, but he caught himself and looked out through changed eyes.

The old man's face appeared different. Nuances of expression were visible where before he had seemed impenetrable. The boy gazed wonderingly and barely noticed when the pipe was removed from his nerveless fingers.

"Too loosely tethered," he heard the man say. "We have begun just in time."

"You were going to show me a secret." Deke heard his voice but felt nothing. His tongue and lips were numb, his eyes glazed, the pupils dilated.

His mind swam. He saw the old man's hand reach to touch his heart, and gasped when it made contact. Images flowed across his thoughts in an accelerating rush.

He saw ugly, mushroom clouds spreading their deadly dust over the earth; saw steel and concrete buildings exploding in a nanosecond's flash of nuclear fire. He saw the clouds raining down radioactive deluges that soon turned to snow as the sun's rays were reflected back into space and the planet began to cool. He heard the old one's voice in his head, but the words didn't make much sense.

Further images swept across his mind's eye: of straggling survivors who scurried like animals to find a scrap in the wasteland, of ragged men and women grouping together into scattered tribes and communities.

There were some who turned their backs on the world and barricaded themselves into walled towns; fort dwellers, Deke thought with the contempt all his people felt for such folk.

A moment later the images shifted to display his own people as they had developed over the years. Like the Mongols of ancient times, Deke's ancestors dwelt in the saddle, moving their herds, living off the land.

A man's face appeared among the many, and Deke knew this was the chieftain, but the features, though familiar, were unknown to him.

The old man removed his hand from Deke's breast, and the boy felt as if an intimate connection had been broken, which in fact it had.

"Do you recognize that man?"

Deke waited, aware the question was rhetorical.

"He was your grandfather, my young chief. He laid the foundation for the conquests of your sire's chieftainship. Though Barr later outstripped by far the deeds of his father, Rael Wolfson designed the model of what was to be."

"I never met my grandfather," Deke said. "He died before I was born."

"You favor him somewhat," the old man said. "Like your father."

"So I've been told," Deke replied.

"And yet, superficial resemblance aside, you favor Rael and Barr not at all."

"What do you mean?" Deke was on guard. He knew he was different, but how could this person know that? With difficulty, he tried to order his thoughts. He felt disconnected from his body, and realized what it meant to be "too loosely tethered." The old man hadn't referred to his sanity, but to his Self. As he examined the implications of this meeting, dismayed awareness swelled in his mind. "You didn't find me by chance," he stated flatly.

The old one nodded. "You are as quick as I was told you would be," he said after a pause during which he analyzed the limits to which he could push the boy in this, their first conversation.

"Who told you?" Deke demanded with bitter disappointment. "My mother? My father?"

"Both. But I would have found you in any case." The old man gestured vaguely. "The rocks, the wind, the earth told me to watch for you. I have been waiting a long time."

"Why?" Deke's face was taut with anger and betrayal.

"Because of who you are. Unless you learn everything I teach you, all will be lost."

Deke seemed to feel a wind blowing through him, as if he were hollow and insubstantial. The old man's voice was filled with such compassion and gentle awareness that his anger abruptly died. "What are you doing to me?"

"You are no helpless child," the old man said sharply. "I do nothing. You do it all."

"But who are you?"

"When it is important for you to know, you will."

"You don't expect I'll put myself further in your hands without knowing, do you?"

"You are in your own hands, Master Wolfson. I am merely sent to show you the way."

"The way," Deke repeated, confused.

"Yes. Come. Arise! Destiny awaits." The old man rose and beckoned.

Filled with misgivings, Deke got up and followed him towards the back of the cave, where numerous recesses were hidden in eerie shadows thrown by the sparking fire.

He trailed the old one into darkness that deepened as they moved away from the hearth. He stretched his hands before him to ward off any potential collision either with the walls or, he smiled a grim, grownup smile, his destiny. He thought now of his mother's words on the subject, that each human had his own destiny, or karma, his own purpose for choosing to be born.

They emerged from the passageway into a natural cavern. Crystal rock formations emitted spectral radiance. The quality of light was fey and unearthly. A mist gathered about his feet as Deke came to a halt, staring. His eyes had to be playing tricks, he decided. What he saw couldn't possibly be real.

Stretching as far as he could see were row upon row of metal shelves, and stacked upon those shelves were more books than the boy had seen in his life, more than he had dreamed existed or could exist in his world. He had the oddest feeling that he could walk along those stacks and never reach the end of them, that they, and the cavern in which they were preserved, were infinite in dimension.

"Ruins," he whispered, afraid to disturb the sanctity of the place.

"Stored here is a repository of the most important and essential records, works of literature, technical and scientific manuals extant today. How or why these books are here is not important; that you make use of them in our time together, is." The old man peered intently at the boy.

"What is this place?"

The old one shrugged. "It is a library. Almost any subject you can think of is represented in these texts, and there is a cunning catalog system located over there in that wall of drawers."

"Are only books stored here?" Deke asked. "Or might there be other things, maybe in further grottos?"

"What kinds of things?"

Deke hesitated. In his mind's eye he saw a vision of another underground place filled not with books but with the steel-cold weapons of war.

The old man frowned. "I *see* what you are thinking. Any weapons preserved from ancient days are better left unfound. Look what they wrought! Look what they brought down."

"Maybe the old ways had to be brought down," Deke said thoughtfully.

"Why would you say this?"

"Before one can plant this year's crops, one must cut down last year's withered stalks."

"That is an analogy of youth, my young philosopher." The old man's eyes were rueful. "Sometimes there is still fruit to be gleaned from a withered stalk."

"I'll be expected to make war soon," Deke said. "Until I kill a man in battle, I can't possibly command respect among Wolf fighters. If I can find a better weapon than my enemy has, it's to my advantage."

The old man was chilled by the boy's matter-of-fact tone as he casually discussed taking another human being's life. He looked into Deke's amazingly blue eyes and tried hard to fathom the boy's soul. There was anger in Deke, he decided, but no sadism or evil. The boy was not one of those who would take pleasure in another's pain. Yet he recognized that this was a creature bred to wage war, and to wage it effectively. Establishing dominion was in the nature of Wolfsons; he had known this when first he had planned taking over the boy's education and training some years ago. It was the type of society he would create within his dominion that interested and concerned the old man. Yes, he was very concerned about that, yet he must make no overt attempt to indoctrinate or propagandize the youngster, because he also sensed a deep and abiding stubbornness in Deke, and it would take only one false step on his part to alienate the boy forever.

"Come," he said lightly. "Choose a book to take home with you. I know you read well."

"Aye," Deke responded. He paused, then said without obvious guile but with charm the old man found irresistible, "If you wouldn't mind, I'd be honored if you would choose one for me."

The old man was pleased. He knew the boy had tried deliberately to make him so, but still he was gratified. "I will pick one for you this time," he said, "But next time you must make the choice. Are we agreed?"

"Aye," Deke replied, eagerness growing in him, hungry to discover what secrets these books held. He wondered how many the old man had read, and found himself jealous of his host's superior learning.

"Let us begin at the beginning," the old man said. He pulled a small volume from the shelves and turned to the boy. "Handle this with care. It has been treated to make it resistant to damage, but nevertheless is an ancient thing and fragile."

Deke looked at the cover. "This is a children's book."

"Oh, so it might seem at first. But do not be fooled. It was written this way for a reason, and when next I see you, you will tell me that reason."

The boy's face was doubtful as he turned the volume over in his hand. The title was not inspiring, and he wondered why the old man would want him to read a child's primer on agriculture. What possible interest could a chieftain's son have in such a book?

He read aloud, "Animal Farm, by George Orwell."

"Yes," the old man said with satisfaction.

Later, lying in the furs and blankets provided for him, Deke thought about the book grotto, the *library*, and felt that his brief sojourn there had had about it the timeless quality of a dream. He knew this impression would never fade over the years, that he would carry the experience of his first visit to that place with him for the rest of his life. So many books, he thought sleepily. And if books, perhaps other things. Maybe not here, but somewhere. He felt sure of it. And if they existed, then he would find them.

He would.

The morning sun was dazzling on the fresh snowscape as Deke led Micmac from the cave. His book was carefully tucked away in his carrying sack and he had eaten a light breakfast. He grasped the mare's mane and with a quick spring was on her back. The old man stood by the horse's head, looking up.

"Thank you for your hospitality," Deke said. "I'd like to return, if you'll have me."

The old man nodded. "It is decided." He paused. "Are you certain you can find your way?"

"Aye," Deke said, and it was true. Today in the clear, morning air he knew exactly where he was, often had ridden past this very spot with his friends. What amazed him was that he never had noticed a cave. None of them had. Now that he knew where to look, it seemed impossible to have missed it.

He shook his hair out of his eyes and lifted one hand in salute. Then he turned his horse and headed away from the rocky escarpments towards home.

When next Deke looked back over his shoulder, he saw the old man sitting high atop a great rock, facing into the rising sun. His eyes were closed and his lips moved, and the boy could hear faint chanting. He shivered, for he was having the strangest feeling, the oddest notion. It seemed to him the old man was chanting a prayer of thanks to the spirit of the storm. The thought came and went quickly, but not before a part of him registered and was stupefied by the implications of such a thing. Then, making a face, he faced front again, dismissing the idea as childish superstition. No matter what strange lore he possessed, the old man was only that: an old man. He could no more command the storms than could Deke.

The ride home was laborious and he was glad when he came over the last rise and saw the widespread tents of his city laid out before him.

He had been spotted by lookouts miles previously, and now he saw the reception committee coming out to greet him; men and women who had spent the night searching through the snowstorm, small children for whom the excitement was an interesting novelty, and behind everyone, Barr and Tilva Wolfson. Seeing his parents together and moving as a unit caused the boy an internal lurch, as if events had progressed in his absence and he was now a step out of the earlier rhythms of his life.

Already he was devising the story he would tell them, for he had decided not to mention his encounter with the old man. His friend Mastra, a tall, lean youth with brown skin, crinkly hair, and warm, dark eyes moved into position alongside Micmac, lending his support.

"Where did you go?" Mastra whispered. "What a hornet's nest you've stirred up!"

"Later," Deke murmured back. "Stay close. They won't make a scene if you're here."

Mastra nodded and the two boys' eyes met, the one's dark, the other's light, yet there was a resemblance between them, something in the set of their cheekbones.

Deke's look was one of gratitude for his friend's presence, then he turned to face the mob. He flashed a grin and a roar of greeting went out over the snow separating them. Then he was among them, feeling hands patting him, reaching for him, as the Wolf People welcomed their wandering cub home.

CHAPTER ONE

What makes a man? What distinguishes the man from the boy he was? Strength? Experience? Ceremony?

The General always said that what made a man was his ability or inabilty to face the unknown by himself. Easy to be brave in a group, he reckoned, that's the child's way, the gang mentality. But to be brave when there was no one to witness the bravery or lack of it, that was the measure of a man or woman. And that, he affirmed, was what made the People of the Wolf so special.

Yet even as he told me this, his expression was troubled, as if memory belied his confident words...

— Ourn Rohlvaag; Collected Journals; City of Life, A.D. 3109

T he day dawned warm, and a hot breeze blew off the ruins. Scattered bits of ancient rubble glittered in the sunlight; flashes of fire adding heat to the day. As far as the eye could see lay desolation. Everything was brown or grey, covered with silt-like alkali dust mixed with ash. It seemed nothing could live in this vast wasteland, but that was an illusion. The ruins were home to a variety of creatures, not all of them natural or recognizable. Mostly, people prospered best who avoided the worst devastation zones.

Except for us, Deke thought as he stood with a dozen other boys preparing to be initiated into the mysteries of male adulthood. In the weeks to come more would follow, but these were the season's first, all sons of highly placed men. His friend Mastra alone was fatherless, without traditional rank or status, but from earliest childhood had been included in the events and ceremonies of the highest ranked chiefs. That this was in deference to his friendship with Deke was the official story. The truth was more complicated and only a few understood it completely.

The previous night the boys had been awakened by none-too-gentle, gruff-speaking men who made them dress, put dark sacks over their heads, and led them to horses they were helped to mount. Each was told to remain silent, not to speak for any reason. Then they had ridden away at a stiff trot, each boy trying to quell the trepidation in his heart even as he clung to his horse's mane.

At dawn they had stopped, here, wherever here was. The sacks were removed and they were permitted a few minutes to allow their eyes to adjust to the light. There were two men attending each boy, the men cloaked and masked. The boys had no way of knowing if their own fathers or brothers were among those present. There was one extra man, robed and cowled entirely in black. He stood aside, pointedly ignoring the boys.

When the sun reached a certain angle, the black-robed man faced the group. He stood with the sun behind him, and such was his timing that his cowl eclipsed the light, making a corona of fiery brilliance around his head. Only his eyes were visible, and they glowed redly with ambient brightness. They fixed on each boy in turn, and each tried not to fidget beneath that unsettling gaze.

When the eyes turned to Deke, the chieftain's son lifted his chin defiantly. An unspoken challenge rippled between the two and the others shifted uneasily. It had been a long time since a future leader of the People had been tested.

"So you wish to be men," the robed figure rasped. "Yet you are afraid. You wonder what will happen to you. You fear pain and discomfort. You know nothing about these matters, yet you expect the worst. You are filled with expectations." The red-tinged eyes raked the group. "Little boys, believe me when I tell you that before this ritual is complete your expectations will be scorched out of you, never to return. Your expectations make you emotional. They make you weak. They keep you children." He paused dramatically. "When the ruins have had their way with you, you will have no more expectations." He paused again, then added, "That is, those of you who survive."

A collective shudder went through the boys.

"Now, strip," the man ordered curtly.

The boys looked uncertainly at one another, and some began to unfasten garments.

"Hurry up," said the man. "To enter manhood you must be as naked as the day you entered life. In a sense you are being born anew, and everything you hope to gain must now be found, made, or won." He waited in silence as the boys disrobed. When each stood uncomfortably naked next to his pile of clothes, he nodded to one of the men who brought him a rough, cloth sack. Reaching inside, he removed a hunting knife as long as a man's forearm. With a quick flick of his wrist, he threw it at the feet of the nearest boy, where it struck quivering in the ground. The boy stood transfixed. In rapid succession the man threw knives at the feet of all boys but one. His hooded gaze fell upon the chieftain's son.

"For the People's future leader, expectations are especially dangerous," he said, and there might have been a tinge of regret in his stern voice. "You go into the ruins truly naked, Master Wolfson. We shall see what blood you carry."

Deke's initial expression of surprise changed to one of comprehension. Thirteen boys into the ruins, he thought, twelve knives. He turned to look measuringly at his fellows and saw them watching him. He grinned reassuringly and winked. Then he turned back to the initiation master. "Not that kind," he said with bravado. "Not the blood of betrayal, you hooded hobgoblin!"

The robed man chuckled harshly. "Bravely spoken," he said. Then, to the group, "You have at your disposal all those things you find about you, those things you can make or devise from the environment, or whatever you can win by whatever means you choose. There are no rules." He paused and looked at the naked boys. Some actually shivered though the air was sultry.

"Remember," he added sharply. "These are ruins. Dangers lurk here. Animals, spirits, demons, the ruins themselves: all will test you before you emerge men." He nodded once, curtly. "You must find your way back here. When you get hungry enough and thirsty enough, you will have a vision or spontaneous awareness, and this will change you, help you. Remember! You begin alone, as prey. Those who survive must become predators, and learn the essential lesson of the Wolf." A final time the red-rimmed eyes raked the group. "Pick up your knives. You may not ask questions. The ruins will make every-thing clear."

One by one the boys obeyed.

The black-robed man nodded to the other men. Sacks were whisked over the boys' heads once more, and each was put aboard a horse.

"Remember!" he shouted after them as they departed. "You are on your own! Do what you must!"

The group of riders separated into pairs of men, each leading a blind-folded boy into the ruins, each pair finding a route away from the others.

The sack was stifling. Sound came to him muffled by burlap. Deke couldn't perceive direction or terrain, though it soon became apparent he was accompanied by only two men. He was uncomfortable; the tender skin of his scrotum and buttocks was getting chafed by the rough, leather saddle, and the sun burned ever hotter across his bare shoulders. Sweat broke out on his body as he tried to resign himself to the various physical discomforts, the purpose of which, he suspected, was to soften him up.

They jogged steadily for hours. When they stopped and he was allowed to dismount, they removed the sack from his sweat-drenched head and handed him a skin of water.

"Drink deep, Master Wolfson," one of the men said in a deep, eerily familiar voice. "It's the last ye'll see unless it's by yer own ingenuity."

Deke looked around, trying to get his bearings. The sun was at zenith. He raised the waterbag and drank as much as he could hold, then drank a bit more.

"Good luck," the men said when he handed it back. They mounted their horses and rode away, leading his. He knew he could try to follow their trail, but on horseback they could lay so many false tracks and paths that there was no point in wasting his time. Even now it was certain they weren't heading in any useful direction. He looked at the ruins, trying to find a distinguishing landmark, anything to give him a clue as to where he might be. He'd been on a few forays into the ruins during training, always with a well-armed group, never alone, certainly never naked. Nothing like this, he thought.

The area was depressingly bleak, with dust everywhere and occasional tumbled hills that might conceal anything. Cracks and crevasses and sinkholes stretched as far as he could see. As he scanned the landscape, the hair prickled involuntarily on the back of his neck. He looked quickly behind him and thought he saw a movement. He cast about for something to use as a weapon, anything, and picked up a couple rocks. He could hardly believe something would hunt him in the light of the noon sun, hadn't expected that anything would try until dark. He'd thought he'd have time to prepare.

His neck prickled again, and this time it felt as if a fingernail had trailed lightly up his spine, a very sharp, dangerous fingernail. Again he glanced back. Nothing. His stomach spasmed. He felt too vulnerable standing naked with only rocks in his hands. Attack or retreat? What would Hawk Farflight advise? Hawk was his weapons-master, had been teaching him and the other boys in his manhood group one-on-one combat techniques since they were old enough to grasp knives. When the enemy is unknown, he told himself, make him known.

He took a tentative step away from where he'd seen the movement, hot dust and gravel burning into the soles of his bare feet. Then he paused and waited, remembering everything he'd been told about the ruins, how a man had to be very strong in his head to withstand them, that one's own mind could become one's worst enemy.

Imagination, he finally decided, almost shaking with relief, his knees weak from tension. Nothing more. There was nowhere anything could hide, unless it burrowed into the dust.

With that thought, Deke strained his eyes harder, squinting against the sunlight. Again he felt something watching him, hunting him. Yet again it seemed to come from behind him.

This is crazy, he thought. What could be under the dust...?

This is a bad place, he decided. The Old Man had warned him there were places on the earth intrinsically detrimental to one's health and well-being, and this must be one of them.

Deke stretched his arms and legs, turned three hundred sixty degrees, and tried to get a sense of where he should go, what he should do. His life's training as a warrior helped him maintain his composure for now, but beneath that layer of imperturbability was a place where he realized he might be quite frightened if he allowed himself to feel it.

West, he decided finally, into the setting sun. Sunsets held significance for him on an unspoken level, drawing him, pulling at his center. He didn't know why he felt that way, thought it might be connected to his father's attraction for the West. He knew one day he would spy out the land there, and see if he could find anything worthy of a Wolfson's interest.

In the meantime he realized that when night fell he would need shelter. Demons lurked in ruins: beings without form or shape who attacked humans at their psyches' weakest link, draining their life-force. Demons were attracted to any psychic whiff of fear or weakness, actually becoming stronger in the presence of it. This Deke believed at the deepest levels of his awareness. He knew also that naked and unarmed as he was, he would be particularly attractive to demons.

He clutched the rocks tightly in his hands and picked up his pace. The afternoon progressed. Shadows stretched.

He jogged lightly through the ancient dust, senses tuned to the utmost, his breathing audible but measured. There had to be something he could use. Had to be.

He centered his mind in the way the Old Man had taught him, focusing on the inner creaks and rumblings of his body's functions. He listened to the even thump of his heart and the steady whoosh of his lungs pumping air. These sounds were familiar and reassuring. They had a calming effect, and soon he moved along without the rising swell of anxiety that had been threatening to overpower him.

He saw an antiquated skeleton silhouetted against the sky, standing as if suspended by strings, and blinked against the brilliant sunlight. The image resolved itself into a dead tree: small, shriveled, dry as bone. Its death could have come from drought or radiation, maybe both. He examined the tree critically, then, using one of the sharp stones he'd been carrying in his hands, laboriously cut three, straightish branches, each taller than himself and as thick through the middle as two of his thumbs. Painstakingly, he sharpened an end on each, working carefully so as not to shatter the ancient wood. Though dry, the limbs weren't rotten, and soon he had three crude but serviceable spears.

He hefted one in his right hand, testing it for weight and balance. Primitive, but effective at close range. Certainly possible to kill prey with such a weapon, even, he thought, armed prey.

He gathered the spears under his left arm, took up the rocks, and carefully scanned westward. Was there a dark patch visible out there, something shadowed in the otherwise uniform landscape? It was worth a look. With a quick glance to mark a line from the desiccated tree, he set off at a rapid, ground-covering trot, feeling a little more at home in this particular patch of ruins. He felt he had been helped, that the little tree had been a gift, and he thanked whatever force it was that might have given him aid. He stretched outward with his sensitivity, seeking to find the source of positive energy that now suffused him, but had to satisfy himself with the simple awareness of that energy, and use it to his advantage.

Deke's shadow lengthened behind him as he trotted steadily over the ruins, and the sound of his feet in the dust was no louder than a whisper. The whisper spoke to him in the sibilance of sand, of deserts out of time and mind. He felt the ruins penetrate him body and soul until he knew what they knew, witnessed what they had witnessed. This was his home, his place, his moment in the Universe. Here on earth's graveyard his people had been spawned and he was coming to manhood. All the men he knew had passed through these rites. If they could do it, he could, too. And, he told himself, he would do it better.

He grinned, filled with pride and pleasure in being alive, then stumbled over a chunk of crumbled cement half-buried in sod and came to a startled halt. His breath pumped faster as he stared at the increasingly green stretch of territory which lay before him. There were many tumbled ruins, growing more plentiful the farther he looked. Things lived here. Plants, probably animals. That meant food, water.

He looked back towards the dust desert. Gnawing his dry lips nervously, he tried to decide what to do next, what the authors of this ritual would have intended.

He heard a deep, grunting cough.

His stomach lurched and he gripped a spear in his right hand, turning slowly to find the source.

Deke felt his knees tremble. There was nothing in sight. The sound was inside his head, yet perfectly clear in his ears.

"Ruins help me," he muttered.

Again the sound came, this time stronger. Still Deke could see nothing, strain his eyes though he might. He recognized it now, remembered how the big cats made coughing grunts unlike other animals. He remembered, too, that only one species of cat could be heard inside a man's head, knew his people's wolfdogs followed the *psi* emanations given off by these cats the way bloodhounds of old had trailed prey by scent. Deke thanked his own sensitivity which had given him early warning of the danger. It was possible the cat known as the *esper* tiger was far enough away that he still might escape.

The sun's rays were decidedly longer now. The day was waning. This awareness filled him with renewed anxiety. He had to find shelter. He had no illusions about his chances if the tiger caught him in the open. He was a skilled hunter of deer and rabbit, had even killed a foul-tempered, long-tusked wild boar of the northern forests, but a big cat was something else, especially the stealthy, infinitely cunning, ruins tiger. A male could weigh as much as six hundred pounds and the females often went as high as four.

Deke quartered his gaze across the countryside, squinting carefully at any crack, any crevice rocky and protected enough into which he might squeeze. His instincts told him the tiger had detected him hours ago, had been toying with his psyche the way lesser cats toyed with their prey's physical selves.

The feeling of being sneaked up on was irresistible and he whirled, half-expecting to see the golden, black-striped esper tiger licking its chops behind him. Nothing. Relief made him break into a fresh sweat. He sighed audibly, turned back towards the greening ruins, took a step, then froze. His hands clutched spasmodically at spears that suddenly felt like brittle twigs in his sweating fingers.

Standing not fifty yards in front of him, tail lashing back and forth in nervous jerks, the esper tiger met his eyes with slitted gaze and bared its teeth.

Deke took in the animal's stance, size, and lean ferocity in a glance. Hunger radiated into his mind with palpable energy until he felt a sympathetic twinge in his own stomach. He got a picture of a small, furless rodent swallowed down in two bites, the cat's last meal taken days ago, not nearly sufficient for so large an animal. He saw himself through the tiger's eyes, felt the eager anticipation of a feline about to make a kill.

With a supreme effort, he forced himself to move his body into a more aggressive posture, unconsciously letting his teeth show in a snarl even as he brandished his spears with short jabs towards the cat. The external image of himself radiating into his mind changed. Now he looked less like prey, more like predator. He felt the tiger's increased caution, felt the creature calculating the odds.

Apparently making up its mind, the cat raked the ground with its claws and snarled with vicious power that made every hair on Deke's body rise involuntarily. He knew the terror that rolled through him making his knees weak, making his jaw quiver, was a purely evolutionary limbic response to the ancient confrontation between feline and primate, but knowing this did not reduce his terror. In his mind's eye he could see the long teeth crunching through his ribcage, could feel the slashing claws like razors in his young flesh.

The taste of blood was in his mouth as he took a step backwards.

The tiger paced forward, its every fiber radiating hunger, its entire being focused on the two-legged prey that crept away so temptingly. Here was a substantial meal at last, and the tiger wasn't about to let it escape. It snarled again, with deeper menace. Its tail whipped faster. Deke allowed the rocks and two of the spears he carried to drop onto the mossy turf beside him. He grasped the third, thickest, and longest spear in both hands, bracing himself for the tiger's charge. Part of him recognized the ludicrousness of the picture he presented; the tiger was four times his weight and armed with a far superior array of weapons.

Common sense dictated a hasty withdrawal, but there was nowhere to hide, nowhere to run. If he turned his back, the cat would be on him. His only hope was to make himself too much trouble for such an obviously hungry animal to waste its limited reserves on. With this thought, he stopped retreating, mentally as well as physically, and forced himself to look deep into the tiger's eyes, prepared to will the fierce creature into submission.

Nearby, a pebble skittered across a larger rock. Overhead, a cloud passed in front of the lowering sun. The tiger's gaze twitched so briefly Deke thought he had imagined it.

Now the big cat growled with savagery that made everything that had passed before sound benevolent. Every hair on its body stood up and it lifted its lips to show its immense teeth. In an instant Deke realized the tiger was no longer focusing on him. He flicked his eyes in the direction the tiger was looking and for a second couldn't process what he was seeing. Half its massive body hidden behind a boulder, one front paw resting easily on the bloody carcass of a fresh kill, stood a gigantic, brown bear. It roared a warning at the tiger, barely acknowledging the boy's presence.

Deke stood frozen, unable to take his eyes from the bear's kill. Though horribly torn and mutilated, the carcass was recognizable as that of a thirteen-year-old boy. A quick movement got his attention as the bear rose menacingly onto its hind legs. It loomed enormously over the landscape, a massive animal Deke thought only an idiot would confront willingly. He took an almost imperceptible step back, away from both tiger and bear. While they were engaged with each other, perhaps he could escape. He looked regretfully at the extra spears and rocks he was too frightened to pick up and eased backward, never taking his eyes from the two animals.

At once there was a deafening roar both outside and inside his head. The esper tiger was watching him, and Deke could swear the cat had ordered him to *stay put!* He squeezed his hands around the spear convulsively.

Eyes locked on the cat who flickered its gaze rapidly back and forth between him and the bear, Deke carefully moved his left foot. At the same moment he realized his foot was reaching into empty air, he saw the tiger accelerate towards him in a series of swift bounds. The bear bellowed furiously as Deke lost his balance and fell on his face. He slid back and down on his belly, feet-first through a small hole and into a narrow passageway. Clods of dirt and pebbles showered onto his head as the world disappeared from his frantic view. He still had the spear clutched in his fingers and it jostled his ribs painfully.

Moments later he jerked to a halt. The last of the grit and gravel that had accompanied him down the hole slowed, then stopped. When he looked back the way he had come he couldn't see the opening but could see the light, which reflected around a bend in the passageway and lit the earth dimly nearby.

There was a frustrated snarl above him and he heard claws tearing through the surface dirt. A huge shadow moved across the light, burying him in darkness. He felt a shuddering scream in his head as the esper tiger challenged the bear. Then he froze. He could swear he had felt something move against the soles of his feet. His straining ears picked up a sound like a whimper. The whimper was echoed by a bubbly little growl.

Now what? Deke thought feverishly, his senses reeling from too many successive shocks. Calling on reserves of courage he didn't know he possessed (and steeling himself for an attack by cave rats at the very least) he slithered out of the cramped passage and into the wider cavity that lay beyond. His hand brushed against something soft and fuzzy and he felt a warm, little tongue lick his fingers. Wolf pups! He was in a wolf den! He felt around carefully and located half a dozen of the young creatures. Needle sharp milk teeth closed on his fingers and he calculated that the puppies were perhaps four weeks old. But where was their pack?

His mind automatically catalogued these facts and questions while he listened to the frightening racket outside. One of the puppies whimpered again, and instinctively he murmured soothingly. He wriggled his way back up the passage to see what was going on.

Bare feet scrabbling for a purchase in the packed dirt, spear held protectively in front of him, he poked his head out for a moment, then as quickly pulled it in.

The bear and tiger were facing one another in a standoff, snarling, growling, making threatening gestures, neither willing to precipitate battle. The bear kept itself between the tiger and its kill; the tiger kept itself between the bear and the wolf den. Both were protecting their interests; neither could bring itself to turn away from the other. The esper tiger sent waves of hatred and ferocity directly into the bear's psyche but the bear was unmoved. It had faced down hungry felines before.

Deke could feel the edge of what the tiger was Sending and knew most creatures would have quailed before the onslaught. His own limbs were trembling just from the side impact of the cat's emotional energy broadcast.

Every few moments the bear glanced towards the den. Bears were notorious diggers and Deke dreaded the possibility of the animal deciding it liked boy meat enough to attack the tiger straightaway and take its intended prey. A panicky feeling rose in his throat. Bear claws could cut through the packed earth around the mouth of the den like blades through butter. And what would the tiger do if the bear made such an attack? Which animal would survive to come eat him?

A faint sound reached his ears, penetrating his fear and filling his head with a kaleidoscope of alien and yet familiar emotions: concern, protectiveness, then, with greater clarity, a growing savagery as awareness of the situation grew.

Deke realized he was getting a combination of visual and scent images of the scene outside his hideaway as if perceived from many different angles at once, too many for him to count. A series of sharp howls and barks could be heard, closer now, stronger and more menacing.

The bear turned its head from the tiger to evaluate this new threat. At the same moment, with a spring too fast for the eye to follow clearly, the tiger leapt across the intervening turf and landed on the bear's back. It swiped one massive, razor-clawed paw across the bear's eyes, and bit savagely at its neck.

Bellowing with pain and outrage, the bear beat at the clawing, spitting cat that clung on awkwardly but with tremendous strength.

Deke's head spun as his mind was beset by violent images. Too many viewpoints created a sensory overload, buffeting him with almost physical pain.

He scrabbled his way back up the passageway in time to see the bear shake the frenzied tiger from its shoulders and throw it ten feet. The tiger twisted with quick agility and managed to land on its oversized paws, crouching and glaring furiously both at the half-blinded bear and the swift, silent shapes circling closer in the fading sunlight.

Six or seven wolves had the tiger fairly surrounded. They darted in and out, wove sideways slashing at the striped cat's rear, leaping free when it whirled to face its tormenters. A similar group was attempting to close with the bear, but it had had enough. Turning, it lumbered back to its kill, snatched up the dead body in its jaws, and tried to drag it away, swinging powerful blows with its paws at the harassing wolves as it went. The wolves seemed inclined to let the bear go, more concerned with the safety of the pups in the den. This Deke understood as clearly as if the wolves had told it to him, which in a real sense they had, but in the form of mental images.

Abruptly, he was filled with rage. Maybe it was the sight of the dead boy's head lolling and bumping along the ground that did it; afterwards, he never would be sure what moved him to do the crazy thing he did next.

Shouting at the top of his lungs, he threw himself out of the hole, spear brandished in both hands. He ran after the retreating bear like one possessed, and wolves scattered before him, astonished by this muddy apparition that had burst from their den and was charging their enemy as if he were one of the pack himself. Deke's voice was a hoarse cry amidst the bedlam of roaring, snarling, snapping jaws and hurtling bodies. With all his strength, he drove his makeshift spear into the bear's flank and felt it slide home between two ribs.

The bear let out a surprised grunt and dropped its kill.

Deke's arms were almost jerked from their sockets as the bear whirled to rake him with its claws. Before the beast's motion could be completed, a huge wolf, larger than the rest, slashed at the bear's far flank and two more closed from the rear. Deke was thrown violently to the ground. His hands scrabbled wildly, seeking a rock, anything he could use as a weapon, and his fingers closed over something long and metallic. It was the dead boy's knife.

Grasping desperately, Deke snatched up the dagger and rolled to his feet. His spear still protruded from the bear's side, giving the animal a weird, off-balance appearance. Its movements were hampered by the shaft, and Deke could see dark trails of blood staining the ground.

Behind him the esper tiger was broadcasting waves of increasing anxiety. It tried again and again to flee, now perfectly willing to abandon its potential meal in order to do so. But unlike the bear, which the wild canines had been willing simply to chase away, the tiger was a primeval enemy, and its feline emanations were of a sort no wolf or dog could ignore. The urge to kill the cat was too strong. Carefully, but inexorably, the pack crowded in. Deke turned away as the wolves tore the screaming, thrashing tiger to pieces. It continued broadcasting its insane, rage-filled emanations until the very last, when with shocking abruptness, it was silenced.

Spotting his extra spears lying where he had dropped them an eternity ago, Deke sprinted over, snatched them up, and charged after the bear. Again the wolves made way for him, and if he had had a moment to think about it, he would have been amazed by his own temerity. It seemed they were watching to see what he would do, willing to follow his lead. Images still poured into his mind from their many brains, and strangely there was no hostility towards him. In fact, one wolf took a long sniff at his feet and legs, then actually wagged its tail before returning to the business of the bear.

One of the wolves let out a yelp as the bear's flailing claws laid it open and crushed its skull. Again the wild rage surged through Deke, echoed in kind by the wolf pack. Why he should be so enraged over the death of a wolf escaped him just then, but the power of the emotion carried him back into the melée of colliding furry bodies who now attacked the great bear in deadly earnest. Deke felt infused with their desire for the kill; he could taste flesh and fur between his teeth, could feel the jarring impact of his blade striking into tissue and bone. In a silence which fell so quickly he couldn't pinpoint when it had begun, he realized he was stabbing frenziedly at the fallen bear, his face and limbs streaming with heated blood and shreds of pulsing matter.

Slowly, he came back to himself and looked around. The area surrounding the den resembled a battlefield, with gore splattered everywhere. There was a living wolf's eyes and jaws inches from his face where he crouched over the still-twitching carcass. The wolf's hot breath mingled with his own. His blue eyes met the wolf's yellow ones. Then the wolf licked his cheek.

He rose, flesh dyed scarlet by blood and the reddening fire of the dying sunlight. His breath came in short gasps. One by one the wolves turned their noses skyward and began to howl, and after a time the boy joined them, his breast full to bursting both with awareness of the miracle of his escape, and the joy of his strange, new-found, wild companions.

CHAPTER TWO

...and so it should be remembered, we ought not underestimate the influence our peers have upon our development, for how much of us is who we are when we're alone, and how much is what we see reflected in the eyes around us?

— *Ourn Rohlvaag; Collected Journals; City of Life, A.D. 3109*

I t had been two months previously that Deke's passage to manhood really began.

The first crocuses were poking up through the melting snow, and everywhere in the tent city, the ground was turning to mud. People cursed the mud even while they blessed the warming sun, and shed the layers of heavy clothing they had worn all winter.

Spring was a noisy time of bustling activity. There were tents to be cleaned, domestic animals to be bred, campaigns to be planned. In spring, officials went out across the countryside to order the supplies and devices that, come harvest, were given in tribute to the People of the Wolf. In exchange for his protection, Barr Wolfson extracted a substantial tax from the lands he controlled. The People's presence was a powerful peace-keeping force, and permitted active trade and relations between those who otherwise might have been mortal enemies.

Throughout Wolfson territories, the sub-chiefs of scattered towns and villages prepared for their annual pilgrimage to Barr's Spring Camp. Some of these sub-chiefs were relations to the Wolfsons of Barr's immediate line, some were lieutenants who had served particularly notably in one campaign or another and had been rewarded with control over one of the sub-clans, a position comparable to a regional governorship.

On a sunny day near the end of March, Barr met with his fighting chiefs in the war tent. The men were grizzled veterans who had ridden all their lives under the banner of the Wolfsons, and they were discussing matters pertaining to a small village hidden in the mountains to the north.

Outside, Deke hovered near the tent. He spotted a servant bearing a fresh keg of ale and quickly intercepted the fellow. "I'll take that," he said with a smile.

The servant grinned back. "Thanks, m'lord."

Deke hefted the keg and rattled the knocker. "Ale, gentlemen! May I come in?"

There was an appreciative roar, and he ducked inside.

His father looked at him measuringly. "Thanks, we've developed a thirst with all this talk."

As Deke filled each man's goblet in turn, Barr shoved a cup towards the boy and said, "Fill one for yourself as well, son. It's time you were privy to these discussions. Perhaps you'll learn something."

"That is my sincerest desire," Deke said, meaning it. His eyes met his father's, and there was sudden warmth between them.

By the ruins, Barr thought, it was a pity the lad couldn't be like this more often. His heart went out to the boy, for he sensed Deke's fundamental curiosity about all things pertaining to war, and this filled Barr with satisfaction. At least in this, Deke was a true son of the Wolf.

The men greeted Deke familiarly, and he endured a little good-natured razzing about the workout his boots were getting lately. After his escapade in the blizzard, his father had taken Micmac from him as punishment. He had been afoot ever since.

Hawk Farflight, Barr Wolfson's Number One, picked up the conversation where it had broken off. Keenness of eye and sharpness of intellect had earned him his nickname, and now even he had trouble remembering the name given him at birth.

"It's obvious they need a lesson," he said to the group.

"Aye," another man put in from where he lolled in a canvas chair. He was a man of middle years, fair-haired and handsome. Willie O'Dale could still charm the ladies when he wanted, and his reputation amongst the local farmers' daughters was legendary, rivaled only by his reputation as Barr's foremost war chief.

"Trouble to the north?" Deke asked.

"How'd you know?" O'Dale was surprised.

The boy ignored his question. "Are you going to rescue the villagers?"

Grins appeared among the men and Hawk said, "Would you like that, Deke?"

"You're too romantic, son," Barr said, hiding his own smile. "It's always in our interest to protect loyal friends. Right now bandits are raiding their town. Our spies tell us there aren't many, but they're armed with modern weapons."

"A squadron should be able to handle it," O'Dale said.

"Good," Barr said. "Select the men yourself."

"Aye, my lord," O'Dale said, inclining his head affirmatively.

Barr relaxed and sipped his ale. "I'd like to go myself, but I've other game to catch," he said, a gleam in his eyes.

"You're pushing west," Deke said, the same gleam appearing in his eyes. For a second the resemblance between father and son was striking.

"Aye, boy, west, into the unknown." Barr grinned. "Come, drink up. The day's wasting."

The boy tilted his cup back and drank the bitter brew in a long swallow.

"I think our lad's had a bit of practice before this," O'Dale remarked with a chuckle.

Deke wiped his mouth nonchalantly with the back of his hand. "It's in the blood," he said to general laughter and his father's glow of camaraderie.

Later that afternoon, as O'Dale visited each of the soldiers he wanted to take north, he was too busy to notice Deke watching him avidly. That night the boy paid a visit to one of the men, gifting him with a flagon of wine from his mother's stores which the man accepted gladly for the honor he supposed it represented. He never noticed the unusual flavor hidden beneath the piquant bouquet, and by the time he awakened from his oversight, it was twenty hours later, his horse and weapons were missing, and he was in a terrific mess, compliments of the chieftain's son.

The girl stood at the edge of desolation, her thin, cotton garment whipping tautly in the steady wind that blew warm and humid up from the southlands, carrying on it all the sensations of spring without any of the substance.

She was tall, graceful, deeply tanned, with a surprising auburn cast to her otherwise almost black hair. Her eyes were as changeable as the earth itself: hazel one moment, grey the next, green when her emotions were aroused. Her features were precise and clean, with a high forehead defined by a pronounced widow's peak. At twelve, she was still a girl, but there was a presence about her which bespoke the rising tide of her womanhood, poised on the brink of adolescence.

She stared across the ruins, held in thrall by the totality of the vista. Miles without end of ghosts, she thought, ghosts and demons and will o' the wisps. She kicked the dirt with a moccasined foot, part of her longing to step out into the wasteland. She wondered if the mother she had never known walked out there in spirit form. Loneliness washed through her, and with a jerk of her head, she turned away from the ruins.

"Andara! Andara!"

The girl looked around. There was no one near. She stopped breathing to listen fully in the way she had been taught by her teacher and patron. There was nothing.

Puzzled, Andara pushed a strand of hair away from her face. The voice had seemed clear, eerily familiar.

Shrugging, she turned away from the ancient devastation.

There was a sound of hooves on turf and Andara whirled, right hand going to the wickedly sharp dagger she carried. When necessary, women were trained first to defend themselves in the ruthless style of hand-to-hand combat taught to all youngsters, and if that failed, to take their own lives. It was known the ruins held special dangers for women due to their potential for giving birth to abominations.

A rider approached, mounted bareback on a horse of indeterminate color. Whether grey or brown Andara couldn't tell, and she felt as if her eyes were playing tricks on her. She looked up at the horsewoman who somehow compelled her mount to motionlessness, though the girl saw neither bit nor bridle.

"So," the rider said quietly. "We meet at last."

Andara shivered at the recognition in the woman's voice. She wanted to draw her knife from its sheath, but something held her hand fast. Unexpectedly, her trepidation disappeared. She knew with certainty that this woman would never harm her. Old, she thought, older than the oldest person she'd ever seen. Silvered hair fell across deerskin-clad shoulders, and her face was a weathered landscape broken by deep lines and wrinkles. Black eyes peered from beneath silver eyebrows. "Who are you?"

"Think of me as a friend of the family," the woman said.

"Should I know you?"

The old one shrugged. "Now you do."

The girl's eyes were watchful, betraying nothing.

"You have had good training," said the woman after a time.

"The Lady Tilva is my patron," Andara said proudly. "I'm learning her arts."

"And a good teacher she is." Then, with strange emphasis, "What do you seek, young one?"

The question sliced through Andara's awareness, and she rubbed her forehead as if the old woman's voice had pierced the front of her skull. "I'm not sure," she whispered.

"No?" The black eyes riveted the girl where she stood. Inexplicably, they twinkled. "We will speak again when you are."

The girl radiated confusion. The stranger's words touched her in a way she didn't understand. It was an intimate contact, and Andara felt in an instant as if the old woman knew everything about her. She almost knew who the woman was, but even as she tried to remember, her mind slid away from the knowledge in a most peculiar way. "Who are you?" she asked again.

"I am who I am, as you are who you are," answered the ancient one with an obliqueness Andara found disconcerting. "Remember this moment," she said, and began to move away. Again Andara had no idea how she communicated her desires to the horse, but the animal seemed to understand whatever signal it had been given, for it went willingly.

Andara watched until a fierce itching started in her eyes. She rubbed them hard, blinking furiously. When her vision cleared, the aged rider had disappeared as weirdly as she had come.

She shivered. Suddenly she wanted to be home, in her own tent. Mind turning vertiginously, she trotted rapidly back in the direction of Spring Camp.

Some boys of Deke's manhood group were gathered at a merchant's tent near the bottom of the chieftain's hill, munching sweet biscuits and drinking milk. Their conversation was lively and filled with speculation about Deke's latest adventure. Mastra was there, along with Tim O'Dale, Willie's youngest son, a compact, well-knit boy of thirteen, with fair hair and grey eyes.

Andara drew closer to listen to their conversation.

"His father took his horse last time, what'll he take this time?" one boy asked humorously.

"His balls!" another yelled to the general delight of all.

"I wouldn't be in his boots for anything," someone commented when the hilarity had died down.

From his tone, Andara knew the boy was lying; what he wanted more than anything was to be in Deke's boots. Envy radiated from the entire group, in fact. What infants, she thought.

"There's Andara!" Tim shouted. "Hey, Andara!"

"Hey, yourself," she said coolly, but joined them when he beckoned to her.

"Did you hear the news?" Tim asked, moving over on his bench to give her room.

"Aye," she replied. "When he comes home he'll have killed a man, and all of you will still be children."

The boys hooted derisively. "They'll never let him fight!"

"I never saw Barr Wolfson so angry," Tim mused. "He rode out after them himself."

"What's Deke doing right now, I wonder?" someone said dreamily.

"Andara can tell us, can't you?" Tim turned to her.

"Aye, cast the tiles! Come on, Andara!" the boys chorused loudly, eager for the diversion.

Andara hesitated. "The spirits would be angry if I did it just to satisfy your curiosity," she hedged. "Besides, he's always difficult to get a reading

37

on."

Tim laughed. "That's just Andara's way of saying she isn't good enough to get an accurate throw."

Andara scowled, knowing he was goading her but refusing to rise to the dare. These *children* (and she italicized the word in her mind) simply did not understand how unpredictable were the powers governing the tiles. And Tim was right in one way: she didn't have the skill yet to control those forces. Tilva had explained that she wouldn't have full use of her abilities until she was a grown woman.

"I'm good enough to know when to throw tiles and when not," she told the boys. "Spirits aren't anything to fool with. What if I called a demon?"

The boys fell silent. A shadow seemed to cover the day. What Andara suggested was a real possibility. Demons existed. Every child of the ruins knew that the way he knew the sky was blue and the grass was green.

Pleased with the effect of her words, Andara left the boys ruminating darkly over all the terrors she could evoke simply by mentioning the unmentionable.

It was at the third stop to change horses that Willie discovered the imposter among his soldiers.

Deke was voiding his bladder against a tree and barely had time to adjust his clothing when he felt the older man's hand come down heavily on his shoulder.

After a brief discussion during which he assured the war chief that there was nothing he could do about the situation since no men could be spared to take him home, Willie extracted his promise to behave and put him under the supervision of Sergeant Melak, a swarthy, seasoned warrior who, along with the rest of the men, was much amused to see Deke among them.

They ate and rested at the little way-station, filling cargo pockets with bread and meat to be eaten as they traveled. In the distance, reflecting light from the setting sun, was a village etched into the highest limestone peaks, and when Melak gestured, Deke knew this was their destination.

The light was failing when the Wolf riders moved on. They rode swiftly through the hills and into the mountains, the trail they followed winding upward past rows of dark spruce and pine. The ground was clear of deadfall, the route well-maintained, and this, Deke knew, could only be by his father's design.

The wind increased and grew chillier. They rode without a break, for Willie was eager to reach the town before sunup. The horses' breath steamed whitely in the cold air, made luminescent by starlight. The ground fell away steeply alongside the trail, and the riders were careful to keep clear of the edge. The way grew rockier, more rugged. They rode along a high ridge between two mountains, bared for a while in silhouette against the night sky. Overall, from the east, the moon shone bright and remote.

By midnight, weariness began to settle into the boy's muscles, and a heavy ache started behind his eyes. Though it wasn't uncommon for Wolf soldiers to sleep in the saddle when necessary, he was determined to stay awake and aware like the men with whom he rode.

Despite his resolution, he fell in and out of a doze. A few hours before dawn the troop of horsemen came to a halt. They were almost directly beneath the cluster of unusual buildings carved into the limestone heights.

Willie eyed the town with satisfaction, saw the signs that told him everything was safe. Nevertheless he signaled to two of his men who slipped from their saddles to run silently up stone steps into a house near the edge of town. In minutes they reappeared, and informed their commander the bandits could show up any time.

Before long, guards were scattered strategically on the mountainside, and the rest of the squadron was bedded down in various safe houses, homes belonging to the unofficial town garrison officers. The men slept the light and uneasy sleep of soldiers who know the day will bring killing. The boy slept profoundly and hard, pitching deeply into the embrace of fatigue and warm blankets.

"It is not so much a matter of good and evil, right or wrong. What is nourishing is beneficial. Anything else is not."

"There are no exceptions?"

"None. Oh, it is true one can commit acts which are what I call 'anti-life' and seem to be none the worse for it, but the effects are there, nevertheless, for brujos like us to see."

"Yet you associate with me, when by your definition I and all my people are 'anti-life.'"

The Old Man touched his cheek delicately. "I have hopes for your education."

Deke's dream-Self arose from where he sat outside the brujo's cave. A premonition of danger went through him. "I feel something."

"They are coming," the elderly sorcerer said. "It is time for you to go."

Deke jolted awake, reached out and prodded Melak.

"What is it?" the sergeant growled sleepily. "It's not time yet."

"Get up," Deke said, collecting his weapons.

A low whistle came from outside their stone sleep-room.

"Come on," Deke whispered impatiently, and slipped out the door into the pre-dawn gloom.

"Wait!" Melak said urgently, then cursed under his breath. "Follow me," he told the other men now crowding near. "Cover the boy! If anything happens to him, we're demon bait for sure!"

The soldiers nodded grimly and followed him out.

Willie was waiting and spoke tersely, dispersing the men.

Where's the boy gotten to? Melak wondered as he ran to the position O'Dale had indicated. Thank the ruins Willie hadn't noticed Deke's absence!

Glancing around, the sergeant bemoaned the order which had put that wild son of the devil under his protection. He'd just known something like this was going to happen! He dove around the granite corner of a substantial building and faced down the main street. He felt rather than heard the others of his squadron setting up their ambush. Explosives were scattered throughout the road, ready for an unwary step to trigger them. From above and behind Melak sensed the presence of soldiers taking up stations and took the opportunity to scan for the boy again. Nowhere. It was as if the mountain had swallowed him.

Melak sighed. What would be, would be. Once set in motion, battles had their own rhythms, and if it was ordained that the boy should die today, so be it. Such was the knowledge each Wolf soldier took into battle, chiefs as well as simple warriors. Deke had chosen to be here. Karma would choose the rest.

Word passed up the hillside man to man in the silent battle language of the People. The raiders had been sighted. They were on their way through the town's main gate.

Deke slid through the darkness with swift surety. It was as if he always had known what to do, and now his feet took him automatically to the place where the battle's crisis would be played out, the place where after the raiders' first shock of ambush they would attempt to regroup.

He could sense other soldiers nearby, for it was natural that an attack leader as experienced as Willie would anticipate the trouble spots. He froze where he stood, his mind reliving a conversation held with the Old Man. Whether he had dreamed, imagined, or actually lived the conversation he couldn't recall just now, and he didn't take the time to worry about it. He simply remembered, and acted on it as naturally as if he had been doing it all his life.

"Invisibility is an attitude," the Old Man had said. *"A state of mind."*

"I understand," Deke had answered. *"One must want to be seen."*

40

"We create and re-create our own images constantly in the material world," the brujo had affirmed. *"What would happen if we skipped a few beats in that creative rhythm?"*

"We would skip beats of physical existence," the boy had said thoughtfully. *"But wouldn't that be dangerous?"*

"As dangerous as stopping your own heart," the aged sorcerer had agreed. *"And yet, so long as you act with complete commitment, without doubt, you may become effectively invisible for short periods of time."*

"What happens if you doubt?" Deke had asked, though he thought he knew the answer.

"Ah, young chief, are you so eager to become a ghost?"

The Old Man's soft question had startled the boy, making his mind turn deeper into more complex levels of awareness.

Even as he remembered this, he willed himself to be a shadow among shadows, without fear, and with the total confidence only a child to whom nothing really terrible has ever happened can summon.

He walked past a man who never knew he was there, so close he could have touched the soldier's face, and was filled with elation. He reached a stone trough that would give good cover, crouched behind it, and tried to make his breathing return to normal.

From out of the pre-dawn came the sound of horseshoes striking stone, equipment jingling arrogantly, careless laughter. In silence, the town waited, prepared to welcome the riders to her bosom.

CHAPTER THREE

I found it interesting to compare the General's reaction to conversation with a psychologist to responses from my more conventional patients. In our culture, those first confronted by the science of mental health are often defensive, challenging, as if saying to the doctor, "Let's see what you're made of." For the doctor who watches and listens carefully, these early moments are quite revealing.

It was different with Deke Wolfson. He was interested, observant, cooperative, yet essentially an enigma. There were many ways his training had taught him to deflect a probe without apparent effort, to evade and engage simultaneously.

Often during our meetings I knew it was he, and not I, who directed the conversation. The places he took us had a secondary effect of expanding my own awareness to the point where I believed this was his conscious effort to help me reach enlightenment (according to his cosmology). At the same time I thought I was helping him, he was making me sense worlds of reality I never would have reached on my own. Such were the shamanistic powers of this man that indeed I was forced to change my outlook, for he made me realize that the reality within which I operated was only a part of a greater multidimensional reality, a spiritual continuum within which he and his people were so at home, and where we of Beori, for all our advanced technology, must necessarily be mere tourists.

And then, of course, there were the wolves.

— Ourn Rohlvaag; Collected Journals; City of Life, A.D. 3109

The wolves milled around Deke, snuffling deeply at his scent. A substantial female squeezed down into the den and returned a minute later, her pups tumbling after.

The massive wolf who earlier had turned the bear away paced over and the pack members gave ground before him. He looked measuringly at the boy, his intelligent gaze wary but curious.

Deke stood quietly, not meeting the wolf's eyes directly, making no challenging gestures. He could feel the feather-light touch of the pack's thoughts, and tentatively filled his mind with an image of himself skinning and butchering the bear. The Alpha wolf stepped aside in tacit consent.

Knife clutched in his right hand, Deke strode through the crowding wolves. The bear lay face down where it had fallen. For a moment the boy was at a loss, then once again filled his mind with an image, this one of himself tugging at the bear's foreleg while the wolves grabbed with their teeth to help roll the carcass over.

Without exception the wolves got the idea, and a minute later they succeeded in getting the bear into a position from which Deke could make an incision from breastbone to anus, opening the belly like a purse.

The wolves dove in and hauled the entrails clear as Deke hacked steadily, freeing the huge mass from the boney cavity that contained it. With deft strokes he cut the muscle and sinew binding hide to flesh, and slowly, as the sun deepened in the west, was able to wrestle the bloody bearskin away from its owner.

He rolled the hide into a tight bundle until daylight when he planned to stretch and clean it for curing. Soon he had cut several pounds of meat from the loin, and this he quickly divided into thin slices which he put aside with the fur. Raw meat wasn't his favorite supper, but he knew tonight he would be glad to have it.

Buzzing, biting flies made him aware he was covered in tacky blood. He made a mental picture of wolves lapping water and sent it hopefully towards the Alpha. With instant comprehension several wolves broke away from the gorging pack and by nips and nudges, got Deke moving. They didn't have to go far. This den site had been chosen because of its proximity to fresh water. There was a small pool where water bubbled up amidst a sheltered group of boulders.

After quaffing his thirst, Deke washed himself and his knife, using silty clay from the bottom of the pool to scrub the blood out of his pores.

When he finished, he returned to the den site. He had to force himself to look at the remains of the dead boy. His lips compressed into a grim line when he recognized his cousin, Peter, the son of Barr's sister. Peter's father was the governor of a small but powerful community of warlike tribesmen who lived east of the People's Winter Camp. They considered themselves kin to the Wolfsons by more than the marriage of their leader to Barr Wolfson's sister; indeed, they regarded their clan as an offshoot of the Wolf People proper, connected by common bloodlines, lifestyle, and philosophy. By giving his sister in marriage to Gant Murdock, Barr had insured peace and bound the Murdock clan closer to his own authority.

Deke's mind rested uneasily on Gant as he stared at the mangled Peter Murdock. He had never liked or trusted the man. Gant was hard-drinking and violent with an ugly temper often vented on his three sons.

Deke had always pitied Peter and his two younger brothers. He and his friends didn't see the Murdock boys too often, only at Spring Camp when the weather permitted visiting among the various communities associated with the Wolfsons.

His expression cloudy, Deke began digging a hole to bury his cousin, using a spear to loosen the dirt and scooping it away with his hands. He

44

remembered how just last year he had inadvertently interrupted Gant beating Peter, how when the chieftain's son appeared, Gant had sent Peter off with a final cuff.

Leering drunkenly, he had said to Deke, "Nothing a father doesn't have to do now and again, eh, boy?"

"You do it too often, I think, Uncle," Deke had replied evenly, though his blood boiled at the diminutive "boy."

Gant's expression had darkened with displeasure and he had taken a threatening step towards Deke.

As if by magic, Tilva had appeared from behind a tent, her face pale with anger. "Have a care, kinsman," she had warned softly, steel in her voice. "This is not a path you wish to tread."

With a muttered curse about witches and their filthy offspring, Gant had bowed in drunken burlesque before stumbling away.

"Are you all right?" his mother had asked, her eyes softening as she turned them on her son. He had nodded, gazing back at her. Never had he seen her look more dangerous, or beautiful.

A wolf's cold nose brushed his thigh. With a shiver Deke returned to the present. For a moment it seemed his mother was standing right behind him. He almost could feel the protective aura of her maternal love envelop him. The wolf thrust its muzzle into the palm of his hand and an image of nightfall filled his mind. Shrugging, he pushed away the feeling of homesickness that clogged his throat, the urgent desire for his mother's arms.

By now the hole was big enough to contain the remains of Peter Murdock's meager life. Deke dragged his cousin's body over and rolled it into the shallow grave. Bloated flies crawled across the dead boy's wrecked features as Deke scraped dirt over the corpse. Brushing angrily at tears which fell uncontrollably, he felt his shoulders heave and knew he should say something, anything, over his cousin's grave, but couldn't think what. Finally he whispered, "Go with God, cousin," and tamped the rocks into the earth with particular force to keep scavengers away.

When darkness was full, Deke sat against a rock near the den, exhausted. He chewed on a strip of raw meat while overhead, the stars glittered with cold indifference. The ground felt soft beneath his tired flesh and he curled into a weary ball. His senses remained preternaturally alert as he sank towards sleep. He heard the wolves moving nearby as they settled themselves for the night.

He wondered how the others in his manhood group were faring; how many of them would be sleeping as securely as he this evening; how many still lived. A strange grin touched his lips. What would his mates think if they could see him now? They would be frightened, but whether of the wolves or himself he wasn't sure.

A skittish breeze ruffled his hair and from somewhere in the night came a chittering noise. Deke stiffened tensely. He tried to remember what sounds he had heard on his few training expeditions into the ruins and for the life of him, could not recall a single thing. It was as if his entire existence until this moment had been blotted out.

Sensing his restlessness, several wolves pressed nearer and ranged around him, their noses pointing outward to the ruins. Their clean, musky scent filled his nostrils as an image of wolf cubs sleeping peacefully filled his mind. He relaxed a little, amazed by the level of intelligence these animals displayed. He had always known canines were bright; exposure to his father's domesticated wolves had taught him that, but what he was experiencing went beyond anything he'd ever heard. It occurred to him that it was the high level of *psi*-sensitivity inherent to his own mind which made the wolves able to accept him, as well as his youth. History abounded with tales of children being adopted by wolf packs, and of course, humans adopted wolves on a regular basis.

We're kin, Deke thought, feeling himself bonding subliminally to the pack consciousness. He wished he could share the liberty of his wild brothers, that he, too, could roam freely across this turning world of ruins, for the impending responsibilities of his birthright seemed entirely too onerous and weighty to bear. As he dropped off he thought he would stay with the wolves as long as they permitted it, leaving duty and obligation behind until he had learned everything he could about living wild and running free. His last waking thought concerned a mental picture irresistible to his romantic, boyish nature: he saw himself racing through a moonlit desert of ancient ruins, the leaping, furred forms of his pack supporting and protecting him as they coursed together beneath the infinitely wheeling heavens.

He was having *the* dream again, the strange, near-nightmare that appeared during periods of high stress in his life. The dream was dominated by images of people he'd never seen before but whom he encountered over and again during sleep. It seemed he knew them, had powerful feelings for several of them, particularly a woman or perhaps it was two women; he couldn't be sure, since often they seemed to be different versions of the same individual.

This woman was young and sinuous, attractive in an alien, non-Wolfson way, with soft hands and exotically tilted eyes. She was oddly familiar, and as often happened in the dream since he'd become pubescent, she was touching him provocatively, stirring his senses with raw, sexual power.

Mostly his dream Self didn't try to resist, and on more than one occa-

46

sion he had awakened after an ejaculation that left him shaking with exaltation and longing. Tonight he didn't awaken. Instead he found himself experiencing the alternate dream scenario, in which the woman disappeared when he reached for her and he was left standing in a shattered field of ancient glass while something terrible crept invisibly towards him, some *thing* he sensed with a non-physical portion of his awareness, and which in seeking him out, now had found him.

This thing stalked him for an unknown reason, and Deke had the feeling that if he could only figure it out, he would solve a great mystery intrinsic to his being.

He could hear the thing's claws scrambling through the broken glass as it approached. Part of his mind shouted that he should draw his weapon and fire, but the part directing his actions was certain it would be possible to lay the thing low with a single, focused burst of an ambiguous mental force he knew he was perfectly capable of launching if only he could remember how.

The sound of claws grew louder, but now he thought he heard raucous cries mingled with the irritable snarls of wolves.

He jerked upright, disoriented in the early morning light. The hubbub reached a crescendo, and he watched, still in the grip of his dream, as the wolves chased a persistent group of buzzards away from the bear's carcass.

Deke shuddered and stood up. His body felt rusty and he jogged in place for a few seconds to loosen his muscles. The pups were out of their den and the adult wolves were engaged in a complex series of actions which at first seemed incomprehensible to the boy. He caught a glimmer of fast-paced images: prey running, sand storms rushing, tornadic winds skipping dangerously through the ruins, a polyglot of smells, sounds and sensations. This was communication between pack members, a concerted effort by the adult wolves to impart information to the pups.

Deke entertained himself with the notion of puppy school while he walked off to urinate.

As had become customary in recent weeks, he examined his penis closely and with considerable anxiety. Soon the final ceremony in these rites would take place, and he tried to gauge the pain that was said to be worse than anything he could imagine. He retracted his foreskin and envisioned how he would look as a man, circumcised. No male of his people could return home after the Manhood Ritual until the primitive surgery was complete. Uncircumcised, he would remain a child forever, without the adult status conferred upon even the lowliest soldier or goat-herd.

Deke let go of himself and tried to put the whole business out of his mind. He began to work on the bearskin, using his knife to scrape blood ves-

47

sels and tissue from the inside. His blade wasn't really suited for the task, but he did the best he could, his thoughts preoccupied.

He wondered where the custom of circumcision had originated. Some of the boys his age told grisly tales they'd overheard from older fellows who'd already passed through the rites. According to them, after the boys of a manhood group returned to where the test had begun, the waiting men would seize them up one at a time, hold them to prevent any inadvertent movement, and then do the deed.

Many times Tim O'Dale had demonstrated on a piece of wood the two cuts needed to separate the childish foreskin from the adult organ. Where he had picked up this piece of information only the ruins knew, for tradition demanded new-made men maintain a discrete silence about the details of their ordeal.

Again Deke looked down at himself. His genitals had changed radically in the last year or so, had gained substantially in both size and mass, and he had begun to be quite attached to this visible proof of his encroaching maturity. The thought of someone slashing him with a knife made him shrivel and shrink, literally as well as figuratively.

The day wore on and once again the sun became a burning coppery disk in the sky. When the midday heat grew too fierce, the wolves sought shady places among the moss-covered rocks to nap, rising occasionally to feed from the bear and discourage the turkey buzzards circling lazily overhead. The meat was nearly consumed and Deke knew the pack soon would hunt again. When they did, he decided he would go with them. Soon enough the final part of this ritual would take place, and though he knew he could delay for no more than a couple days before returning to the starting point, he had decided to give himself those days. After that, if he wasn't there to stand up with his fellows he might as well forget about going home or becoming chieftain some day; forget his dreams of conquest and glory.

He gazed wistfully at the wolves where they dozed. It was very peaceful here. There were no parental demands to fulfill, no teachers pushing him to extend himself. Here life was only survival. The first part of the Manhood Rites was concerned solely with keeping one's wits despite hunger, thirst, or most of all, fear. It was about learning self-sufficiency.

Deke wasn't sure what he had learned in the last twenty-four hours except he felt cleansed of the inner turmoil he'd lived with since he was old enough to think about such things. There seemed to be a new clarity to his intellectual processes, as if his awareness had been augmented. Most surprising was the discovery of another feeling that swept all confusion from his mind, and strangely it was this which most astonished him, because he couldn't remember having felt such a thing before. It was happiness, purest happiness, and he was surfeited with it.

Laughter welled up from his belly to ring out in the sultry air. He laughed for a long time until one of the younger wolves approached and delicately licked the streaming tears from his sunburned cheeks.

On the evening of the third day, a boy straggled back to where the men waited in the ruins. He lifted his head tiredly and said with an edge in his thirst-cracked voice,

"Just because I'm back first doesn't mean I cheated."

One of the cloaked men looked at him. "How can you cheat when there're no rules to the game?" he asked rhetorically.

The boy digested this and seemed satisfied. Another man passed the youngster a water bag and some jerked beef.

"What happens now?" the boy asked.

"We wait," said the first man.

"Where's...you know..." The boy gestured to where the ritual master had stood to address them a lifetime earlier.

"Don't worry," someone else said. "When the time's right he'll be here." He paused meaningfully. "And maybe it'll be you'd rather he wasn't!" The man pantomimed a cutting movement with his fingers and everyone smothered laughter as the boy blanched beneath his sunburn.

The first man gestured towards a heap of clothing nearby. "Find your gear," he admonished kindly. "We'll be here a while." He grasped the boy by the shoulder, adding, "Brother."

The exhausted boy's face lit up briefly, then he went to find his clothing.

On the fourth day Mastra wandered in, half-dead with thirst and near-religious rapture. He was given his clothes, food and water like the first boy, and when they were left to themselves the first boy asked, "What happened to you? Did you see anyone else?"

Mastra shook his head, unable to find his voice. It would be days before he could absorb what he had experienced out there in the dust. It would be years before he spoke of it, for even now he wasn't sure if he had acted properly. So much of the past few days was a blur of terror, misery, and discomfort that he wondered if he'd ever want to remember. He also wondered if everyone had been as frightened as he.

Later that afternoon Tim dragged his cut and bloody body back to the group in the desert and declined to discuss what had happened to him. There was a haggard, grim look in his eyes that Mastra had never seen before.

One of the men ministered to the boy with medicine and bandages taken from a saddle bag. He cleaned the wounds after removing many shards of broken glass. Some were turning septic, and the man knew that another day without care would have seen infection, maybe even gangrene. He said nothing about that, however, only complimenting the boy on his fortitude in walking back on feet so lacerated the tendons showed through in places. Every year he participated in these rituals he was more impressed by the dogged courage these boys displayed. Never a whimper came from the young O'Dale, never so much as a complaint passed his lips. His father would be proud.

Seven more boys returned by the end of the fifth day, boys so wasted and exhausted the men knew they'd lose at least one and possibly as many as two more of them.

By consensus agreement no one mentioned the most glaring absence.

But by day six it became apparent to the surviving eight boys (for indeed one had stopped breathing during the night and another had died that morning) that the rest of their friends probably weren't returning.

Mastra and Tim were dumbfounded. It didn't seem possible that Deke was dead. He had always seemed invulnerable to them. But as the minutes and hours passed, they grew increasingly silent as the awareness of loss grew in their minds.

"Never would have believed it," one of the men muttered softly to the others. "Of all, I expected he'd be back."

The men nodded mournfully.

Tim limped painfully over to the adults. "What's the longest anyone's ever stayed out and lived?"

"Seven days," one of the men replied. "And when that one came back he was carrying a demon."

Everyone shivered, the older men exchanging glances as they remembered that time, their masks failing to conceal their disquiet.

"Can't we go look...?" Tim began.

"No," said the first man regretfully. "If someone doesn't return, there's generally nothing left to find."

"It isn't fair," another boy burst out suddenly. "He didn't even have a knife." He remembered how his knife had been the only thing that gave him the courage to face down the cave rats he'd stumbled into by accident.

"That's the way we've always done it," the man said firmly, though the boys could see his sorrow in his body language.

"It's a stupid way," Mastra spoke up, his tone almost vicious. "Any accident could have killed him, maybe a lion, who knows? How can that test someone's fitness to lead? Who among us could kill a lion barehanded?"

"A future leader better have the brains to avoid barehanded combat with a lion," someone else said somberly.

"That's ridiculous," Mastra said, trying to hide his lips' trembling.

"You did," the man pointed out. "I did, in my day."

Mastra turned a look of such bitterness on the man that he was forced to look away.

The seventh day passed gloomily as everyone's hope faded.

On the morning of the eighth day the boys of the manhood group were awakened by a peculiar sound. One by one they opened their eyes to see the ritual leader standing above them on a boulder, swinging a strange object on a long cord in circles over his head. The object was the source of the weird noise.

"Listen," said the black-clad figure from his height, "Today concludes the final stage of your transformation. The sound of my spirit catcher is designed to focus your awareness. Listen!" He swung the object faster and harder, and the otherworldly wail the thing emitted did seem to gather the youngsters' thoughts into a common place of shared consciousness.

"Soon you will be men with all the privileges and responsibilities that entails. We grieve for our fallen comrades, but we move on. We must move on," he repeated. "Are you ready to enter manhood, to fulfill your obligations to clan and kin as have all the men of the Wolf who have gone before you?" The spirit catcher became silent. The leader waited expectantly, his hooded gaze deep and impenetrable. "Answer!" he barked.

"Aye," said the eight boys in unison, startled into obedience.

"Then we can begin," said the black-cowled leader. He signaled to the men who while he had spoken had arranged themselves behind the group. Two men took hold of each boy. The ritual leader laid aside his spirit catcher and turned away. Without warning, he pivoted and brandished a curved blade knapped painstakingly from a nodule of flint so many years previously its history was lost in farthest antiquity.

There was a collective gasp from the boys, and each felt his knees weaken and his scrotum contract. Each felt the hands of his sponsors support him more firmly.

In the absence of the five missing boys, the extra sponsors prepared to assist the ritual leader. One man carried a bowl of an evil-looking unguent prepared for this day by Tilva and her acolyte, Andara Farflight. The unguent contained an anesthetic to de-sensitize that most sensitive part of the male anatomy. Even with this the pain would be nearly insupportable. Only supreme motivation sustained these young men in their quest for adulthood.

A second assistant stopped in front of the boy who had returned first from the ruins. "Drop yer trousers, lad," he said with compassion. He affected

51

not to notice the boy's quaking knees.

The boy loosened his pants and allowed them to fall to his ankles. He gulped audibly as the first hooded assistant smeared a generous dollop of unguent on his retreating organ.

"Look there," the second assistant said, turning the boy's head away as the leader leapt from the boulder to land nimbly in front of him, ritual knife held high.

"By your survival in the ruins you have proved yourself worthy of this honor. Among our people, this manhood ritual binds us, warriors all, into one clan, man to man, brother to brother. Today you receive this mark of manhood as proof of your courage and commitment." With a deft movement he seized the trembling boy's penis and, flicking the exquisitely sharp flint knife expertly, made two swift cuts, freeing the foreskin which he placed in the boy's hand. "Keep this," he intoned. "There is magic in this flesh."

Too stunned to think, the boy slammed his jaws together to keep from crying out. The ritual leader nodded to his assistants who applied another, different paste to the wounded boy, this one an antiseptic, and wrapped the injury in a light bandage of cotton cloth.

Then the group moved on, stopping in front of Mastra, who felt perspiration break out clammily on his forehead. He was faint but forced himself to stand firm. Stoically, he endured the indignity of exposing himself. He thought of Deke, lost out there somewhere in the ruins, most likely dead, for what else could have kept him from this rendezvous? Mastra's spirit was filled with desolation at this thought. He barely felt the leader's two cuts or the application of medicine and bandage. He hardly noticed the bloody bit of tissue thrust into his hand. He couldn't feel anything except anguish and loss that drowned out the merely physical responses of his nervous system. Trying to imagine what the future could hold for him without the dynamic presence of his best friend in it was depressing, and he couldn't bear to pursue that projection. He prayed he would feel the physical pain soon, anything to distract him from the emptiness that consumed him.

Bleakly he watched the ritual master continue down the line to stand before Tim O'Dale, that this primitive and ancient human ritual distinguishing men of the Wolf from all others could be enacted once more.

And then, finally,

"It is done. You are men. Now you may return home to your new lives." The initiation master stood back from the line of sickish young men. Surveying the group, he nodded with satisfaction. The eight had comported themselves perfectly. Even the fatherless one, he thought, then corrected himself. Especially the fatherless one. He hadn't even flinched when the stone blade circled his flesh. Maybe the chieftain's son had been right about that one all along.

Remembering his young apprentice, the Old Man sighed. Such a loss, he thought from behind his ritual cowl. A tragedy for all of us. A disaster, in fact.

He turned away from the manhood group to hide the wetness in his aged eyes, and sorrowfully, sought his horse. Now the thing was done. It would only be a matter of time before...

The Old Man sighed again and mounted. He raised his hand in farewell to the hooded men and boys standing amidst the ruins of the past, and now, though they couldn't understand it, of the future as well.

Overall, the sun beat down, igniting the glittering dust with noonday fire.

Time passed; hot, sunny days and cool nights during which Deke became glad for his bearskin.

On the third day most of the pack ran off to hunt and Deke followed them. He carried his spears in his hands. Around his waist was tied a broad strip of the bear's hide which held his knife and a water bag he had made out of another piece of hide lined with the animal's waterproof bladder, and drawn up into a sack. Twisted sinew held the bag closed. On his feet he wore hide folded over several times into crude but sturdy sandals and held in place by long strips tied at the critical spots. From his neck hung bear claws strung on scraped rawhide. In a pouch with its drawstring pulled tight he carried both the bear's and the tiger's teeth, prised out of their jawbones with considerable effort.

The wolves led him deeper into increasingly green countryside. Every so often one or another of the younger wolves loped back to check his progress and make certain he didn't lose contact with the pack.

By midday he had caught up with the Alpha at the edge of a broad, rolling grassland. The wolves greeted him, bumping and shoving him with their shoulders, tails wagging, ears laid back. By now he was comfortable enough with them that he felt perfectly safe scratching their itchy places as if they were great, tame dogs. He moved up to where the Alpha sat a bit apart gazing across the savannah. Shielding his eyes from the sun, he squinted and thought he saw dark shapes far away in the grass. As if anticipating his question, the Alpha sent him a quick image of wild cattle grazing peacefully. Deke acknowleged the target with an affirmative gesture the Alpha understood more by emotional intent than movement.

The wolves spread out in a line and moved onto the grass. At the center of the line Deke ran stooped over using the lush prairie growth for cover. His stomach ached with hunger and he could practically taste the steak he was going to roast that very day. He had seen some small bushes and a copse of trees not far away and he was determined to have a fire and cook his meat. The bear had sustained him without satisfying his appetite. Today that was going to change. Anticipation made him salivate.

Now the cattle were clearly visible and the pack moved faster, with greater stealth. Deke still ran easily, his breathing even.

A minute or so later a cow lifted her head, chewing a mouthful of grass. Her ears flickered back and forth and she gave a restive snort. Several others raised their heads, moving reflexively to encircle their calves.

The wolves at one end of the line picked up speed and darted amongst the cows, turning them towards their mates at the other end. Deke nodded in appreciation of the wolves' tactic; the cows were galloping madly, flanked on both sides by wolves who herded them as neatly as any herdsman's dogs. He readied a spear in his right hand, running flat out. A signal went from the Alpha to the pack. They wheeled as one and cut a young cow from the herd, widening the space between her and the other cattle by rushing in a loose formation against their flanks and driving them forcibly apart. Wherever a cow tried to gore a wolf with her horns, four wolves descended on her rear, slashing and tearing at her vulnerable hindquarters.

In fewer seconds than he would have believed possible, the wolves had their cow surrounded a quarter mile or so from her sisters. Deke rushed up, breathing hard. The wolves opened a place for him to help make the kill, and he got ready to launch a spear. The cow whirled frantically, butting and charging wolves who leapt aside just in time to avoid contact with her sharp horns or dangerous hooves. As Deke edged closer to get a clear throw, the cow gave a frenzied bellow and broke into a full gallop, charging straight at him. He tried to jump out of the way but the front of her shoulder smashed into him, tossing him aside like a bundle of straw. The ground rushed up and he felt a tremendous pain in the front of his head. A starburst of light went off in his skull and everything became dark. He felt himself falling through that darkness, then felt nothing more.

Movement. Voices. Wailing cries like mothers grieving for the loss of their sons. Strange images. He saw Tilva pacing back and forth. Words came from her lips that weren't rational. He heard the bass rumble of his father's voice and caught a glimpse of his eyes: deep, shadowed, with all the light gone out of them. He felt himself hanging somewhere in the upper corner of his mother's tent, looking down at his parents.

"Hey," he called out, waving his arms.

They paid him no attention. Indeed, it was as if he hadn't spoken.

"Hey!" he called again, louder. "I'm right here!"

They went on talking. He saw his mother's shoulders shake. He tried to touch her reassuringly but his hand passed through her, and that was when he realized he was out of his body.

The scene shifted and they were standing together on the edge of a hill where a funeral pyre had been erected, the cordwood piled beneath it awaiting the flame. Not far away were gathered all the people of his tent city, as well as some who had come from as far away as his mother's ancestral lands.

"Someone's died," he said to himself. He tried to look into the pyre, remembering that his cousin, Peter, had died a scant few days ago. But as he strained to put his vision where he could see who it was, he felt a queer pulling in his midsection and his sight dimmed. For a moment lights whirled and explosions beat painfully within his head. Again there was a feeling of falling through darkness and then his eyes cleared and he saw that the pyre was empty. This funeral, then, was for one whose body had been lost. When his mother lifted her tear-stained face to gaze into Barr's dulled eyes, Deke finally knew.

"No!" he cried to his parents, his gathered relatives, friends and neighbors, all the varied men, women, and children who formed his world. "No! I'm alive! I'm not dead!"

A peculiar look came over Tilva's face, and nearby, Andara Farflight nudged Mastra with an elbow. "Did you hear something?" she whispered.

New tears oozed from the corners of Tilva's eyes. Barr's arm went around her shoulders. "I must be going mad," she told him. "For a second I heard his voice, as if he were standing right here with us!"

Barr nodded. "I heard him, too," he admitted.

"His spirit is near," Andara told Mastra. "I can feel it."

Deke almost screamed his frustration. He moved rapidly through the crowd, frantically trying to touch everyone. Then the lights began exploding across his field of vision and he was falling once more, but now he felt himself spinning as well, and he became aware of pain in his head and sickness in his belly. He felt himself swimming laboriously up a deep well towards a point of steadiness that stayed just out of reach. For a while, the harder he tried to swim up, the sicker he got. From a distance he felt his body convulsing as he vomited up dust and bile. There was the stench of earth and manure in his nostrils and he forced himself to lift his face out of the dirt. The pain in his head was too strong to bear and he vomited weakly until only dry heaves racked his bruised, stiffened muscles.

A low-pitched whine sounded in his ears and he felt a warm tongue pushing his gummed eyelids open.

Several wolves ringed him. It was a young, submissive female who nosed him urgently, sending a repeated image into his lacerated mind, a picture of him standing.

He tried to rise. He didn't make it on the first or even second try. Finally, after resting for a moment and gathering his strength, he willed himself upwards, and without knowing exactly how he got there, tottered feebly on his feet, his hands locked in the fur of the nearest wolf for balance.

He touched his forehead and discovered a large lump and a quantity of dried blood. His nose felt broken, and he ran his fingers over it cautiously. His nostrils, too, were ringed with dry blood. His lips were abraded on the inside where his teeth had struck on impact, but the teeth themselves were intact, thank the ruins. His chest hurt where the bear claw necklace had gashed him. He still had his knife and water bag and he could see his spears lying nearby. Despite being badly bruised and shaken, he had been lucky.

About thirty yards distant, the bloated remains of the cow lay rotting in the sunlight. A good portion had been consumed. Deke counted heads and saw five wolves in the immediate vicinity. No doubt the others had filled their bellies and gone back to the den to care for the pups. A delicate thought like a whisper touched the surface of his mind and painfully he sent back an agreement. Yes, he wanted to head back to the den also, wanted a place of relative familiarity where he could nurse his wounds and try to unscramble his brain, but he wasn't sure he could walk that far. Also he was beginning to become aware of a ravenous hunger. Despite his stomach's recent outrage, his body demanded food, and soon.

He noticed the sun was low in the sky and the light was positively queer. The female wolf nudged his hand and again sent the image of the den, more insistently this time.

He staggered over to the dead cow, wrinkling his nose. His people rarely ate their meat aged, preferring it fresh. But Deke knew some clans liked to eat meat after hanging it for a week or so. This carcass smelled pretty high considering how recently it had been killed. He bent to examine it more closely. Maggots were already crawling through the flesh. Three days, he thought with alarm. It took at least three days, maybe four, for meat left in the sun to reach this state of decay. His stomach lurched, and he retched tiredly. Even starved as he was he couldn't eat that meat. In his current weakness it probably would kill him.

He straightened and put his hands to his head as another agonizing spasm racked his skull. After a few minutes it passed, and he peered around in the strange light like an old man.

Back, he thought a little deliriously. Got to get back before they finish.

Pushing his frailty aside with determination, he gathered his spears and set out after the wolves. It took all his concentration to keep one foot moving after the other, all his will to stay vertical. The young female sent empathic encouragement and stayed abreast of him. Every so often she winced and he realized she was experiencing with him the pain he felt pulsing in his head.

What had taken two hours on the way out to the grassland now took forever. Every step made Deke grit his teeth. Before long he had to stop to rest, and he drank wearily from his water bag. The liquid refreshed him somewhat and his headache retreated slightly. Dehydrated, he thought. How long was I really out?

There was no way to know. The only thing he was sure about was that once again the wolves had saved his life. Lying unconscious on the wide savannah, he should have been easy prey for any passing predator. The wolves had guarded him when he was helpless, and this went against everything he had ever been told about wolves in the wild. Supposedly they attacked when they sensed weakness, even among their own kind.

He climbed to his feet and continued his painful progress.

Night fell soon after they left the grassland. The air was thick, and Deke started to sweat as the humidity rose. The atmosphere grew stifling and began to feel like a wet blanket lying uneasily against his flesh. He could see flashes of lightning in the western sky and began to understand the wolves' apprehension. A storm was coming, and storms at this time of year often produced twisters.

Almost, he felt his eyes fill with tears. It wasn't fair, he told himself bitterly. It was too hard, too pointless, and his head hurt so abominably; how was he supposed to endure any more?

And for what? he asked himself as he drove his unwilling legs forward. Probably it was too late already, probably it was past the day he must be given the mark of manhood with his fellows, or else remain forever cast out from among his people.

He set his jaw stubbornly. No, he told himself. You will not be cast out. You will find the others. And if you don't...he paused and swallowed hard. If you don't, well, you'll worry about that when the time comes.

Sometime around midnight the rain began. Warm droplets splashed off his skin, taking away some of the dirt and sweat. There was thunder but it wasn't too bad and his hopes began to rise. The rain soaked him, loosening the dried blood from his wounds, running in red streamlets down his body.

The downpour increased to a deluge as boy and wolves trudged along. Despite their obvious desire to rejoin the pack, the wolves never left his side.

57

They led him steadily through the tempest, their inner directional systems telling them which way to go. In particular the young female seemed to have an unerring sense of place and time, and stayed close enough for Deke to hold onto her for guidance.

The night was nearly spent by the time the bedraggled group reached the den site. The rain had slackened to a misty drizzle but the air remained unnaturally warm.

Deke collapsed on his soaked bearskin, his head throbbing painfully, his limbs trembling with exhaustion. The rest of the wolves appeared from everywhere and a vigorous greeting ensued.

The Alpha female emerged from her den and approached. She sat near him at the edge of the sodden fur. Her gaze was intent as she studied his ravaged face. She leaned over and began to cleanse his wounds with her tongue. When she had finished to her satisfaction, she lay alongside, and gazing into his eyes, sent him a vivid image. For a second the depleted youngster could hardly believe what he was getting, but the wolf sent the image again and with her muzzle, pushed his face towards her belly.

As dawn broke greyly, Deke suckled greedily as any wolf cub at the she-wolf's breast, his famished body too desperate for nutrition, his mind too numb from his exertions, for him to feel anything but mute gratitude for this intimate gift of survival.

Another day and night passed before Deke was able to drag himself up to walk creakily over to the fresh water spring. When he got there he rested briefly before cleaning his grimy body thoroughly. His head still hurt but now the pain was more manageable, less debilitating.

The weather remained threatening, the air humid and oppressive. The wolves had hunted again during the night, and he watched as they regurgitated partially digested meat for the puppies to eat. Though light-headed from hunger, he swore he'd suck a hundred wolf tits before eating anything puked up out of anyone's belly.

While the pack lolled about with stomachs distended, Deke filled his water bag and prepared to leave. He rolled the bearskin in a tube and tied it with rawhide. He bound his one remaining spear to it and attached a wide strip to use as a shoulder strap.

He turned to face the wolves who looked at him expectantly, understanding exactly what was happening. The puppies, noticeably larger than when he'd first met them, clambered over the adults to gnaw the leather of his make-shift sandals. He knelt and patted each of them. The Alpha female rubbed against him, and he roughed up the fur around her neck. Her mate stood alertly, waiting for the boy to finish with the other pack members. On his signal the five young wolves who had accompanied Deke back from the ill-fated hunting trip gathered nearby.

Deke looked a question at the Alpha. In response, the wolf sent an image of him cutting branches from a stunted tree, and Deke was so astounded his mouth dropped open. How could the wolf know about that?

A series of further images played across his mind, and paramount among them was a moving picture of wolves following boy-tracks backwards through the ruins.

Of course! he thought. These wolves could follow trails using esper ability alone if necessary!

The Alpha sent another series of images, and in these Deke saw himself following phantom boy-tracks backwards through the same ruins. It appeared the wolf was telling him that he, too, could use psi-sensitivity to follow a trail.

Deke nodded, awed by the wild canine's level of comprehension, amazed to think the wolf had gotten the history of his journey out of his own memory, and was playing it back to teach him an important lesson.

When he was certain Deke really understood, the Alpha came over and rested his huge muzzle in the boy's hand. Then he bounded off, calling to his pack to run with him. Except for the Alpha female who chose to remain with her pups and the five young wolves who waited with Deke, all the wolves leaped up and took off after their leader. Their joyous howls floated back to the boy's ears as he set off in the direction from which he'd started his ordeal.

Now he drove his emaciated body without letup. His five companions ranged around him and used their esper talent like radar to sweep the landscape for danger or opportunity, though for Deke opportunity had to be bypassed in favor of covering the maximum distance with the minimum effort, for indeed, his energy reserves were almost exhausted. The milk he had drunk had been rich and nourishing but his growing frame needed calories, lots of calories. Right now his ribs stood out in separate bas-relief and his flanks were sunken hollows. The taut, wiry bands of his adolescent muscles moved independently under skin drawn so tight it seemed they must burst forth and snap like elastic thongs stretched too far.

Before long, they reached the tiny dead tree. Standing in the alkali dust, Deke relived those first terrifying hours after the men had deposited him here to live or die. He cast his mind back through his memory and retrieved the information he needed to find his way. He remembered heading due west after the men had departed. Prior to that the sun had beat first on his left shoulder and then full on his back. He calculated that if he headed a little north of east he should be able to cut his journey shorter by striking diagonally cross-country.

Without further consideration, he started to trot across the burning gravel and sand. The sun was hot even though the day continued hazy and overcast. Soon perspiration was running down his legs and falling into the dust. Around him were many tumbled ruins, chunks of concrete shaped surrealistically over the centuries by wind-blown sand.

Hours passed. Nothing looked familiar. He fell into a tireless rhythm and the wolves loped alongside him. He thought it was due to their presence that no animals stalked him, no will o' the wisp sapped his strength, no living soul appeared to threaten his way.

The sun slanted westward and he began to be filled with anticipation. He should be coming to the rendezvous point soon. For the last several minutes he had been sensing the echo of human thoughts directly ahead. He couldn't quite judge the distance but it felt close. The wolves were picking it up, too. Their esper communications were becoming more agitated and excited.

In a minute or two he circled around a large boulder and came to a halt. There were hoofprints in the sand, but they were faded, made indistinct by the recent rainstorm. Whomever they belonged to had left days ago. He started walking slowly and a few minutes later came to another familiar place. Here the psychic echo was powerful, and with it was a reverberation of physical pain.

Deke's heart beat very fast. This was the spot. There could be no doubt. But everyone was long gone.

His knees went out from under him and he sat down hard. The submissive female lay down by his side and the other wolves also waited, watching him.

So it was all for nothing. He was as good as dead to his people. By returning late he had destroyed himself. No boy was supposed to survive more than seven days alone in the ruins. After seven days even the strongest, most resourceful boys were considered dead or worse than dead. After seven days the manhood group would have given up waiting, even for a chieftain's son.

Deke controlled his despair with an effort and tried to think what to do next. His hand reached out and absently stroked the female wolf at his side. He wondered if she wanted to go home as badly as he did.

That was the key, he realized, going home. He believed he could find the way, but what would happen once he got there?

His expression was somber.

It was simple. Unless he passed through the final part of this test, his ordeal could never be over.

He thought of his father, remembered how old and destroyed he had looked in his out of body nightmare, and knew he could never cause Barr disappointment. Until that dream, he hadn't fully appreciated his father's emotional investment in him, not only in his life, but in his future potential. It hadn't occurred to him how deeply his father loved and needed him. Or, he admitted to himself, how much he needed his father's approval.

With difficulty he ordered his thoughts.

There was only one solution. He must receive the mark of adulthood. He couldn't go home without it. But there was no ritual master to perform the surgery, nor were there any men present to help him withstand the physical agony. He would have to make the two cuts himself and pray he got it right.

He withdrew Peter's knife from his belt and turned it over in his hands. The blade was long and clumsy for such a delicate task, but the edge, at least, was sharp and clean.

The trick to getting the thing done right would be two-fold. First, he had to cut deep enough but not too deep, and second, he had to cut quickly, before his nerves could fully register the pain.

"Ruins help me," he muttered hoarsely. He felt a sudden urge to urinate and got up to do so, sending his stream splashing across the blade. He remembered hearing that fresh urine had antiseptic properties and hoped it was true. He shook the knife until it was essentially dry and strode back and forth for a few minutes breathing deeply. Better to do it now while there was still light and his resolve held.

He grasped the knife firmly in his right hand and took hold of his shrinking penis with his left. Sweat broke out on his face as he raised the knife overhead in ritual fashion and made a special plea for the spirits who guided him to guide him especially well now. With this prayer on his lips, he stretched his foreskin and held on for dear life. Then he brought the blade down in a swift movement no less precise for its speed, and made the first cut.

The abrupt, agonizing pain was shocking, much worse than he'd expected, and his pent-up breath exploded out of him in an involuntary cry. Blood began to drip onto his hand. Gasping, he flipped the knife to make the second cut and screamed as he inadvertently cut too deep, leaving an extra gash just below the head of his penis on the top side. The piece of flesh that had been his foreskin hung from a shred. Desperately, he slashed once more until it was free and dropped to the dust, taking the last remnants of his childhood with it.

With a shout that brought the wolves uneasily to their feet, Deke turned his face to the sky and gave vent to the triumph that flooded his spirit. He'd done it! Like the biblical Abraham, he had circumcised himself! He felt his throat open in an exultant, rising shriek, and this cathartic release of pain and fear turned loose all the tumultuous feelings long buried in his heart, separating him from his past, and setting his mind free.

Then he dropped the knife from a hand grown tremulous and looked down at his wounded organ. As if from a great height he examined the gash anxiously and hoped it wasn't a serious injury. He let the cuts bleed, believing this would help prevent infection. Without success he tried to contain the indescribable torment that had taken up residence between his thighs. The pain was so intense he wondered how he'd ever be able to travel.

He looked up to see the wolves watching him enigmatically. They probably considered him insane, or worse.

His teeth bared in a grin that was mostly grimace and he drank from his water bag, gagging as the warm water touched his parched throat. The wolves slipped off one at a time and he realized when the submissive female came back with dripping jaws that they had found water of their own. If he could persuade his legs to carry him, he could put fresh water in the bag before going on. But for now his legs weren't carrying him anywhere and in the aftermath of his extreme exertion he sank to the ground, barely finding strength to spread his bearskin before he passed out.

The wolves arranged themselves in their usual protective formation, with their noses pointed outward. The sun slipped below the horizon, but in that place of manhood ceremonial deep in the ruins, no one was awake to notice.

CHAPTER FOUR

There is a tendency for those of us who live in a technological society to denigrate, or at the very least, underestimate, anyone raised without the advantages of modern science, but there is a danger here. First, this pre-supposes that with less technical advancement there is less intelligence or sophistication, and that is frequently untrue. Second, it negates the possibility that sciences exist other than our physical ones, and herein lies the real problem...

When I explained to the General that we could not see the way he could, he was unsurprised. He told me none of the humans he had met who lived locked away from the ruins could do so.

As far as feats of actual magic went, I argued that there was no such thing as magic, just science unexplained. This made him laugh, because, he said, like most unenlightened people, I was allowing myself to be distracted by semantic intellectualization, the purpose of which was to keep me unenlightened.

That shut me up, I can tell you.

— Ourn Rohlvaag; Collected Journals; City of Life, A.D. 3109

Tilva was distraught. She stood in the doorway of her pavilion looking at a group of recently erected bachelor tents set at the edge of a small meadow perhaps seventy yards distant. She could see her husband walking circles around one set on a rise apart from the others. Every so often he touched the poles out front supporting the oiled and waxed double canvas tarp that served as door flap, and in fine weather, awning. She knew he was sleeping there (when he slept at all) and that like her, he was remembering.

Despite the immensity of her own heartache, watching Barr's aimless disinterest in life was even more devastating. In their years together she had known him to be a hundred different men depending upon his mood, but never had she seen him so silent and diminished. Day by day she could see his normally ebullient personality unraveling.

She placed her palms on her abdomen and wondered whether to tell him her news now or wait for his grief to fade. It would never go away entirely, she knew, not for him or for her. But there was always hope in new life, and she held that thought close while cradling her pregnant belly tenderly.

Although Tilva knew her son's spirit lived on, she wasn't comforted. She missed his day to day presence more than she could have believed possible. At moments she caught herself turning to address him and then dissolving in tears when she realized what she was doing.

Each day she wanted to connect to the non-physical entities with whom she normally maintained close contact, but something stopped her. It was as if there was a barrier between her and the greater Universe, one her clairvoyance couldn't breach. She couldn't tell if she had constructed it or if her spirit guides had. Either way, it didn't matter. The fact was, she didn't have the heart to go about her business any more than Barr did.

Other families had lost sons as well; more would be lost as the manhood testing continued. The strange juxtapositioning of young boys dying during this springtime season of rebirth made Tilva believe the rites were a form of human sacrifice, designed to propitiate the dangerous forces abroad in their shattered world so the People of the Wolf could continue to thrive and flourish. If true, she thought bitterly, then this year would outshine all others, for this time the People had given up their brightest and best.

As he wandered in and out of the tent that should have been his son's, Barr's mind was bemused, unable to accept the reality of Deke's absence. For the first time in his life he was prey to horrible imaginings. Was the agent of his boy's death human or animal? Had he been injured, gotten lost, left to wander until he died of thirst or hunger? Or, and he squeezed his eyes shut in agony, had his beloved child been taken by a demon?

He leaned his head against a tent pole, exhausted by grief, by the Universe's mercilessness.

Memories played in unending repetition across his vision; pictures of Deke as an infant, as a toddler when their relationship was easy and his son had liked nothing better than to ride before his father in the saddle, pointing at everything that fell under his curious, blue gaze, asking questions and more questions until Barr had laughed and hugged him near, reminding him that tomorrow was another day and he could continue his interrogation then.

Choking, the chieftain banged his forehead softly against the pole, wishing he could batter his thoughts to silence, and find, if not peace, then at least quiet. Instead he found himself reliving events of the previous March, when Deke had stowed away to the stone village with Willie O'Dale, and learned his people's greatest secret.

Though this part of the tale had been told to him later, Barr was sure the leader of the bandits didn't know what hit him when his horse stepped on the pressure grenade. One moment he was vibrantly, alertly alive, his head cocked as he gazed with anticipation at the town that twice previously had yielded up its produce and women for the taking without protest.

And then, in the flash of an instant, he and his horse exploded in a roaring, ripping spray of blood and tissue. Matter of every description spewed on the cobblestones, spraying Deke where he crouched in hiding. He wiped his face, gripping his rifle eagerly. He already had chosen his target, a burly man wearing unusual headgear that covered his face like a bucket turned upside down.

The bandits were in disorder. They shouted frantically to one another as they fought their horses under control, but Willie gave them no time to recover. The rattle of automatic weaponry started as the Wolf soldiers began to fire with deadly accuracy into the surging melée of confused raiders. Forward momentum carried the chaotic horde thundering in Deke's direction. He stood up from behind his cover, raised his rifle to his shoulder, and fired.

The bandits' second-in-command spotted him at the same time as Willie O'Dale and his soldiers. With a shriek of frenzied rage, this man brandished his weapons, thrilled to have a target upon which to vent his frustration and despair. He spurred his horse viciously, determined to ride down the small figure he held personally responsible for his leader's hideous death.

Fire from a dozen rifles tore his horse out from under him, dumping him practically at Deke's feet. Deke hesitated, bayonet poised, filth and grit in his mouth. The man tried to rise; his eyes met Deke's and seemed startled to discover he was looking into the blood-spattered face of a boy. Then realization came over him: his back was broken.

"Do it," he rasped, his face agonized. He glared upwards at the shining blade of Deke's bayonet. "Damn you, do it!"

Deke's expression was complex and unreadable.

He didn't let the bandit suffer.

The rest of it Barr knew by direct experience as well as telling by the principals, and he remembered it now with vivid clarity.

Word passed from one lookout to another as the sun began to set behind the mountains. They acknowledged with respectful hand motions the lone rider and wolfish dog who paced steadily up the long approach to the town.

These were ignored, and the men settled back into their places, sending covert warnings up the mountain to their fellows: Barr Wolfson had arrived; his mood was uncertain; walk softly.

O'Dale was waiting for his commander and friend. He gestured to one of his men to take the horse and as Barr dismounted, said, "I knew you'd be along, m'lord."

"Where is he?" Barr demanded without preamble.

"Sleeping the sleep of all good soldiers. What a boy he is! You should be proud."

"Are you telling me what I should think or feel, Willie?" There was an edge to the chieftain's voice.

"Never, m'lord."

Barr's eyes narrowed as he studied the other man. Willie returned his gaze equably.

Barr laughed and slapped his thighs. "The boy must have done well for you to take up for him!"

"Aye, he's a bloody marvel, and only twelve..."

"Show me to a bath and some grub and tell me your story. Then I'll decide what to do with him," Barr said, looking around for the first time. "I assume our problem's solved, otherwise."

"Aye," Willie agreed. "But come, m'lord, do you want to eat or bathe first?"

"Bath first, then food. And let's have some ale or wine. After all that riding, I need it!" Barr rubbed his hind end meaningfully.

Willie had gotten rooms for Barr at the local inn, an easily defended spot centrally located in the town. Deke occupied one of them, guarded by the faithful Melak and two other soldiers. Servants had drawn hot water in preparation for the chieftain's arrival, and now they ushered him unctuously towards the baths.

As Barr peeled his filthy outer clothing off, he shouted for another tub to be filled for his dog, demanded food and drinking water be brought as well. The innkeeper waved his assistant off to see to it while he lingered a few moments longer, waiting deferentially to be acknowledged by the Wolf chieftain, who could order his death for any or no reason whenever he chose. Though this Wolfson hadn't the reputation for such behavior, one never knew about these people. Far easier to see that the soldiers were soothed in every way possible.

"You, fellow, bring me wine and a barber. My beard needs trimming." Barr grinned at Willie, his good humor restored by the prospect of a hot bath.

"As my lord wishes. Do you require anything else?"

"Have my clothes cleaned up. I rode so fast I forgot a change."

"As soon as my lord has vacated them..." The innkeeper averted his eyes politely.

Barr stripped and stepped into the tub, sighing as he sank back into its heat. "Ah, there's paradise for you," he said while the innkeeper gathered his discarded garments and stole quietly away. "So," he commented when the two men were alone.

O'Dale nodded and sat nearby on a small stool. "What a morning. Should've been here, my lord, should've seen how the boy did. They'll be writing songs about his adventures one day."

"Aye, if he manages to keep from getting himself killed with his infernal recklessness." Barr stretched his legs, rubbing his left knee where an old wound had stiffened it.

"Boys will be boys, m'lord."

"I don't see yours driving you so hard."

Willie shrugged. "They do their share. In different ways." He chuckled. "We sound like a pair of geezers! Did you ever think you'd be worrying about all this domestic mess?"

Barr chuckled with him. "Aye, because I knew I had to have an heir. A legitimate heir," he amended. "There's plenty of my get flourishing around the countryside, but not one of 'em could command the People, even if I acknowledged 'em. And some are good kids, fine little brats, especially..." Barr paused meaningfully. "Well, you know who I mean."

"Aye, but does Deke? Or Tilva?" O'Dale studied his hands judiciously.

"Not the boy, but Tilva might. She finds out most things."

O'Dale remained silent.

"But Deke, now, here's a boy who has the real fire. He'll hold his own and more."

"And if he's challenged?"

"Only one who could challenge him won't."

Willie spoke softly. "You can't know that."

Barr's expression hardened. "I can't protect him from everything. To lead he must stand or fall on his own merit."

"Not to worry," Willie reassured him. "The soldiers love him and after today, they're sure he's protected by spirit magic."

Barr laughed. "Spirits! His mother probably spelled him so!"

Willie laughed also, but with less certainty.

"Aye," Barr rumbled, settling deeper into his bath. "She's probably spelled him a thousand different ways. She'll take it hard when he moves to his own tent."

"They always do," O'Dale agreed. "So, my lord, if you don't need me for anything pressing, I'll go finish wrapping things up."

"Good. Get some rest, my friend. Tomorrow I'm going to show Deke why we guard this town so carefully."

O'Dale's eyebrows rose in surprise.

"Aye," Barr affirmed, "It's time. If he's to be the next chieftain of the People, he has to know the truth about this place. I'm not a youngster any more."

Willie moved towards the door, an involuntary spasm arcing up his spine as he tried to imagine life without Barr Wolfson in command of the People, and failed.

Barr waved his hand in dismissal. "I'll see you in the morning."

"Very good. Sleep well."

"Yes," Barr said to the dog when Willie was gone, "Let's try, at any rate."

Canis yawned widely as if to agree.

The morning sun was bright and glittered off the paving stones as father and son met in the town's central square. Everything was immaculate. Not a sign of the previous day's battle remained.

"How does one tell the difference between memory and dream?" Deke wondered aloud.

Barr eyed his son's troubled expression with grim empathy. "With luck, others will share your memories. And stay the hell out of your dreams."

Deke nodded. "Good morning, Father. When did you arrive?"

"Late yesterday. Come, let's get breakfast. We can talk while we eat." Barr's tone gave nothing away.

A familiar glint appeared in Deke's eyes and Barr noted it with amusement, thinking, Ah, here is where he tries to charm me.

"Are we at peace or at war?" Deke asked bluntly.

"You decide," Barr replied.

"I choose peace," Deke said without hesitation.

"A wise choice," Barr approved. "Perhaps there's hope for you yet."

Deke sighed. "I guess I deserve that."

"Let's eat, son. And don't worry; I won't take anything more from you."

Deke searched his father's face.

"I'm about to give you something. But like most gifts, this one is double-edged."

"What do you mean?"

"Breakfast," Barr said firmly. "Then revelations."

After eating a meal of fried eggs, toasted bread dripping with butter, and a dried fruit compote topped with sweet cream, father and son strolled together down the main street talking about inconsequential matters.

"You'll be a man in two months," Barr said, after a while. "Why did you have to jump the gun?"

Deke shrugged. "It was something to do."

Barr studied his son, realizing he would never get a straight answer to that question. "You're young for this, Deke," he said. "But I'm proud of you. You've always been precocious in these matters. Your teachers tell me you've

shown great progress in your training. And," Barr added with studied casualness, "It has come to my attention that you've met your benefactor."

Deke glanced at his father, then nodded. "He told me you had spoken
for me."

"You'll find that this...teacher is different from your others."

"Did he teach you?" Deke's eyes were intent.

Barr shrugged. "Only your education is important right now."

Deke considered this. Then his expression brightened. "You said you
had a gift."

"Yes, it is a gift of sorts." Barr was silent for a few moments before
saying, "How much do you know about ancient times?"

"A little," Deke replied, caught off guard by the change of subject.

Barr took advantage of his son's perplexity. "You've been trained in
the use of firearms, explosives, blades, and hand-to-hand combat. You'll be
studying tactics and strategy starting this year. Your mother and I have seen
indications you're already adept in these areas as a matter of natural talent, but
only time will tell for sure, and experience."

Their route had taken them to an innocuous building near the edge of
town. Barr nodded to some men who stood nearby. At his gesture, they moved
away. With his hand firmly on his son's shoulder, he propelled Deke inside and
closed the door behind them.

Inside, all was darkness. Barr brought Deke to a halt. "Stand still."

The hair prickled at the base of Deke's skull. He sensed great space,
great depth, and shivered as air moved against his skin.

There was a brief spark as his father struck flint to metal and lit a
kerosene lamp hanging from the wall near the door.

Deke took an involuntary step backwards. He had been standing nearly on the edge of a precipice falling away in a perfect black circle that formed
the opening of a giant cylinder that went down. Everything was sheathed in
metal, and the floor upon which they stood was also metal. A mostly rickety,
frequently interrupted railing wrapped around the lip of the cylindrical hole.
Barr pointed to a spot halfway around the cylinder where steel rungs descended into nothingness.

"What's down there?" Deke asked. He shut his eyes for a second,
almost in pain. He knew without being told, and Barr saw the awareness on his
face.

"Missile," his father said gravely. "Nuke."

"This building...?"

"Built to hide only." Barr looked into his son's eyes. "This is what used
to be called a strategic nuclear device. It was made for long range use. Our vil-

lagers protect this secret for us."

"They're soldiers?" Deke guessed.

"Mostly not. That would make it too obvious."

"Have you ever been down there?"

"Aye. You can go, too, if you like."

"What will I find?"

"Controls. We don't know much about them. There's no way to make the things go."

"More than one?" Deke asked, unnerved.

"Fifteen buildings in this town harbor similar devices."

"Could they still function?"

Barr shrugged. "No way for us to know."

"What good are they?" Deke questioned.

"We can't use them now. That may not always be the case."

"Do you think the answers lie in the west?"

Barr smiled approvingly. "I've plied the habitable lands up and down the eastern edge of this continent for most of my life. Every fort I take, every village I conquer, I look for information. I've never yet found any answers. But in the meantime I've carved a kingdom. Perhaps you will build an empire, eh, my son?"

"The ruins willing," Deke said, his expression becoming grim.

"Yes, ruins willing." Barr paused. "If you want to climb down, do it now. I'll wait."

Deke eyed the blackness uneasily. "The missile is there?"

"Ready and waiting for the right hand to release it, should it ever become necessary, which in truth I pray never happens."

"Light?" Deke asked.

"Not until you reach the bottom."

Deke nodded, realizing this was another test. He worked his way around the perimeter of the pit until he reached the steel rungs, then started down. It took a long time to reach the bottom and light the lamp he found there. He looked carefully at everything, every incomprehensible piece of equipment and gadgetry, every dial and switch, screen and light, trying to absorb it all, to understand it by staring at it.

Nuke, he thought. Nuclear weapon. The great planet-killer. And he was standing alongside it. He reached out a hand and touched the cold metal. A sense of evil power seemed to ooze from the alloy skin. For an instant he felt himself consumed by madness so compelling he wanted to gibber and dance and genuflect about the base of this monstrous thing, this *ruin-maker*, but controlled himself, trembling, and tore his hand away.

What could his father be thinking? he wondered frantically. Such danger here...so crazy to believe anyone could control it. What if someone found it who knew how to make it go? What if it went off by itself? It had been here a long time, after all. And it wasn't the only one. Nukes from the twenty-first century. A waking nightmare bequeathed to future generations.

Deke sat weakly, the strength gone from his knees. His father wanted him to know about this, he thought. Why?

I'm his heir, he acknowledged. This will be my responsibility some day.

He rose, grasped one of the rungs, and blew out the lantern. In the darkness he felt the malevolence of the sinister thing like a throbbing or pulsation that beat at his body surface.

Much sobered, he climbed the ancient rungs until he stood beside Barr once more, who again sensed his feelings as if they'd been spoken aloud.

"I don't know why you've decided to trust me," he said with a quiet openness he rarely displayed before anyone. He looked into his father's eyes, perceiving him in a new way, realizing he wished to be perceived in a new way as well. "But thank you."

"Good," Barr said brusquely, remembering his own emotions when first confronted with this place. "You must never speak of this, even to your mother or friends. Especially not to your friends. Do you understand me, Deke?" He peered intently into Deke's eyes.

"Aye. You're telling me to trust no one."

"That's right. Now you begin to perceive the world as a man and chieftain should." Barr's expression was dark and unreadable.

"But your men...?" Deke said.

"...have been tested. Until you command men and have put them to the test, this must remain our secret. Promise me, Deke."

"Of course," he replied automatically, and his father could see his mind spinning with these new thoughts.

"Now we go home. Now your schooling begins in earnest." Barr clapped his son on the back and blew out the lantern. Then the two moved into the light together, closing the door firmly behind them.

It was late afternoon. Tilva was jolted out of her gloomy ruminations by Andara Farflight, who arrived bearing a covered, cast iron pot filled with a savory leg of lamb cooked with vegetables and herbs. Andara paused at the door, waiting for her patron to say something, and when the older woman didn't, slipped past her to place the pot on a trivit on the table.

Eventually, Tilva spoke absently. "Thank you, dear," she said without

71

turning, "But I couldn't eat anything."

Andara shrugged slightly. "I didn't expect you would," she said. "I didn't bring it for you."

"Barr probably won't want it either," Tilva told the girl. "I'm sorry you went to so much trouble."

The girl stamped her foot impatiently and crossed her arms over her budding chest. "You really don't know, do you?" she asked disbelievingly.

"Know what?" Tilva said, the girl's unusual rudeness finally getting her attention and making her turn around.

"I thought sure you'd be first to know."

"Know know know...what should I know?" Tilva demanded, losing her temper. "What kind of game are you playing?"

"No game," Andara said, moving towards the door. "Come see for yourself!" She ran outside with Tilva following.

Tilva heard a growing pandemonium and turned a baffled look across the meadow towards Barr, who stood frozen like a great statue.

The chieftain came to life, sprinting towards the southwestern edge of Spring Camp where the bedlam originated. He shoved through a crowding mob of people to stand staring, his chest heaving with emotion. Tilva got there a minute later and stood beside him, following his pointed gaze until she, too, stared in shocked disbelief.

Escorted by lookouts who kept an uneasy distance between them, a strange apparition strode draped in a rank bearskin; a filthy scarecrow whose blue eyes blazed with triumph and exultation. Arrayed protectively around him were five wolves who made it clear they belonged with him.

The apparition came to a halt, swaying slightly. It made a gesture to the wolves who settled on their haunches. Gradually silence fell over the crowd.

Tilva started to run, but Barr's iron grip stopped her.

"Wait!" he said, staring at the impossible spectacle.

The apparition spoke. "It's all right," it croaked with a feeble attempt at insouciance. "I'm no boogeyman."

Barr released her and they went to their son, folding him in their arms while around them cheers began to rise from the incredulous mob.

Joyous hands reached to touch Deke as he, his parents, and the company of wolves made their way through the thronging people. Word spread from one edge of the crowd to the other, and the excited voices of the lookouts could be heard as they related what they'd seen before the chieftain's son had donned the bearskin.

"Circumcised himself, by God!" was repeated more than once until it was said close enough for Barr and Tilva to hear. It took a moment to register and then their eyes met in shock behind Deke's back.

Barr looked at his son, took in the grinding exhaustion, the starvation, the dried trails of blood on his legs, the massive bruising on his face, and was consumed by awe and pity. Gently, he stroked Deke's matted hair, smoothing it back from his forehead. Self-control was an art Barr Wolfson had mastered early in life but now it almost failed him. He had to clench his teeth to keep his jaw from trembling.

Tilva had no such compunctions. She held Deke's arm and patted him to be sure he was really there. When they reached her tent she could hardly wait to get him inside where she could appraise his injuries.

"Wait," Deke said, and turned to look over the surging crowd. His eyes sought out and acknowleged the boys of his manhood group. As he looked at each of his friends in turn he could feel their emotions as clearly as if they had drawn him a picture. Joy, shock, and admiration shone from their minds. And underneath everything, a kind of reverence which only boys so recently made men together could feel for one who had transcended fear, desperation, agony, even abandonment, to surpass them all.

Deke's eyes fell on Andara.

Her gaze was fastened adoringly on his face. He wondered why he had never noticed how green her eyes were or how beautiful she was becoming. He smiled into those luminous eyes and was surprised by a desire to kiss her. He blushed furiously and tore his gaze away. Then he looked at his people. Herdsmen, merchants, artisans, soldiers, women and children: their faces reflected amazement, speculation, and the inquisitiveness common to their kind. He realized they expected him to say something and spoke haltingly.

"You can't know how glad I am to be home with all of you," he said, forcing his hoarse voice out over the crowd, his sincerity moving them all.

Approval came from thousands of throats in the form of glad cheers and bellowing.

Barr raised his hand and the crowd slowly subsided again. "You'll get to see him in a day or two. Now he needs to rest."

There was murmured agreement and people began to move away from Tilva's pavilion. Final calls of welcome floated across the little meadow as Deke fastened his over-bright gaze on Andara.

"Please, stay," he said to her. Her emotional aura was especially strong and appealing to him right now and he thought that of everyone he knew, she was the only one he would be able to talk to about his experience.

Tilva's eyes flicked rapidly between the two young people. "Yes, Andara," she agreed, "Stay." Then, to Deke, "Andara made you some food. Do you think you can eat?"

"Aye." He turned to the wolves who watched him expectantly. An image of the pack's den site filled his mind and reluctantly he nodded agreement. In a fast series of images the wolves made it clear he would always be at the edge of their perceptions. One by one they came to him and allowed him to stroke their fur. Then all but the young female turned and trotted away. A lump rose in his throat as she leaned against his leg and put her muzzle in his hand. He scratched gently under her chin and Sent a reassuring image into her awareness.

His eyes fell on Andara again, and he Sent a tentative image into her mind as well, wondering if she would *see* it with her esper sense. She seemed startled, made a face, and hurried into the tent before he could respond. Suppressing a grin, he followed more slowly, the wolf at his side.

Knowing they were forgotten for the moment, his parents exchanged smiles of relief at their son's deliverance. Hundreds of questions were on the tips of their tongues but they forced themselves to wait. There would be ample time to satisfy their curiosity. For now, healing was their overriding concern, and also for now, it was enough.

CHAPTER FIVE

The General and I talked frequently about his esper abilities. He described the way puberty's flood of hormones had begun the process of accelerating his sensitivity, but that his manhood test had sharpened it. And every week thereafter, he told me pensively, as he recalled his adolescent psychic experiences, he had felt his mind expanding, his strength increasing, until he began to wonder what was happening to him, and if he ever would reach a defining limit...

— *Ourn Rohlvaag; Collected Journals; City of Life, A.D. 3109*

Deke floated above his body.

Soon after eating most of the lamb and making Barr promise to feed his wolf, he passed out at the table, sitting upright. His father caught him before he could fall and carried him to his old bed from his former life. If he had been awake he would have protested that he should sleep in his new bachelor's tent. But even from his strange vantage point the bed looked cozy and familiar as they stripped away the hideous bearskin and crude sandals. While his mother sponged dirt and blood from his sun-blackened skin, his father examined the circumcision wounds, marveling, thinking Deke had done the job perfectly. He ordered Andara to bring a bottle of antiseptic lotion and a bandage. Upon her return the girl was only able to get a quick glimpse before the chieftain's broad shoulders blocked her view.

From his disembodied place near the ceiling, Deke watched as Tilva cut free the rawhide belt and deposited it with the knife, waterbag, and pouch on a small table beside the bed. She removed the necklace of claws and held them up mutely for Barr to see. The chieftain shook his head. The claws looked like five-inch sabers to him and he thanked whatever lucky star had been looking after his son. While Tilva swabbed the cuts on Deke's chest, Barr picked up the pouch and opened it, spilling the contents on the table. Breath exploded quietly from his lungs.

"Look here," he said. "Here're the bear's teeth, but these others! Merciful God! They're from a tiger, a ruins tiger! Why is he still alive?"

Tilva looked at the she-wolf lying nearby whose yellow eyes had never left Deke's face from the moment he'd passed out.

Barr followed her glance. "But how..."

"We must be patient," Tilva said.

"This knife..." Barr began, and his voice trailed off. His gaze turned inward as he remembered his own manhood ceremony. Custom dictated he not discuss the ritual. "This knife," he began again, "Is someone else's."

Tilva's eyes met his. Without turning, she spoke to Andara who was clearing away the food. "You can leave that, dear," she said to the girl. "Why not come back in the morning?"

Andara understood instantly. "Of course," she said. "But if I could say one thing first...?"

"Go ahead," Barr told her.

"Deke would never kill a friend to take his knife," she said in a rush, her words tumbling over one another in her need to convince them. "He couldn't. He'd die first."

Barr nodded. "We know that, girl," he said. There was a rare tender note in his voice as he regarded her, liking what he saw.

"Well, then," Andara said. "I guess I'll be off."

Tilva rose to give her a hug. "Thank you, Andara," she said, her tone filled with affection for her acolyte. "Your father is probably looking for you about now."

"Aye," the girl said with an impish grin. "He'll want to hear all my good gossip!"

Tilva laughed happily, thinking how good it felt to laugh again, and Barr joined her.

Andara departed after a final glance towards Deke. She wondered if either of his parents could *see* his energy self hovering above the bed creating a mellow light which Andara sensed with something other than sight, something other than feeling. For a moment that glow was inside her mind as a more than warm presence, and she flushed slightly at the thoughts it aroused in her before Sending him a shy, but equally warm, farewell. Then she slipped from the tent into the gathering twilight.

After Andara was gone, Deke allowed himself to float back into his unconscious body, the effort of remaining outside more than he could manage. Presently he began to snore and his limbs jerked convulsively as his awareness made its complete body/mind connection.

Tilva's fingers probed his forehead gently and he stirred painfully in his sleep. He had gotten a pretty strong concussion, she saw, but was making a good recovery. Heads seemed so much harder on teenagers, she thought. She examined the swelling on the bridge of his nose and the associated bruises under his eyes. His nose was broken but not pushed out of position. Soon enough the swelling would go down and perhaps all he would have to show for it would be a slight bump.

"Will he be all right?" Barr asked when she had finished, his hands absently passing the knife from left to right and back again.

Tilva nodded and looked at the oversized dagger. "Is it a ritual blade?" she asked.

"Aye." Barr's gaze was introspective.

"And he wasn't given one," Tilva pressed.

"That's right," the chieftain said reluctantly. "You should understand one thing about the testing," he continued, wanting her thoughts, and knowing he had to share this information to get them. "There are no rules. Boys must learn to do what is necessary to survive. For boys of our line, it's even more essential, and we start empty-handed." He laid the knife aside.

"There are no moral consequences, is what you're saying," Tilva commented.

Barr couldn't help but smile. Tilva always managed to put her finger on the crux of any ethical issue. "It wouldn't be useful for a leader to feel guilty about doing what he had to do. It would curtail his choices."

"Do you ever feel guilty, husband?" Tilva asked him for the first time in their married life.

"Guilty?" Barr gave the idea due consideration. "No," he said after a while. "But I do feel regret for mistakes made, and particularly waste. Waste of material, of potential, and lately most of all, time." He looked down at his son thoughtfully. "What's happened to him, Tilva? I *saw* him coming before I saw him! He was inside my head as clear as you're standing there!"

"Is that what it was," Tilva murmured to herself. Then aloud, "Andara must have *seen* him that way also."

"You didn't?" Barr was surprised.

"No." A small dart of jealousy came and went in Tilva's heart.

"It was as if his most essential being, the thing that makes him Deke, was inside my head," Barr mused thoughtfully.

"Why did you stop me from going to him?"

"Because the way he looked, he could have been carrying a demon. I was sure if he was coming back after being out so long that he had to have been taken."

"What made you change your mind?"

"Them," Barr said, and gestured to the wolf. "Warm-blooded animals hate demons."

"What would have happened if he was taken?"

"The same thing your people do when it happens down south," Barr said harshly.

Tilva arranged a coverlet over her son's battered body. Taking Barr's hand, she drew him from the alcove and pulled the hangings shut. Raising a finger to her lips, she led him to the rear of the living area where water had been simmering for herbal tea. She poured him a cup and lightly caressed his cheek as she offered him the most comfortable chair in the tent. He kept a grip on her hand and pulled her onto his knee.

"Now tell me what it is you wish to tell me," he said with a good-humored chuckle.

She settled into the broad crook of his arm and pulled at the strands of his red beard. "How do you know I've got something to tell?"

Barr turned her hand and brought the palm to his lips. "I know you," he said. He tightened his arms around her. "So?"

"We're going to have a child early next winter." She waited for his reaction.

"Good God," he said, amazed.

"What are you thinking, my lord?" she asked archly.

"I'm thinking that I hope it's a girl," said Barr with a grin. He kissed her open mouth. "Yes, a nice, little girl who won't grow up and want to slit her brother's throat for the succession."

She burst out laughing. "You are a devil, Barr," she said, trying to get her breath.

His hands slid under her dress and he felt her stomach. "You might be a little rounder," he said, his lips soft against her ear. His hands went lower.

"Come to bed," Tilva invited, heat in her voice.

He spoke against her neck. "We haven't need of a bed."

"You forget, there's a man in the tent."

"It would take an earthquake to wake him."

"We just might cause one, husband," Tilva said, her breathing becoming more languid. Then, sighing, "I've missed you."

"Aye, likewise," Barr said, rising with her in his arms. "That bachelor tent was a cold, lonely place." He carried her through the hangings separating her sleeping quarters from the rest of the tent. "Though my guess is it won't stay that way long." He set her on the bed and began to unfasten her clothing. "Did you see him making cow eyes at Andara?"

"She's too young," Tilva said. "One of us better have a talk with him."

"And with her," he laughed. "She's a precocious wench, and probably that's your doing!"

"You may be right," she said, running her hands voluptuously across his broad chest in a caress that quickly became an embrace. She put her arms around his neck. "I guess I'd better have a talk with her, as well."

"Aye. But not too strict. It's a good match." Barr's mouth found hers again and she gave herself up to the feel of his hard body against her own.

"Mmm," she agreed. She fumbled briefly for the handle to turn down the oil lamp burning brightly on the nightstand, then, as his touch became more insistent, forgot about it.

Morning came, and with it the quiet rustling of people stopping by Tilva's pavilion bearing gifts of food, household goods for Deke's bachelor tent, and most of all, their good wishes.

Barr and Tilva welcomed them all. Tilva had set up a charcoal grill outside where her servants prepared a variety of small foods for anyone who wanted them. Barr shared his people's high spirits, pouring wine himself for anyone with enough foresight to bring a cup. During a lull in visits, he gestured to the heaps of goods piled around the living room and said, "We can set up shop with all these things."

"Deke can set up shop," Tilva corrected him with a smile, complete contentment radiating from her. She laughed as he caught her hand and pulled her into his arms. "Not now," she protested without much strength. "I'm sure we'll have more visitors..."

"They can wait," the chieftain rumbled, kissing her neck. He buried his face in her hair, thankful for getting a second chance with his family. He had come so close to losing both of them, and now with Tilva in his arms again, he knew how miserably angry and unhappy he had been when they were fighting. He didn't know exactly what had tipped the balance, didn't know what had made her decide to forgive him, but he was grateful nonetheless.

Tilva turned and pulled Barr's face to hers. Her fingers twined through his hair and she noticed how the years had fallen away from his features, how compelling his dark eyes were, and how she wanted to lose herself in their depths. During that long period when she was so angry at him, she had forgotten how he made her laugh, how exciting he was to be with. During the years she had hated him for wanting other women when he had her, when his roving eye had made her feel such humiliation and rage that all she wanted to do was slash his face with her nails, she had thought she could never forgive him, didn't even want to try. She had wanted to hurt him the way he had hurt her, yet his ability to grow stern and remote in an instant had made him a difficult target. Too, there was Deke to think of, and for his sake she had known she had to hold her head up and make the best of her situation.

But the night Deke had wandered off in the blizzard, she had let go of her anger. That night she had seen the feeling Barr had for his son, seen his savage determination to find Deke no matter the cost. Tilva had found she couldn't sustain her anger against anyone who loved her child so deeply.

Also that night she finally had understood that it was she who had the power to mend their relationship; he was only waiting for her to give him another chance. It must have been shortly after that in early spring that she had conceived.

This pregnancy was different from her first. When pregnant with Deke she had suffered the kind of sickness all women dread. She had been bloated and bitchy, starving for all sorts of strange foods.

This time she felt wonderful. Her appetite was becoming embarrassing but she barely had a moment's nausea. And now that her son was safe, she found herself experiencing this incredible feeling of semi-arousal which was distracting but too pleasurable to fight. Barr had said he wanted a daughter; she thought she might be able to oblige him. The harmonious changes occurring in her body made her certain she was carrying a girl.

"Wait," she said breathlessly, pushing his hands away. She pulled back the hanging to Deke's sleeping area and peeked in. He was still asleep though now and again he twisted and shook, speaking unintelligibly in a low mumble. She went in and laid a hand across his forehead. She felt fever, and removed the coverlet, searching his wounds for signs of infection. She didn't *see* any, but that didn't mean it wasn't beginning. On the other hand, he might as easily be sick from starvation and exposure. She went to her apothecary of herbal medicines where she selected some dried pieces of bark and put them in a pot with water to simmer.

Barr's expression was questioning.

"He has a touch of fever," she said. "I don't think it's serious. He may have picked up a cold. The wounds are clean."

There was a rattle at the tent flap and Barr called, "Come in!"

Hawk Farflight spoke in his usual soft tone. "I hope I'm not bothering you," he said, entering the tent with a covered platter in his hands. He smiled. "Andara asked me to bring these over. I promised her I wouldn't touch 'em, but I have to tell you she hasn't made anything like this for me lately!" He removed the cover. Inside were two pies. Their aroma wafted through the tent and Tilva's stomach growled while Barr sniffed appreciatively.

"She told me to apologize for them being made from last season's preserves." Hawk looked hungrily at the golden-brown, woven-patterned crusts filled with sweet peaches and black cherries, respectively.

"Why didn't she bring them herself?" asked Tilva.

"I don't know, she said she had something to do. Who can understand Andara, anyway? She's got her own mind, that's for sure." Hawk waved towards Deke's alcove. "How's he doing?"

Tilva went to her cookstove. She removed the simmering pot from the heat and let it steep.

"Exhausted," Barr said.

"Has he said anything?" Hawk asked, his curiosity getting the better of him.

"No," Barr replied. "But I can tell you he tangled with a ruins tiger as well as a brown bear."

Hawk whistled softly, impressed.

Tilva poured off a little of the steeping liquid into a cup. Her eyes made an appeal to Barr, which Hawk intercepted.

"I'll get out of your way," he said, putting the platter on the table. "Andara will be by later, I'm sure."

"Thank her for us, Hawk," Tilva said warmly.

With an affirmative wave of his hand, Hawk ducked out through the door.

"Could you help me?" she asked Barr.

"Of course." As he held aside the drape for Tilva, the she-wolf rose from her place near the bed. Her ears were alert and focused forward. For a second Barr thought she was staring at them, then, as he heard a mournful sniff outside the tent, he chuckled. He looked at the wolf expectantly. "Well, go on," he said, but still she hesitated.

From outside there was another sniff and then a sharp little yip as Canis begged for permission to enter. He had been waiting patiently outside all day, scrounging tidbits from visitors, but could wait no longer. He pushed the tent flap aside with his nose and came in. The she-wolf looked at him. His tail wagged a few times as he eyed her in return. Her tail stood straight out behind her as she stalked delicately over and touched her nose to his. He whipped his cheek alongside hers with an insane look on his face, his tail wagging again, and stamped his front paws. An instant later, the two animals took off through the tent flap, leaping wildly across the little meadow.

Barr laughed and helped Tilva prop Deke's head up so she could pour some of the cooling liquid down his throat. He almost rose to consciousness but as they settled him back down on his pillow, he murmured and subsided, his arm thrown limply to the side, his large, square hand lying open, palm up, so young and vulnerable.

Feeling how bony Deke's shoulders had become, Barr again was overcome by pity. He stroked his son's face lovingly, leaned down to kiss his cheek. He felt Tilva's eyes on him and took her hand.

"He'd never let me do that if he was awake," he said, his expression making her throat constrict. His eyes softened further. "Do you remember how sweet he was as a little fellow?"

Tilva gripped his hand. She wondered if he knew how much she loved this tender side of him, how the intensity of his emotions stirred her own like a mad witch's brew. "Yes," she said. "He was such an affectionate child, so demonstrative." She sighed. "We haven't done too good a job lately, I'm afraid."

"No," Barr agreed. "You're right. That he's survived is a tribute to him, not us. Perhaps we'll do better with the next one." He reached for Tilva's belly, drawn to make contact with the incubating life there.

"Aye," his wife agreed, covering his hand with her own. Their eyes met. Together they rose and walked to the tent door where they looked outside. The two canines had disappeared, and the serving women were resting under a nearby tree.

Tilva called to them. "We won't be taking any more visitors for a few hours," and she tried to keep from jumping as Barr's hand, hidden from sight, touched her intimately. "Deke..." She dug her elbow into her husband's side and whispered, "Will you stop..." Then, to the women, "Deke needs quiet."

The women nodded as, with a jerk, Barr pulled Tilva inside. The tent flap closed. The women exchanged looks and one said, "I don't think that poor, young man is going to get much quiet."

They smothered laughter, though the occasional giggle could still be heard echoing across the meadow.

By late afternoon, visitors started arriving again. Among them were many of Deke's friends who were disappointed to hear that he was still asleep. They were jumping with eagerness to find out about his adventures, or at least, whatever custom decreed he could discuss with them. As they turned away from Tilva's tent, Andara arrived and started inside. She was stopped by Tim's hand on her arm.

"Tell us how he is," he demanded.

"Different," she said, extricating her arm gently.

"That's not very specific," Mastra put in with a little scowl.

"Well," she said with spirit, "That's as specific as I can be."

"Is it true he performed his own...is it true..." One of the boys was having difficulty framing his words. "It is true, isn't it?"

"I didn't see," Andara lied. "But you know he wouldn't have come back otherwise."

The boys exchanged glances, their imaginations working.

"Are you going inside?" Mastra asked enviously.

"I always do this time of day for my lessons," the girl replied nonchalantly. "Can I bring a message for you?"

"Just tell him...just tell him we're waiting," the tall youth said.

"If he wakes up, I'll tell him." Andara moved past him. "But," she said over her shoulder before disappearing within, "He probably already knows."

"What did she mean by that?" Tim asked.

"Come on, Tim, you know what she meant. You felt it, we all did." Mastra began to walk away.

"I know what you're talking about," Tim said, coming after him. "I just can't...it's too strange for me." His grey eyes were troubled. "It's too..."

"You can say it," Mastra told him. "But, you know, he's still Deke."

"I know, I felt it, that's not it at all...it's what's been happening in my head since."

One of the other boys who had been listening to this conversation said eagerly, "It's happening to you, too? Thank the ruins! I thought it was just me."

"No," Mastra said. "I always felt like I could sometimes see things happening in other places, and there were these crazy dreams...but when he came back, he was inside my head. I felt him there, looking out through my eyeballs with me. No," Mastra corrected himself. "I felt him before that, at his funeral, remember?"

The seven other boys of the manhood group nodded to one another solemnly.

"Maybe it's something about the ruins," another boy said. "I felt more alive out there, more alert, more...everything."

"I can't let it go," Tim agreed. "I can't let go of any of it." He pointed to his feet where shattered glass had sliced the soles to ribbons. "I'll carry those scars forever, but they're nothing compared to what's happened here," and he pointed first to his head, then his heart.

"Could you have done what he did?" another boy asked, and with a quick gesture imitated the two cuts.

Everyone winced without being aware he had and felt a twinge where the knife had cut so recently.

Tim thought about it. "I don't know," he said honestly. "I'm glad I didn't have to."

There was general agreement and the boys decided to take a swim in the nearby river. Soon they would have to get back to their schooling, and all wanted to take advantage of this traditional recuperation period given young men after their testing.

Their voices grew more indistinct as they moved away from the tent.

Inside, Andara tried without much success to keep her mind focused. She couldn't keep her thoughts off the alcove just beyond her patron's shoulder. Tilva also was having trouble concentrating, Andara noticed. She seemed misty, pre-occupied, given to wool-gathering. The older woman's gaze returned for the tenth time to the hangings leading to her sleeping quarters, and Andara followed that gaze.

Obviously Tilva wanted to be in there. Andara smiled. She could sense the chieftain's presence in the tent like a powerful force of nature. She cleared her throat and Tilva's eyes refocused.

"Did you say something, dear? I'm sorry...I don't know where my attention is today."

"You seem a little tired, my lady," Andara said. "Perhaps you'd like to lie down for a while?" She glanced meaningfully at Tilva's room. "I can look after Deke."

Tilva looked at her gratefully, almost blushing with how eager she was to return to her bed. But something in the youngster's humorous yet sympathetic expression made her aware that Andara understood precisely what she was feeling, and was happy for her. It was amazing, Tilva thought as she arose, light as a girl, and gave Andara a squeeze, how the world had changed in such a brief time. It felt like being born anew. With studied casualness she said, "Why not try and awaken him? He's slept enough. He needs food, fluids...it'll be easier to feed him if he's up."

Now it was Andara's turn to blush, certain Tilva saw right through her. She knew her benefactor was aware she had commenced her menses almost a year previously, and wondered if that was behind the double entendre. But this wasn't the time to discuss it, not when Tilva was yearning for the marriage-bed like a new bride.

Repressing a grin, Andara lowered her eyes demurely and said, "I'm sure I'll be able to awaken him."

Tilva smiled at her mischievous response, then yawned elaborately and stretched. "I think I will take that nap," she said, and disappeared behind the hangings. Andara heard Barr say something in his deep voice that made Tilva erupt in waves of laughter, and the girl stood up. She couldn't remember when she'd heard her patron laugh so much or with such abandon.

Andara tried to decide what she'd want to eat if she was as starved as Deke. She filled a cook pot with dried oats, water, fresh cream taken from Tilva's cold closet, a handful of raisined fruits, and a liberal quantity of crystalized honey. She added a few sticks of kindling to the smoldering wood fire before setting the pot on a burner, then picked up a large cup and filled it with water from a nearby pitcher. Casting about, she spotted a lidded chamber pot which she also picked up. Then, awkwardly balancing the two objects, she parted the curtain and went into the alcove.

Deke slept on his side, facing the table. His breathing was quiet and rhythmic. The coverlet had slipped back from his shoulder revealing the taut, sunburned skin over protruding bone.

Andara set the glass on the nightstand and the chamber pot on the floor, studying his face. Gaunt as it was, he still was recognizable, but now with the bone structure more prominent, she could see the rugged countenance of the mature man he would become peeking out from the softer, more boyish features she knew so well. "Deke," she called quietly. "Time to wake up."

She took a strand of her own hair and tickled his cheek with it. She grinned as his eyes flew open in sleepy surprise.

"Hi," he said with a yawn that turned to a smile. Then, shyly, "You look very pretty today, Andara." He shifted a little and stretched, wincing at the pain in his stiff muscles and the continued discomfort between his legs, particularly right now after waking up.

Something of his need obviously showed on his face, because Andara gestured to the chamber pot. "Do you have to use this?"

"God, you can't imagine." He started to get up and hesitated, looking at her.

"Maybe I'd better help you..." The girl's voice trailed off.

"I can manage," Deke replied, willing himself not to show his embarrassment.

"Then I'll check your breakfast. Call if you need me."

The instant she was gone he swung his legs over the side of the bed, removed the lid from the pot, and let go, groaning with relief. When he finished, he replaced the lid and put the pot in a corner, amazed by how weak he felt. He practically fell back into bed, his head spinning. He almost gagged, and fought down a bout of nausea. Hungry, he thought. I'm ravenous.

He spotted the cup of water on the nightstand and drained it in a long gulp. Before rearranging his coverlet, he removed the bandage from his penis and examined himself. The flesh was still raw, but at least nothing had fallen off while he slept. The curtains moved and he hurriedly covered himself, putting the bandage on the table.

Andara sat on the edge of the bed, bowl and spoon in hand. "Can you feed yourself?" she asked. "Or would you like me to do it?"

"You do it," he said, enjoying for the moment his role as invalid and hers as nursemaid.

Andara sensed he was playing with her but discovered she rather liked it. She spooned up some cereal, blew on it to cool it, and offered him a mouthful. He could scarcely control himself enough to take it in a civilized fashion.

"Sorry," he said with an apologetic smile. "Here, give me that," and he dragged himself into a sitting position, took the bowl and spoon, and began to shovel the contents into his mouth at enormous speed. He emptied the bowl in moments. "More, please," he said, wiping his mouth on the back of his hand.

"Of course." She got up and indicated the bandage on the table. "You really should have a fresh one," she commented as she carried the bowl out and refilled it. This time she brought back the water pitcher as well and filled his empty cup.

Perched on the side of his bed, she watched him devour a second, and then a third, helping of oatmeal. She could see life coming back into his face as he ate, and when he finished and set the bowl aside, she smiled and waited for him to speak. He sighed and patted his slightly distended belly. "Thank you," he said. "That was the best oatmeal I've ever tasted."

"Well, you know what they say about hunger," Andara replied, and leaned towards him. He jerked as she reached for his forehead. "It's all right," she assured him. "I just want to see how your temperature is. Your mother said you were running a fever." She reached for him again and this time he allowed her to touch him, feeling as if a flame had rushed from her hand across his skin surface. Until the moment her cool hand contacted him he hadn't realized how heated his flesh was.

"I don't like this fever," she said, disquieted by his hot, dry skin. "I'd better check your wounds."

Deke's startled gaze flew to her face, but all he saw there was concern and concentration. "I already did," he mumbled quickly, looking away. This time he was unable to prevent the color from rising on his cheeks.

"Let me give you a fresh bandage at least," the girl said, maintaining her composure with an effort. A wave of feeling pulsed through her and she felt her throat close. She leaped up and hurriedly fled the alcove, her breath leaving her in a rush. She stood outside the hangings for a second, trying to quell the strange, new feelings in her body, desperate not to make a fool of herself.

At the woodstove, she deposited a selection of herbs and bark into a clean pot and brought them to a simmer. While she waited for them to steep, she went to the cold closet, chipped ice from the block inside, and wrapped it in a clean cloth. Pouring the hot mixture into a mug, she returned to the alcove.

"Drink this," she ordered. "It'll reduce your fever, clean your body out. If you drank bad water or ate bad meat, it'll fix you right up."

"You're getting good at this," he commented, his blue eyes watching her over the rim of the cup as he sipped the bitter liquid. He lay back after draining the remainder, exhausted, and she laid the ice pack across his forehead.

Without specific action to take, Andara felt flustered. When she looked at him she felt strange, as if she wanted to do she knew not what. She noticed him watching her and wondered if he felt the same way.

"Where are my parents?" he asked after a while.

Andara blushed. "Um...sleeping."

"Listen," he said, and touched her hand tentatively. "When I'm better, would you like to go somewhere, just us?" He hesitated. "Maybe pack a picnic lunch or something?"

Andara looked at him, surprised. "Won't the others' feelings be hurt?"

He shrugged. "Why?"

"I don't think they like having me around so much."

"Well," said Deke, "I do." He took her hand shyly, afraid she would pull away, but she seemed content to let him hold it.

"I like being here," she whispered, afraid to move for fear he'd let her go. They sat silently holding hands, each acutely aware of the other's touch.

"Where would you like to go?" the girl asked.

"Anywhere," he said, squeezing her hand tighter. "Anywhere at all. Just so we can be alone."

"Alone?" Andara asked nervously.

"I have to be far enough away that everyone's not in my head," Deke tried to explain. "I keep feeling this pressure...these demands...I can't put it into words exactly." He looked earnestly into her eyes. "But I don't feel that way with you."

"How do you feel?" she asked in a low tone.

"At ease," he told her. "I feel at ease."

Impulsively Andara leaned forward and gave him a little kiss on the cheek. Then she jumped up and adjusted his poultice unnecessarily, her heart hammering in her ears.

Instinctively understanding her feelings, he allowed her to fuss over him. When she darted out and returned a moment later with a bottle of antiseptic and a bandage, he said, "I can do that."

"Are you sure? I mean," and Andara felt her face grow hot, "I know how to treat wounds. I won't hurt you."

"I'm sure you won't," Deke said wryly. "That's the problem."

"Oh," she said in an agony of embarrassment, and looked away.

He took the bottle and bandage from her hands. "Turn around."

"Aye, of course."

From behind her back she heard his quick intake of breath as he applied the stinging antibiotic and wrapped himself in the fresh dressing.

"This is a strange way to try and impress a girl, don't you think?" he said when he was finished.

She turned and saw the self-mockery on his face. "Are you trying to?"

"Would you mind if I was?" he countered.

"What do you think?" she returned, as quickly.

"I think I'm getting into murky territory, here," he replied, setting the antiseptic aside and leaning back. "What do you think?"

"I don't know what we're talking about."

"I doubt that." Deke's eyes grew serious. "I'm sure you know more than you let on."

Andara felt her head begin to swim. She knew he was no longer flirting with her, and that he was talking about a far more complicated issue.

"You're like me," he said. "You can get out of yourself. When did you first realize you could do it?"

She was troubled. "I've never talked to anyone about this, except your mother. It's always been my secret."

He took her hand again, and she felt her heart race. "But I want to know all your secrets." His amazingly blue eyes held her gaze. She felt herself falling, slipping, and with a peculiar wrench caught a glimpse of herself and of him as if she were looking down from somewhere else. For an instant she felt the warm glow in her mind as she had when he first came back, and then she was back in her body staring at him. Her breath came in quick gasps. The warmth in her thoughts remained, and she felt him steady her.

"Oh, Deke," she said. "What does it mean?"

"I don't know," he said. "I only know it's important."

They stared at one another, and then as the herbs he had imbibed started to take effect, he began to feel drowsy again.

"Please stay with me until I fall asleep," he said, his face grey with exhaustion. It had taken all his over-taxed energy reserves to connect with Andara outside their bodies, but he was glad for the expenditure. Now he was sure about what before had been only a suspicion. They were alike, the two of them, complementary. A touch of vertigo made his vision swim. "I'll bet you could run with wolves," he murmured, already half-asleep.

Startled, Andara let go of his hand and felt as if an intimate contact had been broken. She was tired herself now, and for a moment considered lying down beside him, then realized how it would look. Reluctantly, she stood up and went to the door. With a backward glance she directed a last thought towards his mind, unsure whether he could perceive it or not, but it seemed to touch his dreams on some level, for he smiled in his sleep.

I love you, she Sent silently, and was gone.

CHAPTER SIX

One thing as psychologists we should always remember: there is no force more potent than first love, for it contains all our hopes and dreams, all our most ardent emotions, all our innocence and trust. Never are we better beings, never are we more human in the most ideal sense of the word, than when we first fall prey to Eros' passion...

— *Ourn Rohlvaag; Collected Journals; City of Life, A.D. 3109*

I n the darkness before dawn Deke jerked upright with a shout. He was about to climb out of bed when his parents hurried in, tousled and sleep disheveled. "Are you all right?" they asked simultaneously.

Deke was confused. "What are you doing here?"

Barr sat on the edge of the bed. "You were yelling. Were you having a bad dream?"

"I don't remember...I don't know." He shivered hard.

Tilva's expression was troubled. "How are you feeling?" she asked. She laid her cheek on his forehead. "Your fever is down."

"Andara gave me something for it."

"I'll have to ask her what it was," she said with a smile. "She's very intuitive with herbs." Then, pushing his hair back, "Is there anything you need? Are you hungry?"

"Starving. But I can wait 'til morning."

"Don't be silly," his mother said. "Andara sent a couple pies this afternoon. Would you like to start with the cherry?"

"Is there milk?"

"I think we can arrange some milk," Tilva replied, amused.

"Let's all have some," Barr suggested.

Tilva laughed outright. "Your father's coveted those pies since they got here," she said.

"So has your mother," said Barr with a broad grin.

When she returned with the pies and a pitcher of cold milk, she went on, "It's no wonder you're having bad dreams. You're so thin; your skeleton's trying to jump out of your skin."

Deke smiled and looked around the alcove. "Where's the wolf?"

"She and Canis took off this afternoon. It was love at first sight, I'm afraid." Barr swallowed a bite of pie, his eyes closing with rapture. "God, that girl makes good pie," he said. "You better marry her, son, because anyone who can bake like this at twelve will no doubt be supernatural by the time she's grown."

Deke gave a muffled laugh, his mouth full. In moments he devoured three quarters of the cherry pie and began on the peach.

"I may do that, Father. But you'll forgive me if I wait a few years?"

"That's wise, son," Tilva said with a meaningful glance at her husband. "She's still a little too young."

Deke looked up from his plate. "For marriage, maybe, but so am I."

"She's a little young for everything," Barr said tactfully.

"She's old enough to have a child," Deke countered.

Tilva was surprised. "How would you know?"

"The same way you do," Deke said.

"Speaking of children," Barr began, "We have a little news of our own." He took his wife's hand and she smiled with such radiance that Deke guessed what was coming next.

"A baby!" he exclaimed with a grin. "I always wanted a sibling. When?"

His parents looked like mischievous children and Deke leaned over to give his mother a hug, then gripped his father's shoulder affectionately. "Early next winter," she replied.

Barr's hand stole around Tilva's waist.

Delicately, Deke allowed his aura to touch theirs, a superficial contact which nonetheless permitted a connection between their nervous systems and his. Tenuously at first, then with more confidence as the connection firmed up, he immersed himself in their emotions. He stopped short of touching their conscious minds, for listening to their thoughts seemed an inexcusable invasion of privacy.

For a few minutes the three sat in mutual harmony more complete than any they had known as a family. Then, reluctantly, Deke withdrew his thought, filled with fleeting sadness. This: here, now, was what he had craved all his young life. It seemed ironic that only when he was going to leave his mother's tent were his parents able to get along.

After a while they stirred. "Why don't you go back to sleep for a while, Deke?" his mother suggested. "It won't be light for a couple of hours yet."

"I'm slept out," he replied.

"Rest a while, then. You can have a bath later, if you're feeling well enough."

Humor sparked in Deke's eyes as he looked at his parents. "Can't wait to go back to bed yourselves, I see," he said with a grin.

His father laughed. "Thank the ruins you're moving into your own tent soon," he said only half-jokingly.

Deke nodded and leaned back comfortably. "I think later this afternoon would be best, if neither of you mind."

A stricken look passed quickly across Tilva's face and was as quickly controlled. "So soon?"

"It's best, Mother," Deke said gently. "Besides, I'm not going very far. Just across the meadow."

"Oh, Deke, it's not the physical distance," Tilva sighed. "You'll understand one day when you have children of your own."

"I understand now," he told her, patting her hand. With a smile, he picked up the book lying on his nightstand and opened it to a page marked in that other incarnation, before his ordeal.

"What are you reading?" his father asked, trying to get a look at the cover.

"Marcus Aurelius," Deke said.

"Read a little from it," his mother suggested.

Deke moved his finger down the page. "'That which rules within, when it is according to nature, is so affected with respect to the events which happen, that it always easily adapts itself to that which is possible and is presented to it.'" He smiled. "I think Marcus Aurelius was a kind of Wolfson, don't you?"

"Maybe he was," Barr said with a chuckle. "Legend has it that the founders of ancient Rome were suckled at the breast of a wolf."

Deke's smile changed, but neither parent could put a finger on just how. "Were they," he said. "I didn't know."

"That's what I call power," Barr continued.

"The suckling or the Empire?" Tilva asked.

"Both," said Barr and Deke simultaneously.

She looked back and forth between them. "You're both wrong," she said. "It's the one who gives suck who has the power, for she's the one who can withhold it."

Father and son were nonplused.

"There's a thought," Deke said after a time.

"Aye," agreed his father.

Tilva smiled contentedly, glad to have had the last word.

In the afternoon Deke rose from bed, still weak, but much better. The dizziness had departed like a bad dream, and when he emerged from his alcove with the coverlet draped modestly about his waist he saw servants filling a portable canvas bathtub, which when covered with some polished boards, doubled as a bench. Now the boards were laid aside and he watched as Andara tossed a handful of leaves into the water and a clean fragrance rose with the steam into the air.

"Not too hot," Deke said with a smile of greeting. "You don't want to parboil me."

The serving women laughed. "It's good to see you up and about, young master," an older woman said. "We'll be out of your way in a few minutes."

"Take your time," he said. He gestured to Andara. "I hate to bother you when you're busy," he said, "But what's that I smell on the stove?"

"Stew," she said, "And fresh bread." She looked him over critically. "You really look dreadful," she told him. "What's worse is that you look so much better!" She burst into laughter at the rueful expression on his face.

"Well," he responded, "You look beautiful." His eyes flickered from her head to her feet and back. She was wearing a grass-green dress that clung to strategic parts of her blossoming shape and set off the color of her eyes and hair.

Andara flushed and looked down. His compliments made her too self-conscious to think straight. "Are you hungry?"

"Constantly," he answered, sitting at the table. "Where are my folks now? Still *sleeping*?" His eyebrows arched comically.

With an appreciative chuckle, she loaded a plate with stew and bread, then got some butter from the cold closet and brought everything to the table.

He ate quickly. When he was finished, he rose and, hitching the coverlet higher, tested the bath water. It was hot, but not unbearable, at least not to his fingers. As far as that most wounded part of his anatomy went, there was only one way to find out.

The servants had departed, and he turned to look at Andara. She was busy clearing the dishes. He picked up the cake of soap that had been left for him and quickly, while she was facing away, dropped the coverlet and slid into the tub, groaning as the heat penetrated his bruises and wounds. He ducked his head under the water for a minute, then began work with the soap. There was crusted blood and dirt all over him, and he realized he smelled bad.

"How could you stand to be near me?" he asked, scrubbing vigorously at his filthy arms and legs, digging the soap under his fingernails to loosen the blood caked there. He soaped his armpits and crotch, taking care with his circumcision cuts.

Andara looked at him over her shoulder and took a bottle from a shelf. "Here's the good soap your mother uses on her hair," she said, and brought it to him, keeping her eyes politely averted.

"Thanks," he said. He poured some into the insane tangle of his greasy, blood-stiffened hair and lathered, then ducked back underwater to rinse. "I need fresh water." He eyed the dirty brown bathwater with disgust.

"I'll call the servants," she said, handing him a clean towel which he wound about his midsection as soon as she turned away.

Later, sitting in a fresh tub, he soaked luxuriously, made drowsy by the heat. Andara pulled up a chair behind him and waved a comb and scissors.

"Don't even bother to argue," she told him. "I'll try not to hurt too much." Her deft fingers began to work through his matted hair, and though at first he was self-conscious to have her performing such a personal task for him, after a while he relaxed into the unconscious sensuality of her skilled hands. Occasionally she found a knot even patient handling couldn't unwind, and then she snipped carefully, trying not to mutilate his hair any more than necessary. Using water from a nearby bucket, she rinsed his hair and then re-applied the sweet-smelling soap, lathering it in gently, taking care around his forehead. When she thought she had washed him sufficiently, she poured warm water over him until he was clean. "That's better," she commented, admiring her work. The heavy mass of red-gold curls was shades lighter. "Now all you have to do is brush your teeth and you'll be almost fit for human company."

"Thanks a lot," he said dryly. "If you wouldn't mind, a tooth brush and powder are in my room on the chest."

She brought both and sat nearby while he brushed until his gums bled. She gave him a clean mug of water which he used to rinse his mouth.

Grinning happily, he reached for the towel but she caught his hand and gave him a fresh one. He held her hand a moment longer than necessary, then drew her a bit closer.

"Would you be upset if I gave you a thank you kiss?" he asked softly. "You've taken such good care of me." Slowly, with a bashful, little smile, he reached for her chin and caressed first her cheek, then her ear. She moved closer, hypnotized by the light in his eyes. She felt his lips touch hers, clinging for a second, then moving away. Her heart was beating in her mouth and she was about to let him kiss her again when they heard the sound of a throat clearing loudly in the doorway and broke apart guiltily.

"Well, this is a fine kettle of fish," said Hawk Farflight, amusement fighting surprise in his voice. "Kissing naked men in bathtubs...what'll you be up to next, girl?"

Andara flushed, then her temper flared. "Didn't anyone ever tell you it isn't good manners to sneak up on people?"

Hawk stared at her for a second, then guffawed. When he had gotten control of himself, he said, "Seeing it's Deke I guess I'll forgive you."

"Don't expect me to apologize, Papa," the girl said tartly, wishing her father could have waited a while before showing up. She could still feel Deke's

93

lips on hers, and there was a peculiar ache in her middle that made her want to feel them again.

"How are you, Deke?" Hawk asked heartily. "Obviously feeling better if you're up to kissing my daughter."

"I'm much better, thank you," Deke said, the rush of his blood still audible in his ears. He stood up, kept his back to them and wrapped the towel around himself. "If you'll excuse me a minute, I'll put on some clothes." He headed for his alcove but they stopped him.

"You have no clothes," Andara said.

"They were burned on your funeral pyre," Hawk explained. "It's customary in cases when men are lost."

"Oh," Deke said.

"I'm sure there's something around you can wear," Andara said.

"Stay here," Hawk said. "I'll have a look." He headed for the door.

Deke turned back to Andara and said, "What about bedding? Is this all of it?" he gestured towards his alcove.

She shrugged mysteriously. Before he could question her further, the door flap opened again, and this time Barr and Tilva came in accompanied by Canis and the she-wolf. They took in the scene at a glance and then they, too, smiled mysteriously.

Deke looked from one to another and stroked the wolf's ears, picking up her contented thoughts almost absently now.

"Looks like you need some gear, son," Barr said in an amused tone. "Why don't we take a walk and see what we can scare up?"

Deke began to realize they were all behaving very strangely, and he smiled, willing to play along. "Okay," he agreed.

"Just tuck that towel in so you don't cause any unnecessary excitement," Tilva added.

"Very funny," said Deke, blushing.

They ducked through the flap and he was surprised to see numerous people gathered. Most he knew personally, including some of his friends who were loitering outside the row of bachelor tents. They smiled at him, some chuckling over his scant garment, others simply caught up in the moment's fun.

His parents led him across the meadow to the bachelor tent set apart from the others. The flap was raised invitingly. Standing nearby were Hawk and Willie, trying without success to control their mirth at their young student's appearance. "Having a problem, Deke?" Willie asked.

"I wasn't," Deke answered good-naturedly.

"Well, go on," Hawk told him.

Deke went inside, Andara and his parents on his heels, with as many friends and neighbors as could squeeze into the doorway behind them.

The tent consisted of two rooms, the front one larger and serving as living area, dining room, kitchen, with the bedroom at the rear.

Deke's eyes widened. Someone had been hard at work. The walls were hung with woven tapestries; some depicted exciting hunts on horseback, others showed stirring battles, still others were more abstract. There were a couple low-slung chairs and an overstuffed couch covered in soft, wool fabric. A broad table with four chairs stood near a small but efficient kitchen containing a counter, cold closet, a cast-iron woodstove with two burners and an oven. Arrayed along one side of the room were new weapons: body daggers, machete, several rifles of varying caliber, a shotgun, a pair of high caliber pistols, and an automatic rapid-fire machine gun. A large chest lay open, crammed with ammunition and explosives. Now that he was a man, he was obligated to carry weapons with more punch than his old slingshot and hunting knife.

He examined the kitchen area next. The counter was supported by several barrels with access panels in front. These contained quantities of grain: wheat flour, cornmeal, barley, and whole oats. All tent kitchens were designed this way for maximum portability. When necessary, the kitchen could be dismantled and packed for travel in very little time. When Deke opened the cold closet, he saw it was stuffed with food prepared by his neighbors to help speed his recovery. There were so many fresh eggs and pickled vegetables, smoked meats, soups and casseroles, that he was speechless.

Next he looked into the bedroom. Dominating the space was a double bed with a blanket rack at its foot. The bed was fully made up and covered with a goose-down quilt. There were intricately woven wool rugs covering the floor. Tapestries covered the walls here as well. Altogether the combined effect of the two rooms was overwhelming. Everything was brand new and immaculate.

"Who did this?" he asked, trying to control his emotions.

"The furnishings come from everyone," Tilva said, and put her arm around him. "The food, likewise. The clothing, which you haven't seen yet because you haven't opened that chest, was mostly made by my women, though I helped with a few special garments. The weapons and ammunition come from your father and his friends." Tilva paused to catch her breath. "Am I leaving anyone out? As for who did all the work of putting it together, that was Andara. We only helped a little at the end."

Deke crossed the room to the clothes chest and swung back the lid. Inside were clothes for all seasons: shirts, sweaters, pants, socks, underwear, everything he needed and all new and beautifully made, with the colorful stitching and exotic embroidery prized among his people. There were two cloaks hanging from pegs set into one of the tent poles, one warm and sheepskin-layered for winter, the other made with waxed canvas to keep off the wet. Both were hooded. There were gloves, scarves, and knitted hats. There were boots as well, high ones and low ones, insulated and not.

There was a bookshelf stacked with his collection of books. Strange rocks, fossils, oddly shaped pieces of fused glass, a chess set, a war helmet, his bear claw necklace, the assortment of bear and tiger teeth, the ritual dagger; all personal memorabilia were arranged neatly on top. A desk with a wooden chair completed the furnishings.

"Thank you, everyone," he said, moved. He looked at Andara, his feelings plain on his face. "I don't know what to say except thank you."

For a moment their eyes locked.

"Use everything in good health," Tilva admonished. "You might want to start with your clothes."

Laughter came from the crowd behind them.

Barr spread his arms and ushered everyone from the room. "Let's give him a little privacy."

Gradually the crush thinned and Deke was left standing alone in the bedroom. The wolf put her muzzle in his palm and he petted her reflexively.

"So, girl, what do you think? This'll take some getting used to."

Mastra poked his head in. "Hey!" he said with a grin.

Deke grinned back. "Hey, yourself."

"Pretty fancy," Mastra said. "Look at this floor...rugs three deep an' each one thicker than the other!"

"I know. I'll be soft as a fort dweller in a month!"

They laughed together.

"That Andara!" Mastra shook his head. "She's had us fetching and carrying like mules the last two days."

Deke rummaged through the clothes chest, withdrawing underwear, pants and a short-sleeved shirt. He pulled off the damp towel and was about to step into his underwear when Mastra said, gesturing, "How's your prick, anyway? Has it healed yet?"

Deke shrugged and examined himself. "Still damn sore. See, here, where I cut too deep? That one really bled." He put on his underwear, carefully arranging himself inside before reaching for his pants. "How's yours?"

Mastra also shrugged. "Mine looks about the same, but more healed." He smiled slyly. "Bigger, of course."

Deke laughed at the old joke. "In your dreams," he said. "Hurts like hell in the morning, though," he added, buttoning up the fly of his pants.

"Doesn't it!" Mastra shook his head, then fell silent. He watched his friend pull on a woven cotton shirt and sit on the edge of the bed.

Deke bounced up and down for a second, testing the mattress. "You know," he said, "I thought I'd never be able to come home. I thought I'd be out howling at the moon for the rest of my life."

"Did you see anyone else?" Mastra asked.

Deke looked at the ceiling. "Aye," he said slowly. "I buried Pete Murdock out there."

Mastra's whole expression was a question.

"A bear got him," Deke explained. "A tiger was hunting me until a brown bear showed up." His gaze turned inward. "The bear had already eaten most of his insides when I got there."

Mastra realized his mouth was open. He closed it hurriedly.

Deke picked up the ritual knife on the shelf. "This belonged to Peter," he said, turning it over in his hand. "This is what I killed the bear with."

"You killed a bear?" asked Mastra, flabbergasted.

"The wolves helped me," Deke explained.

"How?" Mastra couldn't stop himself. He knew it was impolite to question anyone about his manhood experience, but he had to know.

"I don't know, it's kind of a blur," Deke said. "I speared it, I remember that. The bastard was carrying Peter off like a dinner pail."

"Weren't you scared?" Mastra asked the un-askable.

Deke looked his friend in the eye. "At first I was; when the tiger was stalking me. But afterwards when I attacked the bear, no. No, all I could see was its blood on the ground. I think I must have been crazy." He remembered the chaos of blood and hurtling bodies. By the look of shock on his friend's face, he knew he had inadvertently Sent Mastra a clear image of that moment. After a long pause, he said, "Now, give. What happened to you?"

"I don't want to talk about it," Mastra said in a nearly inaudible voice. "I don't think I did so well as you," he admitted painfully.

"You made it back in time," Deke pointed out, disturbed by his shift in mood. "That's more than I was able to do."

"No one could possibly do more than what you did," Mastra said flatly. "Not in our group or any other. What I want to know is how you do it." He probed with sudden intensity. "How do you get inside people's heads?"

Deke sighed. "I don't know, I really don't. Do you know how you use your eyes to see? Or how you hear? That's how it is for me. Like seeing. Or listening. Or anything else that comes naturally."

"I wish I could do it," Mastra whispered, ashamed of his jealousy.

"My father says most gifts are two-edged," Deke said.

"What're your two edges?"

"I can get out," Deke said slowly, "But everything else gets in."

Mastra digested this. "Everything?"

"If I let it. It's a lot of work keeping everyone out."

The two looked at one another.

"We're getting too serious," Deke said, changing the subject. "What do you think about this? Our own places, you have to admit that's pretty good. We can stay up all night drinking...girls...think of it!"

Mastra smiled. "Girls...Tim says he's going to have 'em two at a time!"

Deke laughed. "Good for him! What about you?"

"I've been looking," Mastra said.

"Really! Who?"

"None of your business, you'll just steal her from me." Mastra grinned.

"I'd never do that," Deke said, laughing.

"Who are you going after?" Mastra asked.

Deke smiled. "Don't you know?"

"Haven't a clue," his friend replied.

"Then you'll have to wait and see," Deke told him. "The Spring Festival's soon; I heard my mother's ladies talking about it. You do know how to dance, don't you?"

"Watch my dust," Mastra bragged.

They laughed together.

Mastra gestured towards the wolf. "Have you given her a name yet?"

"I thought I'd let Andara name her," Deke said with a little smile.

Mastra raised his eyebrows but said nothing.

Deke stood up and slid his feet into a pair of soft, leather moccasins. He was tempted to make contact more directly with his friend's mind but controlled the urge. It was important not to become too dependent on his esper ability, and besides, if he didn't mind his own business, he was sure the people he cared about would begin to hate him.

"I'm going to take a walk and say hello to the others. Want to come?"

Mastra nodded. He was glad beyond words for his friend's return from beyond the flames, and yet, and yet...

He squirmed with inner discomfort, hating himself for having had the thought, however brief, that when Deke was gone, he no longer had felt himself to be eclipsed by his friend's adventures and accomplishments. For a short while, he actually had believed he might have some worth. Despising himself, he followed Deke from the tent, wondering why he had these thoughts, and hoping his friend never discovered them.

Outside, the two boys made slow progress as everyone they met stopped and greeted Deke, slapping him on the back fondly, expressing how happy they were to see him up and about.

Inside Tim's tent, the manhood group was even more effusive in their rowdy way, with boys crowding near, punching him lightly on the shoulders, shaking his hand vigorously.

Self-consciously, Tim offered mugs all around and filled them with table wine, all he could find at short notice. This was the first time he had hosted the group, and he was anxious to make everyone comfortable. "Anyone hungry?"

All the boys were, so Tim brought out a sack of sweet oatmeal biscuits which he passed around.

They raised their mugs in a toast.

"What should we toast?" Tim asked.

"Ourselves," Deke answered. "Most definitely."

"I like that," Tim said. "To all of us!" he bellowed, raising his mug again.

"Aye, to all of us!" the others shouted.

Everyone downed his wine, some with more relish than others, but each with the pleased awareness that now he was a man and could do as he wished.

As Deke looked at his friends, he felt a strange foreshadowing. He saw them as they'd be in the future, these boys who would become the men who would serve as his advisors, commanders, and governors. He gazed carefully into their faces, trying to plumb their souls without resorting to empathic contact. They were good friends, he thought, decent and worthy. Their loyalty should never be a problem. Ingrained within them was the common history of their people, and it was a proud history. None would ever stoop to a despicable act. Among the Wolf People, honor was everything, honor and the courage to defend it. He raised his mug again and said with the spontaneous warmth for which he was well known,

"To you, my friends. May the ruins grant us many victories together."

The boys were surprised, but after a moment, raised their voices in a deafening clamor, their approval obvious.

Then Tim raised his mug. "To Deke," he said. "Welcome home."

"Aye," Mastra agreed, "Welcome home, brother."

"Aye," the others chorused. "Welcome home."

It was long after dark before the party broke up, the boys departing for their own tents.

Deke was the last to leave.

Tim caught him by the arm. "Are you really all right?" he asked, peering intently into his friend's eyes.

"A little bruised, that's all," Deke replied. His head was swimming. "Good party, Tim, but next time invite some women!"

Tim grinned. "You know some of those fellows aren't really ready for that, even though they pretend they are."

Deke laughed. "Are you ready?"

"I was born ready!" Tim affirmed. "Listen, I'm ready now! Isn't there somewhere we can go? You know, I've always wanted to try one of those places..."

"You go ahead," Deke said. He gestured to his crotch. "I'm not putting this anywhere except into a new bandage."

Tim was interested. "How was it to do the two cuts yourself?"

"In my case it was more like three cuts," Deke said.

Tim shuddered. "I keep trying to imagine how you could do it...I would have run away backwards from the knife if I wasn't being held!"

"One thing's sure," and Deke's expression became serious. "I can't imagine anything worse. So I guess if I could stand that, I can stand anything."

Tim's eyes were filled with admiration and too much wine. "Sure you won't change your mind about buying a woman? You know they'll do anything you ask! Maybe if one used just her tongue really carefully..."

Deke started to chuckle. "You really are funny, you know that? If even a butterfly put her tongue on me I'd probably scream. Go on, enjoy yourself. Right now I'm happy I can still piss!"

"Ah, it wouldn't be any fun alone," Tim said with mock sadness.

"Why? You don't need me for what you want to do."

"No, but to brag to after...oh, well."

Deke shook his head. "See you, Timmy," he said, turning away.

"Aye," his friend replied with a wave.

In his own tent (and he savored the words 'own tent') Deke looked around for something to use as a bandage and was surprised to find a bottle of antiseptic and several clean dressings on the table. There also was a pot simmering on the back burner that hadn't been there when he left, and when he looked inside he saw the remains of the stew Andara had given him earlier.

Ravenous again, he got a spoon. Before long he had eaten it all, and he dipped some water, leaving the pot in a basin on the counter to soak.

Heading for the bedroom, he looked around for the wolf. She had trotted away towards his mother's tent earlier, no doubt to fool with Canis. As her image firmed up in his mind, the door flap moved and she trotted in, panting happily. He Sent her an image of wolves greeting one another and her tail wagged. Then he found a bowl which he filled from the water barrel in the

100

kitchen, setting it near the counter. She walked over to it, lapped gratefully, then sent him a picture of a fresh kill. "Hungry, eh?" he asked, and went to the cold closet. "If you'd gotten here sooner you could have had stew." He took out a pot roast and some bread and sliced off a generous quantity of both which he put in another bowl with some of the gravy.

Delicately the she-wolf sniffed the bowl's contents, then took a lick. In moments she decided the meal was satisfactory, and before long, the bowl was empty.

"Good," Deke said, yawning. He pulled off his shirt and doused the lantern on the table. With the wolf at his heel, he went to the bedroom, turned back the bed, kicked off his moccasins, stripped away the rest of his clothes, let them drop to the floor. Seconds later he was asleep in his new bed, and the wolf jumped up lightly, turned in a circle, then curled in a ball near him.

In sleep their minds merged and the random images went back and forth swiftly. In this dream dance he heard a name, and knew it was hers. *Hopi.* This was the name he *saw* Andara would suggest.

The dream changed, and he could still feel the she-wolf's presence in his psyche, as if she were standing a little to the side and behind him. On the horizon he could see darkness looming, worse than the worst twister weather, while on the wind there came the howling of wolves. The exotic-eyed, alabaster-skinned woman was there, and he wasn't sure if she'd just appeared or if she'd always been there. Her hands clung to his arm and she was pressed tightly to him, looking where he looked with an expression of fear so great it was almost madness. At first he thought she was frightened for herself and felt contempt, but then he realized she was frightened for him, and that changed everything.

What was really strange was how tall he seemed to be, how broad and powerful. Clutched in his right hand was a weapon, he wasn't sure what kind, he had never seen anything like it in his life. But it looked more dangerous by far than any simple rifle — it looked like it spat nuclear fire itself. It was about the size of a tripod mount machine gun, but he wore it slung with a strap over his shoulder.

Before them lay a plain of shattered glass, and for some reason he knew he had to go out onto that plain. The unusual woman didn't want him to go, and he felt torn between her emotions and his own need to do whatever it was he had come to do.

On a deeper level of awareness he realized this was a new variation on his dream and he wondered where his nemesis was, the one that stalked him through this ravaged, sharp-edged landscape. No sooner did this thought appear in his mind than he felt the dreadful presence searching for him, trying to pinpoint his location, but for the moment, at least, failing, passing him by.

His dream self pulled the woman into his arms, and there, on the edge of the glittering devastation, they embraced with passion he had never imagined possible. When they broke apart and he looked into her eyes, he saw she had become Andara, but an older, even more beautiful Andara, with lips made tumescent by his kisses and eyes burning hot as green flames...

With a curse, Deke jerked awake and tore the covers and bandage off his erect penis, the onset of pain after the pleasurable sensations of his dream making him almost snarl. He stalked around the tent for several minutes, waiting for his erection to go down. His thoughts were filled with his dream and how it had felt to be making love to a grown-up Andara, and these thoughts were not conducive to his purpose.

He hoped it wouldn't be necessary to use cold water but if anything, he was getting harder, and if this didn't stop he was going to open that damned cut again.

Andara, Andara. He couldn't get her out of his mind, couldn't stop thinking about her. They'd been best friends all their lives, and yet he felt he hardly knew her. The girl he'd known had been always wild, sometimes petulant, definitely stimulating, but now it was as if her very aroma had changed and all he wanted was to be close to her. He longed to touch her in the ways he knew men touched women when they wanted to arouse them, the way his dream self seemed to do so skillfully.

Resignedly, he got back into bed. His situation hadn't improved, and he couldn't even relieve himself with his hand as he had before he went to the ruins.

God, he thought desperately. What am I going to do? His flesh was hot and cold simultaneously.

Feeling lonely and irascible, Deke turned on his side and tried to empty his mind. How stupid, he thought as he chased sleep futilely. How stupid and inconvenient to be circumcised at thirteen, when every other minute his penis behaved as if it had a life of its own.

Days passed, and Deke and his friends resumed their training, spending half of each day practicing with their new firearms and working at hand to hand combat techniques that would enable them to dispatch opponents speedily. Little competitions grew up, encouraged by the older men who supervised these classes.

Watching the youngsters grappling with each other, Willie O'Dale nodded approvingly. They were getting good, very good indeed. Soon he would let them compete against older manhood groups so they could practice against those with superior strength and skill.

Also every day, two hours were spent in the classroom, a one room tent equipped with chalkboard, tables, and chairs. Here the boys studied military history, strategy, and tactics. When they were younger they had learned reading and writing, as well as mathematics. Some had learned their lessons better than others, Deke thought with a grin, watching his friends struggle vainly with their schoolwork.

Learning came easily to him. He had begun reading before he was three, taught by his mother. It had been the only way to keep him occupied when she had work to do. Math was simpler still, because for him it was like a language, the substitution of symbols for concepts, and this he found almost reflexive. He had a superior grasp of spatial relationships; he could look at a chess board and see the potential lines of attack and defense as a series of actions whose probabilities for success or failure appeared in his mind as a form of living images. From one move, he could extrapolate all others, but his particular talent came from the ability to predict which were most likely to play out in any given situation.

On this day, a week after moving into his own tent, Deke listened to Willie discourse on seige techniques, half his attention elsewhere. His gaze rested on the open door through which he saw his mother and Andara pass by carrying baskets laden with fresh herbs they'd been gathering. He sighed, wishing he could escape. The day outside was beautiful; sunny, warm, with a soft breeze on which he could smell flowers.

"Deke!" Willie said suddenly, his voice peremptory. "How would you invest a fort defended with heavy artillery and rockets?"

Deke's mind snapped back to the blackboard, where the war chief had drawn a diagram showing an enemy's walled defenses.

"At night, I'd have our gunners pound the gate to keep the fort dwellers occupied and let them think they know what we're about. Then I'd send volunteers in over the walls here, here, here, and here," he indicated on the board, "To sabatoge their guns and take control of their defenses. By sunup the fort would be ours."

"How do you know the walls wouldn't be guarded?"

"They would be, of course," Deke replied. "What difference does that make? Wolf soldiers can slip past even the most alert fort dweller."

"What if the alarm was given?" Willie watched Deke's face with fascination, seeing the predatory look there.

"Then we'd have to mine the walls," Deke said, boyishly happy at even an imaginary prospect of blowing something up. "We'd pound 'em so hard, lob so many shells into their homes, they'd have to surrender. No fixed defense can stand up to a determined and mobile attacker."

"Good point," Willie said. "Anyone else have a comment?"

There was a negative mumble from the others.

"All right, then. That's it for today."

The boys stood up, stretching.

Deke hurried out the door. With a wave to his friends, he moved off towards his mother's tent, leaving them staring after him. Funny, he mused, how sensitive he was about his feelings for Andara. He knew his friends would tease him mercilessly if they knew, and this was something he didn't want ridiculed. Besides, since his return from the manhood test, he had discovered there was a new distance between them. What he had done separated them, seemed to make more apparent the differences between who they were and who they were going to become. Now that they were men, the democracy of boyhood relations was fading, and the fact that one day he would be chieftain over them was becoming more apparent. He noticed they now deferred to him in most things, and though in some ways this was flattering, it made him feel very isolated.

Andara, on the other hand, was as impudent as ever. When he was with her he could be himself. There was no need for him to maintain a barrier in his mind to prevent the influx of the confused mental babble that overflowed unconsciously from other people, because she had received the same training he had from his mother. And then there was her sensitivity which he sensed was on par with his own, though with interesting differences perhaps attributable to gender.

Deke came up to his mother's pavilion and paused, running his hands through his unruly curls to smooth them, adjusting his clothes more neatly. He rattled the knocker and stuck his head inside.

They were arranging herbs in bunches on the table. The assortment of greenery filled the room with its many-textured fragrances, and he thought he smelled a few he recognized.

The she-wolf lay quietly inside the door. Interestingly, she tended to follow Andara if Deke was otherwise engaged. Tilva looked up with a smile of welcome.

"You know," she said, "You really have to give that wolf a name."

Deke kissed her cheek. "You're right, Mother," he said, and turned to Andara. "I thought you might be able to think of a good one," he said, filling his eyes with her, so glad to see her he wanted to grab her, but his mother's presence inhibited him.

The girl's face became radiant. "You want me to name her?" she asked disbelievingly.

104

"No one else will do," he assured her.

"Let me think about it," said Andara, her mind chaotic.

"Take your time," he said.

Tilva watched this little interplay with a complicated smile. Part of her was amused and impressed by her son's natural gallantry, part was concerned about their relatively young ages, but the biggest part wholeheartedly approved the budding romantic feelings between them. Instinctively she knew Andara was a good match for her son, would look after him well in areas where he needed looking after. Nodding to herself she said aloud,

"Andara, I think I can spare you for a while. I'm just going to hang these on the rack to dry. Oh, and by the way, why don't you stay to supper? Barr's chef is preparing something special. Ask your father if he'd like to join us as well. You're invited, too," Tilva said to her son, smiling to see the hollows in his cheeks beginning to fill, the bruises gone.

"Good," Deke said. He looked at Andara. "You heard her, you're free. Want to go for a ride? Micmac needs some exercise."

"Go ahead, child," Tilva encouraged, though Andara needed no urging. "Make sure you get back by suppertime, Deke. Your father wants to see you."

"I will," he said, holding the door flap for Andara.

They rode side by side over rolling green landscape past a small farming hamlet where men and women could be seen working the fields.

Deke rode bareback with only a hackamore as was his wont. Micmac pranced a little beneath him, sensing his nervous energy, but basically she was a well-mannered horse and behaved herself. Andara's mount was a twelve-year-old gelding named Romeo, and she, too, rode without saddle or bridle. These horses were trained to the touch of a toe or knee and were intuitive to their riders' wishes. It helped that their riders had been aboard horses since before they could walk.

Occasionally their legs touched and when this happened they jumped, moving their horses apart. But the horses always moved back towards each other companionably, and finally, not daring to look at one another, Deke and Andara allowed their legs to be pressed together.

Off to one side and a little behind, the she-wolf kept pace, occasionally darting after some small animal. Her mind radiated steadily at a low frequency, just enough of a broadcast for them to be aware of her presence.

Deke reached across and took Andara's hand, twining his fingers through hers, wanting to bring her palm to his lips but not having the nerve. They held hands, their legs touched, and tentatively their minds reached out for one another, the physical contact speeding the connection.

Around them the world became vague as they focused inward. Andara could feel him in her mind, much stronger now than before. She perceived his emotional presence clearly, and realized he was laying his mind open before hers, that she might enter freely. Unable to resist his invitation, she allowed herself to go where he drew her and found herself being swept along inexorably, carried on a rising torrent of feeling. She felt lost in it, overwhelmed by his naked longing until she experienced an answering surge in her own psyche.

Reluctantly, Deke dissolved the connection and looked at her. In her eyes he saw the same things he felt: joy, arousal, and wonder at this mystery which had caught them up. "Let's walk," he said, sliding down from Micmac's back. She nodded and joined him. They took their horses' lead ropes and strolled slowly through the tall grass.

"The Spring Festival's next week," Deke said. "Are you going with anyone?"

She smiled and tossed her head. The warm breeze stirred her dark hair and she brushed it back. "That depends."

"On what?" he asked.

"On you," she replied.

"Does that mean you'll go with me?"

"If you ask," she said, her eyes hazel and twinkling in the sunlight.

He looked at the sky, then back at her. "Will you go with me?"

"Aye," she said.

He took her hand again and they walked dreamily through a patch of yellow and pink wildflowers. Insects buzzed lazily in the warm air.

"Deke," Andara said, tugging on his hand. She pointed to a small creek bubbling against the tall grass. "Let's let the horses drink," she suggested.

"All right," he said, finding it unaccountably difficult to speak. His heart beat a little faster as they led their horses to the stream, hobbled them loosely, and turned them free to graze. Andara slipped off her moccasins and rolled her pants above the knee. Then she waded into the water, exclaiming at the cold. She looked at him expectantly, and sighing, he followed suit.

When he stood in the icy streamlet next to her, he said, "Well, now you've got me here, what are you going to do with me?"

She glanced at him sidelong from behind dark lashes. "I want you to kiss me."

"Here, in this freezing water?" He began to laugh.

"Yes," she said. "That way we won't get too carried away."

"I want to get carried away," he said, and stopped laughing.

"I know," she told him. "But you scare me."

"Why?" he asked quietly. "Don't you know I'd never do anything to hurt you?"

"I know," she said. "But accidents happen."

He touched her hair lightly and moved nearer, hardly feeling the cold water swirling around his legs. "Nothing between us will ever be an accident," he said, his voice grave. "Everything is going to be because it's meant to be."

"You don't understand," she said and put her arms around his waist. "You scare me because you make me want to let you do the things you showed me in your thoughts."

"Andara," he said, acutely aware of her arms around him. "I only want to do those things if you want to do them, too." His breath was warm against her cheek.

"Maybe we can do some of those things," she murmured.

"Which ones?"

In answer she brushed his lips with her own and moved her hands up his back until her fingers tangled in his hair. "Now really kiss me," she whispered.

He looked into her eyes and saw they had become as green as in his dream a few nights earlier. Her breath was sweet and he leaned down to her, clutching her tightly so she wouldn't feel his trembling. Then he kissed her, and after a moment her mouth opened beneath his and she made a little sound as he tasted her with his tongue.

"More," she said, pulling his face to hers.

He kissed her again, her reaction giving him confidence.

"Ruins!" he gasped when they broke apart. "Let's get out of this water!"

She kissed his lower lip. "If we get out of the water we have to stop."

"I want to kiss you all day," he said. "What harm is there in that?"

"None, as long as we stay here."

"Nothing will happen, Andara. I can't even think of it yet."

"You're thinking of it," she said. "I can feel it."

Deke groaned. "Thinking is all I can do."

"I doubt that," she said. "Tilva warned me that circumcisions heal quickly."

"My God," he said. "Is that what you talk about!" He laughed a little, then squeezed her. Taking her hand, he led her out of the creek bed.

The wolf appeared from a successful foray after a vole, licking her lips. She stood in the water drinking, then came and shook all over them. They laughed and Deke grabbed Andara, swinging her in a full circle before hugging her to him in an excess of high spirits. Then he sat on the edge of the stream, dangling his legs. She sat next to him, her shoulder touching his, and he put his arm around her.

They watched the wolf for a while.

"I thought of a name," Andara said, and turned to look at him.

"Mmm?" His eyes were almost closed as he inhaled her fragrance and wondered if she wore scent or if that was her natural aroma.

"Yes," she continued, "I think she should be called Hopi."

He buried his face in her hair, and she felt him smile as his lips moved to her ear. "It's perfect," he said, moving his hand to her back and slipping his fingers under the hem of her blouse until he could feel the smooth, supple flesh of her waist.

She leaned back against his touch, her palms going to his chest. She could feel his heart beating as wildly as hers and drew him down until they lay facing one another on the grass. An ant walked across his brow, and gently, she brushed it away. "No kissing," she breathed.

He took one hand, kissed it, then put it back on his chest, inside his shirt. "Are you sure?" he asked, running his fingers down her side until his hand rested on her hip.

"Aye," she said without conviction, feeling as if something was wrong with her respiration. Her breathing was coming very fast; when he reached between the back of her thighs, she jerked and caught his hand in hers. "Stop," she said. "I feel so strange..."

"But I'm not kissing you," he said innocently, and shifted closer.

"No," she said, moving away until she felt him caress her again. "What are you doing?" She felt his knee slide between her legs.

"I just want to hold you. As close as we can get."

He slithered nearer until her warmth was against the length of his body, wrapped his arms around her, and held her, gazing into her eyes. Slowly, her arms stole around him, too, and she felt a deep, involuntary pulse of erotic excitement as she realized exactly what she was feeling pressed rigidly against her pelvis.

"I wish we were older," she said.

"Why?" His lips circled her ear, then moved to her throat.

"Because then we wouldn't have to stop."

"How much older?" His voice was deeper than she'd ever heard it.

"Some," she said.

"Does it matter so much?" His hands were under her shirt again, moving across her bare skin.

"Yes," she said, her mind filled with cascading imagery of their two young bodies naked together, rising and falling as they made love fully. "Stop," she begged, her nipples aching as he brushed them with his fingers. She felt his lips on hers and for a moment gave herself up to him, drawing his tongue deep into her mouth before shoving him away and jumping to her feet. She stood over him, panting, her breast heaving.

Deke lay where he was. He reached for the hand she offered to pull him up and clasped it in his. "Andara," he said, tugging until she sat beside him again. "I have to tell you something." His gaze held hers. "I'm out of my mind over you. I can't concentrate, can't think; you're in my thoughts every minute." He played with her fingers. "All I want is to be with you."

"I feel the same way," she said, looking away.

"I know you aren't really ready for this," he said.

"Oh, yes, I am." She turned back with a wry smile. "I just don't want a big belly yet."

"Is that what you're afraid of?"

"Not just that."

"Tell me," he pleaded. "Am I doing something wrong?"

"Ruins, no!" She laughed and transferred his hand to her lap where she turned it over and traced the lines on his palm. "Hmm," she said, "Looks like a long life line, very long. And look: your heart and your head lines are connected by this line here."

"What's that one?" he asked, interested.

"That's your fate line," she told him.

"What does that mean?"

"Wait...see how these lines make a triangle over here? That's called the triangle of determination." She smiled at him and he felt his heart thumping madly at how lovely she looked. Then she looked into his eyes and said, "It means you like to get what you want."

"Will I get what I want?"

She raised her eyebrows. "That depends," she said, a teasing note in her voice.

"On what?"

"On you, of course."

"What else do you see?"

Andara studied his palm closely. "Well, you're a genius, but we knew that. Talents in lots of areas. But there's something here, later in your life..." She looked at her own palm for comparison. "Look!" she told him. "I have the same snarl of lines in the same spot on my life line, too! How strange!"

"What does it mean?" he asked, disquieted.

"It means...something is going to happen," she said, and her eyes grew dark. For a second he felt as if someone else was looking out at him and he shivered. "Something big," she repeated. "Something that will change everything we know."

"What about us?" he continued, sensing the augmentation of personality he had thus far seen happen only with his mother. "What will happen to us?"

Her voice was strong and distinct. "Many of our people are going to be involved," she told him. "Something is stirring in the West, something in the ruins." And then she began to shiver at the inner vision she saw, a vision of wind and darkness and something inexplicable that she couldn't identify, couldn't even bear to acknowlege fully.

He called her name urgently. "Andara! Andara!"

She came back to herself to find his arms around her. He gazed at her with concern.

"Are you all right? I think spirits were talking through you!" He held her until she stopped trembling. "What did you *see*?"

"I *saw* something...oh, Deke, you must not do this thing...!"

"What thing, my sweet Andara?"

She shook her head, unwilling to lend credence to her fear by talking about it.

He rose in a swift movement, taking her with him. "Come on," he suggested. "Let's catch our horses and go back. It's getting late."

She touched his face and looked earnestly into his eyes. "Promise me," she said.

"Promise you what?"

"Promise you'll be careful when you go into the West," she whispered.

"Am I going somewhere?" His expression was humorous.

"You will be," she said, suddenly grim.

"I've dreamed of going west all my life," he mused thoughtfully.

"Why?" she asked. "What could possibly be there that you need to find?"

A strange smile passed fleetingly across his lean features. Then, lightly, "Why, my destiny, of course."

Andara stared at him, then made a face. "You're joking again," she said, "And this is serious."

He caught Romeo and unhobbled him. "Let me give you a leg up."

She grabbed the horse's mane and jumped onto his back, disdaining any assistance.

He had Micmac's hobbles off in another moment. Before he mounted, he stood next to Andara, looking up at her. "I didn't mean to make fun," he said. "And I wasn't really joking." His blue eyes were sincere. "But you did say I have a long life line, so maybe there isn't anything to worry about."

She tossed her head. "There are worse things than dying, Deke Wolfson," she said. "Don't you know that?"

He jumped onto Micmac's back. "I know it." He drummed his heels on the mare's sides. "Come on!" he shouted. "I'll race you!"

Andara urged Romeo forward, bending low over his neck as he picked up speed.

Behind them, the she-wolf followed at an easy lope. Overhead the sky was purple and gold as the sun sank in a blaze of red fire towards the horizon.

Dinner was finished. They lounged around the table conversing, the adults taking care not to smile or stare too openly at the two young people who thought their blushing exchanges of sidelong glances had gone unnoticed. Under the table Deke's hand found Andara's and he smiled blissfully.

Barr studied his son. He didn't know where to begin talking about what needed discussing.

Eventually, sensing his father's scrutiny, Deke looked up and met his eyes. "Was there something you wanted to talk to me about, Father?"

"Aye," said the chieftain. "It's not an easy subject. Our traditions demand discretion in these matters."

"Some traditions aren't useful," Deke said simply. "I'll answer whatever question you have."

"It's about the ritual knife you brought back from the ruins," Barr said reluctantly.

"Ah," Deke said with a quick nod. "Mastra told you?"

"He didn't say a thing," Hawk put in quickly. "I overheard you talking from outside your tent. Completely inadvertantly, I assure you."

"Of course," Deke nodded.

"Point being, I'm not the only one who heard," Hawk continued.

"Is there a problem?" Deke asked.

"Gant Murdock is always a problem," Tilva said.

"All I did was bury his son. I'd think he'd be grateful."

"There's a rumor going around Camp about that damned knife," Hawk said in his softest tone.

"I see," Deke said. "People think I took it from Peter and then buried him, is that it?"

"None of our folk," Hawk assured him.

"Gant's clan?" Deke found himself inexplicably bitter. He let go of Andara's hand and got up to pace.

"There's no judgment being made," Barr said firmly. "Everyone understands about the Manhood Rites."

"No one understands anything," Deke said. "I took Peter's knife after a bear killed him. Then I killed the bear. I took the claws, teeth, and hide. Anyone who doesn't believe the bear killed Peter can go dig up his grave. I'll be happy to take 'em to the spot. Unless they think I'd gut and eat another boy's innards, I think his body will speak for itself."

"Deke..." Tilva spoke soothingly.

"No, Mother." Deke faced his father, anger galvanizing his movements. "You can be sure if anyone in Gant's clan is talking about murder, Gant not only knows about it but is encouraging it!"

"He's probably right," Hawk said to Barr. "Murdock's behind the rumor."

"But what's his purpose?" Tilva asked.

"His purpose is to challenge the succession," Deke said tightly.

Barr's eyes grew hard. "That'll be the day," he said.

"He'll do it, Father, and he'll do it when all the clan leaders are assembled. Probably at the Festival." Deke paused. "He's been looking for an excuse to come after me."

"Why?" Barr rasped.

"I've been less than polite to him," Deke admitted. "And now that I'm a man..."

"You think he'll call you out at the Festival?" Tilva's expression was horrified.

"I'm sure of it," Deke said.

"Gant Murdock is a dangerous fighter," Barr said slowly.

"So is your son," Hawk told him.

"Deke's good, but he's not grown yet."

"Don't worry," Deke said. "Gant will back down."

"Never," Barr said.

"Oh, aye," Deke said, his tone very certain. "He'll back down."

Barr met his son's eyes and realized he had no real idea what his capabilities might be.

"There's something else," Deke continued.

"What's that?" Tilva asked, astonished by this angry, self-assured stranger walking around in her son's body.

"He may be counting on you to interfere, Father," Deke said, and stopped pacing. He looked earnestly at Barr. "You must avoid that, at least in the way he expects. You can't fight my duel for me. The political cost would be too great."

Barr's lips tightened. "He couldn't possibly be after my position. The People would never follow him."

"It's true, he's a drunkard and a brutal piece of dog manure, but he's ambitious. He knows the People wouldn't accept him, but they might accept one of his sons. He's married to your sister. He has a blood claim."

There was a long silence. With fascination, Barr watched his son. "What else?"

"His argument will be that the People shouldn't be governed by witchcraft and magic. He'll try to play on what happened when I came back from the ruins." He paused, almost choking with his anger. "He'll say that a witch's whelp has no business as chieftain of the People."

"Whatever else happens, you can't afford to let him back down," Andara put in from her place at the table.

Deke looked at her in surprise. "Huh? Why not?"

"You must kill him, put him down like a rabid animal. Otherwise," her gaze was meaningful, "He'll be back."

"If I kill him than I have to kill all his kin, too," Deke said. "They would avenge him, sure. I'd have to spend the rest of my life watching my back."

"What's the solution, then?" Hawk asked.

"We'll call off the Festival," Tilva said.

"This situation isn't going to go away," Barr said. "We might as well deal with it."

Deke thought for a moment, then said, "Everyone's invited, right?"

"Of course," Tilva replied. "You know that."

"What do you have in mind, son?" Barr asked.

"When you taught me to play chess, you always told me never to make a purely defensive move," Deke said. "A move should be both offensive and defensive simultaneously, eh?"

"Yes," Barr replied, wondering what his son was getting at.

"There's an action you can take that will checkmate Gant. And the best part is, it won't require vendetta by his relatives. In fact, I wouldn't be surprised if he ends up quite isolated." Deke stared at his father, almost willing him to see the solution.

Barr's brows knit as he thought about it and realized his son already had given him the clue. His expression cleared and he clapped Deke on the back warmly. "You'll make a great chieftain one day," he said quietly, his eyes showing his approval. "You think quickly and well. and the best part is, we can kill several birds with this particular stone."

"Aye," Deke said, his teeth showing as he smiled.

Both father and son's eyes glittered with grim anticipation.

"Whatever you're planning, killing him still would be best," Andara insisted. "The hell with his relatives. Most of them would probably be glad to be rid of him."

Deke turned to Andara quizzically, her vehemence surprising him.

"You're not usually this bloodthirsty," he said.

She folded her hands in her lap and looked down. The she-wolf rose and sat beside her, laying her head on the girl's knee.

"I see we all have reasons to want this man removed," Tilva said, disquieted.

Deke's expression was concerned. He could feel the emotional block Andara had put up to keep unwanted questions at bay, and respected it. He didn't need empathy to know Gant Murdock had affronted Andara in some way, and that gave him one more reason to want his uncle destroyed.

Tilva gazed at her son and her husband, alike in so many ways, both committed to the protection of what they regarded as theirs. She saw the hardening jaws, the narrowing eyes, and experienced a feeling of great security. She rested her hands on her belly, unconsciously cradling the new life there. With such men between her and the harsh exigencies of their violent world, she would always feel safe, for surely nothing could ever harm her.

CHAPTER SEVEN

"You keep asking who I really am and what really goes on between my ears, as if by understanding either of those two things you would have a better concept of how I do what I do. So I'll tell you, on the off chance that knowing this will make you come closer to your greater Self." The General fastened his gaze on me and I could not look away from his eyes. I was riveted in my seat without the strength or will to move. His attention had the effect of draining my motivation, making me content simply to sit and listen.

"I am a free-floating consciousness, as you are, as everyone is, focused for now through this physical form in this earth plane reality. The main difference between us is that I can also focus elsewhere in space and time while still maintaining a living link with my physical self. And there are infinite alternate realities, infinite universes, if you will, each replete with infinite possibility and probability, that I am able to tap both for information and energy enhancement.

"Now, is that of any use to you?"

And with a snapping sensation, whatever connection he had made with me was broken, and I realized he had said not a word aloud, that I had heard him speaking inside my head.

— Ourn Rohlvaag; Collected Journals; City of Life, A.D. 3109

O n the evening of the Spring Festival, guests arrived in a steady stream at the meadow where the celebration was to be held. Several enormous, open tents had been erected to hold the food and drink. The area was decorated with hundreds of tiny lanterns strung on cord stretched between tent poles, and in the gathering dusk, the light they cast sparkled cheerfully, making the meadow into a fairyland. The grass sward had been cut short and cleared of debris. Woodchuck holes had been filled so that no inebriated guest might stumble inadvertantly into one and break a leg, as had happened at one Springtime Festival. Heaps of firewood stood placed strategically, awaiting full darkness before being set ablaze. Musicians were grouped under one of the open pavilions playing quietly, but that would change once the party got going.

In Tilva's tent, Barr examined himself critically in a mirror, trimmed a little more hair from the left side of his beard, then turned to his wife. She was dressed in a silver gown that accentuated her long legs and high bosom. Her pregnancy wasn't noticeable yet, except to one who knew. To anyone else she simply looked especially curvaceous; ripe, he smiled to himself, like a delectable fruit ready for plucking.

"What are you smiling about?" she asked, smiling with him.

"You look good enough to eat," he told her.

"You can," she said, "Later, if things go well."

"Everything is prepared," he said. "I've spoken to Leah and she's ready. She's wanted this for years anyway."

"I know," Tilva said quietly. On too many occasions Barr's sister had confided her husband's perverse cruelties, things no sister could tell a brother. Gant Murdock never left a visible mark on his wife; that would bring Barr Wolfson's wrath down on him in an open declaration of hostility. The credo of Tilva's healing profession demanded confidentiality, and Leah had sworn her to secrecy, so she never had revealed to Barr exactly what his poor sister endured in her marriage.

"You mustn't worry," Barr said gently.

Tilva laughed a little. "You could as soon tell the day not to begin."

"I know how you feel, but my instincts tell me Gant is the one who should be frightened," he said, taking her arms and looking into her eyes.

"Oh, Barr, Deke's only thirteen..."

"Aye." He was serious. "I never knew anyone unarmed to kill a tiger, much less a bear. And as far as taming a pack of wild wolves, well, you tell me. These are not inconsequential achievements."

Tilva allowed him to hold her for a moment, taking strength from his strength. "I know you're right," she said, "At least here." She tapped her forehead. "But my heart knows differently."

"All life is possibility and potential, my darling Tilva," he reminded her tenderly.

"You're actually looking forward to this," she observed, amazed.

"Of course," he affirmed. "Nothing gives me more pleasure than crushing an insect under my boot who doesn't know his place."

"Is that what he is? An insect?"

"He's worse than an insect," Barr said, his face setting in ruthless lines. "If he challenges my son or my authority, then it's war, pure and simple."

"Will he?"

"That's what we shall see. Now, let's get ready, it's almost time for us to make our grand entrance." The chieftain fastened the final button on his new formal shirt.

"Where's Deke?" Tilva admired the way the garment hugged his muscular torso.

"He'll meet us. He's escorting Andara, if you recall."

"Oh, yes," and she smiled, despite herself.

Andara was nearly ready when her father told her Deke had arrived. She put the final touches on her make-up (for the first time she had rouged her

116

lips and applied eye shadow in a shade that darkened her eyes to emerald) and took a last look at herself in the full length mirror that had belonged to her mother. She was wearing a dress that also had been her mother's, altered to fit her own figure. It rippled with color; in one light it was burnished gold, in another deep garnet, and in yet another, rich green matching her eyes. When she moved, a slash up the side revealed her leg to the thigh.

She nodded to her reflection, satisfied. Around her neck she wore an ancient jade pendant, and jade miniatures dangled from her pierced ears. Her arms were bare to the shoulder. On her right she wore a bicep bracelet in the shape of an elongated tiger with jewels for eyes, as well as a matching smaller tiger wound around her left forefinger.

Dabbing on a generous amount of her usual perfume, she slipped her formal dagger into a sheath hidden in the back waistband of her dress and hoped she wouldn't need it.

When she appeared from the rear of the tent, Deke's eyes widened and he expelled breath from between his lips in an appreciative whistle.

"Ruins," he said, "You look incredible!"

She laughed coquettishly. "Do you really think so?"

"Am I lying?" Deke asked Hawk who stood nearby apparently struck dumb by his daughter's transformation from tomboy to temptress. The older man found his voice.

"No, lad, you're sure not lying." Hawk rubbed his face ruefully, thinking how like her mother Andara was. "You're going to be the belle of the Festival," he told his daughter.

Andara looked Deke over. "You don't look so bad yourself," she said.

He was wearing a loose-fitting blue tunic, belted at the waist, over fitted, black trousers. The tunic had the effect of accentuating his wide shoulders and narrow waist, and Andara thought how cleverly Tilva had rendered the garment, how its color heightened the already dramatic hue of his eyes. She noticed the ritual dagger worn ostentatiously on his leather belt.

He saw her eyes go there. "No point in hiding it or pretending it isn't what everyone is interested in," he said.

"This isn't a game," she reminded him, her gaze troubled.

"Aye, it is," he replied seriously. "Just a dangerous one."

"How do you know he won't fight you?"

"Did I say that?"

"You said he'd back down."

"Correct. But I may have to persuade him a little first."

"Do you really think you can take him?"

Deke shrugged.

Andara shivered though the air was mild. She couldn't put her finger on why she felt Gant Murdock must die. She'd tried earlier in the day to cast the tiles, hoping her spirit guide would give her more information, but had been unsuccessful. No answer had been forthcoming. So on her own, using a deep meditative trance, she had attempted to divine the future, but all she had accomplished was to unnerve herself more thoroughly. This presentiment of danger weighed on her, filling her with anxiety. She understood and even admired Deke's insistence on a non-lethal solution to Gant Murdock, but she couldn't agree with it. No, she wanted to see Gant lying lifeless at Deke's feet, his blood draining into the earth.

Something of her feelings was visible on her face and Deke exchanged glances with Hawk.

"Are you coming, Papa?" Andara pushed her thoughts aside with an effort.

"I'll be along," Hawk answered. "You two go ahead. Oh, and Deke," Hawk's eyes held a warning, "Gant is especially dangerous on the counter-stroke, so watch for it."

Deke nodded.

Hawk looked him over, nodding, satisfied with what he saw. The youngster had made a full recovery from his ordeal, healing with the speed only youth provides. He had put back some of the flesh he had lost and although lean, his musculature was more pronounced. Hawk could swear the boy had grown taller in the last few weeks, shooting up like spring grass. "Remember! Gant fights dirty, uses every filthy trick in the book."

Deke grinned. "You've already taught me 'most every filthy trick yourself."

"Aye, but you keep sharp, do y'hear me? Don't make me look bad."

"Don't worry," Deke assured him.

Most of Deke's friends had arrived at the meadow by the time he and Andara got there, as had thousands of other revelers dressed in their gaudiest finery. People from every level of their society were gathered, and Andara pointed to the tents where entertainers made last minute preparations. It was customary at these festivals for artists from across Barr's domains to present themselves and their work for the chieftain and his wife to review. There was great competition among these folk, because it was the chieftain's habit to patronize those whose work caught his eye. Anyone who could show him something completely original, whether it was written, painted, performed as music or drama was certain to receive a financial boon. Anyone who invented a labor-saving device, or most especially, a new weapon, received support for life.

In the tents where food and drink were laid out, people were filling plates and mugs with an assortment of the finest delicacies available in Spring Camp and its environs, and these were considerable. Venison, beef, mutton, fowl, and fresh fish were prepared in a hundred ways, as were heaps of vegetables and legumes, raw and cooked. Breads of every variety, sweet and multigrain, were stacked within easy reach. There were entire tables given over to decadent desserts: ice cream, pies, cakes, puddings, trifles...the variety and quantity seemed endless.

"Do you want something to drink?" Deke asked Andara, raising his voice over the building tumult.

She nodded, and they wound their way through the throngs. The musicians were playing a lively tune that got Deke's feet tapping, and he squeezed Andara's hand, unable to suppress his nervous excitement. He noted the way every male they passed turned to gawk at her and was filled with pride by right of association. The emotions around him were varied and overlapping, washing across his mind like a confusing waterfall. It was impossible to get more than quick impressions from each individual before they were lost in the generalized roar of the mob psyche which surrounded them. There was a basically happy tone in that psyche, and most people seemed to be anticipating a good time. A great deal of warmth was directed at him, and when he and Andara had gotten some fruit punch and joined his friends, he could feel himself surrounded by a cocoon of protective benevolence. People smiled at them, and Tim O'Dale, accompanied by a pretty, dark-eyed girl of fourteen whom Deke knew only slightly, greeted him loudly, obviously well-begun on the alcoholic beverages. He introduced the girl as Callie, daughter of a minor chief from an eastern clan.

Mastra's eyes widened when he saw Andara and Deke. He took in their clasped hands and raised his brows, saying, "So this is what you've been up to! Well, well, well!"

"Be nice," Andara warned, dreading any of the dark youth's barbed witticisms.

None of the other boys in the group had thought to bring girls, and they looked a little enviously at Deke and Tim, then forgot their jealousy as a group of laughing young women walked by, drawing their attention.

At the place of honor, near enough to the tents for easy access but not so near that the crowds reached it, was a long table lined with comfortable chairs. Here the chiefs would sit, with a good view of the festivities. Some already had arrived with wives or concubines and were finding their places, greeting old friends and comrades in arms.

Deke's eyes went there briefly, then moved away. Gant Murdock was nowhere in sight. He sipped his juice, scanning the crowd. At his side, he could feel Andara do the same.

There was a fanfare from the musicians, and Deke saw his parents making their way through the mob, which slowly parted to permit them entrance, then closed up behind them as friends and well-wishers shouted greetings and reached to shake hands. It was a long progress into the meadow because Barr and Tilva wanted to re-establish connections with everyone, making sure each individual felt he or she had been singled out for attention. Deke was impressed by the easy familiarity his parents, and particularly his father, had with their people. They joked, laughed, remembered everyone's names, congratulated this one or that on the birth of a child, commiserated with losses suffered, and swapped memories of successful campaigns and skirmishes. He noted with some interest that after being acknowledged personally, each party seemed to gain in self-esteem, and the better they felt about themselves, the better they felt about their chieftain.

Deke saw Andara watching their almost royal progress with an enigmatic expression, and put his arm around her shoulders, whispering, "What's bothering you?"

Startled, she said, "Nothing," even though she sensed he didn't believe her. She was having the most peculiar feeling as she watched Barr and Tilva, certain she never again would see them together like this at a Spring Festival. She felt a tentative probe touch her mind and composed herself. Of all things, she didn't want Deke *seeing* that in her thoughts, especially not tonight.

Though his curiosity was piqued, he forced himself to respect her boundaries. She had made it clear where she would allow him to go in her psyche, and what the consequences of trespass would be. Truthfully, he didn't want to experience those consequences. He was aware that Andara was every bit as proud and stubborn as he was, and he knew how he would feel if anyone violated his privacy. With a sigh, he held her nearer, and that small gesture did more to center her than any other he could have taken. Gratefully, she leaned back against him, Sending him an image so blatantly sexual he felt an answering throb between his thighs and murmured, "Behave yourself."

She smiled, her mouth curving humorously. His response gave her a subtle feeling of power and she found she liked it. Now, with his arms around her, some of her fears were retreating. Her spirits lifted and soon her mood grew more attuned to his; his excitement and anticipation became her own.

Eventually Barr and Tilva arrived at the center of the long table, and Deke saw that his Aunt Leah was waiting for them. There was a formal greeting, and then she was seated at Barr's right side. Tilva sat to his left, and beyond her stood Hawk, his sharp eyes watching everything around him with the intensity of his namesake. Beyond Leah stood Willie O'Dale, and behind him were several soldiers, discreetly armed with pistols and body blades. The seat next to Leah was empty.

Occasionally someone approached the long table and paid formal respects to the chieftain, sometimes requesting an appointment at a later date for the settling of minor disputes, sometimes being referred to Barr's secretary for rulings to be handed down in writing. Altogether, even at a social occasion like this one, Deke observed, his father got an enormous amount of work done.

By now the darkness was complete. Stars appeared overhead in their thousands. The Milky Way was a wash of misty light, and Deke pointed as several rockets were released to explode in a shower of fireworks. The crowd cheered, and moments later the musicians began to play again. Another roar went up as one by one the bonfires were lit. Soon the field was illuminated by the shifting flames from dozens of fires. Eating and drinking began in earnest, and the noise from thousands of bellowed conversations created a hubbub which, with the music, was deafening. The boys looked at one another, grinning.

"What're you drinking, Deke?" Tim sniffed the cup. "Fruit punch? You're drinking fruit punch?" His voice was incredulous.

"I want to keep my wits about me," Deke explained.

"Why? Expecting trouble?" Tim's grey eyes were instantly alert.

Deke shrugged. "Maybe."

Tim's hand went to his knife. "Who?"

"Gant Murdock."

Mastra couldn't help but listen. "What's his problem?"

"Some of his people overheard me telling you about Peter," Deke told him.

Mastra glanced around uneasily, looking for members of the Murdock clan.

"What about Peter?" Tim asked.

At Deke's nod, Mastra said, "A bear killed him. Deke killed the bear, then buried Peter. But Deke's got his knife." Mastra gestured to the ritual dagger.

"The Murdocks think he murdered Peter?" Tim's eyes began to burn.

One of the other boys leaned closer. "Any Murdock who comes near should be encouraged to leave," he said, his voice betraying his outrage. "Violently."

A generalized mutter went through the group as they expressed agreement.

"Aye, brother, stay near us." Tim grasped Deke's bicep. "We'll take it as a privilege to rough up some of that bunch! Never did like 'em, anyway. Even Pete...always was a weakling."

"Thanks," Deke replied, "But leave Gant to me. No matter what happens, don't interfere with him, all right?"

"Aye," Tim said reluctantly.

"You can have any of his friends who try to interfere, but not him, not Gant. This is a blood matter."

The boys nodded. A blood matter had to be settled by the principals.

Deke was gratified to see their commitment. He gave Andara's shoulders a squeeze and said, "Come on, let's have a little fun!" He drew her towards a clear area in front of the musicians' tent where people were clapping and whooping with the music. A group of professional dancers whirled and gyrated wildly, first on their hands, then on their feet, finally flying through the air.

Deke and Andara grinned at one another. The dance reached a crescendo of spectacular acrobatics, then ended with the music. The crowd cheered appreciatively, then, as the musicians began to play another song, one with a slower, more sensual beat, couples began to pair off for dancing.

Deke took Andara in his arms confidently. After his mother, Andara had been his first dancing partner. They had practiced together many times under Tilva's critical tutelage.

Tonight, though, everything was vastly different. Deke was startled by the way her flesh felt under his hands, for her skimpy dress was made of an ultra-fine weave that clung like a second skin. In the leaping firelight from a nearby bonfire, her hair was as dark as the space between the stars, and it fell in lustrous cascades across her shoulders. He had never seen her wear makeup before, and the way her mouth looked made him hungry to cover it with his own. When she pressed closer he put his hand in the small of her back to better guide her and his fingers encountered her dagger. Surprised, he looked into her eyes questioningly.

In response she shrugged and said, "The others aren't the only ones who'd be happy to dispose of a few Murdocks."

He frowned slightly, troubled by her words. He often watched Andara practice with a blade, knew she was very good. She had been taught by her father, the People's acknowledged master of knife fighting. Andara fought with either hand equally, and her speed and blurring hand changes made her a difficult opponent.

"I hope it doesn't come to that," he said as they moved together, both exceedingly aware of the subtle pressures being exerted on their skin by one another's bodies.

"Look over there," she said, inclining her head across the dance space.

He laughed out loud. Several of his friends had convinced some girls to dance with them, and though they twirled with determination, their spastic motions and lunges could hardly be called dancing. The girls endured these shenanigans as best they could, occasionally having to be quick to avoid being stepped on or jostled too roughly.

"Forget them," Deke said, pulling her closer. When she moved her hips suggestively against his, he practically saw stars. "Who knows," he whispered into her ear, "Maybe Gant won't show up at all."

"Wouldn't that be a blessing," Andara murmured, sliding her hands over his shoulders and around his neck. She met his eyes and saw they were huge, luminous in the uneven light. For a moment it seemed she was plummeting through them, then she realized he was in her head again, and the intensity of sensation this evoked made her weak-kneed. His desire was a living thing in her mind, and she wanted to drag him away to the fields and woods where she could open herself to him completely. She had never imagined she could feel anything this deeply, never imagined she could be filled with such overwhelming need for the touch of another human being.

Deke was hypnotized by her combined emanation of perfume, pressure, and pheremones. He tried to keep his mind focused on his purpose and failed utterly. His head swam with erotic possibilities. He knew she was inciting him deliberately, knew she felt safe here in the bubble of privacy created by their secret communication in the midst of the crowd. It seemed to heighten the intimacy of every heated touch, making him want to put his mouth and hands on all her most mysterious places.

"God," he whispered, clutching her to him desperately.

She hugged him back, and sought his lips with hers as the music ended with a flourish. Breathlessly, they moved apart.

He looked around, immersed in unreality. In all that heaving multitude, only his connection to Andara felt solid, and he took a few seconds to orient himself.

She put her arm around his waist, looping her fingers through his belt. "Let's get something to eat."

"If you like," he said hoarsely, his body aching for hers.

"Are you all right?" she asked, an amused note finding its way into her voice.

"Aye," he lied.

"Are you sure?" she persisted, looking up at his face.

He caught her free hand, and before she could stop him, pressed the palm to his crotch. He grinned when she jerked away as if burned and slapped him on the back of the wrist, hard. She looked to see if anyone had noticed what he'd done and was relieved to find no one had.

"That was crude, you animal," she said, looking into his glowing eyes, laughing despite herself.

"I can feel how much you like torturing me," he reminded her.

"I don't mean to torture you," Andara said contritely, trying to keep the mischief out of her voice.

"It would embarrass the hell out of us both if I lost control in public," Deke said, smiling.

"Would you?" she asked, wide-eyed. "Would you really lose control?"

"Aye," he said, leading her towards the food tents. "I still feel your hand. I can't tell you how much I want you to touch me like that again."

Andara blushed. "I know. What are we going to do?"

"I don't know," he said, though his mind could conjure a thousand things. "Look, my father is getting ready to address the guests." Thank the ruins, he added silently.

There was a blare of brass from the musicians that carried to the farthest parts of the meadow. Gradually the multitude fell silent. Attention turned towards the table where Barr Wolfson stood on a small platform placed on the spot his chair had occupied. In his left hand he held an ornate goblet filled with wine. He raised it towards the crowd.

"Welcome, everyone," he said, pitching his voice to reach each person gathered there. "You are all welcome. I offer this toast in your honor, and hope you enjoy yourselves in health and happiness." He drained his cup while the crowd shouted approval and drank with him.

Barr handed his goblet to Tilva who placed it on the table. He waved for silence and again the throng settled.

"Tonight I have some public business to attend to, and you'll forgive me if I do it immediately, while the clan chiefs are present." He looked pointedly down the table and everyone's eyes noticed the empty chair for the first time. "I see not all the chiefs are present," Barr said, allowing some displeasure to show on his face. He spoke to the crowd. "Do any of you see Gant Murdock?"

Deke watched people turn to look at each other, and nodded to himself.

When Barr judged he had given them long enough, he spoke in a low voice to three of the armed men waiting behind Willie. "Find him. Bring him here."

The men nodded and disappeared into the crowd.

"Tonight I have an unpleasant task to perform," he told the assembled chiefs and citizens. "But I think you'll agree with my reasons for intervention. Bear in mind that it's always easier to raise someone up than to remove him, which is why until now I've been reluctant to interfere. Also, since much of this is a personal matter, a matter of family and family relations, I had hoped it could be resolved by the principals. I had hoped a word to the wise would be sufficient." Barr looked out over the sea of heads. "It was not."

There was a commotion at the far edge of the crowd, growing louder as it approached.

"I see we've found our absentee ally," Barr said lightly, though his eyes were deadly serious. The public affront Gant had made by not appearing at the chieftain's festival had confirmed Barr's decision and he watched his men hustle Gant along with a minimum of ceremony. When his brother-in-law stood swaying before him, his bloodshot eyes filled with hatred, Barr looked him over contemptuously. "Where was he?" he asked his men.

"Passed out in the latrine," one of them said, his mouth twisting sardonically.

"Gant Murdock," Barr said, his cold tone and stern gaze making those standing nearby glad his anger was not falling on them. "Recently my sister made me aware that your treatment of her is brutal beyond belief. This would be bad enough in any case, but it becomes much more serious because of your position. Chiefs are expected to lead by example, and this you have failed to do. You've abused your family and your inferiors, and by the ruins, it must stop." Barr fixed his dark stare on the man who now stood sullenly looking at the ground. "Look at me, kinsman," he ordered, his voice filled with such natural authority that it didn't occur to Gant to disobey.

"I could never remain chieftain of the People if I allowed any of my governors to abuse our folk. I could never remain head of my own family if I allowed one member to abuse another."

Gant shifted uneasily before the steady perusal of his chieftain. A sense of growing apprehension came over him as he forced himself to stand still and pretend indifference. He couldn't stop his eyes from darting back and forth while he calculated the odds of being able to get to Barr Wolfson before the chieftain's bodyguards cut him down. It almost would be worth dying to feel his blade stab into Barr's heart. Rage and hatred filled Gant's being and he had to clench his fists to control himself. He stared stonily up at the man who by marrying a witch from the south and siring a son on her had betrayed his own people. The chieftain had allowed the southern evil to come to power over all of them. He knew the witch's offspring had killed his son, the son he had hoped might someday be maneuvered to sit in the chieftain's tent. Now those dreams were dead as ruins, and Gant was consumed by jealousy and hatred, blaming Barr Wolfson and his family for his personal inadequacies.

"Is that so, my lord?" Gant said sarcastically, ready to defy the chieftain for the honor of his clan.

Barr studied Gant with the fascination of one who has discovered a new species of snake and is trying to decide how best to dissect it.

"Well?" he said.

"What about your family, Barr Wolfson? Your son murdered Peter! You know it, you're trying to protect him!"

"What proof do you have for this absurd charge?" Barr asked.

"Look at him! He's so arrogant he's even wearing Peter's ritual blade tonight!" Gant pointed to Deke where he stood some yards away, watching alertly.

"Are you accusing my son of murdering Peter during the Manhood Ritual?" Barr glanced out at the crowd. On cue, a soldier standing nearby said,

"There's no such thing as murder during Manhoods! Everyone knows that, Murdock! There are no rules!"

"Besides," someone else chimed in, "I have it on good authority that your boy was killed by a bear."

"I claim the ancient right!" Gant shouted over the rising clamor. "I make challenge! Let God and the Universe decide!"

Barr quieted the crowd with a gesture. "Before you make your challenge, let me explain your situation so you understand that what you are doing will gain you nothing, and might in fact end with you in such straits as no sane man could wish for." The chieftain held Gant riveted in place by the sheer force of his personality. "Gant Murdock, you are hereby divorced from my sister, Leah, by her request and my personal decree. Your sons belong to Leah and are now under my protection. You may see them with supervision, but if you ever lay a hand on them you will answer to me.

"Also," Barr continued, "You are removed from your position as regional governor. Your Number One is appointed governor in your place on a temporary basis. If he proves reliable, he may keep his position. If not, he will be replaced as quickly."

A hush lay over the crowd, broken only by the occasional cry of an infant.

"Due to the nature of your transgressions, I now call for a vote among the chiefs to confirm my decision. All in favor, say, 'Aye.' All against, 'Nay.'"

"Aye!" they roared in unison, banging mugs on the table for emphasis.

"Now," said Barr with satisfaction. "Our blood ties are severed. Your ambition is at an end. Do you still wish to make challenge as is your right?"

Gant's head was spinning from the speed with which his disaster had overtaken him. He looked from face to face along the table until his eyes stopped on Leah. Never taking his gaze from her, he spoke softly, "Aye, I still make challenge, Wolfson."

"Do you challenge me, Murdock?" A ripple went through the crowd at the chieftain's lethal tone. A sense of rising excitement filled the air.

"I challenge *him*." Gant pointed at Deke. "The witch's whelp." With a sneer he faced Barr. "He killed my son. Now I'll kill yours."

There was a heavy silence. Barr glanced towards his son.

Giving Andara's hand a final squeeze, Deke walked into the lantern-light, using his sensitivity to tap the mood of the people. He picked up shock, surprise, outrage, and as the people looked from the mature man to the wiry youth, a dangerous groundswell of violence.

"Good evening, Father," he said, inclining his head towards the chieftain. He looked expressionlessly at Gant. "I accept your challenge, Uncle," he said. "But remember this: No matter what happens, you lose. Kill me and you will be outcast. If you don't, well," Deke stroked the bridge of his nose delicately, "You'll wish you had." He drew the ritual knife from its sheath. "This is the knife I used to avenge your son," he said, his tone somber. "I give you this one opportunity to change your mind, Uncle. Leave quietly. Otherwise..."

Gant chuckled gutterally. "Otherwise what, you unnatural little son of a bitch? You'll murder me, too? Look at him," he exhorted the crowd, "Not even nervous! Killed two men in March, my son in May. Hey, killer, how many more will you see dead this year?"

"Just one," Deke said, the unexpected menace in his tone chilling the air. Then, flipping the knife in his hand and holding it ready, "En garde, Uncle!"

Barr stepped down from his platform and spoke swiftly. "You both know the way this works. If either of you is wounded and can't continue, the other retains the right of deciding life or death. If either of you capitulates, the other wins all your goods and possessions by default, and still decides whether you live or die." He raised his voice so the rapt crowd could hear. "No one may interfere! Stand clear and give them room." Moving back to sit beside Tilva once more, he shouted, "You will begin at my signal! Gant Murdock, if you are unarmed, arm yourself now."

Gant reached inside his sleeve and withdrew a body dagger which had been strapped to his forearm. He held it with the accomplished ease of a professional fighter. Though some of his muscle had gone to fat around the middle, his burly frame was powerful still. Red-rimmed eyes squinted beneath overhanging brows, and his pale, flaccid lips parted in a smile that was both treacherous and insinuating. He passed the knife from one hand to the other with eager anticipation.

Tilva touched her husband's hand. She couldn't help thinking Gant

127

looked like a crazed beast facing her son. Though approaching Gant in height, Deke was barely two thirds his weight, and to his mother, the disparity looked insurmountable.

Barr patted her hand reassuringly, then spoke again.

"If both of you are ready?" He looked from Gant to his son and back again.

Deke nodded, his attention now wholly focused on Gant Murdock. The knife felt alive in his hand, almost thrumming with energy. He slashed it back and forth through the air to get a feel for its balance.

Gant snarled in the affirmative, showing teeth stained yellow in his beard.

"Then begin." At Barr's nod, a roar went out across the meadow as people strained to see better.

Gant circled slowly to the right, and jeered at Deke using terms so vulgar that even many of the watching soldiers were repelled. His knife caught the light as he feinted left, lunged at the youth who watched him silently, and was surprised when his thrust missed completely. Now Deke stood a little to the side of him, still waiting in silence, watching Gant's frustration.

Gant attacked again, this time flipping his knife at the last instant into his left hand and bringing it in low towards Deke's right kidney, or where he thought Deke's kidney should be. Once again the knife passed through air, and this time Deke was behind him. Before Gant could turn to defend himself, he felt a hard boot kick him in the rump. Bellowing with anger, he whirled in time to see Deke's little smile as he moved away.

The crowd laughed, and several catcalls rang out.

Deke studied his uncle, calculating the effects of the alcohol the man had consumed over the course of the day. He sent a subtle probe into Gant's mind. This contact was highly unpleasant. Unlike other minds Deke had touched with his sensitivity, his uncle's was filled with images so disgusting he had trouble remaining there. Violence was the predominant emotion, and Deke could *see* where that violence had last been bestowed.

His lips tightened as he got a moving image of Gant stealing into the room his two young sons shared in their mother's tent. In the image, the room was dark, and the two little boys whimpered in their beds. Apparently making up his mind between the two, their father ripped the bedding off one of the boys, peeled his nightclothes away, and threw him face down. What followed was so repugnant, the child's moans and cries so wretched, that Deke was nearly too distracted to anticipate Gant's next lunge. He avoided being cut only by the merest fraction, the clash of steel loud as he parried Gant's blade.

"Come closer, pretty killer," Gant crooned softly so only Deke could hear him, trying to edge inside his guard. At the same time he lunged again, but Deke *saw* the movement in his mind before it happened, and was able to deflect the slash once more with a quick chopping motion.

Another image filled Deke's mind as Gant's eyes fell on Andara where she watched attentively from her place at the edge of the informal arena. Gant licked his lips and leered. "When I've killed you, I'll take your little girlfriend and show her what a real man is like!"

Deke continued to circle silently.

"Aye," Gant continued, goading him. "I'll give it to her up the ass and stretch her 'til she screams... Just like Leah." His grin was horrible to see.

Until that moment Deke's plan had been to exhaust his uncle, make a fool of him, then turn him loose without possessions or status to live or die as an outcast. Now, however, he could feel rage building inside him, rage almost too strong to contain. With that rage his esper capacity surged powerfully, driven by his rampaging emotions. At once he understood why Andara felt as she did about Gant; his uncle's mind flickered with the echo of an encounter where she had escaped being raped only by slimmest accident.

He Sent his thoughts into Gant's mind with savage fury. His uncle's head whipped around in pain and dismay. Deke's eyes blazed like suns as he stalked closer, his rigid expression so threatening that Gant inadvertently took a step backwards.

Before Gant could gather his wits, he said softly, half-speaking in his uncle's mind, "Fire ants, Uncle...don't you see them? They're everywhere, crawling up your pants, inside your clothes..."

His piercing gaze held Gant's in thrall as the man began to squirm. Images and sensations flooded across the clan chief's mind and body and he gave a terrified little cry. He stared at the chieftain's son in horror, then began slapping himself all over, writhing and twisting at an imaginary agony only he saw and felt. He forced himself to brandish his knife as Deke approached. "Get away from me, you witch-spawned devil!" He slashed back and forth through the space separating them.

"Black widows," Deke whispered ecstatically, the upsurge of energy in his brain and body flooding him, shocking him with what suddenly felt too strong, out of control.

Gant Murdock screamed, his expression becoming wild, insane. His blade trembled in his fingers, and Deke looked at his hand.

"There's one on your knife, Uncle," he breathed.

With a panicky gasp, Gant threw the knife to the ground.

"Careful," Deke murmured. "They're all over you. One false move and..." He shrugged. "Maybe your heart'll stop."

Gant stared at Deke, tears starting down his cheeks while little blubbering noises issued from his mouth. He stood frozen, unable to make himself move. He could see scores of the little spiders spinning their silk from his arms and chest. "Help me," he begged, at once abject and sniveling.

"Do you surrender?" Deke demanded, putting the point of his blade to Gant's throat under the chin.

"Anything, aye, whatever you say, just get them off me!" Gant's tone was pleading, broken by his wretched sobs.

"Even if I tell you I'll cut your throat?" Deke leaned closer, repulsed by Gant's fetid breath, but wanting the humiliation to be complete.

"Cut my throat, aye, better than this, please, cut me, nephew, anything you say," Gant gibbered frenziedly.

Deke removed his knife from Gant's jugular. He picked up Gant's blade from the grass and said loudly, "Wise decision, Uncle." He withdrew his thought from Gant's mind, and his breathing returned to normal.

Gradually, Gant came back to himself. He looked in bewilderment at the silent throng, unable to understand exactly what had happened to him. The only thing he did understand was that he had been beaten by this miserable boy, this boy whose eyes he dared not meet for some strange reason.

"You spelled me," was the only thing he could say, and he said it in a hoarse whisper that reflected his recent terror. "You used witchcraft on me!"

"Don't blame me for your delirium tremens, Uncle," Deke said with a cold smile. "Maybe if you stopped drinking you'd fight better."

Cheers and applause broke out along the front edge of the multitude, spreading backward as word was passed to those who had been unable to press close enough to see anything. No one really understood what had happened except that Gant Murdock had faltered inexplicably and the chieftain's son had taken advantage of his weakness to disarm him.

Friendly hands reached out for Deke from every direction, and he felt himself being swept up by the mob and raised to their shoulders. They marched him around the field in an overwhelming bedlam of approval, while the musicians played a triumphant tune and Barr signaled to his soldiers to take Gant into custody.

Gant's eyes beseeched several members of his clan for assistance, but they turned impassive faces away from him. He turned a hate-filled glare upon Barr Wolfson, as well as on Leah. "Filthy whore!" he shouted to his ex-wife. "You'll pay for this betrayal! As will you all, you high and mighty chiefs!"

"Shut him up and take him out of here," Barr said irritably, tired of Gant Murdock and the trouble he'd caused. He took Tilva's hand in his and gave her a glad smile which was returned so beautifully he had to kiss her.

Their embrace prompted another outbreak of cheering among the revelers.

Soon the dancing, whooping mob deposited Deke back where he started and he found himself surrounded by friends who shook his hand and slapped his back. His eyes searched the crowd and when he spotted Andara, waved her over. She pushed past people, making slow progress until Barr observed her difficulty and with a few quick commands, got his men to open a way. They practically deposited her at Deke's side, and he put his arm around her. She squeezed him joyously, proud and happy for his victory. She had *seen* the shifting energy of the emotionally charged images he had put in Gant's mind, had felt that last overwhelming upsurge of power, and approved wholeheartedly. She felt certain he had frightened Gant Murdock enough that the man wouldn't dare bother them again. Besides, Gant's fate was exile into the wilderness, where his odds for survival were essentially non-existent.

Flushed with his triumph, Deke leaned to kiss her. While the happy voices of his people surrounded him, he became lost in the amazing warmth that traveled from her mind to his.

After a while, she moved her lips away. His friends opened a path through the crowd for them and they approached the chieftain. Barr vaulted the table to grab his son in a bear hug, lifting him off the ground with a happy bellow. Tilva's arrival was more sedate but just as joyous. For a while Deke was besieged by another round of congratulations, and someone thrust a drink into his hand, demanding a toast. He raised the mug high and those within hailing distance shouted encouragement.

"To my Aunt Leah's freedom! To all our continued happiness and prosperity! But most of all, to winning, for without winning where would we Wolf People be?"

So deafening was the response to this last that it seemed mass hysteria was on the verge of breaking out. But the crowd managed to contain itself, and after a while with many thanks and apologies, Deke waved them back to their revelry. He rejoined Andara and his parents, shaking Hawk's hand, accepting another bear hug from Willie.

Then he and Andara were sharing a chair at the long table while servants piled their plates high with choice tidbits. Their cups were refilled, and when Deke tasted the liquid he smiled, for mixed skillfully with grain alcohol and several different fruit juices was the pungent undertaste of psilocybin mushrooms. This was paz, a drink he and Andara never before had been permitted to imbibe. He clinked his cup against hers and they drank deeply.

Around them the chiefs re-fought the duel, and more than once laughter rang out as they remembered Gant's surprise when Deke had kicked him. Before long, the music became more compelling, and after drinking several more toasts, Deke and Andara got up and wandered out into the crowd.

Here and there people jigged up and down to the music, while others were busily engaged in noisy conversation, but everyone they passed reached out to pat Deke or shake his hand. Even those from the Murdock clan were friendly, offering congratulations with genuine sincerity.

Soon they had moved beyond the edge of the light, and the music and revelry became farther away, less overwhelming. By mutual unspoken agreement they walked dreamily until they reached a large oak tree, where Andara leaned for a few seconds, trying to analyze the patterns made by the warm, night breeze in the leaves overhead. Her head was tilted up, her smooth throat bared. Unable to stop himself, the psychedelic liquor strong in his bloodstream, Deke put his hands on the tree trunk to either side of her, imprisoning her between himself and the oak. He leaned down and put his lips in the hollow of her colloarbone, feeling the pulse there. She grabbed two handsful of his hair and pulled his face to hers, her lips fevered and hot against his cheek. Then she kissed his mouth, teasing him with her tongue until he responded in kind. She felt his heart hammering against her and put her arms around his waist, pulling him by the belt until his pelvis touched hers.

The sky came alive with fireworks and they stood together, bemused. Tentatively, Deke took her hand and kissed it, then, running his fingers across the smooth fabric covering her torso, held her while she mimicked his caress. Her hand slipped lower and a moment later she felt his engorged organ straining against his trousers. She took a deep breath and looked up at him. He kissed her lips and then she said quietly,

"I want to see you."

For a second he wasn't sure he'd heard correctly. "You what?"

"Will you show me?" She touched him again and he swallowed.

"All right," he agreed, beside himself with a combination of eagerness and shy excitement. He began to unbutton his pants, and then her fingers were there helping him. In a moment she found the drawstring of his underwear and untied it, exposing him to the night air. Her breathing was as ragged as his and she stared with hot eyes at his rigidly extended penis. Her look embarrassed him but he forced himself to stand quietly while she gazed her fill. His erection felt huge, like a clumsy, heavy club between his thighs.

"It's so big," she said wonderingly. "Is everyone's?"

He felt the blush on his face, glad there was enough darkness to hide his self-consciousness. "I don't know," he said huskily.

"What do I do now?" she asked.

"What do you want to do?"

She touched him fleetingly and was amazed by how soft and smooth,

132

how hot and resilient, his skin was.

"Something like that," he said. "Don't be afraid, I won't break."

Andara pressed herself to him more closely, and reached out for his mind. She got a picture which was pretty much self-explanatory, and understood what he wanted but was too shy to ask for. She began to move her hand on him with more confidence until she heard his breathing quicken.

"Am I hurting you?" she asked, and stopped, remembering that it was little more than three weeks since his circumcision.

"God, no!" He pressed her hand more firmly around him and she felt an accompanying throb as he squeezed her grip tighter. "Don't stop," he said, shutting his eyes and burying his lips in her hair.

A series of images rushed through her mind consisting of some visual cues but mainly a kind of sensory feedback transmitting his turbulent feelings to her body, and as her touch grew more assured, she believed she could feel what he felt. He moved her hand faster and now his hips were thrusting uncontrollably.

"Oh, God, Andara!" he cried out, and she felt him leap and jerk in her hand while his semen jetted in pulsing splashes against her skin. For several moments his muscles spasmed and then she heard him draw a shuddering breath. She stroked him a few more times, sliding her fingers sensually over the slippery head of his penis. His trembling subsided and he looked at her, eyes filled with astonishment and adoration. She stretched to kiss him, and he put his arms around her.

They kissed for a long time, exploring each other's mouths. When they separated and looked into one another's eyes, a further unspoken communication passed between them, and tantalizingly, Andara spread her legs a little. She hiked up her gown until her thighs were visible and pushed his hand up between them. Startled, he realized she had nothing on under her dress.

Almost afraid to breathe, he felt her moisture on his fingertips and instinctively pressed his hand gently against her. A little moan escaped her lips and his hand was suddenly wet. A corresponding pulse between his own legs made him twitch slightly, but then he kissed her again, his hand moving deeper with slow pressure. She threw her head back, inviting his lips to travel to her breasts, but he continued down until he was kneeling in front of her. He slid her dress higher, gently parted her legs even further, and before she realized exactly what he was doing, began to kiss her. So shocking was this that she gasped loudly, and then as she felt his tongue and lips caressing her most private place, she began to experience things she'd never felt before, hadn't even imagined she was capable of feeling. His mouth was alternately fast and slow, and in moments she found herself moving against him eagerly. Something was

133

happening to her, a rising tide of feeling so strange and yet so pleasurable that she couldn't catch her breath.

Her fingers twined through his hair and she opened her legs wider, pressing herself to him with little cries of encouragement. She felt the rough bark of the oak against her back and jerked with surprise as he lifted one of her legs and placed it over his shoulder. His tongue explored her ever more deeply, his lips suckled her most sensitive parts with greater urgency, and his presence in her mind became overpowering. His hands cupped her buttocks, then, before she understood exactly what was happening to her, she heard herself shout as if from a distance, while sensations like exquisite waves made her body convulse, rocking her to her core. The sensations went on for many long seconds until her knees gave way and she crumpled to the ground beside him. He caught her and gazed at her tenderly. She looked at him, saw her moisture dewing his face and touched his cheek with her fingertips.

"I want to make love to you," he whispered, and kissed her lingeringly. He ran his hands over her body, touching her nipples, and pulled her against him, his penis seeking her vulva with a life of its own.

She pushed him away, frightened and a little overwhelmed by what he had done to her. At the same time she yearned for him to fill her completely.

"I want to be in you, here," he said, his fingers parting her pubic hair again and slipping inside. He could feel how open she was, how she still pulsed with excitement. He kissed her again, deeply, with a growing sense of what she liked, what moved her. He knew she was ready, knew that tonight, if he insisted, she would let him do what he wanted.

She felt him between her thighs, felt his marvelous smoothness slide against her and for a split second almost gave herself over to his desire. They looked down at themselves and heard each other's breathing coming in rapid gasps. Then she pushed him off her with an abrupt movement, closed her legs, and stood up, rearranging her clothing.

He lay back on the grass, watching her tidy herself. After a minute, he jacknifed to his feet and pulled up his pants, buttoning his fly with shaking fingers.

When they were dressed again, she leaned against him, seeking his lips with her own.

Gently, he smoothed the tangle of hair away from her forehead. Holding her face in his hands, he gazed into her eyes and thought they looked like wild forest pools with the firelight sparkling in them. He was overwhelmed by emotion and kissed her with undiminished ardor. His entire being felt entangled with hers, and he embraced her, grateful for what she had already given him, but aching for more.

"Please, come to my tent," he said, his hands roaming across her back, creating heat wherever they passed. "Nothing will happen you don't want to happen. I just..." His voice trailed off, then he continued. "I just want to hold you tonight."

Andara looked at his face, her thoughts touching his, wondering at his sudden vulnerability. And then she understood, realized how frightened he was beneath all his excited sexuality. The reaction from what he had done to his uncle was setting in, accentuated by the powerful intoxicants in his system.

At that moment his mind was completely open to her and she found this too potent to resist.

"All right," she said, her empathy for him magnified a hundredfold by their new intimacy. She felt a twinge deep inside as he touched her. "But I have to stop home for a change of clothes."

"Come on," he said, taking her hand. He looked back at the ongoing celebration, the music, the dancing, all of it, and shivered at the sense of surrealism washing through him. His gaze fell on Andara's hand clasped in his and he had the odd thought that she was like a life line holding him tethered to the earth. Without her, he would fly off somewhere and, perhaps, never find his way home.

Tonight he had nearly lost control of his esper ability, nearly been overpowered by the ecstatic flow of energy and power through his body. Almost, he had been unable to contain it and keep it focused on his uncle.

He shivered again, more intensely, and Andara felt it, felt his distress as if it were her own. She slipped her arm around him, and pressed herself to his side. His arm went around her, and holding onto one another for support, they made their way home.

Later that night, as the sounds of the festival ebbed, then ended, Barr and Tilva lay in bed together, each thinking the same thoughts until with the synchronicity that comes to two people who've shared a life for many years, they looked at one another and began to speak at the same time. They laughed, which broke the tension that had been building up in the room, and Tilva settled more comfortably against his broad chest, her fingers twirling clumps of hair into little points.

"So what do you think happened?" Barr asked bluntly. "Was it sorcery?"

Tilva sighed. "What you call sorcery many would call science."

"Don't bandy words, woman, I'm serious." He softened the sting of his words with a kiss. "Was it magic? Did he spell Gant?"

"It isn't that simple," she replied. "The Universe being what it is...our

135

son can connect with certain forces, obviously. I don't think of it as magic."

"What then?"

"I think of it as a sensitivity. There's something about his mind that lets his consciousness be in more than one place at a time."

Barr looked at her quizzically. "This couldn't have anything to do with how long he was out during his Manhoods, could it?" His tone was worried.

"It does seem that his experience out there sharpened it, but I've always known about his sensitivity. I just didn't realize how strong it was." She looked earnestly into his eyes and he knew she was sharing some of her secret lore with him. "There are many adepts, as we are called among ourselves, who can receive the thoughts and emotions of others. Some can even Send on occasion. But Deke...he Sends with more power than I imagined a human could. I felt some of what he Sent at Gant." She shivered violently. "I wouldn't have wanted to feel more."

"I felt it, too," Barr admitted.

They were silent for a while.

"What does it mean?" he finally asked hesitantly.

"He's still our boy," she said firmly. "Whatever it means."

"I think he might be a dangerous boy," her husband said. "A very dangerous boy," he repeated to himself.

"Aye," Tilva agreed, "Dangerous indeed, but only to his enemies. Deke has a good heart, which anyone who knows him for more than five minutes immediately sees."

"But how did he get this sensitivity? Why is it getting stronger?"

"The sensitivity he was born with. Perhaps you must blame me for helping to nurture it with my teaching. But, husband, you have that same sensitivity. If you could have been taught when you were a babe the way I taught Deke and Andara, you, too, would be able to do what he, and she, does."

"Andara!" The chieftain's astonishment changed to acceptance as he thought about it.

"You know, Barr, it isn't magic or sorcery that gives humans power. It's enlightenment."

"Aye," he said, and kissed her leisurely, drawing her against him. His hand stole across her abdomen in a loving caress. "And you," he muttered, losing himself in her rising emotion, "Are my enlightenment."

Their embrace deepened and soon they were aware of nothing further except their need for one another, centering.

In the tent where he was being held under guard, Gant Murdock cursed and mumbled to himself in a drunken stupor, surrounded by his own filth. His eyes jerked back and forth, his features twitched uncontrollably, and spittle oozed from the corners of his mouth. Now and then a cackle rose from his throat and he stabbed the air viciously with an imaginary blade, in his mind's eye seeing Deke Wolfson's face slashed to pieces, with bloody sockets where his eyes had been. Over and over he stabbed the face that had mocked him and the eyes that had terrified him.

Tomorrow he would be exiled into the wilderness. Most likely he would die there. He writhed at the thought. But before madness overwhelmed him once again, he swore an oath before God and the Universe, that he would have his vengeance on Barr Wolfson and his unnatural offspring, that before he died they would suffer horribly for what they had done to him this day.

CHAPTER EIGHT

When pressed, he would discuss the habits of the female adepts of his people, but I never felt the General gave me a satisfactory explanation. When it came to understanding the nature of energy, event, and experience, he told me only an adept could interpret properly this trinity which comprised the essence of reality. For others, amateurs all, there would always be distortions caused by the quite natural tendency to adjust the interpretation into a form more pleasing to the individual psyche.

He was amused when he explained at our first meeting how he had assumed I was an adept, and had thought this a powerful combination, adept and president. When I described the true nature of what I did, he was even more amused, for to the General, psychology was merely a tool for obtaining what he wished, for understanding and manipulating human beings, and so he assumed such was my purpose as well.

And for a while, nothing I did or said could disabuse him of that notion, to my chagrin.

— Ourn Rohlvaag; Collected Journals; City of Life, A.D. 3109

I t was late summer and the day was sultry. Since morning the humidity had been rising and in Spring Camp people moved laconically, too hot to be interested in much beyond a cool drink and a shady spot in which to relax.

That morning, before the heat became unbearable, Deke had gone shopping in the merchants' district of the city where he had haggled for nearly an hour with a gem seller over an opal the size of his thumbnail set in solid gold and hung from a matching gold chain. The opal was of the rarest black variety, and ancient. Within its occult darkness, colorful flames sparked, and when Deke saw it, he knew he had to buy it for Andara. Now it nestled safely in a small, wrapped package in his pocket.

Since that night of madness at the Spring Festival, their relationship had come to a standstill. It seemed Andara was taking pains to make sure they were never alone, and on those rare occasions when he managed to corner her, she never allowed him more than a quick hug or peck on the cheek. She was happy to spend time with him in public, but as far as physical contact went, he was stymied.

So frustrating was this behavior that he finally sought out his father for advice.

Barr was amused but hid it well. He listened to Deke's complaint, then invited his son to walk with him along the river's edge. They scaled flat stones across the surface the way they had when Deke was a toddler.

"There's no point in trying to understand women," Barr told him. "In all my years, I've learned only one thing."

"What's that, Father?"

"That I know nothing." Barr laughed for a while. "You know, Deke," he said more seriously, "You can't rush young women. They need time to adjust to your needs and especially their own. From what you've let slip, things might have moved too fast for her. Why not try slowing down? Make sure she knows you still like her for herself."

"I'm pretty sure she knows that," Deke said.

"Maybe so, but once sex comes into the equation, women want you to reassure them that you're interested in more than their bodies. They want us to crave their souls, but what they don't understand is that for the male, the most direct route to the soul is through that gateway to paradise right between their legs!"

Father and son laughed together.

"She won't even let me knock at that gate," Deke commented wryly.

"You might try buying her a gift, something personal, something expensive. Sometimes that makes a woman look kindlier on a man." Barr rested his hand on Deke's shoulder affectionately. "Now, if your problem is more immediate, there are other alternatives."

Deke looked at him questioningly.

"There are places I could take you where for a fee you could try your luck with a professional," Barr suggested offhandedly. "When I was your age my father took me to a courtesan."

"I'm not interested in some old hag," Deke said with a grimace.

"Who's talking about an old hag?" Barr demanded. "I'm talking about beautiful women of every size, shape, and age, who'll show you what to do and let you practice 'til you get it right."

"Is that what you did?" Deke asked, interested.

"Aye, at first. It's not a bad thing for a man to develop some skills between the sheets," Barr said nostalgically. "But then, I wasn't in love."

Deke sent a stone skimming across the river. "Is it that obvious?"

"You've got all the classic signs," Barr replied with a little smile. "You've been besotted for weeks; your instructors tell me your mind isn't on your work or training. And your mother informs me you've become quite forgetful."

Deke sighed and scrubbed his hands down his face. "It's true," he said miserably. "She's in my thoughts all the time."

Barr was sympathetic. "Listen, Deke," he said. "When you're young, sex is a big deal, maybe the biggest deal. But I think there's something else going on between you and Andara, and maybe you should talk to her about it."

"It's not an easy subject," his son said slowly. He paused, trying to find words to describe what he wanted to say.

"You don't have to tell me if you don't want to," Barr said gently.

Deke eyed his father consideringly. "Have you ever felt like you were inside someone else's head?"

"I can't say I have, except with your mother. But perhaps all lovers feel that way at certain times."

"I have to fight not to feel that way," Deke said. He kicked at a tussock of grass almost angrily. "Father," he said, "Do you remember what happened with Gant Murdock?"

At the mention of the former governor's name Barr's expression hardened. "Aye," he said, "May he rot in hell for all eternity."

"That night...that night something happened inside me. I can't stop thinking about what I did. Father," he turned eyes so troubled on Barr that the chieftain's heart went out to him. "I didn't fight him fair. What I did was a cheat. I didn't even try to fight him fair."

"There's no cheating in a duel," Barr said matter-of-factly. "You mustn't beat yourself over this. It won't change what happened, and it could hurt you. Your objectives when fighting are first to stay alive and avoid injury, and second to overcome your enemy."

Deke smiled a little. "Hawk taught me that first thing when I was small."

"That's right, and you should never forget it." Barr was earnest. "Gant Murdock was a grown man, an experienced fighter. You did what had to be done. I'm glad you did it; you solved several problems in one clean sweep. If you hadn't done it, you'd likely not be standing here worrying about it, and frankly, son, your mother and I couldn't survive attending another funeral for you." Barr clapped him on the back and said, "Come, let's have a swim. It's hotter than hell. Tomorrow you can go down to Merchant Row and find some special bauble for Andara. Flowers are also a nice touch. Women love flowers. Roses, maybe. This has been a good season for them. I think we passed some good ones a ways back."

Deke grinned, realizing he felt a lot better. He touched his father's arm. "Thanks," he said gratefully.

Barr returned the grin, thinking that since falling in love his son had become like an open book. "Any time. By the way, I don't know if Willie spoke to you yet, but we're planning a run into the northwest mountains. Scouting parties have reported a rich series of mining towns with coal enough to power our steel forges forever. I'd like you to come along as commander of a skirmishing party. You can tell your manhood group to come along, too. They can form part of your command."

Deke looked at his father in disbelief. "Commander?" he said in amazement.

"That's right, Deke. There's only one way to learn to command men in battle," Barr Wolfson said, his dark eyes gleaming, "And that's to do it." He looked his son over, seeing the eagerness, the anticipation, and knew that matters of adolescent love were banished from his mind completely. Deke's eyes were sharply focused as he considered the implications of command in a real battle.

"There'll be a staff meeting in the war tent tonight after supper," Barr said, stripping his sweat-drenched shirt over his head and kicking off his moccasins. "You'll come. Now, let's swim."

And so it was that next day Deke left Merchant's Row with the opal in his pocket and a new determination in his heart. He stopped where he and his father had taken their swim the day before, and collected a plentiful bouquet of roses, stripping thorns from the stems with his knife, tying them together with ribbon taken from his mother's pavilion. Then, trying to ignore the butterflies in his stomach, he headed for Andara's tent, hoping she would be alone.

When he got there, she was engaged in an animated conversation with her father which he could hear from outside, and he hesitated, trying to decide whether to interrupt and drop off his gifts, or insist on speaking with her alone, which he thought would be too ill-mannered for him to pull off successfully.

He stood outside the door flap, shifting uncomfortably from one foot to the other, becoming more self-conscious by the moment. Finally, unable to bear it any longer and unwilling for Hawk to witness whatever was going to happen or not happen, he sighed with disappointment and gently laid the roses in the doorway. Then, silently, he stole away.

Inside the tent Andara sensed his presence at the door and wondered why he didn't come in. She excused herself from her conversation and went to look outside. No one was there, and she also sighed, wishing Deke had stayed. Her gaze fell and she saw the roses. She knelt to pick them up, saw how carefully they had been arranged and trimmed, and pressed them to her face, inhaling their odor. Tears of remorse slipped from her eyes to fall on the petals. She carried the flowers inside and laid them on the table.

Hawk watched her hands lovingly caress each bloom before transporting it into a crystal vase. His eyebrows went up and he said, "Lovers' quarrel?"

Andara wiped her eyes and shook her head, not trusting her voice.

"Want to talk about it?" her father asked.

Again she shook her head. This was not something she could talk to anyone about. The only person with whom she might have considered discussing it was Tilva, but Tilva was Deke's mother, and Andara felt too strange discussing these matters with her.

When she finished with the roses, she stood gazing at them for several seconds, lost in thought. She didn't have to send any part of her awareness into Deke's mind to understand what he was feeling. She knew her behavior was hurtful, but she didn't know how else to handle it. That night, and her heart skipped a few beats, that amazing, incredible night, had been so emotionally overwhelming that she was having trouble processing everything. When they had gone back to his tent they had slept together fully clothed on his bed. He had respected her wishes perfectly, hadn't been pushy in any way, had been content simply to hold her as he had said he would.

But since then she had felt nervous around him, as if she couldn't look at him. The feelings he had evoked in her, the way he'd made her want him, were nearly irresistible, but it wasn't that which upset her. No, what frightened her was her own behavior, the way she had manipulated his feelings to satisfy her curiosity, and even more, to gain power over him.

But how to explain to him (or anyone) that she only did it to make him love her the way she loved him? He had said he was out of his mind over her, but she was sure that was only sex talking through him.

That night under the oak Andara had deliberately tried to capture not only his imagination, but his soul. She realized she had succeeded better than planned because of the way events had spiraled out of control. Tilva had warned her that love spells, spells cast with the brain and not with any potion or philtre, especially tended to rebound against the caster. The kind of spell an adept threw worked because it was a contact of the mind. Still, the last thing she had expected was to lose control of herself. Sex was talking through her, too, and it was difficult to know what it was saying.

She was desperately afraid that if she gave him more of what he wanted, and truthfully, what she wanted also, at his age he might grow tired of her and seek new challenges elsewhere with other women.

But it was difficult to keep her distance from him, especially when she saw the naked adoration in his eyes. And now when he had made this tender, lover-like gesture... She could feel the message inherent in his gift, knew he was telling her he would wait forever if that was what she wanted.

By the ruins, she thought, her confusion monumental, why couldn't this have happened when we were older? She covered her face with her hands and ran into her own room, needing to get out from under her father's gaze. Loneliness swept through her, and she dried her eyes. She picked up her carrying sack, strapped on her dagger, and went back to the kitchen, where she threw a few items of food into the sack and filled a canteen.

"Where are you going?" Hawk asked, his eyes concerned.

"Just for a ride," she told him.

"Be back before dark," he said.

"Don't worry."

"Take this." Hawk handed her a rifle and a pouch filled with cartridges. She looked at him wonderingly.

"You're of an age now where you shouldn't be wandering around unarmed. You know it makes me nervous to have you riding the countryside alone, but at least with this," Hawk gestured to the weapon, "I'll know you can defend yourself. Aside from which, a rifle makes a lot of noise, so if you ever get into trouble, just fire off a shot and I'll come running."

"Oh, Papa," she said, and gave him a swift hug.

"Stay away from the ruins," he warned, his eyes serious.

"Don't worry," she said. "I just need to do a little thinking."

"Thinking is always good," he replied, kissing the top of her head.

A few minutes later, Andara got Romeo from the stables and rode out of the city, the sun blazing down on her shoulders.

And a few minutes after that, Deke rode after her, the she-wolf trotting alongside him. He sent an image into Hopi's awareness and Hopi sent back an affirmative along with an image of Andara's trail out to the grasslands. Deke nodded. If she wouldn't let him be with her, at least he could keep an eye on her. He didn't like Andara riding alone any more than Hawk did. Besides, maybe the right situation would come up and he could give her the necklace.

He smiled dreamily. Aye, he'd give her the necklace and she would forgive him for whatever he'd done that had spooked her so badly. And then maybe she'd be willing to try again.

So caught up in his pleasant daydream was he, that he almost didn't notice Andara had stopped, tethered her horse, and was walking along thoughtfully, too inwardly focused to see him despite his carelessness.

He slipped his rifle out of its saddle sheath and slung it over his shoulder, checked to be sure his body daggers were accessible. Then he tied Micmac loosely and with a "keep close" signal to Hopi, moved silently after Andara, using the tall grass and occasional rocks or bushes for cover.

She came to a halt at the edge of the grass, where the greenery began to fade into the wasteland beyond. Here she stood motionlessly, staring out across the ruins. An errant wind ruffled her dark hair and he saw her close her eyes, her lips moving soundlessly. A prickle of apprehension went up his spine as he watched her, and he flattened into the tall grass, making himself as near a part of it as he possibly could, thinking like the grass, becoming the grass in

144

essence, so she wouldn't detect his presence with her esper sense. At his side, Hopi imitated him in every detail.

Andara spread her arms wide and extended her fingers, turning three hundred sixty degrees around. With a sense of déjà vu, he remembered doing the same thing in the ruins during his manhood test. Another prickle touched his spine as the wind increased noticeably, blowing straight out of the devastation towards Andara. Hopi whined softly and he stroked her head reassuringly.

His eyes began to itch and he rubbed them. When his vision cleared, he saw the wind had subsided and a rider had appeared as if from nowhere, astride a horse of indeterminate color. The rider approached Andara, and she stood her ground, waiting fearlessly.

Deke blinked several times, sure he was seeing things. But when the rider reached Andara at last and dismounted, he knew. He felt his mouth hanging open in amazement. It was the Old Man.

Andara looked at the ancient woman whose horse might have been grey or might have been brown, and nodded in greeting.

"Well met, young one," the woman said in her surprisingly strong, rich voice.

"I knew you'd be here," Andara replied.

"Yes." The ancient one peered into the girl's face, and something in her expression softened. "So," she said. "You have figured out what it is you seek."

"Aye," Andara answered.

"And what is that?"

"Knowledge," the girl said.

"Ah," said the old one. "You wish to become a woman of knowledge, an adept, is that correct?"

"Yes," Andara said. "My patron told me you could teach me."

"Do you have the commitment?" asked the old woman with a probing glance.

"I doubt you'll be disappointed." Andara inclined her head proudly.

"My disappointment is not important," the crone said sternly. "Your Lady has spoken to me about you. It may be you have some promise." She paused. "Meanwhile, pay attention to the world around you. Watch everything."

"I already do," Andara said.

"Not closely enough. You missed something this very minute," and the ancient one was back astride her horse with Andara having no idea how she had gotten there. The old woman lifted a hand in farewell. "We will meet again soon," she said. Then she looked pointedly where Deke lay hidden in the grass. "As for you, young chief, you still have a lot to learn about stealth. We will resume your studies when the seasons turn again."

Andara's eyes widened as she stared at the place the old woman was looking. Then they began itching and she had to rub them.

The itching was in Deke's eyes, too, as he rose to his feet. That final admonition from the Old Man had come with the impact of a slap. He blinked hard, and saw Andara doing the same. He approached slowly, his color high from having been caught following, not only by her, but by someone he had assumed was his personal teacher. It made him feel odd to know Andara also had a relationship with the elderly brujo. Curiosity helped him get over his embarrassment, however, and by the time he reached her, he was able to speak almost normally.

"I didn't know you knew the Old Man," he began.

"Old Man? What are you talking about?" Andara looked at him as if he was deranged, not sure how she felt about being followed.

"The Old Man, the person you were just talking to," Deke said. He gestured towards the ruins. "Where'd he go? Where'd he come from?"

"He?" Andara said. "You mean she."

"She?" Now Deke was truly confused. "You saw a woman?"

"Of course," Andara said impatiently. "What did you see?"

"I met with that Old Man all last winter in a cave," Deke told her. "I haven't seen him since we came to Spring Camp."

"I met the Old Woman this spring for the first time," Andara said wonderingly, "Here, at Spring Camp."

"What's he teaching you?" he demanded, taking her by the arms and looking into her eyes. "And why?"

Andara tried to shrug his hands off her, his insistence seeming too presumptuous. "What business is it of yours?" she flared, losing her temper.

Surprised by her anger, he dropped his hands and took a step back. "You're right," he said. "None." Without another word, he turned and walked back to where he had tethered Micmac. He vaulted to her back and in a second she was at her top speed, running as if the devil himself was chasing her.

Andara watched them go, knowing that not Romeo or any other horse could catch Micmac at that pace. When they were gone, she was overcome by misery and sat in the grass, berating herself for her stupidity. After a while she felt Hopi's nose against her palm and stood up, sighing, taking a last look across the ruins.

"Mother," she called, "What do I do now?" For an instant she thought she semsed a maternal presence, almost felt a soft hand touch her cheek, and then, as a breath of air passed across her skin, the presence faded, leaving her feeling hollow, insubstantial.

She climbed despondently onto Romeo's back and turned towards home, the wolf following, her spirits too low even to raise a hand to the sentinels who waved her past their checkpoints. Hopi parted company with her upon arrival and disappeared into the meadow. The tent was empty and she started dinner for her father and herself. As she was adding herbs to the roast she was preparing, an idea occurred to her and she perked up. She put the meat in the oven and went to the cold closet, where she took out the ingredients for a pie. Before long she had it ready for baking and put it in with the covered roasting dish.

Less than an hour later she wrapped the pie in a clean towel and carried it over to what she called Slum Row due to the incipient squalor that seemed ready to break out at any moment. Thirteen-year-old boys were not particularly conscious of the appearance of their tents (hovels, she amended mentally). She walked up the incline to Deke's tent, rattled the knocker, and when there was no answer, went inside. She put the pie on the table and looked around. His things lay strewn about, dropped wherever they happened to fall when he had returned. Knives, ammunition, his rifle...all this as well as the clothes he had worn were everywhere, and quietly, Andara picked up everything. She put the clothes in his laundry basket, the weapons in their storage chests. She went into his bedroom and shook her head. The bed was a chaotic pile of twisted covers and unfolded clean laundry. Clothing lay strewn around here as well, along with a general clutter of books, papers, and writing materials. Andara folded his clothes and stacked them neatly in his chest, made the bed, and straightened up the papers, books, and pens, putting them on the desk. Then, as the thought came to her, she took a small square of coarse paper and, dipping his pen in the ink jar, wrote a quick note which she carried to the dining area and left propped alongside the pie.

Glancing around, taking a moment to admire how good a job she had done on the room's decorations, she slipped out the door, feeling better than she had in weeks.

At the staff meeting in the war tent, Deke was unusually quiet, forcing himself to pay attention only with an effort. His unhappiness was pervasive and eventually the other men fell silent to look at one another knowingly.

"Deke," his father said, touching his shoulder to get his attention. "You'll command a skirmish group of fifty cavalry. Your job will be to lure the defenders out. If they think they're only under attack by a small force of brigands, they're more likely to reveal their own forces."

Deke spoke mechanically. "You want me to provoke them, then?"

"Do whatever you have to do to find out how many fighters they have. Willie?"

"Aye, m'lord. Look here, lad, there appear to be three towns walled tighter'n a virgin's... walled tighter'n any fort we've seen recently. Because of their location, because of the way they're connected behind a common wall and mountain, they have pretty substantial defenses, pretty strong. Lots of solid rock, concrete, and timber palisades." Willie paused. "What we don't know is what weapons are behind those walls."

"Why don't we put a spy in there?" Deke asked. "Wouldn't that give us a more accurate picture than capturing some of their people in a skirmish and interrogating the information out of them?"

"How're you going to get a spy inside?" Willie asked. "They're mighty distrustful. They fired on our scouts."

"Maybe they wouldn't fire on a kid," Deke suggested.

All eyes in the tent went to his face.

"Aye, every culture we've met has that in common: they all protect children."

Hawk and Barr exchanged glances. Then Hawk said, "You don't seem particularly childish these days, Deke."

"I could fake it, act younger. If I'm unarmed, and seem to be a runaway…" Deke's eyes were filled with strange light. "I could pass. We'd be able to know with certainty what they've really got."

"It's too dangerous," Barr told him.

"It wouldn't be for long...we just need to let them feel good about themselves for rescuing a child from the wilderness." Deke smiled with grim humor. "Just a day, I would think. Definitely no more than two."

"It does make sense," Hawk said reluctantly.

"Risky, though," Willie remarked.

"The risk is acceptable," Deke said firmly. He looked at his father. "Pretend it isn't me we're talking about. You know it makes sense."

"It does make sense, Deke, but I still don't like it. We can take those folk anyway, whether you go in or not."

"I'm sure we can, but what about casualties? If I can get an accurate assessment of their weaponry and its location, it's possible we can take those towns without any casualties among our people. If by one soldier risking everything we save lives and gain everything, doesn't that justify the risk?"

"Your points are well taken, Deke. Let me think about it tonight and we'll meet again tomorrow. With luck it won't be so blisteringly bloody hot; otherwise I may call this meeting in the river!" Barr nodded to his men.

Everyone rose, and Barr called after Deke, "Stay a minute, would you, son?"

Deke waited until the others had departed. "Aye, Father?"

"Why do you want to do this, Deke?" Barr peered into his son's eyes worriedly. "What's really going on here?"

"I made a perfectly logical suggestion," Deke replied.

"Too logical. You're always too logical when you're doing things for your own reasons. Now, the truth. Tell me you're not planning some hare-brained stunt to impress Andara and make me believe it, else this plan is dead right here."

"This has nothing to do with Andara. Besides, she isn't too impressed with me right now. I've pretty much bungled everything. Maybe my talents are better served with bloodshed. I seem to be pretty good at that."

Barr flinched at the cynicism in Deke's voice. "All right, son," he said.

"Also, I've been thinking about the suggestion you made yesterday." Deke's expression was difficult for Barr to read.

"Which suggestion? I made a lot of good ones." Barr tried to keep it light.

"You know, about the courtesan." Deke colored slightly.

"Why have you changed your mind?"

"I'm not sure I've changed it, I'm just thinking about it. But it occurred to me that I'm just too...well..."

"Hmm," Barr said, and scratched his beard. "Too eager, eh?"

"Aye. I thought maybe I'd be able to go slower with Andara if I could sort of..."

"Blow off a little steam," his father finished for him, trying not to smile.

"That's right."

"I think you've a good idea there. But if you do use courtesans, make sure Andara never finds out. Trust me on this, Deke. A girl like that...she'll have your eyes out just for looking. Believe me, I know."

"I do believe you, Father," Deke said, meaning it. "Was there anything else you wanted to discuss with me?"

"No, son. Have you had your supper? Your mother and I would be happy to have you."

"I'm not really hungry, but thanks. I'm planning to try and drown my sorrows tonight. But maybe in the next few weeks, if you get some time... before we go after those towns..."

Comprehension flooded Barr, and impulsively, he grabbed his son and hugged him hard. "Look here, boy. All men like to have a woman before they go into battle. As soldiers we know we might not survive. But if you have the slightest feeling, the slightest premonition that anything's amiss, you really do have to tell me."

"No, it's just in case, as you said. And besides, I haven't decided yet. Maybe it would be bad luck. Maybe I have to have something to look forward to, eh?"

Disturbed by Deke's fatalistic tone, Barr hugged him once more. "You get some sleep. We'll talk again tomorrow." He released his son and watched him walk away from the war tent. "Thank the ruins," he said to himself, "I never fell in love at thirteen."

Deke ducked through the doorway into his tent, Hopi at his heel, and looked around in perplexity. The living area was neat, everything put away. Through the open hangings leading to the bedroom, he could see that room was as tidy. The oil lamp on the table cast a warm glow and he saw there was something wrapped in a towel with a note. Slowly he unbuckled his belt and dropped it with pistol and knife onto a chair. He picked up the paper and unfolded the dish towel. The pie was still warm and smelled delicious. He read Andara's slanted script and tension relaxed in his body. Before long he found himself smiling. His eyes were full as he got a knife and cut into the pie. Ah, he observed, cherry, his favorite. And then he burst into laughter at the absurd symbolism of her gift, knowing it had been her specific intention for him to appreciate her pointed self-mockery and ribald sense of humor. While Hopi watched with interest, he ate the pie with gusto, and his laughter went on for a long time after he had finished.

Plans for the investiture of the triple mining fortress went on apace. Barr had approved Deke's strategy after a sleepless night of consideration, with the additional caveat of having his son be chased virtually to the fort's door by Wolf riders pretending to be brigands in hot pursuit. That would give the subterfuge greater credibility, and Barr wanted to take every step possible to safeguard Deke's life. Still he worried he had made the wrong decision, and refrained from discussing with Tilva any particulars about the campaign.

The mining towns would be hard to get at, the men in the war tent saw when they studied drawings that were becoming ever more accurate as scouts provided increasingly up-to-date observations. The longer they looked at the topographic renderings of the towns, the more they realized how important it would be to have someone inside. They all reached the same conclusion at approximately the same time.

"You know," Willie said tentatively. "It might not be a bad idea for Deke to jimmy the gates."

"Too damn risky," Barr growled immediately.

"But if a clear opportunity arose..." Willie suggested.

Deke's gaze was thoughtful, "You're right. It would simplify everything. But I'll have to see how well guarded the place is, how they feel about people wandering around at night fiddling with things, especially strangers."

"You do that trick you did on the mountain last spring," Willie said knowingly. "I'd put real money on you being able to sneak past anyone."

Deke's mouth turned down at the corners as he remembered his abortive attempt to sneak past Andara. "I'll have to improvise when I get inside," he said. "Have you decided when we're leaving?"

Barr nodded. "First of October, when the heat breaks. That gives us time enough to provision the troops and get last minute intelligence. Plan on being gone a month, because we'll have to spend time garrisoning the towns and encouraging the population to continue working the mines."

"What if they don't want to make the arrangement?" Deke asked.

Barr shrugged. "They'll want to, fort dwellers usually cooperate. It's a matter of enlightened self-interest."

Deke chuckled. "Isn't everything?" he asked rhetorically, to general amusement.

The meeting broke up shortly thereafter.

In Tilva's tent, Andara was cataloguing the herbs that had been picked at high summer, vacuum-packing them in jars that had metal lids with small holes in them, on which a reverse pressure hand pump could be placed to draw out the air. The jars were sealed with dabs of beeswax and labeled with paper fastened to the outside.

The tent flap moved and Deke poked his head in. "Hi," he said. "I hope I'm not bothering you."

"No," Andara said, thankful for work to occupy her hands and attention. Her chest felt tight, and she licked her lips nervously.

Deke watched her dextrously strip leaves from branches into jars.

"Want some help?" he offered.

"Thanks," she agreed, her nervousness increasing as he sat nearby. He smelled like the outdoors: like horses and dogs and the wind when it crossed a patch of wildflowers on a warm, summer evening.

"Where's my mother?" he asked casually.

"Visiting patients," Andara replied.

"I can't believe I've finally caught you alone," he said softly.

Andara's fingers moved more rapidly through the herbs.

He reached out and caught her hands, holding them still. He brought them to his lips, inhaling the spicy scent of whatever medicinal leaf she had been stripping. When he released her, she saw there was a small package folded against her palm. She had been so flustered she hadn't even felt him deposit

151

it there.

"What's this?" she asked, her heart beating erratically.

Deke tried to be offhand. "Open it."

Andara's fingers fumbled the cord away and she removed the wrapping. Lifting the pendant by its chain, she rested the opal in her hand and gazed at it disbelievingly.

"It's very old," Deke said, thrilled with her reaction.

"It's incredible," she said, turning it this way and that in the light.

"It's you," he said simply.

She looked up and met his eyes, her own misted. "Thank you," she whispered. "No one's ever given me anything like this."

"Would you like to put it on?" he asked.

"I would," she replied, and stood up. She carried the stone to a mirror and unfastened the latch.

He stood behind her and took the chain from her hands. "Let me," he said, moving her hair away from her neck, resisting the impulse to kiss her nape. He hooked the latch and let the pendant fall, then looked over her shoulder in the mirror to see the effect of the jewel.

Andara's hand touched the stone. "It's beautiful, Deke," she said.

"You're beautiful," he replied, putting his arms around her.

She stepped back against him and clasped his arms to her. They stared at their reflections in the mirror. He could see her breast heaving and held her tighter.

"I'll be going away for a while," he said after a time.

"Going? Where?" Dismay appeared on her face.

"Northwest," he said, "With the army."

She trembled involuntarily, feeling a dart of dread in her heart.

"Probably we won't get back 'til after the move to Winter Camp," he continued. "I was hoping you'd keep an eye on Hopi for me."

She turned around and looked at him. "Of course," she said, trying to be matter-of-fact. In daydreams she often had imagined him going off with the army, but the reality felt very different. For the first time she realized there was a real possibility he might die in battle. Abruptly, she threw her arms around him and squeezed until he could hardly breathe.

"Good," he said, and stroked her hair gently. "That's settled, then." He smiled, and what he said next made her feel he had been reading her mind. "If anything should happen to me, I'd like it if she could be yours. She feels like a part of you to me already."

"Bite your tongue, Deke Wolfson. You'll draw bad fortune."

"Would you miss me if I was gone?" he asked playfully, looking into her eyes.

She made a face. "Maybe," she said.

"Maybe!"

Andara's laugh was low and earthy. Shyly at first, then with more confidence, she touched his mind and opened hers, inviting him into places she hadn't let him go before. For the first time she allowed him to glimpse the depth of her loneliness and feelings of disconnection. Delicately, his mind responded, his contact sensitive, ethereal. She could barely feel his presence, but knew he was aware of her every nuance of emotion and thought.

His mastery was growing, she realized.

"No," he murmured. "It's not me, it's you that makes it possible. There's no resistance to fight through."

"Deke," she said, basking in the warmth he was putting into her mind. "Who is the Old Woman?"

"For me he's the Old Man," he answered. "He's my teacher."

"What is he teaching you?" she asked.

He smiled wryly. "Isn't this what got us into trouble last time?"

"I like the way you're holding me now better than then," she said, matching his tone.

"Oh, I see," and they laughed. Then, more seriously, he tried to answer her question. "First, he's educating me in the classical sense, through reading and discussion. Second, he's teaching me the ways of a warrior, or man of knowledge."

"What is that, like becoming a witch woman?"

"Aye, maybe," he said. "But the word which most describes his particular lore is *brujo*."

"What does that mean?"

"Sorcerer," Deke replied. "The people who used to live on this continent, the aboriginal people, that is, whom we are partially descended from, had ways of knowledge that used nature's energy to manipulate the world and reality. This is what the Old Man is teaching me." Deke's expression was rueful. "I don't know that I'm doing so well; you heard what he said to me the other day."

"Why do we see him...her...differently?" she asked.

"You mean why do I see a man and you a woman?" Deke shrugged. "Who knows? What I found really strange was the way he appeared in that little wind."

"I can call that wind," Andara whispered, "By putting my thoughts in a certain place, I can open that portal."

"What do you mean, 'open that portal?'" His tone was flabbergasted.

"That's what I call it," she said. "It's like a door, but usually it's more like a window. Sometimes energy comes through it, or since we've been here this spring, the Old Woman has come through. Sometimes I can only look out through it."

"Can you step through it yourself?" Deke asked, fascinated.

Andara shook her head. "I wouldn't dare try."

"Why not?"

"Would you step into something before you had any idea what it was or whether you could step back out again?"

"Under one circumstance," he said.

"What circumstance?" she asked.

"If you needed me to," and he kissed her lips.

There was a flurry at the door and Tilva came in, Canis on her heels. She deposited her medical bag and an armload of packages on the table, and dropped tiredly into a chair, her face flushed. Her pregnancy was showing well and she had put on some weight, which Deke found quite becoming.

"Don't let me interrupt you," she said, leaning back with a sigh.

Deke and Andara laughed and moved apart, the moment broken, but neither minding. They felt easier with one another than they had for weeks.

Andara brought Tilva a cup of cool water, and Tilva said, "Thanks, dear." She noticed the opal and added, "That's lovely, where did you get it?"

"Deke gave it to me," Andara said self-consciously, her fingers going to the jewel again.

"You have good taste," Tilva told her son. "Like your father. He's always had a knack for the right gift, too."

"Are you feeling all right, Mother?" Deke asked, noticing how tired she seemed.

"Yes, very well. Your sister is going to be a big girl."

"Sister?" Deke was surprised.

"Aye," Tilva said with a funny look on her face.

"Is something the matter?" His eyes were concerned.

"She just moved," his mother said and smiled.

"It's strange," Andara said, standing near Tilva. "It feels like there's a fourth person in the room."

Deke moved towards the door. He sensed the conversation was going to turn to babies, nursing, and other female concerns, and all at once felt claustrophobic indoors, craving the open sky.

"I'll see you later," he said. "I have to have a swim or I'll suffocate." He looked at Andara. "You wouldn't want to come, would you?"

Andara looked at Tilva, then back to the pile of herbs on the table. "I

154

should finish this," she said regretfully.

Tilva waved her hand. "Go swimming, Andara. You can finish that later. It'll keep."

"All right, then," Andara said. She smiled happily and followed Deke from the tent.

They found a secluded spot well away from where their friends swam. "Turn around," she said to him.

"No," he replied. "If I can't touch you at least let me look at you."

Andara stamped her foot and scowled. "I never said you couldn't touch me. But now I'm beginning to think that's a good idea!"

Deke laughed. He stepped out of his moccasins and took off his shirt and weapons belt. His pants and underwear were next. For a minute he stood in the sunlight with the breeze stirring his hair and his bronzed skin gleaming over his rippling, lean musculature, and Andara thought how beautiful he was, like one of nature's elementals. He felt her eyes on him and stretched lazily, letting her get used to his nudity. Then, with as much carelessness as he could muster, he strolled to the water's edge, stuck in his toe, and grinned. "Well? Are you coming or not?"

"All right," she grumbled, irritated at how he had gotten the better of her. His nudity was like a dare, and Andara had never been able to turn down a dare. She unbuttoned the cotton dress she was wearing and let it fall. Her undergarments followed and in a moment she, too, was naked. She tilted her head up and walked in up to her knees before she couldn't stand his rapt scrutiny any longer. With a graceful movement, she arced her body in a dive and swam out to the deeper water. In a few moments he joined her and they swam easily, splashing one another occasionally, enjoying the relief from the sweltering heat.

After an hour they climbed out and sprawled on the grass near the riverbank to let the sun dry them. Deke lay on his back with one brown forearm thrown across his eyes to block the light and Andara took the opportunity to study every detail of his body unobserved.

"Are you nervous about going to war?" she asked.

"No," he said, enjoying the warmth of the sun after the cold water.

"Do you look forward to having to shoot and kill people?"

He smiled. "Yes."

"Liar!"

"What makes you think I'm lying?" His tone was mischievous and he glanced at her from the corner of his eye.

"I can't believe you would enjoy that...!"

"Ah, you can't believe it, therefore it can't be true."

155

"Don't twist my words."

Deke was very amused. He kept his arm across his face so she wouldn't see him laugh at her. "I love the idea of war," he said. "Everything about it: the planning, the execution, the rewards. The killing, too, maybe. Does that repel you?"

"Yes," Andara said.

"Now who's the liar?" he chided.

"I've been trained to heal, not kill," argued Andara.

"War gets a man's blood up," Deke said. "In the most literal sense. Don't you think I know that one of the things you like about me is that I've already killed?"

"It's not that I like it, exactly," Andara admitted after a time.

"It's exciting for you, though, I've felt it in your thoughts."

Andara blushed from head to toe.

"I don't mind if you're excited by it. So am I, sometimes." He turned his head to look at her. "I've been wanting to apologize to you," he said.

"For what?" she asked.

"For what I did."

"What did you do?"

"You know." He blushed, knowing only vulgar terms for what he had done to her the night of the festival.

"You didn't do anything wrong." Andara hesitated. "I did."

He stared at her. "What do you mean?"

"I wanted to see you lose control," she said. "Do you hate me for that?"

"Ruins, no!" He chuckled. "Why would I?"

"Because I wanted to control you."

"I'm not sure I understand."

"I manipulated you, you know," and Andara touched his mind in a certain way which had an immediate and obvious effect on him.

Deke swallowed. "Sort of like what I did to you, is that what you're saying?" He went into her mind powerfully, touching those places he knew would stimulate her without his having to lay a hand on her body. "Like that?" he whispered, his breathing changed.

Andara gasped. "Aye!"

He withdrew his thoughts. "We are what we are, Andara," he said, and reached to caress her cheek. "I can no more stay out of your head than you can out of mine. That's not manipulation, it's just natural. You did nothing bad. Everything you did was good. More than good, it was perfect, or almost so."

"What would make it perfect?"

He filled her mind with all his pent-up yearning for her, with every-

156

thing he wanted to do and have done, and said, "If you felt this way about me."

"It's different for me," she said. "For you there are no risks."

"You mean pregnancy?" At her nod, "There are ways to avoid that."

"Not reliable," Andara said.

"There are risks for me, too. If you were to get pregnant it would involve me as much as you. You don't think I'd let you raise our child alone, do you?"

"Deke, we're too young...I'm not ready to raise a child. My God, we're still children ourselves!"

He slid closer and touched her breasts. "Do children do this?" he asked. "Or this?" He kissed her.

She pushed him away breathlessly. "No, they don't," she said. "But that's not the point and you know it."

He sighed. "I know." He looked at her with longing. "I've never been with a girl," he said. "When I make love for the first time, I want it to be with you." He wound his fingers through her hair. "And I want your first time to be with me. We're made for each other, belong together. Do you think I could love any girl who couldn't do what you did to me?" His gaze was fierce, passionate. "What you call manipulation was ecstasy for me. Do you think I mind that your feelings are so strong you want to move me the way I move you? The strength of your feelings is what draws me to you, every bit as much as this," and he touched her lightly between her legs. "More, in fact."

Andara was surprised by the depth of his emotion. What he said made sense. She tried to imagine kissing another boy and realized that it would almost repulse her. It would be simply lips pressing on lips, without all the incredibly rich, exciting, emotional overtones brought to it by their esper connection. She remembered Tilva once trying to explain to her that sex was as much a mental thing as a physical one, and now she thought she understood what that meant.

"Come on," Andara said, getting to her feet and gathering her clothes. "I have to go back."

"Andara," he said, catching her hand. He looked into her eyes. "Will you at least think about it?"

She looked away from him. "Do you really believe I can think about anything else?"

"I'll understand, whatever you decide."

"But you'll find someone who'll do what you want if I don't, won't you?" Andara looked at him shrewdly.

"I suppose. But that someone will be my right hand." He smiled. "I'd rather it was yours."

"You mean you'd do it for yourself?"

Deke burst into laughter. "Ruins, girl, how do you think I get through the days? Or the nights for that matter? My right hand is my best friend!"

Andara giggled.

"Don't you?" He looked into her eyes.

"No!" She blushed furiously. "What a thought!"

"You're not lying," he said wonderingly. "Listen," he said, "You should try it. It feels good and it passes the time."

Andara started to laugh.

"I mean it," he said. "Any time you want some help..."

"God, do all boys do that?"

"To tell the truth, I thought girls did, too. I'm disappointed to hear you don't."

"Why?" Andara was taken aback.

"Because I've spent a lot of nights imagining you touching yourself," he said. "One of my favorite fantasies has you doing that. And then, of course, I come in and take over."

"You're embarrassing me!"

He pulled her against him for a second. "I'll stop, then," he said, embracing her, the feel of her sun-drenched flesh almost more than he could bear. He kissed her mouth and released her. Turning away, he began to pull on his clothes.

Feeling unaccountably let down, Andara sighed and did the same.

CHAPTER NINE

He told me that for him violence, sexual love, and grief were all tan-gled up, intertwined so closely he could hardly separate one from the other. When I told him I did not think this a particularly healthy combination, he looked at me with more bitterness and self-condemnation than I have ever seen in another human being's eyes and said,

"Don't you think I know exactly who and what I am and how my choic-es have formed me? Are you really equipped to pass judgement on those choic-es? How different we are, Madam Psychologist, for I would never presume to judge you or the choices you have made in your life, even though," and he paused before adding with great delicacy, "I am perfectly capable of plumbing their most primal sources..."

...and perhaps it was his remarkable ability to establish an empathic connection that made me feel this way, but for a time it was as if I viewed a panoramic tapestry of images revealing many of the extraordinary events of his life, and I knew a moment of great doubt, that my pretensions to understanding the psychology of this man must be pointless, because so many of the precon-ceptions of our science simply were not designed for such as he...

— Ourn Rohlvaag; Collected Journals; City of Life, A.D. 3109

T he army wound its way over the rolling countryside like a long, many-legged caterpillar, spread out over a distance of miles. There were twenty thousand men, many on horseback, many driving the scores of supply and ammunition wagons, others guiding mule-drawn artillery pieces and assorted seige rockets, still others tramping on foot.

At their head Barr Wolfson rode the new war stallion he had purchased recently, and he held the animal back with an iron hand on the reins. The horse wanted to run, put in high spirits by the crisp, dry October weather and the barely repressed excitement of his rider. He was a magnificent creature, eight-een hands at the withers, deep russet in color, with a black mane and tail and an arching head carried proudly. Barr had bought him for his speed and strength, and had hopes of actually beating Micmac with this one.

To his right, Hawk rode a quiet gelding trained in all the arts of mount-ed warfare a Wolf soldier required. He could be guided by heel and toe contact alone if necessary, leaving his rider's hands free to fire a rifle or hack at an enemy. Hawk watched Barr wrestling the stallion and smiled, knowing that before long his friend would have the beast under full control. Barr's patience with animals was legendary among the People.

Strung out to the sides of the army, several mounted groups of riders guarded the vulnerable flanks and rear, and it was among these that Deke and his friends rode, trotting along in a haze of dust thrown up by the movement of men and materials.

He watched his friends calling happily to one another, thrilled to have been included on this trip. Their excitement made him smile and he wondered if they would be as cheerful after thirty or forty hours in the saddle. Last night he had seen Tim and his older brother Sean with a horde of other soldiers besieging the courtesan district, and he wondered if his friends had met with success.

Deke sighed, growing more introspective. He had thought about accompanying them but decided against it. Preparations for the journey had kept him so busy that somehow the opportunity to work on Andara had escaped him. On the few occasions he had managed to catch her alone, they were interrupted. Last night at dinner with his parents and her father, he had hoped they would get some time alone, but Hawk never allowed her out of his sight, as if he knew exactly what Deke had in mind and was determined to prevent it.

If Barr hadn't kept Hawk aside in conversation after the meal, Deke wouldn't even have gotten a chance to say goodbye privately.

He sighed again, remembering that leave-taking, his body stirring now as he thought about her.

They had slipped out the tent door and around back. The ground had been rumbling and vibrating from the passage of heavy wagons moving north through the city when he caught her in his arms against a tent pole and kissed her hard. Her ardor had been no less than his, and when he had gone into her thoughts, she had welcomed him with a yielding warmth that only made him wilder. She had encouraged him to put his hands all over her, opening the top of her dress so he could feel her breasts, parting her legs so he could press himself against her more fully. He had known she understood his need when she slipped her hand inside his pants to caress him.

"Come to my tent later," he had whispered as she moved her hand on him.

"He'll never let me out of his sight tonight," she had said, kissing him again and again, gasping when he put his hand between her thighs and fondled her.

"Then tell him," Deke had said, groaning as she touched him with more assurance.

"How?" she had asked, her lips feverish, her eyes glazing as he gently fluttered his fingers inside her. "Oh, Papa, I want to make love to Deke tonight, so you'll understand if I just..." and she had jerked, pressing herself harder onto his hand. "My God," she had murmured throatily and found his lips again, drawing his tongue into her mouth.

At that moment they had heard Hawk call to her and she had raised her voice in a shout, "Coming, Papa!" before he covered her mouth with his again, moving his fingers faster and harder, feeling her move her hand the same way, until he couldn't hold back any longer. He had felt his ejaculation starting and pressed his fingers deeply into her, riding her with his hand as she began to spasm against him.

They had arranged their clothing just in time before Hawk came around the back of the tent. He had looked at their flushed faces, her smudged lip rouge, and said gruffly, "Time to go, daughter. Say your goodbyes."

"Go along. I'll be there in a second," she had said, her eyes locked on Deke's.

Hawk had cleared his throat and glanced from one to the other.

"Please, Papa," she had said again.

He had grunted awkwardly and left them.

"Deke," she had said fervently. "Come back to me, you hear?"

He had kissed her passionately. "I will," he had promised, almost unable to speak past his tumultuous emotions.

"When you do..." She had caressed him boldly, moving her hands lasciviously across his chest, around his back, across his buttocks, back to his loins, "I'll be waiting."

They had kissed once more, and then she had run off into the night and left him standing there, feeling so lonely he had thought his heart would break.

Deke came back from his reverie slowly. He could still feel that final caress. For a moment he looked around and couldn't for the life of him figure out what he was doing there, but then Micmac moved a little to get clear of the dust and he patted her neck.

They rode all day and made camp at sunset in a pretty river valley. The next morning before dawn they were on their way again. The countryside began to change, growing more rugged and mountainous. This area reminded Deke of the path Willie's squadron had taken to the stone village months previously. He could see they were heading well west of that place now, following a trail that began to narrow drastically the higher they went.

Soon no more than three men could walk abreast, and he and his friends were forced to shift their positions inward. Here there was no danger of flanking attacks; more likely they would be attacked from above with boulders and landslides. Scouts rode ahead to prevent any such harassment.

They saw almost no one. Occasionally a herdsman with dogs and sheep would disappear into the mountains before they got to him, but otherwise it seemed word had preceded them and the populace was making itself scarce.

On the third day they had trouble moving the wheeled vehicles through a particularly difficult river crossing. The water wasn't deep but it was fast and cold. All the soldiers pitched in to haul horses and wagons by main brute strength across the river. The cursing and yelling of the men, the raucous screams and squeals from the animals, were unbelievable, and as Deke hauled and pulled on a terrified horse's lead rope he sent a tentative probe into the animal's mind. In a second the horse became docile and followed him willingly over the slippery rocks. He handed the lead to a waiting soldier and went to get another frantic animal. The soldier grinned knowingly at his friend and said,

"See that? Like his Pa."

On the afternoon of the fourth day the army pitched camp. They would travel no farther until Deke had gone inside the fort.

That evening in his tent after the staff meeting, Barr sat with Deke at the table. Barr was drinking wine but Deke stuck to water. They talked casually for a while, then Barr said, "Are you sure you're clear on what you're doing?"

Deke nodded. "Don't worry, Father. It'll be all right."

Barr looked at his son with great fondness, proud of his intelligence and courage. He wondered if Deke knew how he felt, if his sensitivity, as Tilva called it, made him aware of everything people thought and felt.

With uncanny timing, Deke looked up from the map and met his father's eyes, and Barr was sure it was no coincidence.

"Look, Father," Deke said gently, pointing to the artist's rendering of the gate. "From this drawing it looks like the gate moves on tracks. And these openings in the walls...they'll only accomodate riflemen, but perhaps some of the wall sections open to permit artillery fire."

"Perhaps," Barr agreed, sipping his wine thoughtfully.

"Well," Deke said with a yawn, "I guess I'll turn in."

"Why not throw your bedroll on that cot over there tonight? It'd give me pleasure to share my tent with a genuine hero." The chieftain grinned at the look of surprise on Deke's face. "Aye, they're writing songs about you down where the infantrymen are camped."

Deke flushed. "Why, for ruins' sake?"

"The soldiers know you're risking your life to prevent the loss of theirs. As an act of bravura, you hardly could have chosen better. These men will follow you anywhere, now."

Deke went to get his bedroll and Micmac's saddle from the tent he normally shared with Mastra and Tim. When he returned, he unrolled his blankets and spread them on the cot. He stepped outside for a minute to urinate against a tree, looking up at the sky. Through the colorful autumn branches he could see the moon was at a little less than half, and on the increase. A moment later

162

Barr was standing nearby doing the same thing, and when they finished, he said,

"I want to be home before the dark of the moon. After that, the baby could come at any time, and your mother will rest easier if we're back safe before she starts labor."

"What about the garrison?" Deke asked, pulling off boots and socks, stripping out of his dusty clothing and sliding between his blankets.

"I'll leave Willie in charge so we can head back earlier. We'll travel with just a couple hundred horse and let the rest of the army follow in its own time."

"Good," Deke said, stretching. "The only thing about the army that I don't like, Father, is giving up my nice comfortable bed in my nice comfortable tent with my nice comfortable bath tub!"

Barr laughed.

"Aye," Deke said and his tone became dreamy. "I hate to admit how much I like soft living."

"Everyone does," Barr agreed. His cot was prepared for him and he undressed, turned off the lamp on the table, and got into his blankets. The air was growing chilly and they were glad for their warm bedrolls. Soon Barr heard his son's breathing become regular and knew he was sleeping. He listened for a while, wondering how anyone could sleep so easily on the eve of such tremendous risk. It was a great gift for a soldier, he thought, envying him.

He sighed, and a shiver of foreboding went through him. The moment passed, but not before he admitted to himself how frightened he was for Deke, how helpless he felt to protect him. One thing was certain: if those miserable fort dwellers touched a hair on his boy's head, such destruction would rain down on their lives as they had never imagined in their worst nightmares. This thought gave Barr satisfaction, and eventually he was able to doze off.

"The chase better start from inside the edge of the woods," Deke told the group of soldiers who were going to pursue him. "We don't know if they have telescopes watching from the walls, but I'm assuming they do. The lookouts are there, see? Those slotted openings...it would take a hell of a shot from outside to kill anyone."

Barr frowned. He and Hawk exchanged glances. Then the chieftain said,

"That's a run without cover for half a mile, Deke. You make sure you bob and weave. And you chasers, fire a few shots so it looks like he's dodging your bullets, right? Now, Deke, better take off all your weapons. I'm even thinking you should doff your cloak. Makes you look too mature. Muss up your

163

hair and let's get some dirt smudges on your face. Tear up your clothes some, too. Make it look like you've been running a while."

Hawk took Deke's cloak. "Maybe it would help if you could cry a little," he said.

Deke chuckled. "Get me an onion from the food stores," he said to Mastra.

Barr nodded assent and Mastra trotted off.

"Look here, Deke," Barr said seriously. "I want you out of there by the second night, no later."

"Don't worry, Father," he said. "I hope to be out long before that." He swigged from a water skin and gave up his weapons belt. Next came the body daggers. By the time he finished, Mastra had returned with the onion and he rubbed it into his eyes. Tears streamed down his cheeks and everyone smiled. He sniffled experimentally. "Aye, that'll work. Better give me a piece to carry in case I need more at the last minute. Is everyone ready?"

The chasers mounted their horses and moved towards the tree line.

Barr gave Deke a hard hug. "I know you'll do what has to be done."

"Aye," Deke said and hugged him back.

Hawk gripped his shoulder. "Remember your training! It may be all that can protect you now."

Deke nodded, then signaled to the riders. "Give me a couple minutes head start," he said, "Then come running."

Picking a spot with a steep incline leading down to the approach to the fort, Deke took a few deep breaths to center himself. Now the nervousness was coming, and muttering a quick prayer to his spirit guides, he flung himself down the slope. Such was his timing that he tumbled head over heels out of the woods. He picked himself up as if exhausted, and began to run towards the massive walls, screaming at the top of his lungs.

A rifle shot rang out and he saw dirt kick up nearby. He twisted in mid-stride and sprinted off at another angle.

"Don't shoot!" he shouted. "Help me! Please help me!"

A minute later a dozen riders galloped out of the woods after him, whooping and firing their rifles over his head. There was more gunfire from the walls, and Deke could see the shots going past him but he continued running and begging for help from the riflemen whose weapons pointed out through the slotted guard posts. As he pelted up to the gate he took the onion slice out of his pocket, rubbed his eyes with it once more, and tossed it into the dirt. He pounded on the wall, feigning desperation, and looked back over his shoulder. His pursuers had stopped and were waving their rifles defiantly while the riflemen above fired steadily to scare off what they thought was a group of raiders.

Deke heard a sound at the gate, heard it repeat itself twice, and then the gate began to move sideways. It opened just enough to admit him and he fell through as it shut tight behind him. Two more gates slid to and were locked into position. Deke stayed on his hands and knees for a second, gasping air into his lungs. He saw three sets of black shoes near him and scrabbled his way to the nearest pair, grabbing at the owner's ankles and babbling wild thanks, pretending to weep with gratitude.

Hands helped him to his feet and made him look up.

Three men dressed entirely in black stared severely at him. Around each of their necks was a large cross made out of some kind of grey metal. Deke recognized the symbol as that of the ancient Christian religion. He remembered reading about their beliefs last winter.

Questions came at him in a rush.

"Who art thou?"

"From whence come ye?"

"Dost thou accept Jesus Christ as thy Savior?" The first man peered closely at Deke.

A crowd gathered, men dressed like the first three, women in black dresses that covered them from chin to toe, with hats to hide and contain their hair.

"What ails thee? Canst thou speak?" the first man demanded.

"He is frightened, Jubal," said a middle-aged woman with a stern face but a soft voice. "He is just a boy."

"What is thy name, boy?" the man called Jubal asked.

Deke told him.

"Deke? Is that short for Deacon?"

"Aye," Deke lied, remembering that there was some religious significance to the term "deacon."

"Then thy folk are Christian," Jubal said.

"Oh, aye, your grace, we follow the teachings of Jesus Christ." Deke bobbed his head, willing to agree with anything the man said.

"Thou speakest strangely, boy. From whence come ye?"

"My people live east of here. We're a small village, farmers mostly."

"Thou hast the look of outdoor living," said Jubal.

"Thank you for helping me," Deke said. "Those men..."

"Why didst such villains chase thee, Deacon?"

Deke pretended to shudder. "They attacked my village. My parents, everyone...dead. I managed to get away, but they came after. I've been running so long..."

"Poor lost lamb of God," said the stern-faced woman piously.

"Glory to His Name," repeated the crowd in unison.

"Amen," Jubal said with fervor.

"Art thou hungry, boy?" asked the woman.

"Aye, I am," Deke said, looking around curiously. He rubbed his burning eyes and the onion oils still on his fingers made the tears flow again.

"Wait, Sara," said Jubal. "How do we know he carries no servant of Satan?"

"Bring the dogs," a man in the crowd shouted.

"Amen, brother!" others agreed loudly. "Bring the dogs!"

"Stand fast, boy," Jubal commanded, clutching his cross in his hand while two boys in their middle teens ran off.

Deke turned his tear-streaked face towards the woman. The lightest contact with her mind convinced him that under her forbidding exterior she had a kind heart, and sympathy was more likely from her than any of these others.

"What is this place?" he asked.

"This is God's town of Root," Sara informed him.

Soon the teenagers reappeared with half a dozen nondescript canines, each well over a hundred pounds. The dogs dragged on their leashes, barking loudly. The crowd stood back as the boys loosed the animals and allowed them to run towards Deke.

Deke stood still, and Sent his thoughts towards the excited beasts. They stopped barking and snapping and came to stand around him, sniffing his legs and putting their heads under his hands to be petted.

"He's clean," Jubal said, "Thanks be to Jesus."

"Amen," the crowd chanted.

"Sara, take him to our house and let him wash and eat. Then clothe him properly." Jubal looked over Deke's garments with distaste. "He is dressed like an infidel."

"Art thou willing to work, boy?" Sara asked as she led him away towards a row of grim, unpainted, wooden buildings.

"Aye," Deke said. "Thank you for helping me, sister. Those men would have killed me, sure."

"Poor motherless thing," said the woman. "Thou art lucky to be safe under our Lord's protection."

"Aye," Deke agreed. "God brought me here for certain."

They walked past the row of buildings and Deke heard a strange cry, then another, and as he strained his ears he could also hear what sounded like muffled, rhythmic thumping. He glanced around uneasily. "What is that?"

She walked on. "That is our Lord's vengeance falling on the wicked."

"I'm sorry, I don't understand."

"Didst not thy people punish any who broke God's commandments?"

"Aye, by exile, usually."

"There is no exit from this place," Sara said, and looked at him. "Except by birth and death, none arrive, none leave."

"But you let me in."

"God hath said, 'Protect the innocent.' Thou art a boy, we could do naught else."

A final, tortured cry followed them as they walked along the dusty street, rising to a shriek before being cut off abruptly.

Sara glanced around quickly, then whispered, "Thou might be sorry to have come to Root."

Deke looked at the crowded housing, the dreary, colorless landscape, and had to agree. Not so much as a flower grew in front of these buildings. No blade of grass, tree, or shrub softened the harshness of the street. Soot clouds wafted from every chimney, an acrid, foul-smelling smoke that made him wrinkle his nose.

He studied the layout of the town. Beyond it he could see another cluster of buildings, and beyond that another. Behind everything was the mountain, cutting off his view at the back of the defile. The buildings were set into a deep notch between steep, rocky slopes, then closed off from the world by high outer walls and ramparts.

"How do you grow your food?" he questioned.

"We grow nothing here," she replied, "Except Godly folk."

"What do you eat?"

"Look there," she said, pointing. "Do ye see that track winding up the mountain?" At his nod, "We draw coal up in carts and drop it over the other side. In return we receive what we need: cloth, food, everything. It has been thus forever. The Lord provideth."

What a crazy system, Deke thought.

"Thou wilt likely be assigned a job very like that," she continued, and led him onto the stoop of a small, wooden structure. She opened the door and gestured him inside. He hesitated, filled with sudden, stifling claustrophobia, but controlled himself and entered the house. He was in a bare room containing only a cooking space, a table, and four straight-backed wooden chairs. There was one window looking out into the street. A door led to what Deke supposed was another room or hallway.

"Come, Deacon," said the woman, gesturing to the doorway. "Thou canst wear something of Jubal's; thou art close in height."

Deke followed her through the door and down a hall to a tiny room with a tub. There was a hand pump which Sara began to work until water spouted and filled the bath. She removed a piece of brown soap from a cupboard and handed it to him.

"Cleanse thyself," she said. "I will bring more suitable clothes." She left him standing alone in the little room.

So far, so good, he thought, stripping and climbing into the icy water gingerly. He lathered himself with the coarse, rather strong soap and rinsed, pumping water over his head to get the suds out of his hair. The door opened a crack and a hand pushed a stack of black clothing inside before withdrawing.

As soon as he was clean Deke dried himself with the ragged towel he found, and dressed. The garments felt stiff and strange against his skin, but the color would make it easier for him to avoid detection after dark. Except for being loose around the middle, everything fit well enough.

He emerged from the bathroom after draining and rinsing the tub, carrying his neatly folded clothes with him.

Sara almost smiled when she saw him. "Ah," she said, "Now thou look proper. Thou art a handsome young man, Deacon."

"Thank you," Deke replied, listening with half an ear, trying to imagine how he would escape from this place. There was a peculiar, stuffy feeling in the air, a negative vibration that made him very uncomfortable. "When next do you go to church?" he asked. "I'd like to give thanks for my deliverance."

Sara nodded approvingly. "We go morning and evening except Sundays when we worship for half a day, then attend the church social. Thou may accompany Jubal and me this very eve. Meantime, take some food, I recollect my own boy always wanted to eat."

"Where is he now, sister?"

"Dead, Deacon," she said, her grief still in the forefront of her mind for him to *see*.

"I'm sorry," he said.

"He was the same age as thee, about," she said, reminiscing. "Fifteen or so."

"Actually, I'm thirteen," he told her.

"Thou art tall and sturdy for thirteen," she said thoughtfully. She took some oats from a closet and put them in a pot with water.

"Can I help, sister?"

"Nay, sit and rest. Thou look to have had a hard time of it, Deacon." Sara stirred the oatmeal. "Thou may sleep in his room, if that suits thee."

"Thank you," he replied, his mind touching hers to be certain nothing was being hidden from him. "It's kind of you to take me in this way."

"Truly, it pleases me to do so," said Sara. "Thou art a special young man, I can see that."

"Not so special," he said, feeling a twinge of guilt for the way he was deceiving this kind woman.

"When Jubal sees how devout thou art, he, too, will be pleased."

"Was your son devout?" he asked, wanting to keep her talking so he wouldn't have to answer any questions.

"Our Seth was the most devout boy in Root," she said and wiped a tear from her cheek with a rag.

"How did he pass over?"

Sara looked into his amazingly blue eyes, wondering what it was about this boy that made her feel she could tell him anything. "It was an accident," she whispered. "That is what they told to me."

Deke's expression was attentive, sympathetic.

"He was of the group who haul carts up the mountain," she continued. "Someone ahead let a cart get away. It came back down the tracks, taking more carts with it." She dabbed more tears away. "Seth could not get clear."

"You don't sound convinced it was an accident," he said.

"I should not say more," she replied. "Of course it was an accident." Her voice grew biting. "What reason could Jubal have for killing our son?"

"Was he on the mountain, too?"

"He was. His hand it was that released the brake on the first cart. He swears it was an accident."

"Perhaps it was," Deke said soothingly.

"Nay, thou canst never understand how it was between those two. Jubal loved Seth deeply but Seth...was not like other boys."

"Tell me about him." His eyes were gently compelling.

"Seth," she whispered, "Loved another boy."

"So Jubal thought that was an abomination."

"Thou understandeth much for one so young." She shrugged and wiped her eyes again. "Jubal tried punishment, prayer...he pleaded with Seth to change, but Seth would not."

"Those who prefer their own sex can never change," Deke said. "God made them that way for His own reasons."

Sara ladled some of the cooked oats into a bowl and placed it and a spoon before him. "Eat, Deacon. The food is plain, but it nourishes."

"I'm grateful, sister," he said and tasted the oatmeal. It was plain indeed, more like glue than cereal, but he spooned it up doggedly, wanting to please the woman. He felt sorry for her, sorry for anyone who had to live in this hidebound, claustrophobic society.

"Does your husband work?" he asked after a while.

"He is in charge of the mine."

"That sounds important."

"It is," Sara said without pleasure. "That is why we live in this fine house."

"Well, it is a fine house," Deke said with as much sincerity as he could muster.

"Do thine own people live in houses?"

"Different," he said. "We work the fields, raise animals."

"What was thy work?" she asked.

"Boys my age are expected to do a little of everything," he answered. "Mostly we're always learning." He paused. "When will your husband return? I'm eager to see more of your town, especially the church. Is there only one?"

"We have only one, and one shepherd for our flock."

"Is he a good shepherd?"

"The finest, Deacon. When he preacheth, Satan himself flees. Thou shalt see him for thyself."

Deke finished the oatmeal. "Thanks for this food."

"Thou must have been very hungry to forget to say grace," Sara said.

"Aye," he agreed, wondering what "grace" was. "Starved. I've had nothing for days."

"I am sure the good Lord will forgive thee, and I will not tell."

"Thank you, sister."

"It is my pleasure. But always remember grace when Jubal is here, Deacon. He will punish thee, otherwise."

"I'll remember," Deke said, a grim note coming into his voice.

"Please," she insisted. "I would hate to see thee harmed."

"Thank you for your concern. Would you like to show me around Root? Is that permitted?"

"Jubal would be displeased if I usurped that function from him," Sara said. "My work is here, about the house, and also in the church, doing good works for others."

"Oh," he said, disappointed.

"I am sure Jubal will escort thee," she said. "If thou like, thou might rest a while, until he returns. Then, when we go to church, thou might ask him to show thee the town, perhaps even the mine."

"All right," he agreed.

He followed her to a small room in the back of the house. Inside there was a narrow bed, a small bureau, and a straight-backed chair.

"Do not forget thy prayers," she said. "God be with thee, Deacon."

"And you, sister."

She closed the door and he gave a sigh of relief. The room was practically a cubicle, and the one window on the back wall was tiny and set high. He climbed on the chair to look out and saw he was facing the defensive walls, with a good view of the rampart. From where he stood, there was no sign of heavy guns at all, and he felt exhilaration rise in him. Unless there was something stowed on the mountain he couldn't see, it appeared Root's only defense was its physical inaccessibility and the strength of its walls.

He did see quite a few men patrolling those walls; in fact, there were armed men wandering casually about the whole area, and it occurred to Deke that the people of Root were guarded very carefully. Apparently devotion to their God wasn't enough to keep them obedient.

He got down from the chair and stretched out on the bed. It was as hard as a board, and when he looked under the covers he found he indeed was lying on solid wood covered with a couple blankets. Shifting uncomfortably, he smiled, thinking about his field cot back in his father's tent, and how he'd be happy to have it right now.

Sighing, he tried to doze. There were only a few things more he wanted to check, and then, with any luck, he would be out of this forbidding place and back in the world before first light tomorrow.

The church was by far the most impressive structure in any of the three cramped towns. It was ancient, made entirely of stone, with a tall steeple and wide, carved oak doors. At the moment those doors were thrown open and a black-clad stream of the faithful was flowing through them.

Deke walked between Sara and her husband, Jubal. Each held him by the hand. He wasn't sure if they did this out of nostalgic feelings for their son, or to keep him from bolting.

Jubal was a man of middle height, with a soft hand but firm grip. He looked at least sixty, and under his tall, formal, square hat his hair was thin and lackluster. He was clean-shaven with putty-colored skin and pale, cold eyes. Every now and then he threw a glance at Deke, and when he did, Deke had to keep himself from flinching. He could almost believe Sara's story about her son was true, just from the way this man looked. There was a feeling of hidden threat, something sinister and deadly lurking just behind those emotionless eyes. When he tried to contact Jubal's mind he found it so convoluted and controlled, he quickly became disoriented and had to withdraw.

It didn't take much extrapolation for him to see that the citizens of Root were essentially slaves, in part to their religious beliefs and their hereditary fear of the outside world, but mostly to the thugs led by this ruthless man who kept them under strict guard as if they were prisoners.

As they walked up the steps into the church, Jubal turned a long, con-

171

sidering look on him. Deke felt the intensity of that flat stare and tensed, wondering what it meant. On his left, Sara squeezed his hand reassuringly, and in a moment they were inside the stone building's chill gloom.

The interior was as stark as the rest of Root, the narrow pews filling with gaunt parishioners. At the pulpit an imposing man with bushy eyebrows and an icy self-possession stood watching the people file in, and when his gaze fell on Deke, his black eyes lidded over in an expression Deke found more than unsettling. The man licked his lips delicately.

Soon the church was full and with a rustling murmur everyone knelt and prayed silently for a few minutes. Deke imitated the others, keeping his eyes lowered, but reached out with his sensitivity to get a feel for the emotions of the people around him, especially the man at the pulpit. There were pathways into the man's mind but they were circuitous. When he arrived at the center of consciousness, he was permeated by malevolence and could barely bring himself to analyze the man's inner, behavioral patterns. He *saw* cruelty and sadism in large measure, along with the echo of tortures inflicted upon others, teenage boys in particular being the special targets of the man's perverse passion.

Shaken, Deke withdrew his awareness. He took his seat with the rest of the congregation and opened the book thrust into his hand by Jubal, beginning to understand why his life had been spared.

"Canst thou read?" Jubal asked in a low tone.

"No," Deke lied, deciding the less they thought he knew, the more they would reveal about themselves.

"Then listen, and learn," said Jubal.

Deke nodded submissively.

Sara patted his hand comfortingly, and he was grateful for her presence. As long as she was there, he didn't think Jubal or the minister would assault him, but he couldn't count on that. He searched her mind swiftly to the deepest levels and found no conscious awareness of the preacher's secret desire, or her husband's complicity in it.

After a long drone of prayers read from the same book everyone held, the minister raised his hand for quiet. In an unnatural instant, the congregation obeyed. Not so much as a whisper or cough disturbed the absolute silence.

"Today God hath seen fit to bring a new lamb into the fold," he said. His eyes went to Deke. "Stand," he ordered, "And let the people of Root know thee."

Deke rose and glanced around the church. He saw all eyes turn to him curiously. He looked back at the minister, whose devouring gaze belied his bland expression. He could feel the man's dark, sexual hunger like a whiplash

172

in his mind and looked at Jubal, surprising a look of eager anticipation on his face as well. Here and there among the congregation were others he sensed were connected to Jubal and the minister, and he made sure he registered them carefully, impressing their faces and auras into his memory.

The minister gestured him to sit, and then, ignoring him completely, began to deliver a vehement sermon filled with dire promises of hellfire and damnation for any human transgression. When he began to enumerate those tortures which would be inflicted for the slightest sin committed in this life and even in the afterlife, Deke felt his stomach turn. How anyone could submit himself to this ranting distortion was incredible to him. Nothing in his life had prepared him for this sort of vicious dogma, and he tried to control his revulsion, afraid of what would happen if anyone suspected his feelings.

For an hour or more the minister's exhortations went on, his voice rising and falling dramatically, holding his congregation spellbound. When he concluded and the people got up to leave, he approached Jubal and Sara and walked with them to the door.

"This is Deacon, Reverend," Sara said in a pleasant tone which failed to hide her growing disquiet from Deke's mental probe. "He's a devout boy who reveres God."

"Bless his...heart," the minister said, his gaze flicking towards Deke's thighs before climbing slowly up his body to fall like poisonous velvet on his face.

"This is our minister," Sara told Deke. "The Reverend Uriah."

"Shake his hand, Deacon," Jubal ordered.

Deke put out his hand. The minister grasped it in his own papery claw, and while pretending to shake heartily, caressed the palm with his fingers in a highly suggestive manner. The insinuating touch made Deke flush, and his sensitivity took a leap in power. With a startled sound, Uriah retracted his hand as if burned.

Deke stared down at the floor, knowing his fury was visible on his face. When he glanced up again, he surprised a strange, measuring look on the minister's features. Jubal's lips were compressed into a thin line, and Sara glanced back and forth between the two men worriedly. She grasped Deke's hand, shielding him from their scrutiny with her body.

"Well," she said to the minister through an atmosphere abruptly thick with threat, "'Twas a fine sermon, Reverend. But supper hour approaches, and I must prepare food. Deacon? Wouldst thou assist me?"

"Aye," Deke agreed quickly. "Pleased to have met you," he said to the minister, still smoldering, but concealing it.

"Oh, no," said Uriah. A vein in his neck pulsed and his eyes raked the boy with barely contained excitement. "The pleasure is all mine."

"I will join thee presently," Jubal told Sara.

She nodded acquiescence and led Deke away. He could feel her restrain a desire to hurry, and looked back over his shoulder to see the two men's heads draw together in whispered conversation. He shuddered involuntarily.

"Thou art in grave danger," Sara told him when they turned the corner and were out of sight.

"I know," he replied. "I think you were right about Seth," he added.

"How couldst thou know this?" Sara asked.

"Trust me, sister," he said earnestly. "I mean only good to come to you."

"I believe thee, Deacon," she said and looked into his eyes. "I know not why, but I am certain sure thy arrival here was no accident."

His expression was questioning.

"Yes, I believe thou art God sent," she said. "I feel it here," and she touched her breast over her heart.

They reached Sara's house and went inside.

"I do not know what to do to protect thee," she said.

"I can take care of myself," he said. "You mustn't give Jubal and Uriah any excuse to harm you."

She looked at him levelly. "I swear I didst not know until I saw how Uriah looked at thee that he and Jubal were together concerning Seth."

"You're a good woman," he told her, taking her hand between his, sending a reassuring touch into her mind. "But now I must know a few things."

"What things?"

"How many men guard the walls and gate?"

Sara drew breath sharply. "Sure thou art not considering escape!"

"Please," he said, his eyes intent on hers.

"Because thou wilt never succeed," she informed him. "No one has ever escaped from Root."

"What about over the mountain?"

"None that I have heard of," she replied.

"Have people tried?"

"Oh, Deacon, in times past some made the attempt. Either they were shot on the spot or taken back for punishment."

"Who inflicts the punishment?"

"Uriah," she said slowly. "Always he has said it is God's work."

"He likes to hurt boys, doesn't he?"

"I never would have believed so until today." Her expression was disquieted, and Deke realized the poor woman was being forced to confront issues

174

beyond her ability to absorb. "I have never seen him display such a lust before." She covered her face with her hands. "I thought he was a good, godly man. When Seth went to him, I thought it was for piety's sake, not..." Her voice trailed off. "If I had not seen him look so...filthily at thee, I should not have put it together."

Deke said gently, "I think Seth was going to tell about the two of them, and that's why he was killed."

Sara looked penetratingly at him. "Thou art very wise for thirteen, Deacon. Who art thou, really?"

"I am who I am, as you are who you are."

"Nay, that is no answer," she said.

"It's the only answer I can give for now," he said, and patted her hand. "I think they'll come for me tonight. Whatever happens, don't interfere. It could be dangerous."

"Thou art good to worry for me, Deacon." She began to prepare food, more oatmeal, with a few pallid carrots and some colorless beans.

"How many guards?" he asked again. "Do they stay on duty all night?"

"The gate is always guarded, as are the walls," Sara said reluctantly. "There are at least a dozen at the heights all the time."

"What about when everyone's at church?"

"There are fewer then, but how many? I could not tell thee."

"Do your people use weapons other than firearms?"

Sara was puzzled. "What other weapons are there?"

"Have you ever seen big guns, placed permanently either in the walls or on the surrounding hills?"

"Big guns...?"

"Aye," and he gestured with his hands, "So big at the muzzle end and maybe as wide as this room in length?"

"Never," Sara said with certainty.

"Not even behind the town on the mountain?"

"Nay, Deacon, but why must thou know these things?"

Before Deke could think of an acceptable answer, there was a sound at the door and Sara quickly lifted her finger to her lips in warning. Then, raising her voice in greeting, she called, "Supper will be ready in a few minutes, Jubal."

After the tasteless meal was concluded, Jubal eyed Deke. "Tomorow I will show thee thy work," he said.

Deke nodded. "I look forward to it."

"I am sure. Such a devout boy must be eager to exert himself on behalf of the Lord." There was thinly veiled sarcasm in Jubal's voice and, hearing it,

Sara looked away. "Thou shouldst sleep now, Deacon," he said reasonably. "Thou shalt start early, after church."

"Aye, and thank you both for the food and shelter," Deke replied.

"Thou art welcome," Sara said. "Sleep well."

Deke was lying on his back when he heard the key slide into the lock on his door. He was on his feet in an instant, and silently tried the knob. He was locked in.

He stood in front of the door trying to decide what to do, realizing there was no time to waste. Making up his mind, he breathed deeply a few times and centered his thoughts, preparing himself. Then, drawing energy in the ways the Old Man had taught him, he lashed out with his right foot. With a splintering crash, the door burst open, broken nearly in half. He slipped through, and as Jubal rushed at him from the front room brandishing a long cooking knife, he feinted to one side, tripping the man with a quick blow to the back of the knee. Jubal stumbled, flailing with the knife. Before he could figure out exactly what was happening, his wrist was grabbed and twisted viciously until he cried out and dropped the blade. His arm was wrenched up behind his back and he heard the bone give way with a loud crack. He started to scream, but at once the front of his shirt was stuffed into his mouth to silence him. A hard knee drove into his testicles, sending him to the floor with eyes bulging in pain and terror.

"Murdering bastard," Deke said through gritted teeth. "So you thought you'd do to me what you did to Seth. You and that minister both... How many of your people have you killed? How many have you tortured?" Jubal cowered helplessly while the burning eyes bore into his. "Say hello to God for me, brother," Deke said with quiet ferocity. In the next moment, with a quick movement, he snapped Jubal's neck.

Arising from the limp form, he found himself facing Sara, who stared at him with undisguised horror.

"I'm sorry, sister," he said quickly, "But I couldn't let him live. He would have raised an alarm. Worse, he might have harmed you."

She looked from her dead husband to the boy, unable to take in what had occurred. It had been so fast, and the boy had moved with such blinding speed, the whole attack couldn't have taken ten seconds from the time he kicked in the door.

"How...what..." Sara couldn't marshall her thoughts.

"I have to leave, sister. For your own safety I'll tie you up. Otherwise they'll think you helped me."

She nodded numbly.

He tore away strips of Jubal's jacket and used them to bind her hands and feet. Then he bound her to one of the wooden chairs. Leaning down, he kissed her cheek. "Don't despair."

"Jesus be with thee, Deacon," she whispered.

"And with you," Deke replied. "I won't forget your kindness." Then he gagged her, picked up the knife, and stole from the house.

Outside, all was darkness. Directly overhead he could see a few stars shining down, but otherwise the only light came from coal oil lanterns burning in windows, throwing their glow out onto the street. There were footsteps and he sent a psychic probe into the night to seek the source, shrinking back into a shadow until whomever it was went past. A moment later he slid onto the street, moving from house to house cautiously, the kitchen knife clasped in his hand.

He looked back the way he had come and saw a tall figure approaching Sara's house. He cursed under his breath and ran back, waiting tensely beside the stoop. There was a commotion inside, then voices, and then Uriah came clattering down the steps at a run. Deke stuck his foot out and the minister fell heavily into the dusty street. Before he could make a sound, Deke had the knife poised under his ear and said, "We meet again, Reverend." When the minister tried to answer, he said, "Sh! A word and you're dead."

Uriah was silent.

"Do you want to live?" Deke's voice was a whisper in the man's ear.

Uriah nodded once.

"Good. Lie still." Deke used the knife to cut strips away from the minister's long frock coat and tied his hands behind his back. He searched him quickly but thoroughly, removing an unusual handgun from Uriah's waistband, along with a pocketful of shells.

Dragging the minister none-too-gently to his feet, Deke prodded him with the gun and said, "We're going to walk together to the gate. If you don't convince the guards to open it, I'll end your life. Do you understand?"

Uriah started to say something but Deke whipped the knife quickly across his face in front of his eyes and he clamped his jaw shut. A trickle of blood started from a shallow cut on his cheekbone.

"You may nod if you understand," Deke told him.

Uriah nodded.

"Good," Deke said in a curt whisper. He jammed the gun under the minister's ribcage and took his arm above the elbow in a tight grip. "Let's go."

They walked like old friends through the quiet streets, and on the few occasions they saw guards, Deke drew the reverend closer, pressing the gun deeper into his flesh. Obviously the sight of the tall minister with a teenage boy at night was a familiar one, for the guards barely acknowledged them before hurrying away.

When they reached the gate, Deke said, "Tell them to open it."

"They won't." Uriah said with a cold smile.

Instantly the knife was against his crotch. "Convince them."

The minister swallowed. He called out loudly. "Open the gates!"

A head poked from the wall above them. "Reverend Uriah! What art thou doing?"

"Don't ask questions, just do it!" the minister's voice cracked with tension.

"Thou knoweth we canst not do that," said the man.

Deke looked up at the man and said to the minister, "Tell him to come down. Tell them all to come down."

"Come down!"

Several men climbed down the ladders to the ground.

"What is happening, Reverend?" one of them asked.

"This young man hath determined he wishes to leave our town," Uriah said from between clenched teeth, feeling the sharp edge of the blade pressing against his scrotum. "I think it wouldst be best if we let him."

"What about the law, Reverend?"

"A plague take the law! He'll emasculate me if thou dost not obey!"

The men looked at where Deke held the knife and each of them swallowed uncomfortably.

Deke allowed his thoughts to pass from one man to another, filling their minds with the image of their minister's testicles cut free and dropped in the dirt. At the same time he pushed a little harder on the knife and Uriah shrieked thinly.

"By Jesus Christ Our Lord make up thy minds he's going to cut me!" he said in a rush.

Deke shifted the image he was broadcasting so that each man felt the knife at his own scrotum, and after a beat the first one said, "What dost it matter? Let the boy go. He'll soon die outside. Bandits will get him and that will be his end."

"Open the gate," Deke said, his tone commanding.

With a nod, the men moved to obey. Moments later the triple gates were sliding open and Deke took the minister with him as he went through.

"Thou art free, devil," Uriah hissed angrily. "What dost thou need me for?"

"Insurance," Deke said shortly. "Keep walking."

The gates began to slide closed behind them.

"Wait for me!" Uriah called urgently to the men. "Thou must let me go!" He struggled briefly with Deke until the gun prodded him again.

"Walk or die," Deke said, breathing in the night air deeply. It was cold, and the grass underfoot crackled with hoarfrost. He shoved the minister along impatiently.

A voice came out of the darkness. "Who's there? Identify yourself!"

When Deke had done so, there was a roar from the woods and soldiers poured out to surround him and the minister. In seconds their guns were pointing at Uriah, and Deke could relax. Barr Wolfson appeared from nowhere, his huge arms windmilling men out of the way.

"Deke, boy, we almost shot you! And who's your friend?"

Deke tried to act casual. "He's not my friend, but he sure wanted to be! Hell, he wanted to be real friendly!"

Barr approached the minister who cringed before the massive chieftain's baleful glance. "Ah, one of those?" He looked the man in the eye. "So, you thought you'd sodomize my son, eh? Bad choice. Very bad choice."

"Wait, Father," Deke said.

"Don't you want him dead?"

"I do. But I have other plans for him. Let's hold him prisoner for the time being."

Barr nodded and spoke to his men. "You heard Deke. Put him under guard." Then, to his son, "What news have you got for us?"

"No artillery at all. We could have blasted through at any time." Deke put the gun in his waistband and said, "Can I get something to eat? You wouldn't believe what they fed me in there."

Barr laughed. "Aye. Tomorrow we'll take the fort," he said to his men. "But tonight we'll celebrate." He peered into Deke's eyes. "Does that sit well with you, son?"

"Aye, Father, better than well. There's just one more thing."

"Aye?" The chieftain waited expectantly.

"Most of the people in there are under the control of that man I took prisoner and his friends. If we can get the leaders and armed guards out of the way, a lot of those folk will be very grateful for kind treatment. I recommend our men be forbidden to ransack the place. There's nothing of value besides the coal. I didn't see so much as a flower, much less any valuables."

Barr studied Deke for a moment, then nodded. "This is your show, son. You can tell the men yourself, when you lead them inside."

Deke looked sharply at his father, sure he'd misheard.

"Aye, Deke, you'll take the fort; it's only fair. Your plan, your victory."

Deke blinked several times. Then he nodded, not trusting his voice.

With a pleased grin, Barr threw an arm across his son's shoulders and together they walked through the crowding soldiers back to camp, while around them the men cheered their approval.

At dawn, Deke led the attack. He ordered the heavy artillery to bombard the gate, with every gun firing simultaneously. When the smoke cleared, the gates were gone, completely blown apart. Inside, the Wolf soldiers could see black-clad figures running about frantically.

Deke ordered a volley to be fired at the walls. There was a deafening roar as the artillerymen obeyed. A section of stone and timber gave way, with splinters and rocks shooting like jagged bullets in every direction. "Again," he commanded. "Let's flatten 'em."

For the next few minutes the big guns leaped and bucked, growing hot to the touch. Young men carried off the empty artillery shells to be transported home for re-use. Others brought more live ammunition to be launched.

Mastra and Tim stood near Deke, smiles of delight on their faces at the noise and destruction. They looked at the tall minister where he sat trussed like a roast ready for the oven. A powerful youth of about sixteen stood over him, watching alertly.

"That should do it," Barr said to Deke, when the guns fell silent. Beyond the downed walls they could see little damage to the town proper, and Deke nodded with satisfaction.

When the Wolf riders were mounted, he addressed them quickly. "Remember! No firing on civilians unless they're armed. These are poor people with nothing to steal. We'll have control of their coal, that's enough. Everyone understand?"

The soldiers nodded.

"There are three streets running back towards the mountain. Hawk, you take the left with your men. Willie, the right side is yours. My father and I will go up the middle." He turned to his manhood group. "Follow me. Watch out for sniper fire. The buildings are close and many are three stories high."

Without further comment, he gave Micmac his heels and cantered up the grassy incline towards the mounds of smoking debris that once had been forty-foot ramparts, with four hundred cavalry riders right behind him.

The horsemen galloped into the town, their voices raised in terrifying yells designed to intimidate the enemy, their rifles quartering the streets in search of armed targets. There was little resistance. Most of the defenders had been on the walls and when the walls went, so had they. Sporadic gunfire crackled but was silenced by the professional warriors whose weapons spat with deadly accuracy.

Hawk's hundred and thirty peeled off to the left, the horses leaping chunks of rock thrown from the walls. Willie's group moved right, and Barr fanned the central attackers in a protective screen around his son lest any of these people recognize Deke and be holding a grudge.

Most of them fled before the horsemen, darting into buildings, flattening against walls, in some cases simply running back and forth screaming. In less time than Barr would have believed possible when planning this assault back at Spring Camp, the fort was under control. Except for an occasional shout or gunshot, all was quiet.

"Mastra, gather the populace in front of the church," Deke said. "Tim, take a squadron inside and make sure everyone's out. Watch out in there; it's dark and there are lots of hiding places."

Both boys nodded and galloped off. Deke looked for his father and saw him riding with some of his men towards the back of the defile where the mountain's bulk covered the town in shadow.

From behind him a soldier rode up, wiping dust from his face. Deke turned and his face lit with recognition. "Melak," he said with pleasure.

"Well met, chief," said the dark soldier, a grin spreading across his face. "Good day's work. All our battles should be so easy."

"Aye," Deke agreed, "But then we'd get soft."

Melak laughed. "So, is there anything I can do for you?"

"Yes," Deke told him. "Get word to our men outside and have them bring me that preacher."

Melak nodded and rode away.

Deke leaned on his pommel and looked around. Soldiers were entering buildings up and down the streets, escorting the citizens of Root towards the church. The townspeople looked dusty and shaken and weren't putting up a fight. The soldiers were obeying his orders, and handled the population with restraint.

Deke smiled, supremely happy.

Before long the townspeople were gathered in front of the church. Wolf riders circled at a swift canter, keeping them herded together.

Barr, Hawk, and Willie rode to where Deke waited on the main street. "How's the mine look, Father?" Deke asked.

Barr smiled. "Perfect. I'd thought they might destroy the place before letting us have it, but these people haven't got a lot of fight in them."

"No," Deke agreed. "They've had it beaten out of them."

"What do you want to do about them?" Barr asked, indicating the populace.

"I'll have a word with them now, if you don't mind."

Barr spread his hands in an affirmative gesture.

Deke paced Micmac towards the crowd, and the soldiers shoved people out of his way. He rode directly to the steps of the church where he turned the mare and sat quietly, his eyes searching the crowd. When he saw Sara standing at the far edge, he breathed a sigh of relief. He continued to gaze at the people, sending his thoughts out to feel their mood. Fear, anxiety, and uncertainty were the prevailing emotions.

Gradually as he perused them, they fell silent, hardly able to believe this youth was in command of the army that had invaded their town and destroyed the defenses that had protected them for so many centuries.

Deke spoke in a voice that carried well across the square. "All men who worked for Jubal or the Reverend Uriah, come forward now. If you come willingly and swear allegiance peacefully, no further action will be taken against you. If I have to pick you out, and you may believe I know who you are, it will not go as easily for you."

There was a murmur from the crowd and five men walked forward.

"Swear allegiance to Barr Wolfson and the Wolf People, now and forever. If you break this oath, your lives will be forfeit."

The men so swore.

"I know there were more of you," Deke said to them.

"They were killed at the walls," one man said.

"I'll verify that later," Deke said. "Meanwhile, you can return to your lives. Of course, you are no longer in charge of anything, but that seems a small price to pay for the terror you've inflicted on your people." With a gesture he ordered them back into the crowd. Then, raising his voice again, he continued.

"You now live under Wolfson law. You will find that to be an improvement. You are all free to come and go as you wish. You will have no need for walls because we will protect you. Each of you may decide for yourself if you wish to stay here and continue to live as you always have, or leave and try life in one of our many clans or villages. In exchange for protection under our laws, all we ask from you is a fair percentage of your coal production, an amount to be decided when we see what your output is." He paused and saw that Sara was looking at him in shock and disbelief. Pointing to her, he said in an aside to Mastra, "Bring that woman here. Gently!"

Mastra nodded and rode through the crowd until he was at her side. "He wants you," he told her, and turned his horse to follow her as she walked towards the church.

When she arrived, Deke smiled reassuringly. "Wait," he said to her. He spoke to the crowd again. "You are free to practice your religion as you see fit. If you still want to drag coal up the mountain and drop it off the other side for food, that's fine. We'll attend to those folk soon enough. I recommend you establish trade with our people, and we will send advisors to help re-organize your economy accordingly. In the meantime, you may consider yourselves free."

From where he sat with Hawk and Willie watching his son, Barr saw Melak returning with the minister. An anticipatory grin played at the corners of his mouth as he waited, his pride enormous, to see what surprising thing Deke would do next.

Melak rode next to Uriah, leading the minister who was thrown over the back of a pack mule like a bale of trade goods. He came alongside Deke and said, "Here he is, m'lord. What do you want me to do with him?"

"Get him down and untie him. But keep your gun on him, he's not a very nice man." Deke looked down to see Sara's mouth twitch with amusement at his understatement.

He raised his voice to the crowd, who, when they realized it was the minister slung over the mule's back, began to murmur. They quieted beneath his crystalline gaze.

"Many of you probably think this Uriah is a good and decent man. Those of you with sons know otherwise. Certainly there are many young men and boys who've been the victims of this creature's appetites who will testify to his crimes. He has inflicted unspeakable punishments against you in the name of your God, and in this one area Wolfson law will forbid you to live as you always have done. There will be no more beatings, whippings, or tortures for religious purposes. Your Jesus Christ preached peace and love. Root is going to become the most peaceful, loving town in our domain. Any of you who don't like that may depart for the wilderness today."

Deke waited for this to sink in, then continued. "Now, there is just one further thing to take care of, and that concerns how we will dispense justice in this matter of the Reverend Uriah."

He looked out across the crowd. "Anyone who has been abused or tortured by this so-called man of God, come forward. Don't be afraid; no one will hurt you."

There was hesitation, and then Sara stepped forward, her head high. She looked challengingly at her friends and neighbors. "I'll speak first," she said softly. She faced the minister. "Thou helped my husband plan the murder of my son," she accused, her eyes wide with her own daring. "Jubal hast already paid for that crime. How wilt thou make payment? What canst thou do to repay me for my son?"

Another woman came out of the crowd to stand near Sara. "Thou savaged my boy so badly he hath been bedridden for over a year and it is said he will never recover."

Still a third woman emerged and shouted at the minister, "Miserable excuse for piety, thou hast killed my brother and my son! I think Deacon shouldst have thine eyes for his buttons!"

Voices began to ring out from the gathered citizenry, and an angry rumble went through them as they listened to the shouted accusations.

Throughout all this Uriah stood silently, his eyes lowered.

When the accusations trailed to an end, Deke addressed the townspeople. "Since you have been the victims of Reverend Uriah's crimes, it is only right that you decide his fate. Name his punishment."

Scores of suggestions, some humorous, others vulgar, but most exceedingly unpleasant, were screamed out across the crowd. The prevailing sentiment called for him to be strung up by his testicles and lashed with a bullwhip until dead. When it was realized that this was what the Root citizenry wanted, disbelieving laughter broke out amongst the Wolf soldiers.

"You men who used to work for him," Deke called. "You will inflict the punishment. As for the rest of you, I suggest you re-think your sentence. It is an odd fact but true, torture does more damage to the torturer than the one tortured. But whatever you decide, sentence will be carried out tomorrow at dawn." Deke spoke to Melak. "Disperse the crowd," he said. "Put guards on the minister; we don't want him murdered before he can be executed."

Melak laughed. "Aye, chief, that's good thinking."

Deke dismounted and stood near Sara. "Well met, sister," he said with a cocky grin.

"Deacon," she said with a look of wonder. "How didst this come to be? I canst hardly believe what thou art...!"

"What am I?" he asked, his eyes filled with laughter.

"Thou must be a prophet of the Lord at the very least. How else canst I explain all thou hast wrought in so little time? Like Moses, thou hast struck away our chains and freed us from a dreadful bondage."

Deke chuckled. "I'm hardly an agent of the Almighty. I'm just a soldier in training, Ma'am."

"Thou maketh jests with me, Deacon, but I know. I knew when first thou arrived here."

"What did you know, sister?"

"I knew thou wouldst change all our lives."

"I'm glad to have done it," Deke said, taking her hand. "I'm glad I could repay your kindness." His eyes were warm.

"Thank thee," Sara told him. "By tomorrow, all here will thank thee."

"Sister," Deke patted her on the shoulder. "We'll talk again."

"Ride with Jesus, Deacon," Sara said as he sprang onto Micmac's

184

back.

"Call me Deke," he said with a grin and cantered away, followed by the boys of his manhood group.

CHAPTER TEN

There are pivotal events in every life, events we can point to later and say, "Here is where a certain behavior was rooted."

There were many of these events in the General's early life, making it difficult for me to pinpoint precisely where most of his dysfunctional behaviors originated, but there was one upheaval in particular that ultimately proved so scarring, so devastating, one can see the logical progression of every development that came thereafter...

— Ourn Rohlvaag; Collected Journals; City of Life, A.D. 3109

O n a chill, grey dawn near the end of October, two hundred heavily armed riders headed south out of the mountains. At their head, Deke and Barr rode side by side, with Hawk just behind Barr, and Melak a little behind and to Deke's right. Since the day they had conquered Root, the soldier had attached himself to Deke as his personal bodyguard. No matter how Deke tried to convince Melak that he could look after himself, he met with no success. With stolid determination, Melak refused to be dissuaded. Since Barr agreed with Melak, Deke finally gave up arguing. As the sergeant repeated to anyone who would listen, Deke's propensity for adventure made it mandatory that someone be available to watch his back, and Melak felt he was best qualified for the job.

The journey home to rendezvous with the People at Winter Camp would be hard and cold, though without the slower, more ponderous elements of the army, not much lengthier in time than the ride up to Root. Winter Camp lay some three hundred miles south of Spring Camp, in a sheltered valley near a stretch of ruins and wild pine barrens.

The horses' breath steamed in the frigid air, and their hooves broke through the brittle, morning ice layering every puddle and mud hole on the trail. The mountains were stark, clothed in damp mist which penetrated one's bones.

Barr's left knee was bothering him and he longed for Tilva's herb drinks and liniments that always made the old wound easier to bear in cold weather. His mind rested on his wife, and he smiled a little, looking forward to their reunion. He wondered how everyone was getting on at home, and whether the autumn migration had gone smoothly.

Deke pulled the hood of his cloak over his head and hunched his shoulders into the sheepskin liner, glad they were on their way. He was bored by the administrative details that went into re-organizing Root as a viable town and wasn't looking forward to the time when those details would become his full responsibility.

He frowned as he remembered the day the townspeople had executed the Reverend Uriah.

Under orders, the Wolf soldiers had made themselves scarce, though most found inconspicuous positions from which they could watch as the townspeople erected a crude scaffold with a trapdoor through which the prisoner would fall.

They had dragged the minister screaming up the stairs to the top. There they had read him a list of crimes which had been committed by him directly, or those in which he had been complicitous with Jubal. The reading had gone on a long time. Afterwards, they had asked if he had anything to say for himself. He had thought for a minute, then looked straight at Deke, speaking in a voice that made Deke think he was possessed by at least twenty demons.

"If I had known sooner how diabolically clever thou art, I should have understood why I wast compelled to risk everything to possess thee. Aside from thy natural beauty, thou art filled with Satan's brilliance, and even for my own life's sake, I couldst not resist thee." Uriah had paused and looked down at the faces of his congregation. "Now, do what thou wilt, and be damned to ye! I'll see thee in hell, Deacon!" he had shouted, his black eyes filled with rage that bordered on madness.

The men who once had been his servants had stripped him naked, bound his hands behind him, and slipped a noose around his genitals. Before anyone could say another word, the trapdoor had slammed open under his feet.

Uriah's scream had gone off the scale as he dropped through and flipped like a hooked fish. The impact with which he hit the end of the rope would have killed him had it been around his neck, but due to the noose's positioning, there instead had been a meaty, tearing sound, and Uriah had dropped to the ground, minus his masculinity.

Swiftly the five former servants had seized him and tied him to the side of the scaffold. The minister had been in shock, bleeding badly. Each man in turn had struck a blow with a long whip, and one by one every person in the town had walked by and wielded the lash. Before Uriah passed out from pain and blood loss, one of the men had walked under the scaffold and collected the minister's severed sexual organs. With hammer and nail, the man had fastened them to the wooden post in front of Uriah's eyes.

Even now, nearly a month later, Deke could hear the blows of that hammer, and was sickened by the memory.

The weather worsened during the next few days, with an icy drizzle turning first to sleet, and then to snow driven by a thin but cutting wind. Nonetheless, the horsemen made fairly good time, and Deke was grateful that the main body of the army would follow after.

As they drew nearer to Winter Camp, they were forced to stop for half a day when the wind and snow were too fierce to see anything beyond their horses' noses. The riders huddled under tarpaulins near sputtering fires, fighting to stay warm.

Barr was restless and irritable, frustrated by the delay. If the weather would cooperate, they could be home in no more than a couple hours even at their slowest pace.

Deke's mood was no better, but for different reasons. Early that morning he had begun to be filled with a strange anxiety, a tension which made him edgy as a buck when the hunter's on his trail. It was as if someone was scratching inside his skull with a knife, wearing a groove that eventually must drive him either to bolt or commit an act of violence. He didn't know why he felt this way, but as the day progressed and he tried to keep his extremities from freezing, he felt that if the snow didn't stop soon, he would lose his mind.

During the night the storm blew itself out. The wind died and before dawn the stars came out, while in the east the last of the shrinking crescent moon appeared like a livid wound against the sky.

Deke's sleep was disturbed and he jerked and twitched like a dog hunting in its dreams. His own dreams were tumbled, confused, overlaid with growing dread. He nearly awakened several times, but somehow slept on, gripped by images too awful for his sleeping mind to contemplate. These images whirled vaguely just beneath the threshold of his consciousness, until finally, in the way dream visions do, they rose to the surface in a burst of terrible clarity. He jerked upright, his eyes wide and staring, every muscle rigid with horror and fear.

"Mother!" he cried, and leaped to his feet, fighting free of the blankets.

Barr awakened and looked at him askance. "Son, what..."

"Come on," Deke said, and ran to where Micmac was tethered with his father's stallion. He threw his saddle on her back and in an instant had it girthed securely. She whinnied loudly in protest at this rough treatment, but he got her bridle on and quickly checked to make sure his weapons were at hand.

His father had followed and now grabbed the reins. "What is it, Deke? Tell me what's going on!"

"Mother...oh, God." Tears stood trembling at the edge of Deke's lashes as he fought for control. He leaped into the saddle and looked down at his father's frightened expression.

"What about your mother?" Barr demanded.

"God, Papa, I think she's dying!" Deke's voice was a hoarse shout, his face agonized.

Barr registered the ghastly pallor on Deke's features and knew if his son had called him that name from earliest childhood he was on the verge of hysteria.

"Hang on," he said, and saddled his own horse swiftly. He called to the soldiers who now were waking from the commotion. Hawk ran up with Melak on his heels.

"Follow as quickly as you can," Barr ordered, his voice harsher than Hawk had ever heard it. Then he swung aboard the russet stallion, who reared. Sawing savagely at the reins, Barr fought the horse to a standstill.

Glancing back to be sure his father was with him, Deke dug his heels into Micmac's sides, and with a cry of animal desperation, urged her to a run. In moments she was racing away across the countryside, her hoofbeats muffled by the recent snowfall.

Cursing at the stallion, Barr drove him to a gallop, following the barely illuminated path his son had cut through the phosphorescent snowfield. Overhead, the sky wheeled slowly in its indifferent majesty, and soon the ethereal moon was covered over by dark clouds. Moments later, its delicate glow dimmed, then, abruptly, was snuffed out.

Tilva and Andara finally had gotten the last of their pharmacopeia organized and put away. It had been the last thing they unpacked after the long trip from Spring Camp, but now it was done and they could relax. Andara had supervised most of the move, directing servants with the easy assurance of a lifetime. Her patron's pregnancy was so advanced that she practically waddled, and tired very easily.

Tilva rubbed the small of her back where it ached almost all the time and half-sat, half-fell into an easy chair. She smiled at Andara, noticing how grown-up the girl was becoming, and how beautiful. Each day Andara seemed to ripen further, and with a start, she realized her acolyte's thirteenth birthday was almost upon them, the fifth of November it would be. She beckoned the girl to her and gave her an affectionate squeeze. "Thank you for doing all this work, Andara," she said. "I don't think I could have managed it without you."

Andara returned the hug with a gesture of dismissal. "Please, it was my pleasure, my lady. Would you like some tea? The stove's set up and I have to start a fire anyway."

"I'd like that," Tilva said. "Perhaps some raspberry leaf added would be good. I'll be in labor soon enough," she added, her hands going to her enormous stomach.

"How do you feel?" Andara asked.

"Ready," Tilva said with a wry grin. "Ready to have this little one out here in the world."

"What does it feel like to carry a baby?" Andara wondered while she built a fire in the stove and put water on to boil. She selected a variety of soothing herbs including the raspberry leaf Tilva had requested and put them in a cup. For herself she made chamomille with a dash of mint.

"Heavy," Tilva told her. "Like being a turtle on its back."

"I mean in here," and the girl pointed to her forehead.

"Ah," Tilva said thoughtfully. "With this one, there is definitely a communication of some kind between us. I almost know her name already."

"What is it?" Andara asked, interested.

"No, that has to wait for Barr to come home," Tilva said. "I promised we'd name her together."

"What is it like being married?" Andara took out honey and set it on the table with a spoon.

Tilva's eyes sharpened, but the girl deliberately busied herself at the stove. "It's like a bed of roses," she said. "Sometimes wonderful, but then there are thorns."

"How do you stand it when he's gone? I mean," and she blushed, "Worrying about him and all that?"

Tilva laughed. "Barr Wolfson can take care of himself better than any man I ever saw," she said. "Besides, you know perfectly well, when it's your time there's no point in fighting it. These decisions are often made before we're born for reasons we may never understand, so worry doesn't serve much purpose."

"That's all well and good to say," Andara muttered to herself.

"Deke is pretty good at taking care of himself, too," Tilva said pointedly.

"Accidents happen," Andara said.

"There are no accidents," Tilva said. "There are only probability and karma, and these two forces guide Deke as well as they guide you. If you are meant to be together, you will be."

"What do you think?" Andara asked quickly.

Tilva smiled. "I believe your karmas are intertwined. I'm sure that's why your mother asked me to teach and look after you when she lay dying." Her expression was musing as she remembered. Then she met Andara's eyes. "You will always be my first daughter, Andara. Whatever else happens, I've always loved you as if you were my very own."

Andara's eyes filled and she swallowed hard. "You're the only mother I've ever known," she whispered. "That's why it's so important to have your blessing."

"My blessing?" Understanding lit Tilva's eyes. "Oh, my darling girl, of course you do! Can't you tell? I think I've always seen you together in my mind's eye, ever since you were infants."

"I'm in love with him," Andara said, looking at her.

"That's good, because I know he's in love with you."

"How can you be sure?"

"A mother knows things," Tilva said with a small smile.

"Do you think we're too young?"

"Chronological age is only one way of counting maturity," Tilva replied. "It's my belief that you are linked through many lifetimes, many experiences. Neither of you is typical for your age, as you know. I take some of the credit for that; my training had the effect of making you grow up swiftly."

"Do you think we're too young for..." Andara blushed and fell silent.

Tilva's gaze was penetrating. "Has that already become an issue?"

"Aye," Andara replied. "Not," she added hurriedly, "That we've done anything yet."

"You've come close, though, haven't you?" Tilva's eyes were sympathetic.

Andara nodded, embarrassed.

"Do you know what to do to avoid pregnancy?" Tilva asked, becoming practical.

Andara nodded again, her embarrassment growing.

"You know there are no perfect methods, I suppose."

"I know, that's what worries me most."

Tilva sighed. She considered all the answers she could give and finally decided on the one that felt truest to her own heart. Altogether, that was usually the best approach. "Andara, you're both very young, but life being what it is and our futures being so unpredictable, I see no reason to put off any joy you might be able to find. I wasn't much older than you when I married Barr, and I don't regret a day of it."

"Were you...I mean, did you..." Andara was having trouble expressing herself clearly.

"What would you like to know?" Amusement battled with Tilva's concern for her protégé.

"Did it hurt the first time?" Andara asked, her face crimson.

"Aye," Tilva responded. "I got over it."

"Why does it hurt women at first?"

Tilva shrugged. "Maybe it's nature's way of making sure we pick the right man. Sex for women is rarely casual the way it can be for men. We are, after all, left with the consequences." She gestured to her swollen abdomen.

"I'm scared to have a child," Andara admitted.

"That's normal at your age."

They were silent for a while and Andara served the tea. Tilva sipped hers thoughtfully. "How does your father feel about this?"

"Ruins, I've not discussed it with him!" Andara laughed aloud at the idea. "He's so skittish trying to protect my virtue, I could never talk to him about it."

"It's difficult for men with their daughters," Tilva smiled. "I remember how my own fought against me leaving with Barr."

"That must have been so frightening for you," Andara said.

"When the soldiers came into our town, I was terrified. I was even more terrified by Barr at first. But he promised peace between our people if I came away with him as his wife. He wanted to marry me from the moment our eyes met."

"What did you want?"

"I wanted it, too," Tilva admitted. "I've never told anyone this, but when I saw him, it was as if I recognized him. And besides, he was so exciting and masculine compared to the men I knew, he filled me with emotion right from the beginning."

"I guess it's in the blood, then," Andara said.

"Aye," Tilva said, smiling. "Follow your heart, Andara. Don't worry about what other people expect you to do. If you always follow your heart's true path, you can never take a misstep in life. If you feel you are ready for mature love, then who is anyone to tell you differently? Ultimately you know yourself better than any other. Only you can be the final arbiter in your own life."

Andara came and gave Tilva a swift kiss. "Thank you, my lady," she said. "I do love him, you know. I think I'd die if he didn't want me."

"But he does," Tilva told her. "And he'll be back any day now."

"Aye," and Andara's expression grew dreamy.

For the next few days Andara and Tilva were confined indoors by a nasty patch of weather that started with an ice storm and graduated to a snow-storm before ending the day before Andara's birthday. That evening they listened to the wind dying and played backgammon to pass the time. After losing her third game in a row, Andara said, "The luck is all yours tonight, my lady. I think I'll quit while I still have a few shreds of dignity left."

Tilva laughed merrily, very pleased with herself. She put away the game and said, "Yes, I'm feeling very lucky these days, it's true."

They ate their dinner and fed Canis and Hopi when they came in from outside. Hopi had come into season shortly after the army had departed, and in the way of canines everywhere, Canis had bred her repeatedly during her receptive period. Now Tilva and Andara were looking forward to signs that Hopi was pregnant, and they eyed her speculatively while she bolted her food.

"I'm sure she is," Andara said. "Look how shiny her coat is! And her aura! She has the same look in her eye you had at the beginning!" The girl laughed.

Tilva joined her. "You're right. Barr will be happy; puppies and a new baby!"

As if sensing she was the subject of their discussion, Hopi came and sat between them, receiving their petting hands as if it were her due. Canis, as was typical for him, lay down a little distance away, watching them with his great, dark eyes. He yawned widely and put his head on his paws. Andara also yawned and stood up.

"I think I'll turn in," she said. "I'm very tired tonight for some reason."

"Sleep well, dear," Tilva said.

"You, too, my lady." Andara gave her a kiss, then went into the alcove that once had belonged to Deke, where she now slept while her father was away. She let the hangings at the door fall closed and got undressed. Rinsing her face and hands in the bowl at one side of the sleeping area, she poured fresh water from a pitcher into a cup and brushed her teeth quickly. When she was finished, she used the chamber pot and climbed into bed, pulling the down-filled comforter around her shoulders. It was chilly in the tent and she snaked one arm out to turn off the oil lamp. A moment later she saw light from the main room enter as Hopi pushed her nose between the hangings and came in. She rested her head on the edge of the bed and Andara could feel her tail wagging. She patted the bed and Hopi jumped up, circling once and curling into a ball against Andara's feet. The she-wolf sent an image into Andara's mind of Deke sleeping, and Andara wondered if that meant Deke was somewhere near enough for Hopi to perceive using her esper sense, or if it had something to do with the alcove and bed they shared.

She didn't know which it was, but now that the wolf had put the idea in her mind, she found her thoughts turning in his direction. She felt warmth between her legs just thinking about him, and turned on her side, trying to sleep. Maybe he would return tomorrow. That would be the best birthday present she could imagine. It had been too lonely in the tent city with him gone. Sighing, she rolled over again and Hopi shifted against her feet. After a while her breathing evened and she fell asleep.

In the main living area, Tilva had dozed off while reading. She woke up having to use the chamber pot and pushed herself upright with difficulty. After relieving herself, she felt restless, and stuck her head outside into the night air. It was cold and crisp and the snow looked very pretty covering the city and ground. The stars were bright overhead, and she decided to take a walk and get some fresh air. She thought she'd gather some pine nuts for a special dish she wanted to prepare for Andara's birthday dinner the following day, and put on a warm cloak over her nightgown. Gathering up a collecting basket, she went out through the tent flap. Canis rose to follow.

They walked through the pristine, white world in silence. Tilva gazed delightedly at the sliver-moon where it recently had risen in the pre-dawn gloaming. The air smelled incredible; the scent of wood smoke wafting from Winter Camp's many stoves serving to accentuate the purity of the atmosphere.

After walking for several minutes Tilva came to the edge of the pine barrens, and now the night was filled with the scent of evergreens. Her senses felt unusually acute as she took in the beauty of the natural world around her. She held her stomach cradled in her hands, gazing at the stars and sky, and could feel a most profound connection with the living earth on which she stood, could feel the earth's energy rising through her body, filling her with light. For an instant she felt joy more intense than she could remember, and gave herself over to the emotion completely. She was about to reach for a pine cone when beside her, Canis gave a low growl.

She looked at the wolfish dog whose every hair was standing up on his back, making him seem even larger. He lifted his lips in a more concentrated snarl, baring his long fangs ferociously. When she looked up she saw a group of horsemen standing motionlessly just inside the tree line. The collecting basket fell from her fingers. The riders moved clear of the trees, and her heart gave a lurch. Gant Murdock spurred his horse towards her, his red-rimmed eyes filled with a cruel and sullen glow.

Tilva turned to run, unwieldy with her pregnancy, and the riders galloped after her. Canis leaped for one of the men and pulled him from his horse. In a second he had nearly decapitated the man and went after another. The sound of his jaws crunching through a man's leg was followed by the sharp report of a rifle, and the dog gave a sudden yelp and fell back. He struggled to his feet, dragging himself after the attacking riders, his snarls and growls terrible to hear. There was another rifle shot and Canis jerked, then lay still.

Gant rode Tilva down, and as he passed he knocked her to the ground. She heaved herself up, fear making her wild, and continued running, holding her stomach with her hands.

Gant turned his horse and jumped off. The men with him did the same. They closed in on her remorselessly, and she drew her dagger from its sheath and slashed the air between them, her breath coming in quick gasps.

"Come now, sister-in-law," Gant said, extending his hand for the knife with a grin so evil Tilva knew he meant to murder her. "Don't make this difficult."

"When my husband finds out what you've done, he'll kill you," she said between gritted teeth, her fear for her unborn daughter too strong to contain. She put her left hand protectively across her stomach.

Gant's foot shot out and he kicked the knife from her hand. In an instant he had her wrists in a grip so tight she couldn't move. He leaned closer, his sour breath and foul body odor filling her nostrils, sickening her. Nuzzling her cheek, he said, "A pity you're carrying, sister-in-law, else I'd not be able to restrain myself...as it is, pregnant women wilt my stalk." He slid a body dagger from the sheath strapped to his forearm and put it to her breast. "Don't worry," he whispered, his expression filled with sadistic glee. "I'll be quick."

Tilva lunged away from him, but before she took two steps she felt his hand come down on her shoulder and grab her hard. There was a sudden burning pain in her back and she gasped. He spun her around and plunged the blade again, into her stomach. Tilva screamed in agony. The knife thrust into her breast, twisting, and then, knowing she was almost finished, she concentrated the last of her remaining energy into a massive outflow of psychic force to make a Sending, and as consciousness began to fade from her mind, she called her son's name.

Gant threw her limp body into the snow and wiped his knife blade on his pants. He stood for a moment watching the snow darken beneath her, then climbed onto his horse. With a gesture to his men, he started back to the pine barrens, and after a second, they followed.

Tilva was barely aware of them leaving. She could feel her life ebbing fast. Suddenly her body convulsed and she felt her uterus contract. A gush of liquid flowed from between her legs and she moaned weakly. In a moment there was another contraction, this one more powerful, followed by a third of even greater intensity.

As she lay writhing in the ice and snow, her dying body, in a desperate attempt to preserve her baby's life, ejected her infant daughter in a torrent of blood and amniotic fluids.

"I'm sorry, baby," she whispered, the tears falling from her eyes to mingle with the blood on the snow. "...so sorry..." she said again, and felt everything grow dimmer while she struggled to remain conscious. She could see her baby's arms and legs flail feebly and tried to reach out for her, but failed.

In the east, the sky began to lighten as the new day began.

Deke drove Micmac at a swift gallop, his mind filled with the awareness of his mother's scream for help. Wind-forced tears streamed unheeded across his cheeks to freeze on his skin. While he rode, he probed outwards with his sensitivity, seeking his mother's location. He could feel her somewhere ahead, and with all his strength, projected his thoughts across the intervening distance separating them, putting images of comfort and succor into her weakening consciousness, placing images of himself and his love for her into her mind that she might somehow find the strength to live long enough for him to get to her. Concentrating with a part of himself he never knew existed, he projected his own energy and life force into her, joining that energy to hers that he might help support her body's functions a little longer.

So intent was he that he almost overshot his mark, and pulled Micmac to a skidding halt in the snow near the pine barrens.

He took in the dead man and Canis in a sweeping glance, then ran to where his mother lay with something in the snow between her legs. What he saw when he got there almost unhinged his mind, but with desperate control he sent a tentative probe into his mother's thoughts and felt that she still lived, though barely. In one motion he swept off his sheepskin-lined cloak and put it over her and the infant he could feel was dead. He stroked her face and kissed her forehead, the tears flowing freely now, and cradled her head and shoulders in his lap as he sat in the snow. Her mind responded to his emotional contact and her lips moved. He bent down to put his ear near her mouth and strained to hear.

"Deke," she breathed. "Love you more than life itself...tell your father I'm sorry; sorry and..." She struggled briefly then continued. "...and that I'll love him...love him 'til time ends..."

"Mother," Deke said, his expression stricken. "Please, don't...!"

"Goodbye, my son..." Her body relaxed against him as her breath sighed away.

"Mother." Deke caressed her cheek, knowing her spirit was no longer attached to her body. He kissed her lips tenderly and as he was drawing the cloak to cover her face, he heard the thunder of his father's horse. He looked up as Barr dismounted. "She's gone, Papa," he said, his voice breaking. "She's gone."

Barr knelt beside them, took Tilva from Deke's arms and held her, laying his cheek alongside hers. He rocked her for a minute, the mute grief in his eyes tearing Deke's heart.

"She told me to tell you...she told me to tell you she was sorry, and that she would love you until time ends." Deke's throat closed and he fought down the sob that tried to force its way out. He knew that once started, he'd never stop, and there was still something that had to be done, something he had to tell his father.

Barr squeezed his eyes shut and shook all over.

"Father." Deke touched his shoulder and the chieftain opened his eyes to look at him. "Father, I know who did this," he said.

"So do I," Barr rasped. "May God forgive me for not killing him when I had the chance. Andara was right all along, and I didn't listen to her."

"It's my fault," Deke said bleakly. "I was the one who had to be so smart..."

"No, Deke. This is not on your head. I made the decision."

"The responsibility belongs to us both, then," Deke said, his heart beginning to fill with such hatred he could hardly breathe.

"Aye," Barr agreed, and for an instant Deke saw a red flicker in his father's dark eyes.

There was the sound of hoofbeats on the frozen ground, scores of them, and in a minute the Wolf riders clattered to a halt nearby. Hawk jumped from his saddle and approached Barr and Deke. When he saw Tilva his expression changed to one of shock and sorrow. He looked around and his experienced eyes read the signs that told him what had happened.

Barr rose, laying Tilva gently in the snow. His face filled with rage that made Hawk take a step backwards. The chieftain pulled his .45 from its belt holster and stormed over to the russet stallion.

With an inarticulate cry of anguish and fury, and before anyone could make a move to stop him, he put the muzzle to the horse's head and jerked the trigger. The sound of the shot echoed across the countryside and everyone recoiled in consternation as the animal fell dead.

"Goddamned horse is too slow," he whispered, glaring around, daring anyone to disagree with him. "If he had gotten here just a little sooner..." The chieftain's voice trailed off and he looked at Hawk, the pain in his eyes almost too much for his friend to bear. "Make a litter," he said. "We'll bring her home. And then Deke and I will take care of Gant Murdock." His dark gaze scanned the area, taking in everything. He looked at Canis and his lips tightened. "Don't forget the wolf; we'll send them onward together."

Hawk gestured to Melak who quickly organized several soldiers. They made two litters, one to carry Tilva and the infant, one for Canis. Silently, consumed by their sorrow, they headed for Winter Camp, and Tilva's pavilion.

Andara awakened abruptly from dream into nightmare. Hopi leaped off the bed when the soldiers came in and ran to the outer room. Throwing on her clothes, Andara came out of the alcove, saw Barr with Deke and her father, saw their faces, then looked to where the men were carrying the litters into Tilva's room. Barr followed, saying, "Put her on the bed."

Awareness grew in Andara's mind, and she stared at Deke, starting to reach for his thoughts, but something stopped her. His expression was closed off, filled with unspoken suffering. Taken aback, she pushed past the soldiers into Tilva's room with a cry of realization. Her father's hands caught and pulled her into his arms.

"What...how..." Andara struggled to free herself. Then she saw Barr's eyes and sent a quick probe into his mind. She felt buffeted by the force of his emotions and withdrew after a moment. "Gant Murdock," she whispered.

"Deke," Barr said with an effort.

"I'm here." Deke appeared and took his father's arm. His face still had that strange look, Andara saw, cold and withdrawn, almost unrecognizable.

"Can your wolf backtrack the trail?"

"Aye," he said.

"Andara." Barr looked at the girl. "Please, stay with her. She would have wanted you to be here. We'll have the funeral tomorrow."

Tears streamed from Andara's eyes. Her throat closed and she couldn't speak. She nodded.

"Thank you," Barr said, his voice hoarse with the effort of maintaining control. Andara's heart went out to him and instinctively, she sent a part of herself into his mind again, this time touching his thoughts sympathetically.

"Tell the men to get fresh mounts," Barr ordered Melak. "Bring horses for me and Deke and get our gear transferred."

"Aye, m'lord." Melak ran to comply.

"He came with several men," Deke said, his voice strained, as if forcing words out was more effort than he could manage. "All from the Murdock clan."

"How do you know?" Hawk asked.

"They left their stench-filled echo behind," he said, and Andara shivered at the savagery in his tone. "We'll find them at the Murdock camp."

"If his clan has given him shelter..." Barr's voice broke off as he contemplated his son.

"This is vendetta," Deke said, his tone deadly. Everyone in the room stared at him. "Two hundred of us will be enough."

Barr nodded. He went to the bedside, took Deke's cloak from Tilva's body, and drew the bedcovers over her. Of their own volition his fingers trailed

199

through her hair and caressed her cheek. Then he covered her face. He handed the cloak to Deke, who, ignoring the blood, wrapped it around himself, drawing the hood low over his eyes.

"Let's go," Barr said and left the room, Hawk following.

Andara caught Deke's arm and he stopped, unable to look at her. He knew if he met her eyes or allowed her into his mind the stiff-lipped control he maintained at such great cost would shatter, leaving him helpless as a babe for the work he had to do.

"Deke," she whispered, her grief searing his lacerated spirit. "Deke," she repeated, and then, knowing he was unable to reply, took his hand and brought it to her lips. His fingers clenched into a fist and he pulled away from her. He followed his father outside where the soldiers had brought fresh horses and were transferring Micmac's saddle and bridle quickly, with a minimum of fuss.

Seconds later he was in the saddle again, astride a tall, speckled, grey mare whose breath made plumes of smoke in the freezing air. His father mounted the bay gelding brought for him and pulled alongside Deke. The two exchanged glances and turned their horses back to the pine barrens. Deke Sent a mental call to Hopi who loped ahead. She reached the place where the Murdock clansman still lay in the snow. Sniffing around, she came to where Canis had fallen and howled with haunting mournfulness. Deke clenched his jaw, the stark loneliness of the she-wolf's cry making his chest hurt. Hopi found the place where Gant Murdock had gotten off his horse. She snarled fiercely, her hackles rising. Deke sent her a series of images which she acknowledged by backtracking the riders to the edge of the pines. She paused for a moment to make certain Deke understood, then took off into the barrens, following the trail at a pace that forced the soldiers to gallop after her.

They followed the wolf over icy pine needles and through whipping branches that lashed their faces. Every one of the two hundred men was filled with the same lethal rage that consumed the chieftain and his son, joined in a commonality of emotion born out of their grief at the passing of this gentle woman who had been their people's most gifted healer. Most of the men could remember times when Tilva had saved the lives of soldiers who should have died from gangrene or other complications from wounds received during battle. They remembered her abroad in the night delivering babies, tending the sick, comforting the dying. When they thought of how she had died, in pain and terror for her baby, their souls burned to avenge her, to spill blood in such quantities as would drown their pain and quiet the madness they saw in their chieftain's eyes.

They rode for an hour or more before the trail led out of the pines and into open country. Now the riders had no need of the wolf; the tracks were perfectly visible in the snow and they pounded along at a swift canter. They could see the trail indeed led towards the Murdock camp, and all nodded grimly at this confirmation of Deke's earlier statement. His intuitiveness pleased them, reminded them of his mother and how she also had known things in advance.

People were just getting up and about in the Murdock camp when the Wolf riders thundered into their tent village. Men of the Murdock clan rushed from their homes to see the grim-faced soldiers lower their weapons and point them at anyone and everyone they saw. There was a staccato rattle of gunfire and people on the ground began dying. The horsemen circled through the village, seeking Gant Murdock and his associates.

"Bring me his Number One," Barr shouted to Hawk. "I want Murdock alive," he told his men.

Deke had his rifle across his forearm and snapped the bayonet onto the end. He saw a man running frantically and pulled one of his body daggers from its forearm sheath. With a quick flip of his wrist, the dagger flew through the air and landed in the man's back. Deke galloped past, the emotion rising in him as he looked for Gant. With his bayonet he slashed into any tent he passed, looked inside, then moved on when he didn't see his uncle. He tried to Send his awareness out to search but discovered he couldn't separate from the insane anger that flooded him with bloodlust. He wanted to immerse himself in blood, feel his hands swimming in it.

When they found Gant, he was asleep in a drunken stupor. Melak dragged him up from his bed and brought him out of his tent. Gant looked around blearily, unable to grasp what was going on. The screams and yells of his people filled his ears and he stood stunned as a man ran up to him and was dropped by a bullet to the back of his head. Brains exploded in Gant's face as the man's forward momentum carried him into the former governor.

Deke jerked his bayonet out of the Murdock soldier he had just killed and swung his machete at a charging man whose horrible scream cut off as the blade sliced into his throat. Two Murdock clansmen groveled in the snow begging for mercy and he dismounted, striding towards them as if in a dream. One reached out to clutch his knees, and with a sudden motion, he slashed with the machete and the man had no hands. Deke's next blow split his skull in half. He stabbed his bayonet into the second man, twisting it viciously to do maximum damage, while the man shrieked in terror and agony that left Deke completely unmoved.

A young girl dressed only in nightclothes screamed by, and he watched as one of the soldiers cut her down mercilessly. Vendetta of this kind launched against a community could only be satisfied by its complete destruction. He climbed onto the speckled grey and rode systematically through the village, seeking more victims. He was aware there was something wrong with him, knew it wasn't like him to have so little feeling for helpless innocents, but he was beyond caring now. His pain was too strong, still burned too brightly for him to stop the flow of Murdock blood which was the only thing he felt could ease his agony. He finally saw Melak and two other soldiers holding Gant and spurred the grey over. He could hardly lift his arm but he managed to sheathe the machete and approach the stolid sergeant.

Moments later, Barr joined them, and as the chieftain looked at the blood-spattered face of his son, he saw the emotional disconnection and grew frightened for Deke's sanity. Deke's right arm was bloodied to the shoulder; his bayonet dripped with bits of flesh and bone. There was a look in his blue eyes Barr had never seen before: grief and a killing rage unquenched even by the many deaths he had inflicted.

Barr's gaze fell on Gant.

"What do you want to do with him, m'lord?" Melak asked, looking up at the chieftain.

Barr glanced around, saw Hawk dragging a man roped behind his horse. When Hawk reached his friend, he said, "Here's the Number One, all wrapped up for you."

"Get up," Barr ordered the man, his voice made more terrible for the quiet cruelty in it.

The man slowly rose to his feet, looking up at the chieftain.

"You know the law," Barr grated, "Yet you sheltered him. Why?"

"It was only going to be for the winter," the man said sullenly.

"Do you know what he did this dawn?" Barr's rage rippled between them like something fiery and alive.

The man looked away, unable to meet his eyes.

Barr's foot lashed out and struck the man with such force that his larynx was crushed instantly. The man fell to his knees, struggling vainly to get air past his broken windpipe. Hawk made as if to shoot him, but Barr restrained his hand. "Let him choke to death," he said. "Slowly."

He turned his attention back to Gant Murdock. For a long time, while the Number One gagged and retched hideously, Barr regarded the former governor.

After a while, at his horse's feet, the man expired, eyes bulging, face purple.

Melak spoke again. "What're your orders, m'lord?"

Deke stared at Gant with silent hatred, waiting for his father to pass sentence, barely able to restrain his murderous passion.

Finally, his eyes turning inward, his voice devoid of all emotion, Barr said, "Crucify him."

Inside the graceful pavilion, Andara and the servants cleaned Tilva's body, washing away the blood and dressing her in fresh clothes. They did the same for the dead infant, swaddling her in clean, soft fabric and laying her against Tilva's torso. All of them wept with pity when they placed the baby inside the crook of her mother's arm.

Andara could hardly cope with the magnitude of her grief. She remembered how happy Tilva had been the previous evening and burst into fresh tears, unable to believe this had happened. She touched her patron's cool cheek with trembling fingers and opened her mind to sense the world around her in the way she had been taught from earliest childhood, seeking any trace of Tilva's spirit.

There was nothing.

The servants finished what they were doing, bundled up the blood-drenched clothes, and withdrew quietly, leaving Andara alone with her sorrow.

She tried to imagine what would happen to her without Tilva's presence in her life. The People would need another trained healer, and Andara knew she was the logical choice despite her age and inexperience. Though she had assisted in surgeries of all sorts, she never had performed a serious one herself. As far as making diagnoses went, she knew she had talent, but without the years of further training she would have gained at Tilva's side, she was afraid she might be more of a danger than a help. Only in herb lore was she in any way adept-proficient, yet even so, it would take time for her to reach her full potential.

Her thoughts went to Deke and Barr and she began to cry again. She sensed that despite the vastness of his loss: wife, daughter, even his dog, the chieftain would find a way to cope. It was Deke she worried about, because he never had experienced death in a personal way. No one close to him had ever died. And to have the death occur in this way...Andara was afraid of what the shock might do to him. His love for his mother had always been so profound, even protective, particularly when his parents were fighting.

She sighed a sigh that felt neverending. Then she sat in the easy chair near the bed, wrapping herself in a blanket from the rack at its foot. Her eyes fell on Tilva's still features, and she thought how even after such a death her patron's face remained ethereally beautiful. A sob worked its way out of her throat as she remembered that Tilva was only thirty-three.

Andara leaned back and closed her eyes. She curled into a ball with the blanket clutched in her fingers, and soon, emotionally exhausted, dozed.

She was awakened by the touch of a hand on her shoulder. Opening her eyes, she saw the chieftain standing over her, swaying with exhaustion. Her gaze went quickly to the spring-wound fort clock on the nightstand and she saw that it was early evening. Rising from the chair, she turned up the oil lamp and the shadows retreated.

"I'll take over," Barr said quietly, his dark eyes haunted and bloodshot. His clothes were covered with dried blood and dirt, and the hugeness of the sorrow radiating from him made her throat hurt.

"Is there anything I can get for you, my lord?" she asked. "Something to eat or drink...?"

He shook his head wordlessly and sat in the chair she had vacated.

Andara walked from the room and stepped outside where she called for servants. When they arrived, she told them to fill the tub in the living area. This they did, and then she ushered them out. She got a fire going in the stove and put a pot of water on to boil. Then she walked back into the bedroom with determination and stood over Barr.

His expression was harsh, unreadable to her.

"My lord," she said, and touched him. Immediately she was flooded with turbulent, grief-filled images. "My lord," she whispered, "You must get out of those clothes. They're wet and you'll catch pneumonia."

He looked at her briefly, his eyes overflowing with sadness. After a moment he turned his gaze back to where Tilva lay.

"Please," Andara said, and touched his shoulder gently.

"Go away," he said.

"My lord, I won't leave until you let me help you." Andara's voice was stubborn, and once again the chieftain looked at her.

"Can't you let me alone?" he said.

"No," Andara said firmly. "Come, I've drawn a hot bath, and I want you to get into it. Don't make me call for help."

Barr's eyes went to her face, took in her set expression. "Andara, your father is waiting for you at his tent."

"He can wait a little longer. Please, my lord, don't fight me on this. You know Tilva would agree with me."

At the mention of his wife's name, Barr's lips twisted and he covered his face with his hands. His shoulders shook uncontrollably and before Andara understood exactly what was happening, his arms went around her waist. Clotted, choking sounds came from him, and instinctively the girl embraced him, pressing his face to her and making small, comforting noises. His weeping was heartrending and tears started from Andara's eyes again while she stroked his hair and tried to breathe past his strangled grip.

After a while his weeping subsided and he turned his bearded face up to look into her eyes, his own filled with the depth of his suffering. She smoothed his hair away from his forehead and said,

"Come, please, you'll feel better if you bathe."

Sighing, he rose unsteadily and went with her to the living area, where he dropped his weapons and stripped off his clothing while she looked away. He climbed into the tub and the water's heat began to warm his chilled flesh. Mechanically, he began to soap himself.

Andara poured a cup of very strong chamomille tea with extract of poppy added. She wanted Barr to sleep, knew that sleep would help heal and prepare him for the emotional turmoil the following day would bring. She added an oversized dollop of grain alcohol and a liberal quantity of honey and brought him the steaming cup. "Drink this, my lord. It will help you."

He looked at her expression, saw she wouldn't leave until he complied, and took the cup. He caught her hand in his for a moment and squeezed it.

Andara nodded. She patted his hand and watched while he drank down the tea. "Are you sure you won't eat something?"

He shook his head, thinking that after today he might never eat again.

"Will you be all right tonight?" Andara was worried.

"I'll stay here," he said. Then, speaking with tremendous effort, he added, "Would you stop by Deke's tent? I'd rest easier knowing you were with him."

Andara's face was a question.

"I'm not sure what he might do if left alone tonight," Barr admitted.

"I'll see to him," she said.

Barr's features relaxed slightly, and Andara knew the opiate was working, acting quickly on his empty stomach.

"Thank you, Andara," he said.

She nodded and brought him a cotton bath towel and a fresh change of warm clothing. "Don't worry about the tub; the servants can take care of it in the morning," she said. Then she put on her cloak and stepped into a pair of sheepskin boots. "If you need me I'll be at Deke's. Please send for me if there's anything I can do for you."

Barr nodded.

In a moment she went out the tent door into the evening air. It was very cold, far below freezing, and the snow squeaked against the soles of her boots. She walked to Deke's bachelor tent which now was located in a choice spot near his father's. Since the move to Winter Camp, the newly made bachelors had scattered their tents through the city as was customary, each living wherever he wanted.

Andara rattled the knocker at the door and when there was no answer, went in. Hopi greeted her with a little whimper and she patted the wolf. She looked around the room. It was dark, the oil lamp on the table turned off. A faint glow from the bedroom was the only light. Turning up the table lamp made the room spring into definition and she gasped in shock. Deke was sitting in one of the easy chairs, motionless. His eyes were open but stared blankly straight ahead. His face, his clothes, his hands; every part of him was covered in caked, dried blood. She went to him and touched him but got no response. Fear rose in her and she said loudly, "Deke! What are you doing?"

His gaze went past her, focused on something only he could see.

She touched his cheek and was frightened by how cold his skin was. In a minute she had wood in the stove and a fire started. She left the stove door open to let the heat into the room. Taking his hands, she chafed his flesh vigorously, trying to get his circulation going. When he made no response, she said in a voice tinged with panic, "Come on, Deke, help me! Please don't do this..."

She tried to put her thoughts into his mind but was rebuffed by a defensive screen too strong to penetrate no matter what she did. Tears started in her eyes again and she wiped them away angrily.

She ran to the tent door and called for servants. When they arrived, she said, "Fill a tub, please, as hot as you can get it."

The servants complied, and before long the tub was steaming in the center of the room. She thanked them and when they had gone, tied fast the tent flap, loaded more wood into the stove and went back to Deke's side. He still sat as if transfixed, staring at nothing whatsoever.

Hopi thrust her muzzle into Andara's hand worriedly, and she stroked the wolf's head. The girl searched briefly, saw there was no water bowl or food dish set out, and took care of both. Then she went back to Deke, wondering what to do next. She peeled the blood-soaked cloak off him and hung it on a peg. The body daggers came off with a clatter. The heavy, wool sweater followed, and she struggled it over his head and off his arms, throwing the sodden garment on a towel on the floor. She untied the doeskin shirt underneath, and was shocked to see that this, too, was saturated with blood. When she got it off him, fighting his apathy all the way, she saw that the skin on his chest also was slick with blood.

"Deke," she said, "Stand up. You've got to help me, do you hear?" She rubbed his arms briskly, felt how cold and stiff they were, how frozen all his body was, and knew she had to get him into the tub. She pulled him to his feet and he stood quietly, his rough breathing the only sound he made.

Andara unbuckled his weapons belt and put it on a table. His boots were destroyed, with blood pooled inside them. Grimacing, she pulled off his socks and dropped them with his other clothes. The strings on his doeskin trousers were swollen and wet and she struggled with the knots. Finally, frustrated, she took a paring knife from the kitchen and cut the thongs. She pulled the stiffened leather down, lifting his feet one at a time to free them from the pants legs. He allowed her to remove his long woolen underwear and then followed her docilely to the tub.

She quickly checked him over, looking for any wound that might account for the blood on his body and found nothing at all. All this blood, then, came from another or others. She looked at his right hand, saw the blood under his fingernails and ground into the calluses on his palm, and shivered.

Moving him by small steps, she lifted his right foot and put it inside the tub, then his left until he stood in the water, so motionless and inwardly focused that she didn't know what to do to call him back. Once again she Sent a probe towards his mind, but this time subtly so he wouldn't detect it, and this lighter touch made contact with his awareness beneath his conscious mind's defense system. What she *saw* there frightened and shocked her anew. She pursed her lips and tried to get him to sit down. He resisted, his knees locked, his eyes wide and startled. A small cry escaped him and for a second he looked like someone struggling to wake from a nightmare, and failing. His body trembled as he was racked by shivering. His teeth chattered behind his blued lips and she reached for him to make sure he didn't fall.

Deciding abruptly, she kicked off her boots, stripped off her socks and pants, unbuttoned her shirt and took that off as well. Her undergarments were next, and then she climbed into the tub with him. She pressed herself to him, trying to warm him with her body. She took his arms and put them around her, reached up and kissed his cold cheek gently.

"Please, Deke," she pleaded, her voice filled with her misery. "You promised you'd come back to me, don't you remember?"

She felt the muscles in his arms tighten and then he was hugging her suffocatingly. His breathing was ragged in her ear and she allowed him to hold her until after a while she looked into his eyes. They were wide and anguished, but no longer remote. She took a step away and sat down in the water, drawing him into the intense heat with her. He gasped when she took a small bucket, dipped it in the water and poured it over his head. She did it again, then began to soap him thoroughly. She was on her knees between his legs washing his chest when she felt him touch her mind tentatively. She froze, afraid to move lest she startle him back into his previous near-catatonia. He looked into her eyes and with a relieved exhalation of breath, she leaned closer and kissed him with wild tenderness. His mouth responded to hers and slowly he ran his hands over her soap-slick fingers. She caught his hands and washed them carefully, rubbing until all the blood was out from under his nails. She was soaping his neck and shoulders when she felt his fingers touch her breasts, gently caressing her nipples before cupping them against his palms. Covering his hands with her slippery ones, she began to slide them across her skin, until they were around her hips. He pulled her closer, running his fingers across the small of her back and up her spine.

"Close your eyes," she whispered, and when he complied, she washed his face, rinsed him, and shampooed his hair. While she did this, his palms roamed her body slowly and dreamily, as if there was nothing in his mind guiding his actions. She pinioned his hands and rinsed his hair, finished washing his upper body, and sat back against the far end of the tub. She began to soap his legs and feet while he watched and soon worked her way to his thighs.

His breath caught in his throat. He felt her at the edges of his consciousness and was about to open his thoughts when he remembered, and clamped down his defenses. She let out a cry of pain at the unexpected surge of energy that blocked her contact and stared at him in disbelief. It had felt like the mental equivalent of a punch in the solar plexus.

Furious, she said, "I don't know what you did that you're trying to hide from me. But by God and all the ruins, if you ever do that to me again, I'll walk out of here and we'll be through."

His eyes flew open at the anger in her words and he slammed his awareness into hers with stunning force, making her feel some of the terror and loneliness ravaging his mind and spirit, forcing her to perceive that when he had closed his mind to her, he hadn't realized it would affect her the way it did.

She couldn't believe his strength. In the month since she last had connected with him in this way, his capabilities had grown much more powerful. And in his current state of mind, every contact was augmented by the rampaging force of his emotions. It occurred to her that he had no real idea how strong his esper sense had become, that now he could wound with a thought. Her anger receded, replaced by compassion greater than she had ever felt for another human being.

Deke's turmoil was monumental. Her threat to walk out nearly made him shut down again, but he fought to remain aware and connected. He reached for her, pulling her against him, his lips seeking hers with desperate need. She kissed him back, unable to resist the flow of energy rising in his mind. He moved his lips away and kissed her ear, her neck, her throat. Then he whispered, "I'm sorry, so sorry. I didn't know that would hurt you." He covered her mouth with his own again, holding her close. His heart pounded in his chest and then convulsively, he shoved her away. "But if I tell you what I did, you'll hate me forever." His voice became almost too low to hear. "And you'd be right," he added, his gaze turning inward again.

Anxiously, Andara kissed his eyes, his ears, his lips. "I could never hate you," she told him fervently. "But if you don't tell me, you'll hate yourself, and that might be worse."

"I already do," he said in the same low tone, and Andara shivered at the despair in his eyes. He seemed to consider for a moment, then said even more quietly so that she had to lean in to hear him, "And I keep thinking there's only one way to make reparation for what I've done, what I've caused to happen." The self-loathing in his eyes frightened her with its violence. Altogether she perceived a level of repressed violence in him so unlike his normal personality that she was unnerved. What was most disturbing was that the violence was not turned out into the world any more, but inward against himself. She felt a strong urge to hide his weapons but realized that if self-destruction was his goal, she couldn't stop him. She looked into his eyes, felt his soul's damage from the events of this day; her birthday, Andara remembered with a start. She sighed, and continued her line of thought. She believed he was so damaged that without immediate healing he either would find a way to kill himself directly, or would do it in the slow, indirect way those consumed by guilt and grief did, pulling away from the world until they were isolated emotionally, and simply perished.

No, Andara said to herself, setting her jaw stubbornly. She wasn't going to permit that to happen. Her love for him was too powerful, her love for his mother too much a part of who she was, for her ever to permit harm to come to him.

She moved against him swiftly, snaking her arms up across his chest to his shoulders, sending the water surging as she slid against his body. Her legs moved over his and she felt him stir against her thigh. She drew his mouth to hers, kissing him with seeking awareness that made his heart pound in his throat. Her hands smoothed his wet hair away from his temples and she kissed him again, filled with yearning that made her want to devour his lips with her own. She felt him pull her even nearer and closed her eyes, her breathing coming more rapidly.

When she opened them again she saw he was watching her while they kissed and she was startled by his strange expression.

He moved away from her, then stood up, taking her with him. Picking up a bucket of fresh water from outside the tub, he gently poured it over her, rinsing away the bathwater. A minute later she did the same for him and they stepped out together. She handed him a towel and he unfolded it and wrapped it around her shoulders. The feel of her body was reassuring until he realized she wasn't planning to go anywhere, that she intended to spend the night. He dropped his hands and stared at her, nervous as a cat.

Glancing at him sidelong from under her black lashes, Andara perceived his emotions as clearly as if they were written on his forehead. She dried herself and then wrapped a fresh towel around him, rubbing him all over with it, pausing every so often to reassure herself that his body temperature had risen and the chill was out of his flesh. She got a blanket from the rack at the foot of his bed and put it over his shoulders. She put on her heavy woolen shirt, then went to the kitchen where she set water on the stove to boil and took eggs and bread from the cold closet. He stood still, his eyes following her every move, his body churning with too many feelings to sort through. Her everyday motions as she fried half a dozen eggs and warmed the bread, melting butter into it, acted as a balm to his mind. He pulled a chair away from the table and sat, dropping his head into his hands. For a second he could feel the grief welling up inside him and his lips trembled.

Pain moved in waves through his body and he stifled a choking sob, not wanting Andara to see him weep like a baby. When he looked up out of eyes made luminous by his unshed tears, his vision played tricks on him. He saw her dark hair lying against the woolen fabric of her shirt and her slim but strong back, and something wrenched internally in his mind. For a moment it was as if he saw his mother preparing a meal for him as she had done daily for most of his life, and he looked away, drawing the blanket across his face to control the spasming of his features.

Somewhere inside him a part of his being was curled into a fetal position, and all that part wanted was his mother. He wanted her gentle hands pulling the tangles out of his heavy curls, her comforting way of putting misfortune into proper perspective. He wanted to feel her arms around him and the security of all the unconditional love she had rendered to him. Never in his life had he felt he had to prove anything to her; he always had known she accepted him exactly as he was, and that she treasured him beyond words.

Now she was gone, and the empty, cold feeling that had taken up residence around his heart made him want to die. He had even gone so far over the course of this day as to think of the various ways he could kill himself, and the only thing that had stopped him was that he could do no more harm to anyone he loved. He simply could not do that to his father or, and Deke gazed longingly at her where she flipped the eggs expertly onto a plate, to Andara. But he wanted to, yearned to hear the chaotic roar of his life silenced in one final act of bloodletting.

For a while during the massacre of the Murdock clan, he had felt his pain disappear, and had been filled with a rage so exquisite he had felt drunk with it, giddy with the sense of his own dark power. The killings, the blood, the screams: all had taken him out of himself to a level of transcendent energy where he knew he had become one with a force that pumped straight from the Universe into his limbic brain. And while he had swung his machete, he had known a feeling so dangerous to his sanity and soul that he was ravished by it.

Andara brought the eggs and bread along with a fork. She steeped some chamomille with opium as she had for his father, added grain whiskey in a generous dollop, some honey to sweeten it, and poured him a cup. After a moment, she poured one for herself as well.

"Eat," she told him.

He picked up the fork, and though he thought he had no appetite, once started he realized he was starving, and bolted the eggs, swabbing up the yolks with the bread.

"Good," she said, with satisfaction. "At least your body wants to live."

He looked at her sharply, feeling as if she had been reading his mind. It gave him an odd internal jolt to remember that she could do what he did, and that perhaps she could do it without his knowledge.

"Drink some of this," she said, pushing the cup towards him.

"What is it?" he asked, and she squeezed his hand, glad he was present enough to be interested.

"It'll make you feel good; warm, and a little sleepy," she said.

"Like the smoke."

She raised her brows questioningly.

"The Old Man showed me where to find the ingredients," Deke told her. "I'm sure..." His voice dropped and he forced himself to continue. "I'm sure my mother keeps...kept most of them."

"We'll look for them sometime," she told him.

He sipped the steaming liquid and looked at her where she sat perched on a wooden chair, her bare legs tucked under her and the place where her thighs met hidden tantalizingly behind a tail of her shirt. Realizing he was staring, he flushed and looked away, wondering how he could be thinking about that at a time like this.

He looked up to find Andara's eyes on him, and as he watched, she deliberately shifted her position so the shirt tail fell aside. His heart skipped a beat and he forced himself to drink more tea. Something strange was happening to him, something inside his head and body simultaneously. It felt like a hundred static-electric shocks pricking him everywhere at once and he stared at her, unable to imagine what she was doing, but aware she was doing something.

Andara concentrated, wondering if her attempt to touch that part of his electromagnetic essence which Tilva had referred to as *chi* had been successful. She could feel the imbalance inside him, but didn't know if she could change it to help him regain his emotional equilibrium. She saw him grow restless and withdrew her contact. Now she sipped her tea thoughtfully, meeting his eyes. She Sent a different kind of touch into his thoughts, and on an unspoken level, using something other than words, asked him to open his mind to her, and let her *see* what he was hiding.

He covered his face with his hands and shook his head. "No," he said aloud.

She pulled his hands away and made him look at her. "Yes," she said. "You must. For your life, Deke."

"Not now," he said, pulling away from her, standing up, beginning to pace. He wrapped the blanket tighter, almost, she thought, as if he were protecting himself.

"Now," she said. "If you care anything at all for me, you must do this."

"I can't," he said, and she saw tears trembling on his lashes. "I can't."

"You can, you must. Right now, with no delay. The longer you wait, the harder it will be."

"It's already too hard. I won't risk it."

"Risk what?"

"Losing you," he whispered.

She arose from her chair and closed her shirt. Catching him by the blanket, she drew him towards the couch and when he was seated, retrieved their cups. Sitting next to him, she faced him and waited expectantly. His blue eyes were desperate, panicky, filled with pain.

She moved nearer and put her hand on his. "Trust me," she told him. "You won't lose me."

"You say that because you don't know," he said miserably. "You think I'm a good person, I've *seen* that in your mind. But you're wrong, Andara. I'm..." He hesitated, then forced himself to go on though his voice fell to a mutter, "I'm a monster." His gaze was tortured. "A monster," he repeated.

"Why would you think that?" She kissed his brow gently.

He grasped her hand, then placed it over his heart. He put his own hand over her heart and reached out for her mind. At once she felt like a rampart being stormed from too many directions to withstand. She grew dizzy and knew that such was his strength she never would be able to block him if he didn't consent to the blockage, for there was no defense against the penetration he was making.

Panting, she started to reel away from him, then realized that was what

212

he was trying to make her do. She firmed her thoughts and instead of fighting, threw open her mind. She could see how this surprised him, but then he leaned closer, his eyes huge and compelling, and in a voice laced with ruthlessness, said,

"You're so sure you want to *see* this, but I know how it will make you feel because I know how it makes me feel..."

"Show me," she murmured. "Stop trying to scare me with how terrible you are, and show me."

He stared at her and again seemed surprised. Her heartbeat under his hand was steady, and he noted her utterly fearless expression. His anger fled, and he kissed her, feeling his innermost self scorched by her quick surge of passion.

Then he moved away and closed his eyes, focusing inward. Psychic brick by psychic brick, he dismantled the defensive wall he had maintained against her, opening himself to her scrutiny. His psyche seemed to quiver as she Sent her thoughts into him, and gently, she put a tendril of comfort into his mind, steadying him.

At first, Andara thought, it was like being in a cyclone of emotion, a storm of feelings so confused and in such moral turmoil that she was carried along roughly, being struck, in a manner of speaking, by images that began to fall like blows upon her consciousness, making her cry out with distress and pity. The images began with Tilva's Sending, and she viewed the events that followed as if through Deke's own eyes, as if she were sharing his eyes, riding just behind his awareness. He showed her what he had seen when he found his mother, how she had died in his arms. He showed her the wild ride through the barrens and across the plain to the Murdock camp, and she was swept along helplessly in the consensual rage of the avenging riders. There was the search for Gant, the killing and more killing, the screams of the dying, the terror, his emotional disconnection from everything except the blood. She heard Barr's sentence passed as if she were there, and then the scene shifted outside the camp where the soldiers had crossed two tent poles into an X and laid them in the snow. She watched in horrified fascination as Gant was dragged struggling and cursing to the poles, stripped, and tied on at all four extremities. The posts were raised and held in position by more poles propped against them and staked into the ground with spikes and rope.

Gant hung in the frigid air, abuse pouring from his mouth. She heard Deke's voice speak, and it sounded strange to hear it from inside his head, as he said, "He could take a long time to die, Father, and we'd have to listen to him the whole while. Let me kill him now."

"I want him to die in agony," Barr was saying. "He doesn't deserve a quick death."

"Let me kill him," Deke begged. "I promise you he'll know agony."

Barr looked at him, and Andara felt he was looking at her as he said, "Is this so important to you, Deke?"

"Aye," Deke said, and Andara felt the darkness swirl through their minds as a dreadful force began to unfold inside him, a force that came from she knew not where. She felt his esper potential jump and was nearly blinded by the rushing power rising through his body, the sheer explosiveness of it. A window seemed to open in the back of his mind and incredibly, more energy poured into him, until with an awful cry he sent a wash of pure hatred at his uncle where he hung on the cross. Gant actually jerked under the force of it, and his eyes bulged with terror.

The speckled grey mare Deke was holding whinnied loudly, and he quieted her with a quick mental contact. He pulled his machete from its sheath and approached Gant Murdock, who struggled desperately against his bonds before sagging back, completely cowed, unable to look at Deke's eyes, acting as if it hurt to look at Deke's eyes.

Running the blade of the machete across Gant's forearm, a thin line of blood appeared, and Deke shook his head. Andara heard him say, "Too sharp." He walked over to a boulder and scraped the edge harshly a few times, then tested it with his thumb. Now it was dull but chipped with jagged little bumps and hooks. "Perfect," he said. He walked back to stand before his uncle once more.

"When I found my mother," he whispered, "I swore I'd take your head for what you did..."

Gant began to babble crazily but Deke turned his gaze on him and he fell silent, his limbs trembling uncontrollably.

"But my father wants you to suffer, Uncle," Deke continued, his voice still low and deadly. "So I'm going to take your head, but slowly, and thus you see my dull blade."

Andara's thoughts were shocked, incredulous. Unable to stop the flow of images, she watched on, sickened by what she witnessed next. Yet despite it all, she found she understood, and in a secret part of her awareness, wondered if she would have had the guts to do the same thing. She watched as he reached up and began his grisly task, felt first the spraying, then the showering of Gant's blood, heard the ghastly shrieks and moans of the man as he swung there, spurting gore across Deke's face, down the front of his clothing, even into his boots.

Eventually the job was done, and Deke grasped his uncle's head in his hand, holding it up by the hair. The soldiers chanted their approval in a rhyth-

214

mic pattern accompanied by stomping and beating their rifles with their knife handles. The sound was frightening, barbaric, and Andara was rapt. Then Deke impaled the head on a spike jammed into the earth. He gazed as if hypnotized across the crowd of soldiers who now roared his name, saw how their savagery matched his own. He felt his father touch his shoulder and spun, his breath rapid and panting, the reek of blood in his nostrils.

"Let's go home now, son," Barr said with great gentleness. "Let's go home."

Andara watched as everyone mounted his horse. Each soldier looked around the destroyed camp, and she felt Deke's gaze quarter back and forth, eyeing the smoking tents and scattered bodies dispassionately, as if they meant nothing whatsoever. This peculiar disconnection persisted until the soldiers rode past a dead woman who had tried to protect her child until the last moment, and now both lay intertwined in death. As Deke's gaze fell on these two, she felt his mind scream with a horror he dared not voice. She could feel his thoughts reeling as he finally understood what they, what he, had done. And she could feel the need that possessed him to set himself free from his pain in the simplest way possible: a bullet through his skull.

Andara broke the connection between them, and he let her go, too ashamed to meet her eyes. She caressed his cheek and turned his face to her.

"I'm glad you did it," she said quietly, filled with grim pleasure at the vengeance taken against Tilva's murderer. "You were right to do it." She kissed his mouth with soft urgency.

Disbelievingly, he looked into her eyes, Sending a part of himself into her thoughts to see if she was lying to him.

"What would be the point?" she said, reading him perfectly. She kissed him again, hungrily. His mouth responded to hers and he reached for her, hardly able to think as realization poured through him.

"I love you, Andara," he told her, holding her in his arms and staring into her eyes. "I've always loved you, always will love you." He pressed her to him in a desperate embrace, his lips feverishly kissing everywhere he could reach. He tilted her chin up and she reached around his neck to pull herself closer. Her hands were locked in his hair and she made a low sound as he kissed her and sent his thoughts into hers again, making the kiss seem to go on forever.

He touched a certain place in her psyche that he knew would move her, made the kiss and the esper contact merge into one until, with a jerk, Andara moved away and stared at him. She tried to catch her breath, but could feel him in her thoughts, putting images there so erotic and heated, she thought she was going to faint.

Overwhelmed, she could barely reciprocate in kind, and she could feel how it stirred him profoundly to make her so. The more she responded to him, the bolder he got, until all at once his mouth was on hers again and his hands were slipping under her shirt to touch her breasts. She arched onto his palms and he caressed her, noticing how full her breasts had become, how they filled his hands. Her nipples hardened under his touch and she made a sound of earthy pleasure.

Their eyes met and they rose together from the couch. The blanket fell from his shoulders as he kissed her again, and the touch of her hands on his body made him groan. He swept her into his arms, and Andara reveled in his easy strength, putting her arms around his neck as he carried her to his bed. He quickly turned back the soft quilt and she sat down, her eyes growing wide with arousal, her heart galloping in her chest. He knelt in front of her, and with trembling fingers, unbuttoned her shirt which he pushed away from her shoulders. He gazed for a long while, his hands freeing her arms from the garment before he tossed it on the floor. Then he caressed her shoulders, aware both of her heated desire and her trepidation, and delicately, with as much sensitivity as he could manage, entered her mind. Simultaneously, he leaned closer and kissed her breasts, drawing the nipples between his lips sensuously. She jerked and grabbed his head, pressing him to her. His mouth was inexorable, and when he moved down and parted her legs, she became weak-kneed with anticipation.

He could feel how his warm breath made the skin flutter on the inside of her thighs, and he kissed her there before looking up at her face. Her eyes were smoldering, her expression openly wanton, and he had to pause for a moment to contain himself. He could feel in her mind how much she wanted him to do what he had done at the festival, and he slipped his hands under her, pulling her to him. When his tongue touched her she moaned, and one of her hands tangled in his hair as she began to move against him. He could sense her rising excitement and deliberately stopped, wanting to draw it out as long as possible. She said his name as he moved his mouth across her belly, kissing her, while his hands clutched her hips. He suckled her breasts again, then stood up, his chest heaving, his pulse loud in his ears. She moved aside so he could sit beside her and then pushed him down on the pillows, lying across his chest and kissing his mouth deeply, her tongue teasing him. He pulled his legs onto the bed and felt her move closer. He found the quilt and drew it over them, creating a warm cocoon in which he could feel her pelvis against his straining erection, and his hands began to roam her body, touching everywhere with wonder. He rolled her over until they lay on their sides, and she put her hand on him. It wasn't enough; she wanted to do more, and she wriggled lower until she felt his smooth skin touch her cheek.

Shyly, tentatively, she kissed him and he threw off the covers, unable to believe what she was doing. When she took him in her mouth he forced himself not to move, not wanting to frighten her. His hand went to her hair, and in an instant she was in his thoughts, feeling his feelings, and as she did, she moved her lips and tongue with more knowledge and confidence. Before long he had to pull her away, his breathing ragged and out of control, his erection harder than he'd ever felt it.

"Deke," she said, her voice husky, and pressed herself to him, unable to keep from touching him between his legs. He moved forward, putting his knee between her thighs, opening them, resting one of her legs over his hip. She threw her head back and moved against him eagerly, holding onto his shoulders. His breath was hot in her ear as he tasted her with his tongue, and he could sense she was ready. He pulled her into his arms and she spread her legs under him. Awkwardly, he lifted her hips and moved until he was poised against her.

"God, now, please," she begged, wanting him inside her. She guided him to her opening and felt him in her mind, his energy filling her. He was gasping in her ear; she could feel him struggling for control as with infinite care, he probed gently, then withdrew, then probed again, until she thought she'd go mad with excitement. "Deke," she whispered, thrusting her hips towards him while he moved tantalizingly away. She felt him link his emotions to hers, and with a distant part of her thoughts, knew he wanted to feel everything she felt, wanted to immerse himself in her feelings. At the same time he began to push into her, penetrating a little, then withdrawing, each time moving a bit deeper, until he felt the constriction of her hymen and heard her grunt of surprise at the sudden, sharp pain, which he could feel as if it had happened to him.

"Are you all right?" he asked, his lips seeking hers.

She kissed him passionately and grabbed his hips, thrusting herself onto him until their pelvic bones nearly met and he cried out with pleasure. Her palms were hot against him as she held him inside her, aware of the pain but not caring. She gripped him with her legs and he began to move in her, small movements at first, as he sought a way to please her without hurting her. She encouraged him, her voice rising, and he made his strokes longer, with deeper pressure, covering her mouth with his, his mind completely entangled with hers. For a moment he felt they were riding the life force of the Universe as they moved together in perfect synchronization. He could feel the tension in her, knew it was pain that was holding her back. He reached into her mind until he found the place where the pain was registering and, as if untying a latch, helped her to disconnect from it.

When Andara felt the pain disappear, she was filled with elation. She moved her hips with him and at each thrust grunted with increasing delight, thrilling to the steady, grinding rhythm he made. She could feel him stretching her, filling her up; could feel him pulse inside her and though she tried to prolong it, suddenly she was there, her entire body arching in ecstasy more soaring than she knew was possible. She felt him shudder as she took him with her and she held him while his breath sobbed in her ear and she felt his spasms viscerally.

For a long time neither of them moved. Deke kissed her lips and started to get off her but she grabbed him and said, "No...stay." Her voice made him throb and he kissed her again. He could feel the sweat pooling between their bodies, and gloried in the incredible eroticism of their embrace. Her thighs were slick with their combined juices and he could feel her soft breasts against his chest. She moved her leg across his and caressed his back all the way to his hips and buttocks, her hands slow now and relaxed.

Eventually he slipped out of her and she made a small sound of disappointment. He shifted until she lay against him, and draped the quilt over them.

For a while they listened to each other's breathing. She turned her mouth to his and kissed him searchingly. "Deke," she murmured as she felt his hands wander across her body.

"Mmm," he said, the depth of his feelings making him inarticulate. The combination of joy in Andara and grief for his mother made him feel like an open wound. He looked at her in wonder, unable to understand how she had taken him from despair to exaltation.

"How soon can we do it again?" she asked.

His eyes widened and for a second she saw the old Deke looking out at her, as a pleased glint flashed in their blue depths. "Soon," he said.

"Good," she said, laying her hand on him. She kissed the corner of his mouth and twined her legs through his, acutely sensitive to every brush of hair, the movement of each muscle, the way his slightly tumescent penis felt against her thigh. She inhaled the scent of his body, thinking how good he smelled, how his fresh sweat made her want to rub herself all over him until she, too, wore that musky odor of pure sex. She felt his mind touch hers, felt his lips in her hair.

His hands were on her again, exploring. He trailed his fingertips across her throat, up her cheek, and around her ear. She caught his hand and kissed each finger, smelling herself on him. When he touched her breasts she sighed, feeling it inside where she was sore.

"You're so beautiful," he said in a whisper that sent a thrill through her body. He cupped her breasts in turn, then moved his hand across her abdomen. Gently he squeezed her thighs, sliding his hand between them and resting on her pubic mound.

She opened her legs, inviting a more intimate caress. His fingers moved inside her, and delicately, he touched her engorged tissues, seeking the places that made her react the most.

He shifted his position until he could kiss her mouth more easily, and pulled her over him, spreading her legs wider until he felt her cover him. She felt him move and such was her positioning that as he stiffened, he penetrated her again, and she pressed herself onto him gingerly, wanting him, but concerned about her soreness. From her care he understood her feelings and sat up, holding her on him until she sat facing him. He kissed her lips which were swollen and inflamed beneath his. "Don't move," he told her.

She squirmed a little and her breathing got faster. He kissed her again, and touched her breasts, looking down where their bodies were joined. He made a deep sound of pleasure as she quivered around him.

"Does that hurt?" he asked, and put his arms around her, shutting his eyes. The room cartwheeled behind his closed lids and he concentrated on maintaining control.

"Not too badly, but you feel so big, so tight," she said with difficulty and squirmed once more.

"No cheating," he said, his lips at her ear, touching her thoughts to ease her discomfort.

"I can't...I have to," she said. A twitch of her muscles made him grit his teeth.

"I dreamed this once," he told her.

Her hands clutched his biceps spasmodically and she felt the pressure increase against her cervix as he seemed to grow even larger. "What?" she asked breathlessly, her eyes glazing. She heard her heart pound and wondered how he could sit still.

"I've dreamed of doing this with you," he said, kissing her lips. Another pulse made him draw breath sharply. "Aye," he said, "You feel so good, so..." Her muscles clenched on him, and he gasped. "God," he muttered and buried his face against her breasts, squeezing her tighter in his arms.

She shifted again. "I don't know how much longer I can stand this." Her voice caught in her throat.

"What do you want to do?"

"I need to move, I need to..." She writhed on him suddenly, catching him by surprise. He almost felt himself go, but controlled himself, panting.

"Look at me," he said, and caressed her hair.

She tried but couldn't concentrate. "God, Deke, you're making me crazy."

"I want you crazy," he said. "I want you wild. I want you to tell me what you need, no matter what it is, and I want to give it to you."

"I need you to love me," she said, her tone alive with grief. "I need you to love me," she repeated softly.

He kissed her, his tongue caressing hers, and felt her undulate against him. She rose a little and looked down to see where he was buried inside her and the sight made her heart jump.

He moved slowly, drawing away slightly, then pulled her back to him. She gasped with excitement.

"More," she said, and moaned as he began to thrust into her. It took her a minute to catch on to his rhythm, but when she did she felt her emotions rising quickly and could do little more than react to him. He pressed his pelvis against hers, sending a vibration through her that made her hold onto his shoulders as if he were the only solid thing in the world. She began to move with him, riding him, and for a time they could hear their bodies slipping together and apart, could hear their mutual sounds of pleasure growing more frenzied and frantic as they strained against each other. Their hands pulled at one another's hips feverishly until with a shout, he drove into her, the strength of his orgasm carrying her with him as they rocked together ecstatically.

Moving away briefly, he changed their positions until they were lying like spoons. He pulled her thigh over him and pushed into her. She groaned. His erection had backed off only slightly, and he began to move in her again, his mouth on hers, his fingers going between her legs to touch her.

"Can you go again?" he asked in a deep rumble, brushing her tangled hair away from her face.

"Aye," she said, her voice clogged with passion.

He let his thoughts flow into hers, sensing her turbulent emotions. In moments he was fully hard again.

"I can't believe how good you feel," she said voluptuously, and slid all the way onto him.

"I know," he said. "I want to be with you like this forever."

"Do you think other people feel this way?" she asked.

"How could they?" he answered. "They don't have you."

She put one arm around his neck, and moments later he touched her thoughts, moving more insistently. Soon she took his hand away from between her legs and put it on her breast. She could feel his increased control and from what his thoughts showed her, knew he wanted to make her shudder and shake with climax after climax. On another level she was aware that while pleasur-

220

ing her he was no longer thinking about his grief, and so she opened herself to him further, emotionally as well as physically. She felt his presence in her mind more intimately, and then he was doing things to her that made her dizzy, until she dug her fingers into his flesh and held on with helpless abandon. As the night grew old, he made love to her over and over, using hands, mouth, and mind in combinations she never would have imagined before he showed her, until finally, in the hours before dawn, they fell apart, exhausted.

Eventually they got up to use the chamber pot, and Andara put more wood in the stove which had burned low. There was a strong chill in the air and she shivered, wrapping her shirt around her shoulders. She boiled water, made more of the potent tea, and brought both cups back to the bedroom.

Deke's eyes followed her with heavy-lidded desire. "If I weren't so tired," he said, turning back the quilt. "Look." He pointed to the bloodstains on the sheet.

"Aye," she said, slipping in beside him and handing him a cup. "Virgin no longer."

She leaned against the headboard and sipped the tea. He watched her over the rim of his cup, slightly unsettled by the blood.

"I'm sorry I hurt you," he said.

She shrugged. "It was worth it."

"You're not sorry?" His eyes caressed her.

"If *I* weren't so tired..." She touched his shoulder lovingly.

"What do we do now?" he asked.

"We drink our tea and go to sleep."

"I don't mean that," he said.

"I know," she said. "But I think we have to go one minute at a time."

His eyes were questioning.

"Aye," she said, unconsciously massaging the muscles of his arm with tired pleasure. "One minute at a time, and maybe we'll be all right."

He covered her hand with his and shook his head. "I don't know if I'll ever be all right again," he said, the sadness in his voice heartbreaking for Andara. "I miss my mother," he told her, and she saw his eyes fill. "I miss..." He shrugged, unable to put his feelings into words.

"You miss your innocence," she said, with complete understanding.

"Aye," he said, marveling at her insight. "That's it."

She drank her tea and set the cup on the nightstand. Then she nestled against him and put her arm across him. He stroked her hair absently, sipping the heady mixture she had brewed. In the aftermath of this insane day he tried to sort his feelings and realized he had no idea what he felt, except for two powerful emotions; he missed his mother and he loved Andara. He had a sudden awful thought that if his mother hadn't gone walking, Gant would have looked for her in her tent, and there he would have found Andara as well. This upset him so much he put his cup aside and enfolded her in his arms, squeezing hard.

"What?" she wondered, returning his embrace but puzzled by its intensity.

"My mother went for that walk to save your life," he said, his voice rough with repressed emotion. "Maybe she wasn't aware of it consciously," he added. "But her soul knew."

Andara froze and looked at him in horror.

"Aye," he said, his voice breaking. He held her tighter, knowing he was going to lose control in a moment. "Gant was coming to her tent when he found her in the barrens. I know it."

Andara shivered. "Of course," she said. "He wouldn't have known she was out walking." Her heart was heavy and yet she had the strangest feeling.

He looked at her. "What?" he asked.

"She made this choice for both of us," she said. "Why?"

"I don't know," he whispered, and now the tears were falling, flowing in torrents from his eyes while he choked and sobbed helplessly and she held him tightly.

"It'll be all right," she said, kissing his streaming eyes tenderly, Sending comfort into his tormented thoughts. "I don't know how, but it will. Everything happens for a reason, and if we don't know the reason, we haven't looked hard enough or thought clearly enough."

His weeping slackened a bit and she knew he had heard her. "I don't care what the reason is," he said. "I'm just glad you're here, alive, with me." He kissed her mouth, tasting salt on both their lips, then moved away slightly. "Your life was my mother's last gift to us."

"In that case," Andara said, pulling him down to lie on the pillows. "We owe her a soul debt. Probably we'll spend a hundred lifetimes repaying it."

"A thousand wouldn't be enough," he said, his voice raw with emotion. "If anything had happened to you, nothing could have kept me here." His eyes were starting to close and he murmured, "Without you, I wouldn't want to live."

She caressed him gently and turned off the oil lamp on the nightstand. Drawing the quilt over them more cozily, she folded herself against him and slipped her leg over his. He was already half asleep but his arms went around her and he muttered,

"Goodnight, sweet Andara."

222

"Goodnight," she whispered, and the tears began to fall from her eyes again as she wept for the woman who in the most real sense had been as much her mother as Deke's. He stirred against her, feeling her distress, and held her closer, rocking her soothingly. In the darkness, his tears mingled with hers on the pillow, and so, grieving, they finally slept.

CHAPTER ELEVEN

When he told me about the events surrounding his mother's death, I couldn't help but feel pity for those poor children, forced into adulthood so precipitously. I told him that murder was virtually non-existent in our society, and that it was difficult for me to imagine the effects of such personal violence on a thirteen-year-old's emotionality.

From what I know of the man, I can extrapolate backwards to recreate the youth he must have been, recognizing the extraordinary intellect and awareness, along with the physical precocity, but as I tried to explain to him, being brilliant and precocious do not make up for lack of life experience, simple lack of time alive on the planet. At thirteen his emotional being could not possibly have been equipped to deal with this profound trauma, and so therefore, the trauma was still alive and living inside him.

Interestingly, he did not argue this point with me. His lack of defensiveness struck me as significant; it was one more example of the authentic quality of his self-knowledge, that he wouldn't waste my time or his with pointless denial.

— Ourn Rohlvaag; Collected Journals; City of Life, A.D. 3109

The morning of Tilva's funeral dawned grey and overcast, and the sky was dark with the threat of snow. The temperature was bitter, and skin left uncovered could freeze in a minute.

Deke awoke slowly, every muscle in his body protesting, and crept out of bed like an old man, leaving Andara bundled warmly in the quilt. He used the chamber pot and wrapped himself in the blanket he'd dropped on the couch the night before. Shivering, he started a fire in the woodstove, patted Hopi who was curled in one of the easy chairs, and put out food for her. There was a skim of ice in the water barrel, and he broke through it and put water in a pot to boil. He added milk and oatmeal along with honey, raisins, and sliced apples and left the covered pot to simmer.

He washed his hands and face, brushed his teeth vigorously, then returned to the stove, checking the oatmeal. It was ready and he filled two bowls, adding butter and cream. He brewed tea using the last of the herbs Andara had brought and, balancing everything carefully, came back to the bedroom. He looked at where she slept and felt his heart constrict.

Setting the bowls and cups on the cluttered nightstand, he dropped his blanket and crawled under the quilt. She stirred sleepily, opened her eyes, and smiled at him so beautifully his body ached. He kissed her lingeringly.

"I made breakfast. Are you hungry?"

"Starving," she said, sleep pitching her voice low. She stretched lazily and sat up. "It's freezing in here." Drawing the quilt over herself, she buttoned the wool shirt she had slept in. He scrabbled over the edge of the bed and got the blanket he had dropped, wrapping it around her shoulders. She reached across him, took one of the cups of tea and tasted it. "My God, Deke, we're going to be unconscious from this, you made it so strong!"

He nodded. "I need an anesthetic today."

Her face paled as she remembered. "Good thinking," she said, feeling the weight of her sadness descend on her again.

"Have some cereal," he suggested. "Do you know when you last ate?"

"Dinner, night before last." She tasted the oatmeal. "It's good," she said, surprised.

He lay half-reclining on the pillows, his bowl balanced on his chest, and watched her eat. "What do you want to tell your father?" he asked after a while.

She looked up, startled.

"What I mean is," he paused. "I'd like you to move in." He squeezed her leg through the covers. "How do you feel about that?"

"Move in?" At his nod, she said, "Are you really ready for that?"

"Aye," he said with certainty. "I like waking up next to you. I like making you breakfast. But if you think it's too soon..."

"I don't know what I think," she said truthfully. "Though now you've brought it up, I guess I can't really imagine sleeping anywhere else. Not," she added, "That we did much sleeping."

"I'd like to do a little more of that not sleeping," Deke said.

"Not 'til I finish breakfast," Andara said. "And use the pot. And bathe. I feel kind of..." She gestured to her crotch and shrugged.

"Crusty," he supplied.

"I was going to say 'sore,' you crude person."

"Well? What about your father? Will he challenge me?"

"I hope not," she said. "I know he feels we're too young for what we did."

"That may be, but the deed is done."

"What are we going to do, tell him since we've already done it, we might as well keep on doing it?"

"That sounds good," Deke said. "I'd like to start doing it again as soon as possible."

"Me, too," Andara admitted, and squeezed his hand.

"So?" He played with her fingers. "Or are you holding out for marriage?"

"No one will marry us," she said. "That you can be sure of!"

"I'm Barr Wolfson's son," he said. "I'll find someone to do it."

"Ruins, you're serious!" She looked at him in astonishment.

"Of course. I want to be with you for the rest of my life."

"Was I that good?" She looked at him sidelong.

He set his bowl down and moved against her, wrapping her in his arms. "Beyond good," he said. "Even if I wanted someone else, you've already ruined it for me."

"I suppose you know you've done the same for me," she told him.

He hugged her, then let her go. "Since neither of us wants anyone else, doesn't it make sense to live together?"

"You feel that way today; how do you know you'll feel the same a week from now or a year from now?"

"How do we know we'll be alive a week from now or a year from now? Who knows what the future holds?"

"Your mother..." Andara hesitated. "Your mother said almost the same thing before she..." Her voice trailed off.

He kissed her and her mouth tasted of apples and oatmeal.

There was the rattle of the knocker at the tent door. They looked at one another, and he said, "Do you want anyone to know you spent the night?"

Again the knocker rattled against the flap.

"I'm not ashamed," she said. "Are you?"

"No." He called towards the door, "Just a minute!" He pulled on pants and a sweater, stuck his feet into sheepskin-lined moccasins, then untied the flap. Hawk Farflight pushed through to stand awkwardly blowing on his hands and stamping his feet.

"'Morning, Deke," Hawk said, eyeing him cautiously, remembering how he had been the previous evening. "Are you all right?"

Deke tied the door closed again, shrugging. "I'm here," he said. "Thanks to your daughter."

"Ah, yes, my daughter." Hawk was silent. Then, "Your father said I might find her here."

"We're eating breakfast. Would you like some?" Deke gestured to the oatmeal. "I made plenty."

"I would, thanks," Hawk said, removing his cloak and laying it over a chair. "Where is she?" he asked, trying to remain casual.

"In bed," Deke replied, as casually.

Hawk's eyes went to the bedroom hangings.

Deke indicated the table. "Why don't you sit down? I'm sure she'll be out when she's presentable." He collected Andara's clothes from the side of the tub. "Excuse me for a second," he said, and brought them into the bedroom.

227

"Ruins," she whispered. "You're handling him well! How can you be so calm?"

"What else can I do?" he whispered back. "There's water in the pitcher," he told her, "And there should be a washcloth, too. You can use my toothbrush, if you don't mind."

She looked at him. "If you were going to give me a cold, you probably did it already."

"Hopefully I didn't give you anything you didn't want," he said. "There's an empty chamber pot over there. Don't leave me alone too long. I haven't the faintest idea what to say to him."

"You're doing fine," she said and got up from the bed.

Outside in the kitchen, Deke filled a bowl and brought it to Hawk at the table. He felt the man's gaze on him and returned it equably.

"Your father said to tell you the funeral will be at midday," Hawk finally said.

Deke nodded.

"Listen, Deke...I know what you're thinking."

"Do you?"

"Aye. You think I'm going to wear you out, don't you?"

"I think you'd like to try," Deke replied.

"Yes, well..." Hawk cleared his throat. "You're wrong, in any case."

Deke's eyebrows went up.

"Just one thing," Hawk said, his voice filling with emotion. "You were gentle with her, weren't you?"

Deke gripped the older man's arm, his affection obvious. "I love her. I'd never do anything to hurt her."

"I know...but yesterday, you weren't in your right mind."

"Aye," Deke agreed.

"I was concerned. You're both so young."

"We're at least a hundred years older today," Deke said sadly.

Hawk began to eat the oatmeal. "You made this?"

"Aye. How's my father?"

"He's older, too."

"I hate for him to be alone. Are you going back?"

"I thought I would."

Andara emerged from the bedroom. "Hi, Papa," she said, with a yawn.

"Are you all right?" Hawk asked quickly.

"In what way?" She didn't intend to make it easy for him.

"Why, in any way you might think," he said lamely.

"Deke, where'd you leave your toothbrush?" she asked. "I couldn't find it anywhere."

"Sorry, it's here." He handed it to her with the powder.

"If you're asking about last night, of course I'm all right," she told Hawk. "In every other way, I'm pretty terrible."

Deke squeezed her shoulders comfortingly and she held his hands around her for a moment.

Hawk watched them, his thoughts spinning. He wondered if they knew how beautiful they were together. Their feelings for one another positively shone from their faces. He rubbed his jaw ruefully. It was hard for him to think of them as adults, yet as he looked at them, he knew they were no longer children. Young, yes, but not children. There was, in fact, nothing childish about either of them, not in the way they carried themselves, nor in the way they related to one another. He sighed, feeling the passage of time and the twinges of arthritis in his joints.

Andara brushed her teeth, then drew on her cloak and stepped into her boots.

Deke and Hawk looked at her askance.

"I have to speak with the servants," she said. "Also I want to get some fresh clothes. I'll be back soon."

Deke caught her hand and kissed it. She kissed his mouth and went out the door, Hopi jumping up to follow.

"Well," Hawk said with a strange smile. "It's obvious she's fine." He finished his bowl of cereal. "Thanks for this," he said and rose.

"If you're going to see my father, I'll come with you," Deke said, anxious at the prospect of being alone.

There was a rattle at the flap and a serving woman stuck her head in.

"Is it all right, m'lords? The young lady said the tub needed draining and some clothes needed to be disposed of..."

"Please," Deke said, "Come in. We were just leaving." He went into his bedroom and put on another sweater as well as a scarf and gloves. On his way past the kitchen, he put more wood in the fire and closed down the damper. Heat began to radiate into the room.

"M'lord? Shall I refill the tub?" The serving woman ran the waxed leather drain hose out through a tiny flap designed for the purpose, pushing it away towards a depression sloping down from the tent.

"Aye," Deke said. "But give it half an hour."

The woman nodded, then said softly, "I'm sorry about your mother, m'lord. She was like a sister, always so kind to me..."

Pain flickered in his eyes.

"If there's anything else I can do, please let me know."

"I will," he replied. "Thank you."

When they got to his mother's tent, he had to force himself to enter. During the night with Andara, Death had retreated into the shadows beyond the glow created by their love-making, but now he could feel its presence again, crouching like a hungry vulture at his shoulder.

Inside it was worse. His mother's echo filled the pavilion, ingrained into all the furniture, the art work; the air itself seemed to resonate with her vibration, and as he inhaled, he could smell her scent as if she simply had stepped out for a moment. His Aunt Leah and her two sons were sitting quietly in the living area, offering silent support if needed. He nodded, acknowledging them politely. He could feel his father's grieving presence radiating nearby, and slowly, filled with sorrow and dread, made himself walk into the bedroom.

When he saw his mother and the infant he closed his eyes, fighting the anguish in his spirit, fighting to keep the rage at bay. He had expected to be fighting only sadness; the rage caught him by surprise. If he could kill Gant Murdock a thousand times he knew he'd barely make a dent in that rage. Clenching his fists, he tried to center his mind in the way he had been taught, and gradually a shred of control returned to him. He exhaled slowly, and crossed the room to where Barr sat near the bed. Leaning down, he kissed his father's bearded cheek, and held his shoulder comfortingly.

Barr looked up in surprise. He saw the grief in his son's eyes, also that sanity had returned to them. With a sigh of relief, he patted Deke's hand. "Is Hawk with you?"

"Aye, Father, he's in the living room with Leah."

"And Andara? She found you...?"

"Aye," Deke said, his tone changing. "She did."

Barr nodded. "That's quite a young woman, son. She has great strength. She'll be a worthy successor to your mother."

"I know." Deke's eyes went back to the bed. Almost it looked as if Tilva was sleeping.

Barr rose heavily, and from the way he moved, Deke knew he hadn't slept at all. "Are you all right?"

"Tired," Barr said. "Very tired. And sick to death of bloodshed. I'm getting old, Deke. I'll be forty-nine my next birthday."

"That's not old," Deke told him.

"I feel as if I've squeezed ten lifetimes into those years," the chieftain said. "And I don't regret any of it. But now, well, we'll see. I believe I'll retire from the army and leave the fighting to you younger men."

"That doesn't seem likely, Father. Come spring, you may feel differ-

230

ently."

"I've done a great deal of thinking since last night," Barr said, putting his arm around Deke's shoulders, his moody gaze traveling to the bed. "And I don't know that anything will change my mind. You're ready to lead forays yourself now. I'll continue to handle the administrative details, but the push west; that'll be for you, son. I don't have the heart for it any more."

"Why not give it some time?" Deke suggested. "It's possible you'll change your mind."

"No," the chieftain said with finality. "My time leading soldiers to war is over." He studied Deke, noticed how tall he was getting, how he was filling out. With a nod to himself, he said aloud, "I'll remain chieftain, but as far as military matters go… Frankly, son, I think you've already surpassed your teachers. I'm sure they'd agree."

Deke didn't know what to say. Standing here with his mother and baby sister lying dead in front of them, he found himself unable to think about anything other than his loss, much less going to war. Besides, the idea of his father retiring unsettled him to his core.

"Don't worry, Deke," Barr said, understanding some of what was going on in his mind. "You'll start small and build, the way I did, the way your grandfather did. It'll seem more natural once begun."

He looked into his father's eyes, sensing many chaotic emotions there. For a moment he felt Barr's heartbreak as if it were his own, and realized that his father's love for his mother had been the primary force motivating his desire to create a kingdom in which people could live without fear. Now it seemed the burden of that creation had grown too wearisome to bear, and he wanted to shift some of it to Deke's younger shoulders. Compassionately, knowing it would relieve Barr's mind, he nodded, and said, "If you think it's best, Father."

Barr hugged him tighter. "Good," he said.

Deke nodded again, and the weight on his spirit grew heavier.

With a final glance at Tilva, Barr moved towards the door and after a moment, Deke followed.

Leah and her sons had departed and Andara had arrived while he was in the bedroom. She was picking through Tilva's herb collection while Hawk sat watching. Choosing several varieties, she put them in pouches and the pouches into her carrying sack. "Good morning, my lord," she said to Barr. "Let me make you some breakfast."

"I'm not hungry," Barr told her.

"Still, you need to keep your strength up." She rummaged in the cold closet, took out bacon, eggs, cheese, and onions. Tossing some butter into a pan, she quickly sautéed the onions, cooked and drained the bacon, and beat several eggs together in a bowl. Adding a little salt and dill weed, she poured the eggs into the pan, layered them with the onions and bacon and placed the cheese overall. In a minute she had the omelet folded and removed it from the burner.

Hawk sniffed appreciatively.

"Please, sit down," Andara told Barr as she slid the eggs onto a plate and put it and a fork on the table.

"Can you believe the way she bullies me," Barr said under his breath, but it was obvious he didn't mind.

"Can I trust you to eat this?" Andara asked the chieftain. "I need to get cleaned up for later. But if you're going to be difficult..."

"I'll make sure he eats," Hawk assured her.

"Make sure you don't eat it, Papa," she said.

"Deke already fed me, remember?"

"Aye," she said and looked at Deke expectantly. "Are you ready?"

"In a minute. Father, you wouldn't have an extra winter cloak you could lend me, would you? Mine's beyond salvaging."

"There's a clean one in my tent. I'll have it sent over to you."

"Thanks," Deke said. He took Andara's arm and wrapped her cloak around her. "We'll see you later."

After they left, Hawk and Barr exchanged glances.

"Well?" Barr asked.

"Well, what?" Hawk returned.

"It's obvious they're lovers," Barr said. "How do you feel about that?"

Hawk leaned back in his chair. "I suppose it's good they were able to comfort one another."

Barr's expression was surprised. "I thought you'd want to clobber him at the very least."

"Clobber Deke?" Hawk laughed shortly. "More likely he'd clobber me! Besides, judging from his condition last night and the way he is today, and knowing my daughter, I'd say it was Andara who made the first move."

Barr almost smiled. "She is a spirited wench, it's true."

"Aye, I can almost feel sorry for the lad."

The two men, such old friends who'd passed through their manhood rites together so long ago, looked knowingly at one another.

Then the chieftain said, "He's man enough to handle her, I'm thinking."

"That's good, because she's a little like wild wisteria; unless you cut it back every so often it'll grow all over you. I mean that only in the best way, of course."

"He needs a strong woman, someone he can't manipulate or push around. It's a good match, the best possible match. Tilva..." His voice cracked but he went on, "Tilva thought so, too."

"Aye," Hawk said. "Next thing they'll probably want to move in together. I can see the signs already."

"Probably." Barr was pensive.

"You don't mind?" Hawk was curious.

Barr shrugged. "Why would I? They're young, in love...the distance from your tent to his is too long for their arms to reach."

"You knew when you sent her over there what would happen, didn't you?" Hawk said, and there was a trace of accusation in his voice.

"Perhaps," Barr admitted. "Are you angry with me?"

"No, I suppose not. It was inevitable, I guess."

"What was?"

"That she'd leave me for another man one day." Hawk sighed. "At least it's Deke, and she isn't going far."

"Listen, I'm grateful to her. She saved Deke's life last night. He was lost. She brought him back. I couldn't have done it, and neither could you."

"We don't have Andara's...attributes," Hawk said with a complex smile.

"No," Barr agreed. "We surely do not."

The funeral pyre had been erected on a hill outside of Winter Camp. From its elevation, one could see the entire tent city spread below, as well as a vista of escarpments and meadows, pine barrens and orchards, fields and farming villages. The light was strange and threw a pale glow across the land, while overhead, clouds piled deeper and thicker, creating a dark and sullen blanket. The wind was light but increasing, and occasionally a gust stirred the snow into swirling ground mists.

As mid-afternoon approached, groups and individuals gathered on the hillside near the pyre, dressed in their warmest furred and quilted garments. Soon everyone from the city had arrived, except the soldiers still traveling home from the town of Root. Thousands of people waited in the plummeting cold, talking quietly, remembering their healer and witch woman. The sorrow in the air was palpable as the Wolf People mourned their leader's wife and child. They had loved Tilva from the day Barr brought her home, welcoming her into their society at every level, celebrating their chieftain's joy by their immediate acceptance of his new wife. They had loved her for herself and her selflessness. Most people could not accept that she was gone, and wondered where they would find so gifted a healer again.

Inside Tilva's pavilion, Deke and Andara stood with their fathers in the living area, preparing to make the long walk to the funeral hill. An honor guard of soldiers would follow directly after, bearing Tilva and the baby, as well as Canis, on raised litters.

Deke found he was unable to look at his father, unable to bear the darkness of Barr's mood. Grief had made Barr's features severe, and there was a fatalistic cast to his shadowed eyes. He could sense Barr's physical exhaustion in the deliberate way he moved, as if he had to think carefully about where to put each foot or hand before placing it.

For the first time in his life, Deke was profoundly depressed. Now that the time was at hand to send his mother's spirit onward, he found himself reliving the special moments of their lives together, as well as odd shreds and snatches of everyday routine that seemed to resonate with significance in his memory. Every bit of advice, every scrap of herb lore and magic she had imparted to him, every caress and kiss, seemed to grow larger in his mind as he remembered her, and he swore he would never let himself forget.

He felt Andara in his mind and opened his awareness to her, not in the all-consuming way he had the night before, but in a quiet, welcoming manner that brought tears to her eyes. She held his hand and he felt her keening sorrow inside his thoughts. He squeezed her hand in return, sharing her grief as she shared his, their empathy complete.

Soon it was time, and Barr spoke to the soldiers who would carry the litters. A moment later he nodded to Hawk, to Deke and Andara, and leading the way, started out of the tent, fastening his cloak against the bitter wind.

They followed, and behind them the soldiers hefted their burdens sadly. Slowly, the small procession wended its way through the city to the outskirts and up the long incline to where the pyre waited, stark against the forbidding sky. A few snowflakes driven by a cold blast of wind struck Deke's face and he buried his chin deeper into his cloak. It was becoming more and more difficult to force his feet forward. He looked at Andara but couldn't see her face past her hood. From the way she trudged at his side, dragging her boots through the snow, he knew she felt the same way he did.

When they reached the top of the hill, the soldiers positioned the two litters in the places prepared for them. Kerosene-soaked cordwood was stacked beneath the pyre; it would take only the touch of a torch to ignite it.

A great sigh of sadness and pity went out across the mourners as they saw Tilva and the infant for the first time. All eyes turned to the chieftain, looking searchingly at his ravaged face. They took in Deke and Andara's rigid expressions, Hawk's wordless sorrow, and another sigh of sympathy arose from the crowd.

Barr walked forward and took up the traditional torch prepared for him, holding it firmly in his right hand. He stood before the pyre gazing at Tilva's face for a long time, then turned to his people.

"Thank you for coming," he said. "Today we're gathered to bid farewell to our people's healer, my beloved wife. All of you knew her kindness and patience, her beauty of body and spirit..." The chieftain's voice broke. He struggled to dominate his emotions and eventually succeeded. He went on. "...her beauty of body and spirit and mind, the warmth and generosity of her nature in all things."

The people called out their agreement, and individual voices rang loudly with spontaneous expressions of grief.

"At times like these, we wonder why God, whom we believe is all of existence, could permit such things to happen, but we must remember that the Universe gathers back to itself with jealous possessiveness those unique souls who simply by existing among us, change our lives for the better. My wife would say..." Again Barr fought for self-control, "My wife would say that everything happens for a reason, that no event is wasted or in vain. I have tried these last hours to understand what reason there could be for this to have occurred, and can come to no good conclusion. I have no answers. All I can do is be grateful my darling Tilva graced my life, my son's life, with her presence even for this short time, and enriched our people's hearts and minds during the years she was among us."

Deke heard Andara sob and put his arm around her. He saw tears on Barr's bearded cheeks, saw his father turn again to the pyre. A murmur rose from the assembled people, rolling like a wave across the multitude. The wind increased, and Barr looked away once more.

His face a study in misery, Hawk approached bearing ritual flint and steel. Eyes on Barr's, he drew the flint across the metal and the spark instantly ignited the kerosene-soaked fabric at the torch's tip.

Barr raised the torch and froze, a growing expression of disbelief on his face.

Andara lifted her head and her hand clutched Deke's cloak. "Look there!" she whispered frantically. "Can you *see*?"

He looked at her as if she were deranged. Then he concentrated and thought he *saw* movement near his father.

Barr stood transfixed while the wind whipped the torch wildly. His eyes were wide, staring, and he was convinced he saw Tilva standing near him, raising her hand to touch his cheek. When the diaphanous glow contacted him, he experienced her love and tenderness as a flood of ineffable yearning that spread through his body and self.

"Look!" Andara said excitedly, and opened her mind to Deke, letting him *see* it through her eyes. Astonished, his muscles jerked involuntarily, and he *saw* what looked like a warm light in the image of his mother, touching Barr's face.

"What does it mean?" he asked, his heart pounding painfully.

"She's here to say goodbye," Andara answered. "But to be able to actualize, even like that..." She shook her head. "So much love needed," she said softly. "Such expenditure of energy... I've heard of such things, but to *see* it...!"

Barr heard Tilva's voice speaking inside his mind in something other than words, other than thought. She was telling him not to worry, that she was all right, that she would love him forever and meet with him in the place he went, dreaming. She told him she would be waiting when he crossed from the physical membrane to the non-physical place of energy at the end of life, and that he wouldn't be alone, that a portion of her awareness would be nearby always, loving him.

He seemed to feel her hand on his where he held the torch, and he sensed she wanted to put the flame to the pyre with him. Her voice filled his mind again, and gently, as he touched flame to wood and the fire leaped up, fueled by the intensifying wind, he heard her say goodbye.

"Goodbye," he whispered, filled with longing and loneliness as he felt her presence dissipate. "Goodbye, my wife."

In a minute the fire grew high and he was forced back. He threw the torch down in the snow where it sputtered feebly for a while before going out.

The pyre became an inferno, the flames reaching higher until nothing on it was visible any more, only a blazing conflagration throwing heat that melted the snow thirty feet away.

Deke watched and felt Andara's hand steal into his. Her thoughts caressed his as she attempted to comfort him. She could feel his distress, and wondered why knowing Tilva's spirit was near hadn't reassured him; in fact, she sensed he was more anguished. Gently, she probed his feelings, and when she understood, took his arm and whispered,

"She could only muster so much energy for this effort. Her focus had to be on your father; he never got the chance to say goodbye and you did. You must not feel she loved you any less because of that."

He put his arms around her and held her close, wrapping her with him inside his cloak and hiding his face against hers.

More wood was heaped on the pyre and Barr moved to stand beside them, head up, hood thrown back, his face filled with a combination of sadness and exultation. A few snowflakes fell from the fecund clouds, clinging to his hair and beard. He patted Deke's shoulder and nodded to Hawk, wondering if anyone else had seen what he had, and if so, whether they understood.

The snow was coming faster now, whipped by the wind as it rose to a gale. The pyre snapped and popped, wood collapsed onto itself. Oblivious to the gathering storm, the People watched their healer's body convert back to the energy from which it had been created. Many of them had sensed a presence near the chieftain, but few understood it the way Andara did. Her training made her able to *see* with absolute clarity what had happened, and she was awed by that *seeing*.

After a while people began to file by, paying last respects and expressing condolences to their chieftain, his heir, and Tilva's acolyte. They looked with curiosity at Andara, realizing that now she was most qualified to take up their healer's mantle, and wondering if she was ready for the responsibility. Something about the quiet way she stood watching the fire seemed to reassure them, and slowly, while the pyre burned down to ash, the last of the mourners passed by, many of them in tears, all rendering support in the best way they knew how.

When nothing remained but a few smoking, charred heaps of wood, Barr looked at Hawk who nodded, then at Deke and Andara. The wind rose to a shriek, and, nearly blinded by the force of the storm, the four moved down the hill away from the sizzling embers now dying in the puddling snow-melt.

When they reached Tilva's pavilion, they saw many packages of food slipped just inside the tent door. By tradition, condolence calls wouldn't begin until the following day, but that didn't stop friends and neighbors from dropping off tempting dishes of all sorts to help comfort the bereaved family.

Andara put the perishables away in the cold closet, preparing two more bundles for storage in Deke's tent. She put water on the stove to boil and set several of the gift packages on the table, along with plates, forks and knives.

She began to feel the silence was oppressive, but didn't know what to say to lighten the atmosphere. Soon she began to serve some of the food and the three came to sit at the table with her. They ate, not very enthusiastically.

"Will you be all right, Father?" Deke asked, his voice heavy with sadness. "We could stay, if you like."

"No, go to your own bed. It looks to be an ugly night." Barr stood up and rumpled his son's hair. "Make sure you take some of that apple crisp and sweet cream. I know how you like it."

"I'll sleep in your old room," Hawk said. "Without Andara home, it looks like if I want to get fed regularly I'm going to have to stay here anyway."

Barr snorted. "Any excuse to eat up all this food. I swear I don't know where you put it."

Hawk smiled slightly at this old complaint. Except for special occasions, Barr ate sparingly, dreading the possibility of middle-age spread.

Deke rose and got his and Andara's cloaks. He wrapped hers around her and fastened his own, drawing up the hood. Accepting the packages from her, he said, "You know where to find us."

When they got to his tent, Hopi leaped up to greet them, putting her paws on his chest and bolting around the room, sending glad images into his mind. She jumped on Andara, washed her face thoroughly with her tongue, then ran through the door flap and into the snow, where she squatted before tearing exuberantly in a huge circle and finally coming back inside. Deke tied fast the door against the fierce blasts of wind and looked at the wolf curiously.

"What's with her, I wonder?" he mused aloud.

"Maybe it's the storm," Andara said, doffing her cloak and hanging it on a peg. "It feels like a big one."

"Aye, maybe," Deke said, shaking the snow from his cloak and putting it next to Andara's. He looked at the two cloaks hanging side by side and felt his insides practically melt. He sighed and went to the stove as if in a dream, loading more wood inside.

Andara looked at his wan expression and poured him half a cup of neat whiskey. "Drink up, Deke," she said kindly. "If anyone ever looked like he needed a drink, you're it."

Deke sipped the whiskey, feeling it burn its way down the back of his throat, warming him, thawing the ice he felt growing around his middle.

He collapsed into a chair with a loud exhalation and stretched his legs out in front of him. Questions crowded his mind but he was too tired to give them voice. He felt as if his emotions were being crushed by sadness and depression. This was different from what he had experienced before the funeral. Then, he had been in limbo, someplace where he recognized what had happened but hadn't fully accepted it. Now he did accept it, and he thought it was because of the finality of funerals, the way they seemed to relegate to the past the reality of one's attachment to the deceased in the present.

He felt Andara's hands on his shoulders as she massaged his muscles with knowing fingers, finding just the right spots to release the tension from his neck. He leaned back to her and she caressed his jaw before slipping her arms over the chair's back and hugging him. He took her hand and guided her around to his lap and into his arms. She curled against his chest and he rested his chin on the top of her head, holding her securely. She felt his tears on her hair and murmured quietly, moved by the depth of his unhappiness.

"Come to bed," she told him.

He shook his head and held her tighter.

"What is it?" she asked.

He struggled to find words. "When I thought she was gone completely, it was easier. To know she lives somewhere and I can't touch her..." His hands clenched and unclenched and she caught them between her own.

"But you know her spirit lives on," Andara said. "I don't understand you."

"There's knowing and knowing," he said. "I'm not saying it's rational."

"Do you ever give any thought to where your sensitivity comes from, why it works the way it does?"

Surprised by the seeming non sequitor, he said, "I think of it as a function of my brain."

"No," she said, "It's a function of your mind, and that's an entirely different thing. It has very little to do with your body at all, except that your body acts to focus the energy from one level to another, in particular from energy essential levels, to this one."

"Your point being...?"

"Extra-sensory abilities come from the spirit world, and that's where your mother lives now. Her energy self is a lot like her physical self was, looks the same, feels much the same to her. If she chooses, she can go to another evolution and move into new realms. Or she may choose to come back to earth, in another incarnation."

"How can you know?" he asked her. "How can you be so sure?"

"Because," she explained, "My spirit guide talks about these things. I know the spirit world exists because I have a relationship with it. You used to, but now that you're a man, you're concentrating more on the physical side of your being. There's nothing wrong with that, but it takes you away from your greater Self, and that distance creates disharmony in your spirit."

"The mystical aspects of sensitivity confuse me," Deke admitted. "When I go into your thoughts or anyone else's, I feel it's something I personally do, but if I had to explain how, I probably couldn't."

"That's because you're too wrapped up in the earth-focused parts of your personality. You haven't listened for the voice that comes at quiet moments and tells you everything you need to know about anything you care to know."

"Whose voice is it?"

"Why, your own greater Self. Whose else?"

He stroked her hair lovingly and considered how much more grounded she was than he, how much more in balance. What his father had called strength was more than that: strength alone was too rigid a term for what she possessed. She had the pervasiveness of water, the ability to find her own level no matter the situation, and to rise to whatever challenge life might throw at her.

At once he wanted to be with her, joined to her physically and emotionally. He tilted her face to his and kissed her, the color of his eyes growing more vivid as his feelings burst from him. She kissed him back as passionately, and he sent his awareness into her from multiple directions, each contact more subtle and stimulating than the one before.

"You say that comes from the spirit world?" he asked, moving his lips from hers to kiss her throat. "How can that be? It's so much a part of me, my emotions..."

"You're a spirit, too, don't you know that?" She kissed him scathingly. "Energy, emotion: these are one and the same. You don't change at death, you simply shed your dense physical vehicle and become who and what you really are."

"What am I?" His mouth was warm and tasted of whiskey.

"You are a free-floating consciousness, made of energy. This," and she prodded his chest, "Is just a vehicle to get around in, a way for you to experience the physical world."

"Why would any free-floating consciousness, as you call it, want to be physical in the first place?"

"I used to ask myself the same thing," she said, her eyes soft as they found his. "But you made it clear to me." She squeezed his arms and said, "Now can we go to bed?"

"Aye," he said, slipping his arms under her and rising.

"This is the best part," she murmured against his chest.

"What is?"

"When you carry me off like a spoil of war and ravish me mercilessly."

His eyes gleamed with excitement. "So you want to be ravished, eh?"

"Aye," she said, blushing. "But in a nice way."

He carried her to the bedroom, tossed her on the bed, ripped her clothes away with mock violence, and proceeded to do that very thing.

When finally she fell back bathed in sweat and he made as if to begin again, she said faintly, "No more, please...I have to rest...don't you get tired?"

"You said you wanted to be ravished."

"You ravish better than anyone I ever dreamed of."

"You inspire me," he said, and moved until he lay alongside her. Steam rose from their heated flesh in the chill air.

"Listen to this wind. You don't think the tent will blow away, do you?" Andara asked, cooling swiftly now that he no longer covered her.

"I hope not," he said, getting up to find another quilt. He ran quickly into the kitchen and put more wood in the stove, then ran back and got under the covers with her. "Brrr," he said. "It's cold...too cold for November." He kissed her and wrapped her in his arms. She adjusted the quilts and sent a mental image to Hopi who came in through the hangings and jumped up on the bed. They petted her until she turned around twice and lay close to them, sharing body heat.

"You know," Deke said, his voice tinged with sadness, "Maybe someday I'll be able to look back and make sense of all this. But right now...nothing seems to have any pattern I can grab ahold of."

She snuggled against him. "So many things have happened so fast, maybe it would be more helpful if you stopped trying to analyze everything, and followed your instincts."

He kissed her and moved his hand to her breast.

"Other instincts," she said, catching his hand and holding it.

"Aye," he agreed. "You may be right."

They lay quietly listening to the sounds of the storm surrounding them, grateful for one another's company. Deke thought about his father, about how lonely he must be feeling, and blinked rapidly to keep the tears from falling. Such sadness, the world was filled with such sadness and blind fury he hardly could bear it. He knew he was like the world, also filled with sadness and fury, but those feelings kept taking turns with the joy and love he felt for Andara. He realized he was confused in a way he never had been before. Previously in his life he had known who he was and what he wanted. Now he knew only that his emotional being had been flayed so deeply he was afraid he never would experience love without feeling grief, never would feel grief without wishing to commit violence, never would experience any of those three without the undercurrent of rage that had taken up residence in his unconscious mind.

Sensing his disquiet, Andara touched his thoughts sympathetically. "It takes time. This won't go away in a day or even a month. But every day it'll be a little less and you'll remember the good things about life, and maybe you'll even want them again."

"A life of blood is what I've sought," he said. "It's been my dream since I was born. I've always known I was a natural conquerer, known it the way other boys know they like to fish or play ball. I've always been able to get people to do what I want, one way or another. I should have known what Gant would do. I should have killed him when I had the chance. Everything that has happened is my fault. I can't forgive myself for any of it, not a single bit. I may

241

learn to live with it, but I'll never forgive myself for what I've done."

"Oh, Deke," Andara said, touched by his misery. "Guilt won't serve any purpose except to make you feel bad."

"Aye," he said, "I'm guilty. Guilty of arrogance and stupidity, and now murder, too."

"It isn't fair for you to take this all on yourself," she said quietly. "Your mother used to tell me that there are some choices we make, and others we simply go along with, for deeper reasons. Gant Murdock being what he was, surely some of the responsibility has to fall on him. You tried to show him mercy. That was a good thing, a humane thing. It would be the wrong lesson to draw from this that mercy leads to disaster."

"You're just trying to make me feel better."

"Yes, but I'm also telling you the truth."

"How'd you get so smart?" he asked as a particularly fierce gust of wind shook the tent violently.

"I'm female," she said. "It comes naturally." She kissed his neck, then felt his cheek in front of his ear. "You're getting a beard."

"Oh, that," he said. "Not much of one."

She touched his face curiously. "Are you going to shave it off?"

"Aye. When it's more impressive, maybe I'll let it grow in."

"You'd be handsome with a beard," Andara said, trying to imagine it. "Aye, very handsome."

He pulled the quilts higher over their heads, enclosing her in his arms more comfortably. Here, with her, he felt safe and at home, secure in the awareness that she wouldn't let him go, that as long as she was with him, he could remain tethered to his physical life. Though a short life, it had been crammed with experiences, each of such a profound nature he felt he'd been alive forever. Short and filled with pain, with so many scars building up on his mind and his body, he felt like a weapon being hammered in a forge, and wondered for what purpose he was being so assiduously prepared.

A shiver shot through his body and Andara murmured comfortingly, holding him nearer. For a moment in the howl of the wind he heard something scrabbling, almost like the dry sound of claws scraping through broken glass, and at the edge of his consciousness, he sensed something seeking him, something alive but unlike any sentient animal he knew to walk his world.

He sat up with a cry, his eyes filled with fear. Andara touched his mind, caught a distant echo of what he sensed, and clutched him nervously.

His breath came harshly as he sat shaking, pulling his awareness in like a net, tearing his thoughts away from that place they had drifted without his knowledge. The feeling of being hunted retreated, and with a groan of relief he

242

put his arms around her.

"God." His voice was more shaken than she'd ever heard it. "It's real," he said, the horror of what he'd felt audible in his tone. "It's not a dream at all." He tried to stop trembling but couldn't. Every muscle in his body quivered against her.

"What isn't a dream? What was that...I *saw* something, but I don't know what it was." Andara's disquiet was as great as his own.

"Thank God, it's gone." He almost wept with relief.

"What's gone? Deke! What's not a dream?"

He lay down and tried to compose himself. "I have this dream," he began, forcing himself to breathe slowly and regularly. "It comes when I'm upset or worried, but sometimes it comes for no reason whatsoever." He described the plain of glass, the presence that sought him, the way he knew he had to face it, whatever *it* was. "But just now, that's the first time I ever felt it waking. And it didn't feel like a dream, Andara. It felt real."

"You're under such stress...could it have been a hallucination?" She put her head on his shoulder and her arm across his chest. "I felt it, but I couldn't tell if it was in you or only visible through you."

"That was no hallucination," Deke said flatly.

"Then what was it?"

"I don't know," he said, beginning to recover. "Last spring, you remember that day by the stream...what did you *see*?"

Andara frowned. "I don't know. It didn't make sense. But it involved you and something terrible. There was darkness and the sound of the wind..."

He tried to quiet his heartbeat. "It's real," he said, unable to believe it, unable to avoid believing it. "Andara," he said, "Will you cast the tiles?"

Foreboding filled her. "Why?"

"I have to know more...I can't live with not knowing."

"Not tonight," she said. "Not in the dark."

"Why not?"

"There are powers abroad which get stronger in the dark," she said. "The best time would be in the afternoon."

"Will you do it?"

She hesitated.

"Please?" He kissed her forehead.

"I'll think about it," she told him. "But I have to warn you, you're difficult to get a reading on."

"What do you mean?"

"I've tried before," and he felt her face grow warm with embarrassment as she admitted this to him. "Often, in fact. I only get the most inconse-

243

quential information about you. Your mother told me she had the same difficulty."

"Is that unusual?"

"Very," she told him.

They were silent for some minutes, then Andara said, "Let's get some sleep."

"'...in that sleep of death, what dreams may come when we have shuffled off this mortal coil...'" Deke whispered the ancient words like a litany.

"What is that?" Andara asked.

"Shakespeare," he replied. "I'm afraid to sleep, Andara, afraid of what dreams may come to me tonight."

She pressed herself to him. "Whatever they are," she told him, "We'll face them together."

While the blizzard bowed and buffeted the tent, they held each other warmly, until after a while they felt the she-wolf stir and crawl under the edge of the quilts with them, drawn to their body heat and companionship. She touched their minds lightly, making images of comfort, and soon they were asleep and knew nothing further.

CHAPTER TWELVE

What can a person do to expiate guilt?

Since the earliest days of civilization, humans have sought ways to rid themselves of guilt's destructive effects. Alcohol, drugs, confession, psychotherapy: at various times most who suffer from these feelings try one or all of these remedies.

When Deke Wolfson first intimated to me his profound sense of guilt for the events culminating in his mother's murder, I knew he was allowing me to glimpse a part of himself he had kept hidden all those years in the hope that somehow there would be penance he could do which would permit him to forgive himself. I explained that no penance could remove a stain which was so entirely self-imposed.

He told me that had always been his greatest fear, that the penance he must endure already had been agreed upon by his greater Self and karma, and he saw no escape save death, for his was a life sentence...

— Ourn Rohlvaag; Collected Journals; City of Life, A.D. 3109

Two weeks after Tilva's funeral the army returned home, men and animals exhausted by the grueling journey through the deep snow.

The blizzard that had started the day of the funeral had continued for three more days, days of frigid temperatures and howling blasts of wind. The People had been amazed, expecting a return of the glaciers at the very least.

During the first week, callers straggled through the mounting snow to sit with their chieftain and his sister, his son and their newest healer, offering gifts and condolences in equal measure. Eventually the blizzard blew itself out, but in its wake temperatures plummeted, and a series of deadly snow squalls continued to pile up the inches until most tents were three-quarters buried.

In the second week, the condolence calls tapered off, and so, too, did the bad weather. Gradually paths were opened up and life resumed in Winter Camp. Barr moved back to his own tent, taking with him many items which held special memories of his eighteen years with his wife. After he was gone from the graceful pavilion and with his permission, Andara turned the space into a clinic, enlisting several of Tilva's serving women to help rearrange everything. She organized the bedroom into a private examining area, and sorted through the voluminous medical texts and notes her patron had accumulated over the years, making everything easily accessible.

Almost immediately she was busy with patients, many of whom came first out of curiosity and a desire to test her knowledge, and then as they saw they couldn't fool her, with real complaints. She kept two servants with her all the time, beginning the process of teaching them how to assist her. And in the meantime, she kept her eyes open for a young girl with interest and talent she could train as her acolyte.

Deke envied her absorption in her work. He himself had nothing much to do, except to deal with the many expressions of sympathy and try to be of comfort to his father, not an easy task when he was so depressed and direction-less himself.

His father, he knew, had his vision experienced at the funeral to sustain him, and there were moments when Deke looked at him and felt he was re-living that event with both joy and wonder. Knowing Tilva's spirit lived on apparently gave him great comfort. When Deke put his thoughts into his father's mind, he became aware that Barr even believed he could hear her speaking to him.

But for him, the aftermath of his mother's passing became a time he would remember later only vaguely, as a blur. His ongoing grief made every-thing around him seem flat and colorless, and he knew if it weren't for Andara he simply would have ceased to function. He could see she was comforted by spending time in Tilva's pavilion, but he had to force himself to enter. So much of his life had happened in that gracious tent, all of it bound up with his moth-er, that merely walking through the flap sent him spiraling into depression.

For the first few days he fought to regain his former equilibrium, but after a while he stopped struggling. He discovered he no longer cared what happened to him, and when at the end of the second week Hawk suggested they blade spar for a while, he agreed with such apathy that the weapons master grew worried.

During practice on a snowy area packed and flattened for the purpose, Deke was sluggish, and Hawk finally grabbed him by his sweater and shook him. "Listen, Deke, if you fight like this you're going to be killed by the first likely challenger. What's wrong with you, anyhow?"

"I just don't care about it right now," Deke replied, his sadness perva-sive. For a moment Hawk was overwhelmed, then the older man said grimly,

"You'd better care. Now, defend yourself for real, else I'll give you a cut that'll make you remember better what you're about next time." Hawk tossed aside his wood-lathe blades and unsheathed his machete, holding it in his right hand, while in his left he held one of his body daggers.

Deke looked at the steel weapons and reluctantly did the same.

Since that day at the Murdock camp, he had cleaned and sharpened the machete's blade, scrubbing the handle until every trace of blood was gone. Yet still the weapon had the power to make him shudder in memory, and now he held it almost gingerly, fearing a resurgence of the dark energy that had flooded him. So distracted was he that he was taken completely by surprise as Hawk feinted to one side, his knife too fast to defend against. Blood began to drip from his forearm, and Deke looked at himself in shock. The cut wasn't deep but it stung and he turned his eyes on Hawk, seeing his teacher's commitment.

An instant later Hawk lunged again, but at the last moment twisted under Deke's ill-timed knife slash and came in low, the machete flashing in the sunlight.

"Ow," Deke said, as the weapon opened a cut on his thigh. He tried to focus his attention, but his mind was slow, ponderous. When Hawk's knife thrust caught him across the ribs, cutting to the bone, he grabbed himself and looked at his blood-covered fingers. He looked into his teacher's eyes and knew if he didn't defend himself with more alacrity, he would end up seriously injured, maybe even crippled. Hawk would feel he had failed in his duty if Deke ever allowed himself to be bested for simple want of trying.

The machete flashed again, and there was a long, wicked cut in Deke's bicep. A second later there was a matching slash across his shoulder.

Blood was flowing freely everywhere on his body, and the sight of it made him angry. He met Hawk's next slash with a vicious parry that flung the older man's knife hand back and made an opening for his own knife to fill the gap. When he moved away, blood dripped from Hawk's hand, and the weapons master grinned fiercely as he began to circle to the left.

"Better," he said. "But not good enough." In a blindingly fast exchange, his machete flew into his left hand, the knife shot into his right, and he crossed both in a double slash that opened two long wounds on Deke's chest. For a second he was afraid he'd gone too far, that the boy was seriously injured, but then he saw the blue eyes first grow furious, then calculating.

Hawk attacked again, but this time, Deke wasn't where he expected him to be, and he felt the prick of a knife point in his back, before the machete blade opened another cut on his hand. Angered, he countered swiftly and felt his own machete strike home into Deke's flank. He heard the boy grunt with pain. Without hesitating, as if he had been waiting for the machete to be engaged for that moment, Deke's foot lashed out and smashed the knife from Hawk's right hand. He stamped down on Hawk's instep with all his strength and heard a bone give way. Using the butt of his machete, he punched Hawk violently in the jaw, sending him flying backwards, disarmed. He then jerked his teacher's machete out of his side where it had stuck fast in a rib.

"Ah," he gritted loudly, as a surge of blood seeped from him. He panted, holding himself painfully. With difficulty he picked up the fallen knife and handed back the machete. Hawk took both in his undamaged hand.

"Your father would be angry if I ever let you get away with being so lazy," Hawk said, staring guiltily at the blood pouring from Deke's side. "Come on, we'd best get you seen to. I didn't mean to hurt you so badly. I thought sure you'd wake up before I did so much damage."

Deke swayed on his feet, and stuck his knife and machete back in their sheaths. Pressing his elbow tightly over the wound in his side, he felt Hawk take his other arm and begin to walk him rapidly towards his mother's tent. On their way they passed Barr, who, when he saw the blood, put his arm around Deke's shoulders and gave Hawk a furious glance before accompanying them inside.

There were several people waiting their turn to see Andara, but when she came from the back room at her assistants' call and saw Deke, she quickly gestured them inside and drew the hangings shut behind them. She looked at her father, saw his wounds weren't serious, and practically hissed at him,

"What did you think you were doing?" She caressed Deke's cheek lovingly and made him sit on the waist-high examining table she had installed in the room. "Lie back," she said, quickly removing his blood-soaked sweater and shirt. She probed the wounds carefully, saw the one in the flank was the most serious, and indicated for Barr to pull off Deke's pants so she could check the thigh slash.

"You are so lucky you didn't cut the artery," she told her father, anger clipping her words short.

"You may not believe this from looking at us," Hawk said, "But he won."

Deke groaned slightly, the wound in his side throbbing more intensely as Andara began to irrigate it.

"What were you fighting about?" Barr asked, his hand resting on Deke's head, disturbed by all the blood.

"Just practicing." Deke set his jaw against the pain.

"Aye, it took a while for your son to get warmed up," Hawk said.

"Andara?" Barr turned to the girl who continued to flood the wound. "How serious is it?"

"Once I get him cleaned and stitched he should be all right," she said. "But he's losing a good bit of blood. Really, Papa, you might have been more careful."

"No," Deke said, "I wasn't paying attention. If he hadn't fought true, I would have been the worse for it. Thanks, Hawk," he said, reaching for his teacher's hand.

"Men," Andara muttered. "Only a man would thank the one who cut him for the pleasure of the wound."

Barr looked at Hawk. "How bad are you?"

"He broke my foot," Hawk replied.

Andara put her assistants to work irrigating Deke's other wounds and kissed his forehead. "Are you in a lot of pain?"

"Not too bad," he lied.

"You'll have to take it easy for a few days. No more fighting." She looked hard at her father.

After a while she cauterized some blood vessels in his side using a probe heated in the stove, then stitched him carefully, wanting to kiss him all over to take away the pain, having to force herself to stay calm and detached. Most of the other wounds could be closed with only a stitch or two, and shortly thereafter she was finished. She put bandages over those cuts that needed them, and gave him a pat. "You should go home and climb into bed. I'll be along directly. Don't try to do anything," she warned. "And don't take a bath."

Deke sat up, feeling the stitches pulling in his skin. He looked at her gratefully. "Thanks," he said, holding her shoulder for support as he hopped unsteadily off the table. She handed him his clothes and looked at Barr.

"Maybe you could give him an arm home?" she asked. "I'm going to see to my father and then finish with those folks out front. I should be there in an hour or so."

"All right," Barr agreed. He watched Deke pull on his trousers laboriously and button them up. He helped him put on his shirt and sweater, then wrapped his own cloak around his son's shoulders, half-supporting him as they walked from the room.

Andara turned to her father and examined his wounds. The cut on his back was barely a pinprick, much more typical of the types of wounds gotten during blade-sparring matches. Deke, it seemed, had exercised considerably more control than had her father, and she wondered what had happened to make his normally laconic nature so explosive. Even the wounds across his hand weren't especially serious, though she did have to do a little very fine stitching to repair one of his tendons which was torn nearly in half.

When she finished, she looked up at him and said, "If you had hurt him seriously I never would have spoken to you again."

"If I hadn't hurt him, the next time might have been with someone who would have killed him for his carelessness," Hawk told her. "I did what I did because I love him, don't ever think otherwise."

"You have a funny way of showing it," Andara told him. "Are you sure it had nothing to do with me?"

"I hardly think so," Hawk said, visibly disturbed by the remark. "He was fighting like he wanted to die, like he wanted me to kill him. I had to do something to wake him up."

"You almost put him to sleep, permanently," Andara said quietly. "That wound in his side...a little deeper..." She shrugged.

"Maybe by so doing I saved his life," he said.

"He's been through a lot, Papa. You might show a little compassion. You might let him finish grieving."

"There's no time for that, girl," Hawk said firmly. "At any time his or even your life could depend on him having his wits about him. Any man who's going to lead the People can't afford to languish in depression. It's my job to see to it he's fit to lead."

"You said something about a broken foot," Andara said.

"Aye," he said, pulling off his boot with a groan. "The miserable wretch crushed it, I think."

"Good," Andara muttered, and examined the instep. "Yes," she said. "It's broken. I'll make you a cast and you can use crutches to stay off it for a few weeks."

"You have mighty little sympathy for your poor father," he said. "You'd think I hadn't been the one who took care of you all these years."

"Deke was so careful not to hurt you seriously...do you know what he could have done to you with a thought?" Andara tried to control her anger and failed. "God, Papa, he may have let you kill him rather than harm you."

Hawk was adamant. "No," he said. "This is something you should be aware of, daughter. He sought my blade intentionally."

"If you thought that, why didn't you stop?" Andara looked at him meaningfully, then pressed firmly on the bones of his instep, pushing them back into position while he clamped his jaws shut in pain. She wrapped the foot in soft bandages and began to layer plaster and gauze until she had built up a sturdy thickness. When she was finished, she gave him a hand and helped him hop into the outer room to let the cast dry. Then she beckoned to the next patient.

On their slow walk back to Deke's tent, Barr peered at his son worriedly. "Was it only a sparring match?"

"I think so," Deke said. "What else?"

"I've never seen Hawk cut anyone so badly in practice before," his father said.

"He was worried, trying to get me mad. Maybe he lost control a little. It was good for me, though."

"Why would he try to get you mad?"

Deke shrugged painfully. "My heart wasn't in it."

"Fighting when you're mad can make you careless. Much better to stay cool."

"I know. But I really wasn't trying. He didn't do anything wrong." Deke raised his head. "Listen!" he said. "Do you hear that?"

Barr cocked his head. "Aye," he said, and smiled slightly. "I've been worried about them."

"Let's go see..."

"Forget it," his father said firmly. "You'll see them soon enough. We're putting you in your bed, like your woman ordered."

"Ah, yes," Deke said, enjoying the words. "My woman."

Barr heard the enjoyment, and was gratified. Soon the sounds of horses, men, and heavy equipment could be heard more clearly as the approaching army forced its way through the waist-high snow.

They reached Deke's tent and went inside. Hopi nosed both of them, putting images of wolves greeting one another into their minds. Barr gave the wolf a pat and helped Deke into the bedroom. While his son removed his destroyed clothes, he rummaged in the chest for a clean, flannel shirt which he handed over, as well as clean underwear.

When Deke was settled under the quilt, Barr went into the kitchen, stirred the embers in the woodstove, and added more wood. Then he came back and sat on the edge of the bed.

"How are you getting along, Father?" Deke asked. "Is it any easier at all?"

Barr shrugged. "Not easier, just more familiar." He rubbed his beard, and Deke thought he saw more silver in it.

Deke nodded, understanding.

Barr studied him thoughtfully. "When you're recovered, I'll show you the maps and charts I've collected of the various routes west. They're very old, and likely the country has changed a good deal since they were drawn, but they will serve as basic indicators of distance and terrain. They show where ancient cities used to lie as well as their surrounding sprawl of smaller communities, so it'll be easy to pinpoint where ruins will be. I have one chart I think you'll find particularly interesting."

Deke's eyebrows went up questioningly.

"Aye, it was drawn by a man who claimed to have made the journey all the way to the sea. He said he'd found a city, but hadn't approached too closely. Said it was crawling with demons, among other things. He said it lay half-submerged on the coastline and stretched for miles. He called it the 'Dead City.'" Barr paused. "Of course, he may simply have been mad," he added. "My father thought so."

"What was your father like?" Deke asked.

"He was a hard man, very hard, but fair. He was unforgiving of mis-

251

takes but quick to reward success. At the strangest times he would surprise me with an act of kindness when I least expected it."

"Did you love him?"

"I respected him enormously," Barr said. "He was a splendid warrior, a pure soldier."

"And your mother? My grandmother?"

"Ah, she was special, son, very special. Probably my better qualities come from her."

"How did she die?"

Barr's voice was somber. "In childbirth."

"The child?"

"Also dead."

"How old were you?"

"I was nine. Leah was four."

"It must have been hard for you."

"Life is usually hard, Deke. Never forget it. Always grab whatever joy you can find, because life is hellbent on stealing it away from us."

"I know," Deke whispered. "Father...how are your dreams?"

Barr's gaze sharpened. "What makes you ask that, son?"

"Do you ever dream about something in the ruins?"

"Like what?"

"Something terrible, inhuman."

"Are you having such dreams?" Barr rested his hand on Deke's ankle and gave him a comforting squeeze through the bedding.

"I've always had them," Deke said, "But now they're changing. And I'm not so sure they're simple dreams."

"What do you think they are?" Barr's voice was stable and reassuring.

"I don't know. You never have such a dream?"

"No," Barr said.

"This dream feels clairvoyant," Deke said. "And I feel it has something to do with the west."

Barr nodded. "The unknown is always frightening. And it's a fact that demons generally are found west of our lands. That's one reason I want to push westward, to dispense with the mysteries and make the unknown known."

"What do demons look like?" Deke asked.

Barr frowned. "They don't look like anything," he said. "But they feel awful, they make us feel awful. You can see them sometimes; often they travel in a little whirlwind, something like what people call a dust devil. But sometimes you don't know they're around until they take someone, and then it's too late."

"Have you ever seen that happen?"

"Aye."

"What did you do?"

"We killed the poor bastard," Barr said. "Quick as we could."

"What happened to the demon?"

"If it's in someone's body and the body dies, it also dies."

"How can a person avoid being taken?"

"If a demon wants you, it gets you. Sooner or later."

"They don't seem to want us very often, do they?"

"It's true, they seem to take others before they take any from our clan."

"Why is that, do you think?"

"Demons rarely go after large, well-armed parties," Barr told him. "With a couple hundred men, you're safe as you can ever be."

"Are our weapons of any use against them?"

"I'm not sure. I do know that well-armed men are more confident, and perhaps that's what makes the difference."

There was a sound in the living area and a second later Andara strode in, bringing the cold air with her. She took off her mittens and cloak and hung them on a peg, then went to Deke, taking his hand and kissing his cheek. "How are you feeling?" she asked solicitously.

"I'm fine," he replied, catching her face and kissing her more thoroughly. "A little sore, and some of the stitches are pulling, but otherwise not too bad. I'm lucky to have such a good witch to look after me."

"Will you stay to supper, my lord?" Andara asked, her color considerably higher after the kiss. "I've got turkey stuffed with cornbread, chestnuts... also candied sweet potatoes."

"Who could resist such an offer?" Barr asked, smiling at her fondly, his experienced eyes noting the flush and approving the way it heightened her fresh beauty. "Are you inviting your father?"

"I'm angry with him," she said, her eyes flashing as she thought about it. "But I guess he'd be too hurt if I took it out on him over food."

"I'll fetch him," Barr said, rising.

"Thank you," Andara said. "It'll take me an hour or so."

"We'll see you then." Barr slung on his cloak and ducked out.

Andara looked at Deke searchingly. "Well?" she asked. "What really happened?"

"It's as we said," he told her. "I needed to be woken up."

Andara kicked off her boots and crawled into bed with him. "I've accustomed myself to the idea that you could get hurt in battle," she said. "But I thought you'd be safe with my own father." She kissed his lips, careful not to

253

bump any of his wounds.

"Why are you really so mad?" he asked, his hand in her hair.

"Just look at you!" she said. "I can't even touch you!"

"Sure you can," he said. "Carefully."

"You've got cuts everywhere," she told him. "And your poor side...that damn blade went right into the bone. By the ruins, I could just kill him."

"He meant well."

She smoothed his hair. "Are you hurting anywhere? I could give you something."

"Maybe later, with dinner." He stroked her face lightly. "I can still touch you, anyway."

"Touch, maybe, but probably we can't make love for a while," Andara said, plainly irritated.

"Now I'm mad at him, too," Deke told her.

"If he had just avoided that slice into your side, we probably could have managed something."

"We probably can manage something anyway," he said. "But it'll be complicated."

"We'll see about that," she said. "Later."

Throughout dinner, the sounds of heavy wagons and artillery rolling through the city's main thoroughfare could be heard, and every so often the ground vibrated and shook as particularly weighty cannon were brought through. The air was alive with the sound of cursing, bellowing soldiers. When the meal was finished, Hawk and Barr excused themselves and went to see Willie O'Dale. Deke would have liked to go with them but knew he wasn't needed, and besides, now his cuts were beginning to hurt in earnest.

Andara noticed he had grown quiet and got up to put a pot of water on to boil. She picked through her herbs and brought out the poppies. These she steeped, making a strong tea sweetened with honey, and gave it to Deke in a cup.

"Drink it quickly," she said. "It should make you feel better. You can have another cup if necessary."

He didn't argue, seeking the relief he knew it would provide. "Willow bark wouldn't work?"

"Willow bark sometimes interferes with clotting," Andara replied.

"Aye, but these poppies..." He rubbed his eyes. "They fool with my head."

There was a rattle at the door and Andara opened the flap. Mastra and Tim stood in the snow, noticeably surprised to see her. "Come in," she said, standing aside.

They ducked through and she tied the flap behind them. The two boys stood awkwardly, their faces somber.

"We came as soon as we heard," Tim finally said. "I'm really sorry, Deke, I don't know what to say."

"Is there anything you need? I know we're probably too late to be of any use," Mastra said sadly.

Andara went back to the table and sat near Deke, taking his hand in hers.

"Thanks," Deke said softly. "But we're all right."

"Do you want anything to eat or drink?" Andara asked them. "There's plenty of turkey and we have ale in the cold closet."

Mastra and Tim looked back and forth between them, then took off their cloaks and sat at the table.

"That sounds great," Mastra said, wishing he knew what else to say. When they had reached the tent city, the murder had been the first news given to the returning army, and all the soldiers were equally shocked. Deke's manhood group was especially upset, because Tilva always had been kind and welcoming to them.

"Deke," Tim said in his blunt way, "They say you killed Gant Murdock."

"Aye," Deke said, and didn't elaborate.

"Your father," Mastra said. "How's he holding up?"

"As you'd expect," Deke replied.

Andara squeezed his hand a little tighter, knowing by his short answers how difficult this conversation was for him. She could feel how he was reliving everything and decided he didn't need to be doing that again, not tonight. She jumped up and put plates in front of Tim and Mastra, pulling turkey, stuffing, and potatoes from the oven where they'd been keeping warm. She got the jug of fresh ale from the cold closet and poured four mugs.

"How was your trip home?" she asked, picking a safe subject and serving out the food.

Tim talked around a mouthful of potatoes. "These are delicious, Andara," he said. "The trip was horrible. We were already on the way when it started to snow, and we could hardly see where we were going."

"Aye," Mastra agreed, pouring gravy over his turkey and stuffing, then digging in with his fork. After a bite, he rolled his eyes with pleasure. "Andara, it's a pity you aren't the cook for the army. War would be a snap if the food wasn't so terrible."

"It'll be good to sleep in a bed again, too," Tim agreed. He studied

Deke judiciously, then noted he was wearing only a shirt and underwear. "I see you don't believe in dressing for dinner."

"It's uncomfortable right now," Deke said and displayed some of his wounds.

"What happened to you?" Mastra asked, his eyes widening.

"Hawk and I were blade-sparring today," Deke told him.

"Hmmph," Andara said under her breath.

"It looks like you got the worst of it," Tim said sympathetically.

"Aye, I guess I did."

"This meal is incredible," Tim continued, helping himself to more turkey while Mastra nodded. "I can't get over how good it is to eat home-cooked food again."

Deke sipped his ale, feeling lightheaded from the opium. He was glad to be anesthetized; it made dealing with his friends easier. He nodded, glancing at Andara. "There's always something delicious to eat around here these days."

When the boys finished eating, Andara put away the food while they shifted to the couch and chairs. She brought her mug and sat with Deke on the couch. He put his arm around her and she rested her hand on his uninjured thigh. Mastra and Tim watched them and exchanged glances, surprised by their casual intimacy.

"Did Deke tell you about Root?" Mastra asked Andara, jealous of the familiar way her hand lay on Deke's leg. He could almost feel that touch on his own inner thigh, and looked away, licking his lips nervously.

"Not too much," she said, aware of his feelings and amused by them. Deliberately she moved her hand higher in a gentle caress. Deke looked at her hand, then Mastra's eyes. When he understood what she was doing, he smiled and took her hand in his, holding it so she wouldn't get into further mischief.

"All right," Tim said, "I'll tell, since Mastra has obviously fallen into a trance...Deke went into the fort as a spy, pretended to be chased by bandits and they let him right in. We were the bandits. Next thing we know, he's coming out of that place with a hostage."

Deke thought back to the town of Root, amazed at how far away and long ago it seemed. He could hardly remember what he had done there, how he had felt in that dreadful place. He remembered killing Jubal, remembered the townspeople executing the minister, but everything else had blurred into the time lived before his mother's murder. He couldn't place himself emotionally in that period; it seemed he had been in his current confusion of grief and rage forever.

Andara sensed his change of mood, and her mind touched his gently.

Do you want them to leave? she asked inside his thoughts.

Let them stay, he responded the same way. *It comforts them to feel they're comforting us.*

She nodded. His sensitivity to his friends' feelings made her want to embrace him, but she restrained the urge, gazing at him with such affection he felt it and was kindled.

"The hostage was a minister who'd abused a lot of young boys in the town, even killed a bunch of them. Deke exposed his crimes to the people, then gave him back to them. You should have seen what they did!" Tim was still amazed as he told it.

"What did they do?" Andara prompted.

"They hung him by his...you know," Tim gestured.

"Testicles?" she asked innocently.

"Not just them, everything." Tim shook his head. "They dropped him through a trapdoor to hang him, but he didn't hang so well."

"What a pity; men so like to be well-hung."

"Aye," Mastra said after a second, shocked by her ribald humor, glancing at Deke and Tim who were chuckling helplessly. "Then they took turns beating him with a whip until he was dead."

"Don't forget the most disgusting part," Tim said gleefully.

"Right, they took his severed organs and nailed 'em up..."

"All right," Deke said quickly. "No need to go on."

"I can take it," Andara assured him. "They nailed them up? Where?"

"Right in front of his nose!" Tim said triumphantly.

"I suppose you applauded?" Andara's voice was caustic.

"No," Tim said. "That would have been too disgusting, even for us."

Mastra continued. "That was the worst thing. The best thing was the way Deke conquered the town."

"Deke conquered the town?" Andara's eyes widened. "You didn't tell me that," she said to him.

"He's too modest," Tim remarked. "He planned the whole thing, spied out the place to be sure there were no secrets that could kill any of our men, then launched a full scale attack. It was great!"

Andara looked at Deke who looked away.

"His father said it was his plan so he should lead the attack."

"The soldiers wrote songs about him," Mastra told her. "They knew the reason he went in alone was to save them from getting hurt."

"Don't embarrass me," Deke said softly.

"Best thing was," Mastra concluded, "We had no casualties, and there were almost none in the civilian population either. Deke had those people eating out of our hands in a day."

"How?" Andara wanted to know.

"He conquered 'em with kindness," Tim said, astonished anew as he remembered. "They were actually cheering and thanking him for having conquered them!"

"They were cheering because I set them free," Deke corrected him.

"Aye, well, it's all one and the same," Tim said admiringly.

Andara squeezed Deke's hand. "I like that story," she said and smiled. "Except for the torture part."

There was silence for a moment, then Tim nudged Mastra. "We ought to let you get some rest. You look pretty cut up. We'll visit again tomorrow."

"Aye," Mastra agreed. "Come on, Andara, we'll walk you home."

"I am home," she said easily. "I live here now."

Tim and Mastra looked at her, amazed. Then they looked at Deke who was kissing her hair possessively.

Mastra swallowed as comprehension filled him.

Tim grinned and eyed Andara appraisingly. "Congratulations," he said. Then to Deke, "You lucky bastard, you caught the prettiest girl of all! Any time you get tired of him, Andara, there's room in my tent..."

"Aye," Mastra agreed, "There's plenty in mine, as well."

Andara gave an earthy chuckle. "In your dreams, boys."

"You can't blame a fellow for trying," Tim said.

"Aye," Mastra said, looking at her searchingly, wondering what it would be like to have her in his bed. From the way she looked, she was happy with her new living arrangement, and Mastra sighed to himself, wondering what Deke had done to get her to move in. Most likely he'd never find out, because he was sure Deke wouldn't discuss their personal life any more than he had when they were sparking before the Spring Festival.

"No wonder Hawk chopped you up," Tim said knowingly.

"Hawk's all right," Deke said, his fingers playing with the ends of Andara's hair.

Mastra watched them enviously for a moment, then sighed again. "Come on, Tim, let's leave the lovers to themselves. We'll go back to our lonely, cold, bachelor tents."

"The others will probably stop by tomorrow," Tim said with a grin. "Just so you don't get caught with your pants down."

"Very funny," Deke said as Andara laughed aloud. "Thanks for coming over," he said.

"Thanks for feeding us," Tim said. "And again, I'm so sorry, Deke. I'll miss her."

"Aye," Mastra said. "Me, too."

When their friends had gone, Andara brought Deke the last of the opium tea along with water for herself and rejoined him on the couch. "How are you feeling?"

"Strange," he said, drinking down the tea. "My head is spinning."

"You should go to bed and rest," she said.

"Aye, in a minute."

Carefully she leaned against him and he put an arm around her, kissing her ear. "Did it make you jealous that Mastra and Tim wanted me to move in with them?" Her tone was teasing.

"No," he said, and kissed her again. "I understand you have to test your powers. Besides, you know manhood groups usually share their girlfriends, don't you?"

Andara sat up and looked at him in disbelief, then, when she was sure he was joking, settled back, a little ruffled.

Deke laughed softly, caressing her neck and shoulders. "I'd have to try and kill anyone who wanted to take you from me," he said. "Even if it was one of them."

"What if I wanted to leave?"

He studied her. "That would be different, obviously."

She put her arms around him carefully. "I'm not hurting you, am I?"

"I'm feeling no pain," he assured her.

She kissed his mouth with slow enjoyment. "I don't want anyone else."

"I'm glad," he said, with feeling. "You want to go to bed?"

"Aye," she said. "Are you sure you're all right?"

"We'll figure it out," he said, rising unsteadily, the opium making him see strange, colorful movements of what looked like light or energy zipping through the air. He buried his lips in her hair and leaned against her as they walked to the bedroom.

"Here," he said when they got there, feeling as if the room was stretching before his eyes. He held her against one of the tent posts and began to unfasten garments dreamily, letting them drop at random while his hands and mouth sought her bare flesh. He felt her untie his underwear and take him in hand.

They heard a rattle at the front door and stopped, listening to see if whoever it was would go away.

The knocker sounded again, more persistently.

"Maybe you better see who it is," she said, too caught up to move.

He pulled up his underwear and put on a pair of loose pants. Making sure the bedroom hangings were closed, he went to the door and opened the flap. A woman he didn't recognise was there, clearly distraught.

"I'm sorry to disturb you, m'lord," she said in a rush. "But I was told the Lady Andara could be found here?"

"Come in," Deke said. "An emergency?"

"Aye, m'lord. My husband...he can't seem to get his breath and he's having chest pains..."

"One second." Deke went to the hangings and poked his head through. "I think you've got a patient with a heart attack," he said, watching her dress swiftly. "Do you need help?"

"No, I'll manage," and she quickly gathered her medical bag, Tilva's old one, Deke noticed. "Go to bed," she said, giving him a quick kiss. "I don't know how long I'll be."

"I'll wait up for you," he said. "Hurry back."

She went out through the hangings and he wrapped her cloak around her. "Let's go," she said to the woman.

When they were gone, Deke put wood in the stove and patted Hopi, his eyes speculative. "You're getting fat," he said to her, touching her thoughts affectionately. He looked closer, noticing how soft and full her coat was getting, how she had an enigmatic female look in her eyes. "What do you know," he said in wonder. He sent an image of puppies nursing to her and felt her stomach and nipples, realizing she was perhaps halfway through her pregnancy. "I'll have to make you a den of your own right here," he told the wolf. He smiled, pleased at the thought that a part of Canis would live on.

Going back to the bedroom, he selected a book from the shelf and stretched out on the bed, protecting his wounded side unconsciously. Hopi jumped up beside him, resting her head on his stomach and gazing into his eyes with complete devotion. He petted her for a while, his mind drifting from the opium. He felt peculiar, connected and disconnected all at once: connected to the texture of the world around him, disconnected from harsh feelings or physical pain, even his own frustrated sexuality. There was the sense that his imagination was wandering in a hundred directions, each more surrealistic than the next.

His reverie meandered along accented by occasional flashes of light and color as well as moments of vertigo. He re-lived the sparring match with Hawk, the way he had been so phlegmatic, absolutely limp in every way. Andara was sure he hadn't fought because he didn't want to hurt her father, but Deke knew better. He had allowed Hawk to inflict the punishment because he knew he deserved it; knew he should be made to feel physical pain to match the psychic pain that held everyone he cared about in thrall and for which he felt responsible. He hadn't fought because he had hoped Hawk would kill him.

His thoughts spun on, and in his opium-filled awareness, they were accompanied by music and colored light formations. He opened his book but was unable to concentrate. The letters were crawling around on the page as if alive, and he could make no sense of them at all.

He allowed his eyes to close for what he thought was only a second but when he opened them he saw Andara getting undressed quietly, trying not to wake him. "When did you get home?" he asked sleepily, swinging his legs over the side of the bed to get undressed and laying his book on the nightstand. He motioned to a clean chamber pot. "Do you need to use this?"

"I used the latrine outside," she said. "Go ahead if you want."

He moved the lid aside and let go, feeling her eyes on him. When he was finished, he covered the pot and put it in its accustomed place. He was drowsy from the opium and quickly slipped out of his clothes and into the bed beside her. "How's your patient?" he asked.

"He'll be fine," she said. "It wasn't a heart attack, just bad indigestion."

"Ruins, you left me for an upset stomach?" Deke shook his head.

"That kind of indigestion feels just like a heart attack. Poor man was terrified." She reached across him and turned off the lamp. "Is Hopi sleeping between us tonight?"

"You get her to move. I don't have the heart. She's pregnant."

"Oh, you noticed?"

"Why didn't you say something if you knew?"

"I knew you'd figure it out," she said, worming her feet under the wolf and wiggling them until Hopi got up and jumped off the bed. Andara moved closer to Deke, her arm sliding across his belly comfortably. "Your sweet body, so cut up...I hate to see you in pain," she said, kissing him, opening her awareness to him.

His thoughts wandered into hers in a fuzzy way, and she smiled, realizing he was absolutely plastered from the opium. He put his arm around her carefully, and said, "Come spring, I'll be taking raiding parties out into the ruins. My father wants to expand westward."

Andara stiffened against him. "Why?"

"It's time."

"You personally will be taking raiding parties?"

"Aye." Deke's gaze was focused elsewhere as he stroked her bare back.

"I suppose after conquering a town that seems only logical."

"It didn't really feel like a conquest," he said, forcing himself to think back. "One thing simply led to the next, like this," and he moved his hand lower to her buttocks, enjoying the sensual curve of her hip against his fingers. "Your skin is so soft, smooth," he said.

"Mm." She put her mouth on his nipple gently. "Yours is like the ruins."

They both started to laugh, giggling madly, until Deke wiped his streaming eyes and begged, "No more...you're killing me...!"

Andara was instantly concerned. "Are you all right? Stitches hurt?"

"Everything hurts," he told her. "But at least this hurt I can deal with."

"I'm sorry you had such a rotten day." She caressed his cheek affectionately.

"It's been a good day," he told her. "I feel more like myself, if you can understand what I mean."

"I do understand," she said. "You feel better because you took a beating. It distracts you, helps ease your guilt."

"Aye," he said, amazed by her.

"I have such hopes that you'll give up all that guilt one day," she said, her voice warm with her love for him.

"I'm trying," he whispered, holding her tighter.

"I know you are," she said tenderly. "I was so proud of you for not hurting my father too badly, even though he deserved it."

"He didn't deserve it. He was trying to help me."

"Still," she said. "I know what you could have done."

"That wouldn't have been fair," Deke said. "I'll fight dirty when it counts, but not sparring with your father."

"Using all your abilities isn't fighting dirty," she said. "It's just...fighting. To me, all fighting is dirty."

"Maybe when you're the Lady Andara, healer and witch woman," he said with a grin she heard rather than saw. "But when you're my Andara and I've got you where I want you, you like it. You like it a lot." He kissed her again, slowly.

"You have a real crude streak, you know that?" she murmured, not minding that he was crude.

"Aye, that's what makes it so good between us," he said.

"You being crude?"

"And you being such a...firecracker," he said.

She laughed. "If I'm a firecracker," she said, her tone heating up as he touched her intimately, "It's because you know how to light my fuse."

"Now, where's that little fuse anyway?" he asked playfully, his fingers sliding between her thighs.

She opened her legs and sighed as he caressed her.

"There," he said, "How's that?"

"Perfect," she told him, putting her hand over his, directing him subtly.

"I'm glad it's winter," he said, propping himself gingerly on his wounded arm to kiss her more completely. "Because I intend to spend as much time as possible right here, if you're agreeable."

"Aye," she said, almost purring.

Carefully he pulled her over him and she opened her legs wider as she positioned herself correctly. In a second she sat up and began to ride him.

"Are you all right?" She closed her eyes with pleasure.

"Aye, just go slowly and quietly," he said, "No sudden movements." After a while, "This isn't so complicated."

"No," she said, before it became impossible to speak any more. "It's not complicated at all."

By morning the opium had worn off and Deke rose to consciousness in a haze of excruciating pain. He groaned as he sat up and used the chamber pot, then fell back weakly into bed. His skin felt hot and he tried to lie quietly, not wanting to wake Andara. The pain was everywhere, every wound alive with it, particularly the one in his side. He lay with the quilt thrown off, bare skin exposed to the morning air, feeling some relief in the cold. All at once he began to shiver and his body was gripped by tremors that wouldn't stop no matter how he tried.

This brought Andara awake with a start, and she turned to him, her expression filled first with concern, then, as she felt his searing flesh, with mounting panic. She jumped up and tucked the quilts around him after a quick examination of his flank which seemed to be the primary source of his fever. The wound was inflamed and she bit her lip worriedly. She knew when bones were compromised as Deke's rib had been, it was difficult to prevent infection.

"Deke, sweetheart," she said to him. "Can you hear me?"

"Aye," he said, turning eyes glazed with fever on her.

"You have an infection," she told him gently. "I'm going to have to open the wound in your side again, but I need to run and get some instruments. Will you be all right for a few minutes?"

He nodded, shuddering violently, and she kissed him quickly before throwing her clothes on, grabbing her cloak, and flying from the tent.

In less than five minutes she was back and moments after that her two assistants hurried into the bedroom with her. She had one of them start a fire in the kitchen woodstove and get water boiling in a large pot where she put several fine probes and scalpels to sterilize. She had the other woman help her roll Deke onto his side with the flank wound up, propping him securely with pillows and rolled towels.

Throughout this she could see his fever increasing before her eyes, and soon his muttered protests became words running together in delirium. She scrubbed her hands in the basin and dried them on a clean cloth.

Quickly she took her fine scissors and cut the stitches holding the wound closed. Immediately she saw the spreading infection. She flushed the gathered blood and pus away and probed into his flesh, seeking the source. In seconds she nodded to herself. It was as she had feared, in the rib.

There was a cold breeze on her shoulder and the hangings at the door parted. Barr came in, throwing his hood back from his shoulders and kneeling by the bedside out of her way. "What's wrong?" he demanded. "The servants said you were in a tizzy."

"His rib is infected," she told him. "I'm going to try and kill the infection."

"How?" he asked, his eyes growing wide with fear as Deke practically convulsed on the bed.

"Any bug that can get him sick this fast is too powerful for my usual herbal concoctions," she said. "Tilva did some experimenting with molds and left a jar of powder she said was very strong. But before I can give him that, I have to reduce the infection, which is spreading fast. If this were summer I'd use maggots, but right now and because of the bone..." She hesitated. "I have to use fire."

"What can I do?" the chieftain asked, the muscles in his jaw clenching.

"Hold him still," Andara said. "And pray."

By this time the fire was going strongly in the woodstove and Andara put her steel probes into the flames to heat. She checked the water on the stove and added a combination of herbs, including bark from magnolia, sumach, and willow to help reduce his fever.

Soon her instruments were ready and she laid them on a freshly laundered cloth on the nightstand. Using a scalpel, she quickly scraped away shreds of necrosed tissue from the wound, examined the bone where the machete had cut into it, and began flushing it with a wash of echinacea and distilled water. She shook her head and got her probes. "Hold him now," she told Barr, and pushed the heated tips against the infected tissues while Deke thrashed and bucked.

"I can't be sure I'm getting the bone," she said, frustrated. "There is one more thing I can try." She took out a bottle filled with black powder and got a long splinter of wood which she lit in the oil lamp. Then, pouring a small mound of the powder into the wound over the rib, she touched the flame to it. Instantly it caught fire, sizzling and flaring as it burned. Deke let out an agonized scream and sweat poured from him as Barr struggled to hold him down. In a few seconds the powder had burned up fully and the flame died. Andara washed and flushed the wound, checking to make sure she could *see* no further sign of infection.

"Maybe that got it," she said after a while, her muscles beginning to cramp from tension. She bathed the sweat from his face tenderly. Now he lay completely still, passed out in a dead faint.

"Where did you learn that?" Barr asked her, awed.

"Tilva taught me how gun powder can cure as well as kill," Andara said, and began to sew him up. When she was finished, she put a bandage over the stitches and had Barr help her wrap him all the way around his body to hold the dressing in place.

Together they settled him on the bed and she sponged him gently before putting the quilts over him. Andara spoke to one of her assistants who brought a cup of the herb tea sweetened with honey. Using a measuring spoon, she dipped out a generous amount of Tilva's mold powder and stirred it into water.

"Hold him up, please," she said. "I need to get this into him."

Barr complied, cradling Deke against his body, while Andara carefully poured the liquid down his throat. She blew on the tea to cool it, and bit by bit, managed to get that into him as well.

Afterwards, while her assistants cleared away the bloody cloths used to prop him up, Andara lifted his eyelids, checked the color of his gums, listened to his heartbeat which was galloping in his chest, and watched his fast, thready breathing with concern. She put a couple pillows under his legs to elevate them and tucked the quilts around him up to the ears.

"How is he?" Barr asked, worried by her expression.

"I've done everything I can," she said, sitting on the edge of the bed, drained. "I'll keep the fluids going into him and more powder. With luck..."

"Luck?" Barr's expression was startled.

Andara touched the chieftain's arm. "I'm frightened for him," she whispered. "My father said he deliberately sought the blade."

Barr digested this, then looked at his son's fever-tormented face. "How long before you know?"

"When his fever breaks." She paused, her expression grim. "Or doesn't."

Barr took Deke's heated hand between his, amazed to see it was as large as his own, and identical in shape. Andara left him for a minute, returning with several icicles which she broke and wrapped in a clean cloth. She laid the cool compress on Deke's forehead and said, "The best thing now is for him to rest."

"Aye," Barr agreed, sighing.

Andara went into the outer room where she spoke briefly with her assistants. Soon she returned with a cup of tea which she gave to Barr and one for herself which she drank slowly, trying to control her terror so the chieftain wouldn't see it. Deke's fever was too high, she couldn't recall seeing one higher. She remembered Tilva telling her about rampaging infections that could encompass enough tissue in a few hours to kill an otherwise healthy person. She found herself following her own advice to Barr, and began praying silently to her spirit guides and the Universe, knowing she couldn't bear the loneliness of her life without Deke in it. Her eyes were on Barr's face and she knew he couldn't face life without his son either. This awareness made her feel great empathy for him, and she watched him hold Deke's hand to his cheek tenderly before placing it back under the quilts.

Soon Deke was tossing and turning again, muttering incomprehensibly, his limbs jerking, tears of pain running from his closed eyes. Andara replaced the cold compress; the first one had melted away in minutes against his heated brow. When she touched him she thought his flesh felt like a furnace burning too hot for safety, and she debated whether to try and reduce his temperature or let his body combat the infection in its own best fashion.

She fought down tears as she battled her uncertainty, aware she wasn't experienced enough to know what to do, and that her ignorance could kill him.

She was about to order the tub brought in and filled with snow when a chill wind stirred the hangings behind her and she turned simultaneously with Barr, both of them staring at the heavily cloaked figure who stood just inside the door. In a moment, the figure threw back its hood and Andara's mouth dropped open.

"Well met, Lord Wolfson," said the Old Man, and Barr nodded.

"Not so well met, Old Man," the chieftain said.

Andara stared silently at the Old One, as she now thought of that person. For a moment she saw the entity through her own and the chieftain's eyes, and perceived both personas shifting back and forth too quickly for her mind to register.

"Our young chief is poised on the edge of decision," the Old One told them.

"Do you know what the decision will be?" Andara asked tensely.

"Only he knows, but I thought I could lend my modest skills and at least reassure you that everything that should be done, has been done."

"Thank you," Andara said gratefully, relief flooding her.

The Old Woman nodded, then went to the bedside. Quickly Andara pulled back the quilts and stood aside as the ancient crone moved her hand across the bandage, feeling the heat there, closing her eyes to better focus on the injury.

Barr watched as the Old Man's touch seemed to quiet Deke's delirium. The brujo removed his hand and when he looked up, Barr gazed expectantly into the aged, jet eyes. Deke began to writhe and moan again and Barr's lips tightened.

"You've done well," Barr heard him say to Andara. "Everything is in order. You must let this fever run its course. He has chosen a trial by fire, both metaphysically and metaphorically speaking, and we cannot interfere."

"I can't just sit by and watch him suffer," Andara said, her tone bleak with the effort of maintaining control.

"Then talk to him, remind him what he has to come back to, that this world still holds joy and mystery worth exploring. He's far away now, connected only by the finest thread..." The ancient one's tone was both sad and thoughtful. "If all else fails, remind him that he came here for a purpose, and that his purpose has yet to be served. Remind him..." the Old One's voice trailed off momentarily before continuing. "Remind him of his promise."

Then both Andara's and Barr's eyes began to itch furiously, and when their vision cleared, the Old One was gone.

Deke hovered near the ceiling, looking down at his body where it lay twisting in agony on the bed, glad to be separated from the experience. He looked fondly at Andara and his father where they sat nearby, and saw the she-wolf next to him, her eyes focused where his awareness floated. He knew Hopi *saw* him and sent a reassuring image into her thoughts. She whimpered, and he distinctly heard her feeling that he should come back to his body. He reassured her again, then, feeling freer than he could remember, felt himself pass through the tent's canvas layers until he was high in the sky, staring down at Winter Camp spread beneath him. Part of him maintained a fraction of connection to his physical self, but this was minimal and didn't distract him at all from his marvelous experience of flight.

For the first time since his mother's death, he felt at peace. Here, rising through the blue, blue world, with the earth growing ever wider below, there were no concerns, no worries, no silly dwelling on problems that had no solutions. There was only freedom, this profound sense of freedom, and he knew this was what he had sought all his life.

He began to be aware of a light source which glowed at the edge of his consciousness, and he turned his perspective until the light was directly in front of him, as he thought of front and back in this non-physical place of unending peace. The light was warm without burning, bright without blinding, and he could feel it draw at his center with such appeal that all he wanted was to move closer.

He realized he was not alone; there were other minds or personalities to either side of him. He strained to see who they were, feeling he would recognize them if he could see just a little more clearly. All at once he sensed a familiar presence and could hardly contain his surge of joy, for now he recognized Tilva in the flow of energy surrounding him.

Mother! he thought to her, and would have wept if that were possible here.

What are you doing here, my son? she asked him.

Trying it on for size, he told her.

Her loving emotion engulfed him and he was tempted to sever his connection with his body on the spot. *Go back*, she thought. *You have unfinished business to attend to, essential business. And there are those waiting who love you...*

I don't want to go back; it's too dark and it hurts too badly. Please, let me stay in the light with you a while longer, Mother.

He felt his plea move her before she firmed her thoughts and told him he must go back, now, without delay, that there was at this point/moment in space and time no place for him, not here...and he felt her regret at this communication.

He looked back along the faint trail of energy that held him bound to his earthly life and made a final plea. *How can you make me leave when I've only just found you again?*

You know this is the right decision, she thought inside his thoughts. *You know what you have to do. Remember the promise, Deke. You must remember the promise.*

What promise? he asked as he felt his awareness sliding away from her, being drawn back down the path of connection away from the light and his mother's love. *What promise?* his thoughts shouted as he fell dizzyingly, and the earth rushed up all around him. He slammed back into his physical situation, overwhelmed by the agony his body was experiencing, fighting to keep from screaming with terror and loss, and failing.

"What promise?" he shouted aloud, startling his father and Andara. For a moment he could see their faces staring at him worriedly, then his vision blurred once more and all he knew was the pain.

Shaken, Barr and Andara looked at each other.

"What does it mean?" she whispered.

"You're the witch woman," he responded. "You tell me."

"I wish I knew," she told him. She watched Deke try to throw off the covers and touched him soothingly, her heart wrung by his anguish and her helplessness in the face of it.

Barr stood and went to the living area where he retrieved an easy chair, placing it near the bed. "I'm getting too old to crouch on the floor," he said.

"Can I get you anything, my lord?" Andara asked.

"No, thank you." He studied her, admiring everything about her. "But I would like it very much if you called me by name now and again, daughter," he said.

She looked at him in surprise, then gave him a smile so lovely, and yet so sad, that his heart lurched.

They sat together, he in the chair, she on the floor next to the bed, and watched Deke jerk and shake, mumbling in a constant flow of disconnected images. On the one occasion Andara tried to go into his thoughts, she felt as if she were in a maelstrom of sharp objects and had to withdraw immediately, overwhelmed by the level of pain he was experiencing. All she could do was murmur comfortingly, not even daring to touch him for fear of hurting him more.

Over the course of the day, people came and went, unnoticed by the three in the bedroom. Andara's assistants gently sent visitors away until Hawk arrived on his crutches looking for Barr and was told what had happened. Shocked, he swung through the hangings and took in the scene around the bed. Pity and remorse filled him as he watched Deke for several long seconds.

"What's this?" he whispered, distraught.

"The cut in his side turned septic," Andara said tiredly.

"Can I do anything?"

"No, Papa."

He flinched at her resigned tone and slowly dropped into a cross-legged position on the floor near the foot, laying his crutches alongside him.

"My fault," he said sorrowfully. "You were right, what you said to me yesterday. I should have stopped."

Andara looked at him sharply. "There's entirely too much guilt in this room," she said, "And I'm sick of it." Tears slid from the corners of her eyes and she brushed them away angrily. She rose and went to the kitchen where she filled a cup with the cooling herbal infusion, added some honey and brought it back. Stirring in some of Tilva's antibiotic powder, she waved Barr over to lift Deke while she carefully poured the liquid down his throat. His skin was parched, hot to the touch, and she wondered how anyone could be that hot and still live. She bathed his face with a cool washcloth while he shivered uncontrollably, shaking as if having a seizure.

It was then she began to be aware of the sound that was coming from everywhere outside the tent and she looked questioningly at her father and the chieftain. Barr arose heavily and went to the outer room. Ducking under the door flap, he stared across the crowd of people who had gathered around Deke's tent to wait for news. Someone called to him and he shook his head. Then, "You should all go home, have supper. It's cold out."

Heads nodded, but no one moved. Barr acknowleged their kindness and support with a grateful gesture, then spoke to the servants who left to fetch food and hot cider from his personal stores to give to anyone who wanted it.

Inside again, he returned to his chair by the bed and saw Deke's movements becoming weaker as he grew more exhausted. He smoothed the sweat-soaked hair back and said in a low voice, "Come on, boy, don't give up on me."

The hours passed. At midnight Andara poured more of the antibiotic and herb liquid down his throat, along with a cup of plain water. She laid her hand gently on his side, feeling the heat beneath the bandage radiating like a brazier full of hot coals. Even such a light touch made him groan in pain and she returned to her place despondently, wondering how much longer he could go on.

Just before dawn she had Barr help unwrap the bandage around his middle and she took the dressing off the wound, examining him meticulously, sniffing the bandage for any hint of corruption. There was none, only some blood and clear serum. She made a fresh dressing and they re-wrapped him while she prepared another cup of antibiotic tea.

After they got it down his throat she sponged him again from head to toe, covered him with a bath sheet, and drew the quilts up, scrutinizing him carefully. His skin was ruddy with fever, almost glowing from the heat of the fire burning within. Sighing, she sat down again and dropped her head wearily against her arm.

At midday they changed the sweat and urine-soaked bedding and sponged him once more. Andara poured water and antibiotic into his mouth, noticing that he hardly thrashed at all as his body tired and he fell into long, protracted periods when he became totally motionless and his breathing grew shallow. At these moments she sat rigidly, unable to relax her muscles until he started moving again.

After one of these times, she grabbed his hand and brought it to her lips. "Deke," she called softly. She kissed him, her tears falling on his fingers. "I think we're losing him," she said in an agony of fear.

Barr gripped her shoulder. "Keep talking to him."

Andara felt some of his strength flow into her and sniffled hard, wiping her eyes on the quilt. As the afternoon wore on and the shadows lengthened, she talked quietly to Deke, reminding him of their childhood together, the escapades they had gotten into when small, the skunk they'd brought to Hawk for a pet, the wonderful races they'd held with their friends across the grasslands at sunset, the time they'd run away together but sneaked back because they were hungry and afraid of demons.

No longer having energy for self-consciousness, she talked about how he made her feel when they made love, how he had made her understand what it meant to be a woman.

Barr and Hawk listened compassionately, moved by the depth of her emotion. When the darkness was full once more, the chieftain interrupted and handed her the medicine cup to refill.

Andara poured the dose of antibiotic tea into Deke's mouth, followed by another cup of water, tired herself now. She was beginning to see things in the air all around him, little flashes of light and dazzling color. When she finished, she laid her head on the edge of the bed and tried to rest her eyes.

At midnight they dosed him again, carrying out the familiar routine quickly. Now it was easier because he was much quieter to handle.

Sometime after that he began twisting and turning again, as if his body was consuming itself for fuel. He cried out several times as a paroxysm of trembling overtook his limbs, and sweat began to flow even more copiously from him. In an instant the bedding was soaked. Shuddering all over, he groaned deeply, drawing several profound breaths. His eyes fluttered open, and for a second he looked around in confusion. His hand closed on Andara's so hard she almost felt the bones crush, and then he said in a completely normal tone as he gazed at her,

"Andara! What are you doing on the floor? Come to bed, I've just had the strangest dream...!" before closing his eyes again. The trembling gradually stopped and slowly his body relaxed. His head fell to one side and he began to snore softly.

Dumbfounded, Andara, Barr, and Hawk exchanged glances. Andara took a cloth and dried Deke's face. She touched his skin all over, hardly able to believe how much cooler he felt.

"Please," she said to the chieftain. "We need to get him into dry bedding."

"His fever..." Barr asked, hardly breathing. "...it broke?"

"Aye," the girl said. She covered her face while her shoulders shook. She felt her father's hand on her arm and patted him gently before peeling back the quilts and tossing them aside. In a few minutes they had the bedding

271

changed and Deke dry. Andara laid her hand on his side again and sent a prayer of thanks to the Universe as she felt how the wound was barely warmer than the surrounding flesh.

"It was the gun powder," she said in wonder. "And Tilva's powder."

"What is that powder?" Hawk asked, amazed.

Andara took a sheaf of note paper from her medical bag. Her fingers ran down through several pages. "Ah," she said. "Here it is, with the recipe for isolating the molds and the dosages. She calls it 'penicillin.'"

"It's a miracle," Barr said quietly, running his hand through Deke's hair, grateful beyond words for his son's deliverance. He felt Tilva had intervened personally to save Deke's life, and thanked her silently, wherever she was, for sending their son back to him.

"Aye," Andara agreed.

"We should eat," Hawk said, a smile lighting his lean features.

Barr laughed and hauled his friend up from the floor as if he weighed nothing. "Aye, for a change, you're not the only one who's starving."

"I'll make something," Andara said, starting for the door.

"No," Barr said firmly, guiding her to the chair and pushing her down in it. "We'll get the food. You rest. You've earned it." He leaned down and kissed her forehead, then her hair.

The two men moved towards the door, and then Andara was alone with Deke. She looked over her shoulder to be sure they were really gone, then squeezed herself onto the bed beside him, putting her arms around him and resting her head against his chest. For a while she simply held him, filled with joy too deep for expression, basking in the relative coolness of his skin against her cheek. There still was fever, but it was much less, barely what accompanied a bad head cold. He moved slightly and murmured something unintelligibly before his hand went to her hair and she felt his body relax even further.

Moments later, without being aware she had done so, she fell asleep.

When Barr and Hawk returned, they looked at their sleeping children for a while until Hawk crutched to the bed and drew the covers over them more completely. He caressed his daughter's cheek and patted Deke's hand where it lay tangled in her hair. "I guess she can wait to eat," he said.

"If you could have seen her in the emergency..."

"Aye," Hawk replied. "She's got a cool head, always did."

"My son's a lucky young man," Barr said thoughtfully.

"So he is," Hawk agreed. "I'm feeling pretty lucky myself, right now."

Barr's eyebrows went up questioningly.

"Sure," Hawk said. "I know you would have felt duty bound to kill me if he had died."

"Don't be foolish," Barr told him. "Andara told me what happened."

Hawk sighed. "I only hope that's the end of it. That cut in his side...he actually threw himself on my blade so he could get my knife from me. I'll have to teach him there are better ways to keep a machete occupied than holding it in your own flesh."

"One would have thought you'd covered that obvious lesson long before this," Barr remarked dryly.

"Aye, but sometimes we miss the obvious."

"Do we? Or do we simply choose not to see it?"

"That's a question for a philosopher," Hawk said, "Not an old war horse like me."

"I'm tired," the chieftain said. "I'm going to my bed."

Hawk nodded, supporting himself on his crutches. "I suppose they'll be all right now."

"Aye, until the next crisis." Barr smiled slightly and drew on his cloak, feeling each of his forty-eight years as if they were a hundred.

Together they walked out into the night and gave the news to the people who waited patiently in the cold. A moment later a roar went up into the sky.

Inside the tent, Deke and Andara felt it touch their sleep. Nestling more closely against one another, they returned to the dream they shared back and forth between them, until after a while, they slept deeply and dreamed no more.

CHAPTER THIRTEEN

In my attempt to construct a basic case history on Deke Wolfson, I was frustrated by the contradictory anomolies of personality which, had they appeared in one of our own people, would have required neurological re-programming at the very best, and lifetime incarceration at the worst.

There was no denying he was a killer, so accomplished at his chosen profession that too much thinking about the subject becomes chilling. And always there is the question one must ask concerning where killing leaves off and murder begins...

The General said one must consider it killing if there was a reason for the deaths involving survival, either for oneself or one's greater community, and murder if the killing was gratuitous or for personal motives.

I tried to convince him that all killing was gratuitous, but this he stubbornly refused to accept. He insisted that anyone who lived in the ruins knew there were some people who just needed killing. He said my inability to recognize the truth in this matter was due to the sheltered life we live here in Beori, as well as essentially wrong-headed, unrealistic thinking, and he offered to spend a month camping in the deep ruins with me, that I might get a better feel for his argument.

Without further discussion, I declined his invitation, and conceded the point.

— Ourn Rohlvaag; Collected Journals; City of Life, A.D. 3109

From his place hidden in the ruins, Deke looked left and right along the line of soldiers tucked amongst the scrub grass, dust, and tumbled piles of concrete. The sun was beginning to rise above the horizon, bringing with it the threat of increasing heat later in the day. Nearby, Melak grinned and whispered,

"Almost time, chief."

Nodding, Deke studied the small fortified town lying at the bottom of a gentle incline. Stone walls enclosed the fort with watchtowers placed every twenty yards. Each tower held an armed man. None had spotted the two hundred crouched in wait outside their battlements, nor suspected that under cover of darkness their main gate had been mined with powerful explosives.

Behind them, hidden from the watchful fort dwellers, the soldiers' horses were tethered to long ropes stretched between boulders.

"How much longer?" whispered Mastra, who was squatting in a clump of brambles behind some rusted metal girders.

Deke covered his lips with his finger and sent a silent signal in the soldiers' battle language towards Willie O'Dale, who waited patiently in the brightening sunlight.

As Willie signaled back, there was a massive explosion in front of the fort, sending the guards in the watchtowers scurrying frenziedly. From their places on the hill, the soldiers fired quickly and accurately, taking out the guards along the wall. In a moment Deke waved to the men and they rushed to their horses. As he leaped onto Micmac's back, Deke shouted to the boys of his manhood group to watch the towers, then gestured to the rest of the soldiers. Seconds later he put his heels to Micmac's sides and she galloped up and over the hill, the rest of the men following. They thundered into the fort between the shattered gates, rifles sweeping back and forth, the air filling with their war whoops and shrieks.

Inside, people had taken shelter within the crowded buildings that stood jammed together, wall to wall. With a series of hand signals, Deke ordered the soldiers to fan out and spread through the streets, locating and neutralizing any defenders.

Except for the armed guards at the ramparts, no one put up a fight. In fifteen minutes the riders had rousted the inhabitants out of their houses, many out of their beds, and gathered them in a frightened huddle in the town's main square.

"Citizens!" Deke shouted above the hubbub, and encouraged by the soldiers, the people quieted. Micmac pranced slightly until Deke's hand steadied her. He looked at the fort's populace, the fourth they'd invaded in the last three weeks. They were not a very prepossessing lot, he thought. Like most fort dwellers, they showed signs of inbreeding, with some badly deformed by genetic overlapping. His eyes narrowed in disgust.

"Swear allegiance to Barr Wolfson and the People of the Wolf, and you may live in peace. We will require some small contribution to offset the costs of this campaign, so I ask what goods you have to offer as tribute, whether foodstuffs or mechanical devices, perhaps valuable trade goods."

The people looked stupidly at one another, and one man, their leader, said, "Why should we give you tribute? What do you offer in exchange?"

"Your lives," Deke replied with a predatory grin. The man was silenced, chilled by this cold-eyed youth in command of these eager warriors.

"We're poor people," he said sullenly.

"Let me be the judge of that," Deke replied. He gestured to Mastra and Tim. "Take a dozen men. Escort this fellow and have him show you anything of value. Bring everything here for inspection."

The boys nodded, and Deke relaxed slightly, his eyes taking in the town, his mind touching the people's thoughts to be sure no one was planning treachery. He rode to where Willie sat his horse and said, "Slim pickings,

Willie. Four forts and not one with even a wench worthy of a soldier's tender attentions, much less any spoils. I have to admit, I'm disappointed."

"We'll hit one worth the effort soon, I'm thinking," O'Dale said, grinning.

"I hope so." Deke rubbed the bridge of his nose thoughtfully, starting to sweat in the heating sunlight. "It'll take a long time to get rich on the rubbish we've liberated these weeks."

"You want to be rich, Deke?" Willie asked curiously.

Deke shrugged. "I'd like to find something worthy of Andara," he said.

"You'll look a long time to find that, my friend," Willie said with a laugh.

"That's true, but she has a fondness for beautiful things, and I like bringing her presents. I know how she hates it when I go."

"They all do, Deke. No woman likes to think of her man in the thick of battle."

"Aye," Deke agreed. "But she's especially protective."

"You give her reason to be," Willie said. "You take too many risks, you're still too quick to engage the enemy..."

"We've had no casualties this spring," Deke argued. "I take no risk without considering the odds. These forts are no challenge, they're barely more than training exercises. As far as engaging quickly, that's the secret to winning battles. Once you know your enemy's mind and resources, time spent ruminating is time wasted."

"Is that a Deke Wolfson war axiom?" Willie asked, amused.

"Why not?" Deke returned, smiling. "When I write my text on attack strategy and close quarter tactics, you can be sure I'll include it. I look forward to the day I can fight a real battle."

Willie frowned. "Pitched battles are hellish confusing and dangerous."

"Maybe," Deke said, not convinced.

Soon the soldiers who had accompanied Mastra and Tim began straggling back bearing burlap sacks filled with assorted trinkets. There was nothing particularly large or valuable but Deke called for tables to be set up and ordered the sacks dumped so their contents could be examined and divided.

"Is this the lot?" he asked.

"Aye, pretty much," Mastra replied.

"Did you find any weapons?"

"Some. Mainly in houses and on the towers," his friend answered.

"All right, let's have a look." Deke paced Micmac over to the long table and looked down.

The soldiers watched, and one called out, "Take something, m'lord!

277

First choice to the commander."

"Aye!" another shouted. "Take a woman!"

Grins appeared on the soldiers' faces. All were aware of Deke's celiba-cy while on raiding expeditions and were hugely amused by it. These two hun-dred were the same who had accompanied him and Barr on the vendetta raid against the Murdock clan months previously. When Deke had sought men for these westerly exploratory probes, the two hundred had volunteered, swearing personal allegiance to him for life. Each remembered how he had served out Gant Murdock with such casual brutality, remembered the killing spree on which he had led them, igniting with his ruthlessness and courage a hot, fanat-ic flame in their hearts. Young men all, they were filled with the same lust for spoils and adventure that moved their commander, and they trusted implicitly in his ability to lead them to it. On this, their third foray into the western ruins, they had sought out any and all communities, ransacking them for valuables, but also, on Deke's specific orders, looking for information concerning the ter-ritories lying to the west.

Deke had asked Willie to accompany them as well, wanting the bene-fit of his experience, knowing he could work comfortably with his father's best war chief. O'Dale had agreed instantly, flattered to have been asked, impressed by how methodically his former student had planned these trips.

When the People had made the move to Spring Camp just before Deke's fourteenth birthday in early April, he had wasted no time in planning a series of expeditions, each making a swing over westering countryside in over-lapping arcs two hundred miles deep. Each expedition would consist of sever-al smaller forays, some lasting no more than a few days, others lasting weeks.

Deke eyed the heaps of jewelry, odd bits and pieces of ancient coins, occasional gold or silver plates or goblets. He drew his machete from its sheath and used it to poke through the skimpy treasure pile. He wasn't sure what he was looking for, but knew he'd recognize it when he found it. His thoughts turned to Andara and his expression softened.

He missed her on these trips. Throughout the winter they had never been separated for more than a few hours. He had been laid up for a month from the machete wound, and during that time Andara had taken such devoted care of him that he was embarrassed by all the attention. They hadn't been able to make love during that period, but there had been other compensations in the form of spectacular meals, stimulating conversation, and many backgammon games played for sexual wagers to be paid off in the future when he was capa-ble again, games that Andara had a habit of winning more often than not, and the results of which she kept strictly tallied in a little notebook. Altogether she had proven to be the best of both worlds for him: a boon companion far more engaging than any of his male friends, and a lover of such explosive passion and tenderness that she positively owned his soul.

Throughout the long, frigid winter, he gradually had begun to heal from the wounds both to his spirit and his body, until by the weeks following the time Hopi gave birth to six squirming, black, blind little puppies in the enclosed, den-like whelping area he and Andara had prepared near the wood-stove, he had known he would recover. Soon he began to feel he was awakening from a long, uneasy sleep, and found himself looking around in wonder, amazed to find the world still existed and life continued to progress despite his protracted emotional hibernation.

From that time he took up the reins of his life once more, grateful to be alive, young, in love and loved by a brilliant and beautiful young woman, more than grateful for the opportunity to fulfill his dreams as he memorized maps and charts and prepared for a spring season of intensive campaigning. Except for the occasional black mood, to those around him, he knew he seemed pretty much as he had been. That this was an act of will was known only to himself and, perhaps, Andara. Once he decided to live, he knew he had to put the past to rest. And so far, with her help, he was managing not only to do this, but also to hold himself in balance.

Something glittered in the dazzling sunlight and Deke was brought back from his daydreaming. He slid the point of the long blade through a necklace that took his breath away. When he held it in his hands, he saw it consisted of emeralds, rubies, and diamonds set in a metal he suspected was platinum. The stones were arranged in a mesh-like spread of interlocking settings, and he could imagine how it would look against Andara's smooth, tanned skin.

He raised the jewels high and the soldiers cheered.

"What about a wench, m'lord?" bellowed a soldier on a sorrel mare. "They don't look too appetizing, it's true, but they probably can do the job."

"I'll pass, Harry," Deke said with a smile, pulling the man's name out of his memory reflexively. "A man'd have to be pretty desperate to want a fort dweller anyhow."

"I've seen some worth the taking," Melak said at his shoulder, his eyes constantly in motion, scanning for any and all danger that might threaten Deke.

"None worth the wrath of a witch woman," Deke said with a grin.

Melak chuckled. "I heard a joke about that very thing, once," he said. "But for the man who was spelled, it wasn't really that funny."

"I've heard that joke," Deke said dryly. "About fifty times in the last several months." He moved Micmac away from the table and gestured the men to make their choices. The day was getting old, and there was no reason to linger in this dreary little fort. He pocketed the necklace, tucking it away carefully.

"A present like that would buy a lot of stiff pricks," Tim said, pulling his horse alongside Deke. "Not that you need to," he added, laughing.

"You still go to those places, eh, Tim?" Deke asked.

"Oh, aye, there's a woman who likes me, does it twice for the price of one."

"You like paying?" Deke was curious.

"Beats doing myself. Not all of us are as lucky as you, brother." Tim looked at him fondly. "So what's next on the agenda? Another fort? Or do we go home?"

"There're about sixty miles more on this leg," Deke told him. "We'll finish covering this area, then head back."

"Aye, I look forward to that," Tim said.

"Better make your selection now," Deke recommended. "Otherwise you'll get the dregs."

Mastra meanwhile was poking through the spoils, looking for a gift he could bring his mother, as well as something that would buy him a young and willing courtesan, for he had decided to try one upon their return to Spring Camp. Soon he found several gold rings and a jeweled bracelet that he liked. He looked up at Deke and smiled.

During his friend's long recuperation, he had come to visit often, bringing interesting news and delicacies prepared by his mother. It hadn't taken him long to recognize that the feeling that lay between Deke and Andara was far stronger than any normal adolescent infatuation, and that the odds of him getting a chance with her were nil. Not, he was sure, that she would have been interested in him when she had Deke, but one could hope. Mastra's smile faded as he climbed aboard his horse. What girl of good family would want a bastard of unknown fathering?

Among the People, the birth of any child was considered a blessing. The earth's population was so decimated, the birth rate so affected by radioactivity in the environment, that the Wolf dominions always welcomed the arrival of healthy new life. So welcome were births that abortion never occurred, except when the mother's life was threatened or in cases where it was known there would be birth defects. Marriage was a convention not always adhered to, and generally speaking, children born out of wedlock were as welcome as any others, as long as the father was known. There were sound genetic concerns involved, as well as issues of upbringing, and having been raised all his life in this culture, Mastra understood and mostly agreed with the philosophy, except, of course, in his own situation.

He never had understood why his mother refused to tell him who his father was, for he was certain his father still lived and was in fact one of the higher-ranked members of the clan. He believed this because his mother received a stipend of support generous enough to take care of all their needs, not to mention his own inclusion in every event and activity of chiefs' sons. Sometimes he thought if he were only more worthy, perhaps his father would declare himself and make him legitimate. So Mastra studied the chiefs, trying to catch one who looked at him the way a father looked on a son, but never had been able to do so. The fact that one hadn't done so in all his fourteen years made him feel bad in his innermost self, with a profoundly low sense of who he was.

Deke sensed Mastra's negative emotions. "You all right?"

"Aye," Mastra said. "Just brooding about life and love."

"No point in brooding about either," Tim said, overhearing. "Brooding never made life work out or women put out."

Mastra and Deke laughed.

When the soldiers had taken their pick, the remaining goods were put back in burlap sacks and tied up for transport home. Deke looked around at the miserable collection of buildings and residents, his expression unconsciously contemptuous. These people were so superstitious about the world outside their walls that the only time they opened their gates was to hunt for meat to supplement their meager truck gardens and fish ponds. They had no form of intercourse with any other communities, acted, in fact, as if other humans were possessed by demons at the very least. At one of the forts they'd ransacked during this trip, the people actually made warding signs at the Wolf riders, believing they were supernatural beings spawned from the ruined wasteland in which their community was built.

As he signaled his men to leave, he rode over to the town's leader and pointed his machete blade peremptorily. "You, fellow, what do you know about the land west of here?"

The man shrugged, watching the blade anxiously.

Deke saw his eyes on the weapon and sheathed it. "Well?"

"There are vagabonds who roam in wagon trains," the man said. "They are traveling entertainers, mostly, who go town to town begging bread in exchange for a show."

"Anyone else? Anyone armed?"

"Other towns," the man answered.

"Armed like you?"

"More."

"How much more?"

The man was silent.

Deke entered his thoughts, giving a little shove to get the fellow talking again.

"Some have cannon," the man then said willingly enough.

"Ah," Deke said, satisfied. "Rockets, too?"

"I've seen such," the man told him.

"Anything else?"

"Rats," the man said, and shivered. "Lots of rats."

"Cave rats?" Deke asked.

"Mind rats," said the town leader.

"We call them cave rats," Deke said.

"Whatever you call them, there're lots of them."

"That's all?" Deke's eyes pressured him, and the leader twitched once, hard.

"Yes," the fellow said, fear in his voice.

"I hope so," Deke said. "For your sake." He shifted his gaze, releasing the man, who stood for a second trembling before he rejoined the rest of the townspeople. Then Deke turned Micmac after the soldiers riding out through the blasted gates, Melak as ever to one side and half a length behind, rifle in hand.

They camped that night in open countryside, and when the sun was setting Deke heard the howls of wolves nearby. He sat for a while listening, wondering if they were his wolves, the ones he'd known during his manhood ritual. It was possible; they weren't far from where his ordeal had been played out. When it was fully dark and everyone was bedded down except the first watch of guards, he slipped from his blankets silently, and with a quick series of breaths to center his mind, placed himself in the spaces between moments until he had penetrated the camp perimeter and was well away from anyone's sight.

Since his out of body experience during the fever, the techniques he had learned from the Old Man had become second nature to him. In the same way he could project his awareness into the minds and world around him, he now could deflect the awarenesses of other minds without their conscious knowledge, and so become effectively invisible. The technique was easiest at night when he could use nature's best camouflage, but he could do it in full daylight as well, with greater expenditure of energy.

Something else had happened to him since that encounter with his mother on the other side of life. He was certain he *saw* shifting patterns of light and energy he believed were spiritual entities, and he wondered how he could have failed to *see* them before. There were times these entities spoke to him, and when he asked them questions, they answered, sometimes cryptically, mostly accurately. The only information they wouldn't give pertained to his personal future. It had taken a while for him to accept that these entities were not figments of his imagination, that they existed independent of his own mind. Andara had helped him understand about non-physically focused personalities, as had the Old Man, though the Old Man referred to them as "helpers." Through use of the smoke during the past winter, the Old Man had led Deke into realms of shifting reality he never would have understood without that experience so close to death. They spoke of personality projection and something the Old Man called "psychotronic forces," the information so esoteric at times that Deke spent hours trying to unravel the meaning and figure out how he might apply these lessons in a practical, physical fashion.

He glanced up at the sky, saw the Great Dipper rising in the east, and sent his awareness across the ruins, seeking the source of the howls, sending images of wolves greeting wolves into the night.

The small chitterings of birds and other nocturnal creatures rose on the air, and Deke allowed his thoughts to spread out, almost slipping from his body to scan through the dust and graveled concrete more effectively.

In a moment he *saw* them with a sense other than sight, feeling them in his mind joyously. He recognized the Alpha and sent a particular greeting image that drew the wolves closer towards him, and minutes later they bounded across the ruins. The Alpha took precedence and sniffed him first, putting his muzzle into his hand and leaning on him like a great dog. Soon all the pack crowded near, re-establishing the connection made a year earlier. The four young wolves who had accompanied him and Hopi back to Spring Camp were bigger now, fully mature, and bumped him affectionately, their thoughts a stream of excited images inside his own.

After a while the Alpha put an image in his mind showing them racing beneath the curving sky, and he sent back an affirmative. He looked around, taking an impression of the place where he stood and fixing it in his awareness. He stripped off his clothes except for his boots and dropped them on the ground. He strapped his weapons belt around his waist, then moved off with the wolves, the night breeze on his bare flesh evoking prisming sense memories until he grew dizzy, caught between past and present.

This season the pack had selected a different location for its den site and as Deke jogged through the ruins in the faint starlight, the wolves showed him images of the spot, also of the Alpha female with her new litter.

He sent the wolves images of humans riding wagons with an interrogative. After a second the Alpha gave him a strong picture of exactly such a group, and by orienting the image under the Dipper in its present position, was able to show Deke in what direction he would find them.

After that, Deke relaxed and allowed his consciousness to range across

283

the countryside, filled with a primitive joy that took him back through the past year to the last time he had run with wolves.

He remembered circumcising himself, remembered telling Tim on his return that if he could do that, he could do anything. Smiling grimly, he almost laughed at how naïve he had been to think that was the worst that could happen to him. He remembered battling the bear, the wolves tearing the esper tiger to pieces, his concussion, the lonely journey home afterwards. All of that paled when compared to the events which had followed.

In this year of coming to manhood, he tried to find the good things that had happened, and naturally at the top of his list was the miracle of his love for Andara, and even more miraculous, her love for him. He considered how the relationship with his father had changed, how much better he understood Barr now, and how much he loved him. There was his new status as leader of this eager band of brigands, and that gave him pleasure of a sort more difficult for him to express, even to himself. It was hard for him to admit how much he enjoyed the taking of a fort or town, hard to acknowledge how the roar of explosives and the crackle of gunfire gave him a thrill equaled only by Andara held in his deepest embrace. There was something about breaching an enemy's defenses he could compare only to that moment he had taken Andara's virginity, and he wondered at the strange juxtaposition he felt between the experiences. Sometimes he felt as if all the mysterious earth was like a woman waiting to be taken, and he wanted to be the one who did the taking.

The wolves adjusted their pace to his, surging in circles around him, their minds broadcasting images of terrain and any animal life they encountered, though when most creatures sensed the pack nearby they made themselves scarce.

Deke's thoughts went to Hopi's litter. They had been born the third week in December on Barr's forty-ninth birthday, and now were six months old. When they were two months old, Deke had picked the pup who most reminded him of Canis and presented it to his father as a belated birthday present. Now the chieftain's mind was distracted by a bright and inquisitive young wolf who sought to chew his clothing and papers as well as anything else he could get his teething mouth on. Deke and Andara had been much amused by this rambunctious puppy's antics and so, they were glad to see, was Barr.

The other pups had remained together and Hopi had begun to take them out into the world to learn the skills of a wild pack. Throughout the latter half of the winter Deke and Andara had participated in this process, realizing some of the young wolves might fall prey to the dangers of the wilderness, but understanding the need to make them self-sufficient.

Soon Deke forced himself to stop thinking and simply enjoyed the sensations of the night as they impacted his body, suspended in a timeless, wordless place of emotional connectivity. He could hardly separate himself from the wolves who leaped and frolicked around him or the living energy of the earth beneath his feet. He felt he could run like this across the ruined landscape forever, but knew his men would be worried. Reluctantly, he began to swing back in a wide circle, and that was when he heard the sound of gunfire coming out of the night.

He ran faster, cutting directly towards the pile of clothing he'd left in the dust. Dressing in a moment, he picked up his rifle and approached the camp where he could see campfires as well as the flash of more gunfire. Curses rose on the air, along with a scream that tapered off to a gurgling moan. Deke burst through the perimeter in time to see his men firing into the ruins. A moment later the gunshots ceased.

"What's going on?" he questioned when Melak appeared at his shoulder.

"We had visitors, but they're gone now."

"Who screamed?" Deke gazed at the group of soldiers who ringed him protectively.

"One of them," a man said.

"Let's have a look," Deke said.

"What happened to you, Chief?" Melak asked. "When these bastards attacked and we saw you gone, we imagined the worst."

"I took a walk," Deke said, and Sent an image out beyond the firelight to the wolves who returned his contact, then communicated farewells.

"Hell of a time to go walking," Melak muttered.

They walked to the perimeter on the other side of camp and examined the masked man lying dead in a bloody patch of gravel.

"This the only one?" Deke asked.

"He's the only one we got," a soldier told him. "There were about twenty; bold sons of bitches to attack such a large party."

"Where's his weapon?" Deke poked the body with his toe.

"His friends must have taken it," the soldier replied.

"They had rifles?"

"Aye," said the soldier. "Primitive single shot; not automatic."

Deke knelt and removed the dead man's mask, then stepped away in disgust. The raider's face was a solid mass of scar tissue, wrinkled and shiny under the soldiers' flickering torchlight. "Burned," he said. "Anything in his pockets to indicate who they were?"

Melak nodded to one of the boys of Deke's manhood group who searched the body, then stood up holding a strange metallic object in his hand.

"Just this," the boy said, handing it over. Melak looked at it and shrugged, passing it to Deke.

"What is it?" he asked.

Deke examined the object carefully, turning it this way and that in his hand. It was cylindrical in shape, approximately six inches by two inches, sheathed entirely in stainless steel, with two rigid, wire prongs at the end. He looked at the prongs, noticing faint marks on the steel from which they protruded. "I'm not sure what it is," he said slowly, "But it fits into something else. You can see where the metal is scratched."

"But what does it do?" asked Mastra, approaching through the circle of soldiers.

"Beats me," Deke said. "We'll hold on to it. It might prove useful." He paused, then spoke to the men. "If all the excitement's over, let's get some rest. Tomorrow we have new game to catch." His eyes gleamed in the torchlight.

Mastra's eyes held a question.

"You'll see," Deke said mysteriously. He slipped the metal object into his pocket and headed back to his bedroll.

"You want us to post more guards?" Melak asked.

"No, I doubt they'll attack again tonight."

Willie joined Deke, followed by Tim. "I don't like it," the older man said. "For so few to attack us...something's not right."

"They must have been testing us," Deke said thoughtfully, "To see our weapons and how skilled we are in using them."

"Aye," Willie agreed, giving him a sidelong glance.

"They weren't mounted?" Deke asked.

"No, we'd have heard 'em sooner if they were." Willie found his blankets and sat down on them.

"Those burn scars on that fellow," Deke said, also sitting on his blankets. "They didn't look natural, somehow."

"What do you mean?" Tim asked, shaking dust from his bedroll and putting it down again carefully.

"Every bit of his face was burned," Deke replied. "Nothing else."

"Maybe a flare-up?" Tim suggested.

"Maybe, but I tell you, it looked deliberate to me. And the mask; were the others wearing masks?"

"Aye," Melak put in from his own bedroll near Deke's.

"It would be interesting to know if they all carry those scars," Deke said.

"What difference does it make?" Mastra asked.

"If they all have them, then it's some form of ritual scarring, and that could make them very dangerous."

"Why?" Mastra was curious.

"We perform a ritual act that binds us as warriors," Deke said. "Their face burning might serve the same purpose."

"They did fight well," Willie said, nodding.

"Imagine the guts it would take to have your face burned that way," Tim said. "They must be tough."

"Aye," his father said.

"I wonder if their women do it, too," Tim said, grinning in the semi-darkness.

"No woman would allow her face to be destroyed that way," Melak scoffed from his bedroll.

"Who knows?" Tim answered. "If it's their custom..."

"Ugh." Mastra shuddered. "Now you're being gross."

"Why?" Tim asked innocently. "Just take her from behind..."

"One thing's for sure," Willie added, "Such a woman could never claim you were interested in her only for her looks."

The men laughed and stretched themselves on their blankets. Before long they slept deeply, and none awoke again until it was time for the guards to be relieved. Willie rose briefly, checked to be sure all was well, then returned to his bed. He felt Deke's questioning gaze on him and gestured reassuringly. With a nod, his former student closed his eyes and Willie saw that he was asleep almost instantly.

Envious of Deke's ability to drop off so quickly, Willie stretched as comfortably as possible on the hard ground, pulling a stone from beneath his backside and tossing it into the night. He studied the boy in the shifting fire-light, noticing how grown up he had become. His body was long now on his bedroll, practically as tall as his father, and though still lean, Willie knew from hand to hand combat practice that he was as strong as a young bull. His physical coordination always had been uncanny for one his age, but now... Willie shook his head.

If Willie had asked him, Deke would have explained that all physical activity began as an act of will, and that if one focused one's will precisely, then superbly accurate movement through the material world became possible. He would have described for his former teacher the strands of luminous energy that drew every action and were focused from one's center. He also would have made it clear he was still a novice at these techniques, and when fully mature could expect far greater control. But Willie didn't ask, because these were areas of learning being overseen by the Old Man, and it never would have occurred to Willie (or anyone else for that matter other than his father or

Andara) to question Deke about his training as a male adept, or brujo.

Every other morning Willie watched Deke shave the patchy red-gold stubble away from his upper lip, chin, and sideburns, remembering how just last fall his skin had been soft as a girl's. He looked at his own son where he slept, seeing the physical changes in him as well, and sighed, feeling the passage of time stealing his youth like a highwayman on his life's path.

It wouldn't be long, he knew, until nights sleeping out on the ground became too uncomfortable for him. Like the others of his manhood group, he would begin to spend more time in the city. Then would this new generation of Wolf riders truly come into their own, and it was his earnest desire that they should be ready.

He closed his eyes, trying to sleep. Eventually he dropped off, the mournful howls of wolves in his ears.

At dawn the soldiers rose, ate jerky and dried fruit, corn biscuits washed down with water, and were in the saddle by the time the sun cleared the horizon.

They headed southwest through the ruins, following Deke who followed the route indicated by the Alpha. By midday the terrain changed, becoming greener, mossier, with many half-buried, weed-covered concrete blocks and boulders strewn seemingly at random. Two hours later, trees and shrubs appeared with patches of tall grass. As the sun's rays began to slant and stretch their shadows, they saw a line of covered wagons drawn by mules camped not too far from a small, exquisite lake nestled among lushly growing verdure.

For a moment no one at the campsite noticed them, then a man's voice rang out and there was a flurry of activity around the wagons. Deke made a hand signal to the soldiers and they quickly spread into ten shifting bands who swept towards the wagon train at a swift gallop from every direction, and before the defenders could fire a shot, they were effectively surrounded and infiltrated. They lowered their weapons, then looked in astonishment at the youth leading the attack. A man came forward, obviously the leader.

"Why, if it isn't Deke Wolfson! Well met, m'lord! You might not remember me from last year's Spring Festival; we entertained all your folk that night." He grinned, relieved to see it was Wolf riders and not those others they had tangled with. "My name's Johnny Carillo, and you are welcome here."

Deke gestured to the soldiers who sheathed their weapons.

"Do you mind if we camp near you?" he asked.

"We'd be honored, m'lord." Johnny Carillo was swarthy, well-built, approximately forty years old, with a sweeping moustache and nut brown eyes both shrewd and cheerful.

Nodding to Willie who began issuing orders to the men, Deke looked around the well-ordered camp and jumped down from Micmac's back. Holding her reins with one hand, he clapped Carillo on the shoulder and said with a friendly grin, "Thanks for the hospitality. What are you doing in these parts, Johnny?"

"Going here and there, entertaining any who'll pay," the man replied.

"Seen any unfriendlies?" Deke's eyes were alert.

Carillo nodded. "Did we ever, m'lord. Don't want to run into their like again any time soon."

"Masked?"

"Aye," Carillo told him. "Tough as scabby old rats, too."

Deke turned to Mastra. "Make sure the men set up a good perimeter defense tonight. Trip-wires, mines, the lot."

"Aye," Mastra said, and rode off to see to it.

"You know these men?" Carillo asked.

"We played with them last night," Deke replied. "Do you know where they come from?"

Carillo nodded. "They live west of here. I've never seen their village; no one has. But their fighters seem at home in the ruins and protect a particular area which I can tell you I have no interest in getting anywhere near!"

"What happened?"

"They attacked us. If we had been sleeping...well, we were fortunate."

"What arms do you folks carry?" Deke wanted to know.

"The usual we've bought from your father. It was enough, thank the ruins." Carillo's eyes were searching as he looked at Deke. "But tell me, m'lord, what brings you to this little oasis in the middle of nowhere? If you don't mind my asking?"

"I don't mind," Deke replied. "We're exploring, contacting new communities. Do you know of any others nearby?"

"There's a miserable little fort northeast of here, but maybe you've already found it since you came from that direction?"

"Aye," Deke replied.

"We're getting ready to eat supper," Carillo said. "Would you like to join me and my family? I'm sorry we can't feed your men, but we can entertain them! If they like good music and dancing, even storytelling, we can give 'em an evening such as they haven't had for a while!"

"Maybe we can help with the food...Tim, organize some men for hunting parties...be quick! I thought I saw ducks and geese on the lake."

"Aye," Tim agreed with a wide grin. He rode away at a canter, shouting to the soldiers.

"Come with me, m'lord," Carillo said. "We'll find a good spot for your horse and feed her, too. We have some oats she'd probably like."

"Thanks," Deke said. "I appreciate it."

An hour later the camp was fully reinforced and guards patrolled the perimeter. Hunting parties began straggling back bearing ducks and geese as well as a number of rabbits. These were quickly stripped, gutted, and set to roast over the many cookfires. There were even two deer caught at dusk coming out to feed, and now they, too, were slowly turning on their spits. The meats had been rubbed with herbs and salt and the air filled with appetizing odors until Deke felt himself salivating. He looked at the lake where it caught light from the fires and setting sun, thinking he'd take a bath after supper.

Most of the entertainers associated with the wagon train were either members of or indirectly related to the Carillo family, and before preparing an area for everyone to eat and watch the promised show, they stopped to renew acquaintanceship with Deke. Before long a grassy area dotted with campfires and torches had been readied. The Wolf riders and Carillo family loaded their mess kits and plates with food, washing down the fresh game and traveling supplies with water and a few jugs of super-potent white-lightning the wagon folk provided.

After the meal, wood was piled on the fires until they flared brightly. Deke accepted a jug from Johnny Carillo and swallowed deeply, choking on the fiery liquid. "Ruins," he wheezed. "That must be nearly pure alcohol!"

"We figure about one hundred forty proof, m'lord," Johnny said with a slightly tipsy smile.

"Don't go too near the fire," Mastra muttered from nearby.

A moment later musicians began to play a wild tune led by flute and fiddle and supported by guitars and hand drums, tambourines, and a string bass. A group of dancers got up, began to whirl madly until the music reached a crescendo, and then with a triumphant phrase, froze. Without pause, the drums began a slower, more insistent beat, and a young woman of perhaps nineteen got up to dance alone. Her dark brown hair fell to her waist and moved when she moved. Equally dark eyes glowed from beneath black brows and her gleaming skin was either comparably dark or deeply suntanned. She danced as if the music lived inside her flesh, so much a part of her that every step, every gesture, seemed a natural expression of the ever more complex rhythm.

The soldiers watched raptly, her striking beauty and fluid movements holding them spellbound. More than one reached to touch her as she flowed past, but she avoided their grasping hands expertly, while making each man feel she danced for him alone. Before long her dance carried her to where Deke sat on a log, his attention as focused as the other men's. She moved more suggestively, her hips and pelvis keeping a rhythm of their own, making him wonder how it would feel to be inside her as she did that. She saw the heat in his expression, how his blue eyes seemed to caress her breasts, and for a moment felt as if a knowing hand had slipped between her thighs to touch her intimately. Gasping at the quick surge of warmth, she danced away from him, her emotions in turmoil. She threw a glance over her shoulder and saw he was grinning mischievously. A little frown formed between her brows as she tried to convince herself he hadn't made that happen, that she must have imagined it.

"Wouldn't you like to lie between those legs tonight?" Tim whispered to Deke, as if reading his mind.

"They are beautiful legs," Willie agreed.

"Aye, she's beautiful," Deke said. "But I have beautiful legs to lie between at home, if I was only looking for that."

"She looks like she wouldn't mind giving you a go or two," Tim said enviously.

"She's not interested in me," Deke told him. "Only my status."

"Who cares?" Mastra asked. "I'd take her in a heartbeat."

"You're not alone," Willie said. "Every man here would be happy to take a chance with her."

"We'd better make sure the soldiers understand about the obligations of guests," Deke said to Willie. "It would be unfortunate if someone behaved inappropriately with that young woman."

"Inappropriately?" Tim grinned. "For me, inappropriate would be letting that go to waste!"

"I know," Deke replied. "But these are friends."

Johnny Carillo came and squatted near Deke. "Do you like her dancing, m'lord?" he asked, offering the jug again.

"She's wonderful," he answered honestly, accepting it and drinking cautiously. "Who is she?"

"My eldest daughter, Nitsa," Johnny said.

"Married?" Deke asked.

"Not yet, though she gets offers."

"I don't doubt it," Deke said, his gaze appreciative as he watched Nitsa spin sinuously across the grass in the leaping torchlight.

"Would you like to be introduced, m'lord?" Johnny's shrewd eyes noted his interest.

"I would," Deke said.

"When she finishes," Johnny said agreeably, thinking what a catch the young Wolfson would be for his daughter, and how in a few years the difference in their ages would become less important.

In a while the dance concluded and Nitsa approached in response to her father's beckoning motion. Her face was glowing with perspiration and she inhaled deeply to catch her breath.

"This is Deke Wolfson, Nitsa," Johnny said, smiling. "M'lord, my daughter."

"How do you do, m'lord," Nitsa said with a curtsey and laughed at the surprise on his face.

"It's a pleasure to meet you," Deke told her, rising to take her hand. "You're very talented." Something electric passed from his fingers to hers.

"Thank you," she said, amazed by how compelling his eyes were, how difficult she was finding it to look away from him. What a handsome boy, she thought, and so confident in his manner. The way he appraised her was frankly sexual and she blushed, embarrassed to find herself stimulated by a boy his age.

"Would you like to join us?" Johnny asked his daughter.

"Later," she replied. "I need to get cleaned up, change."

"It was an honor to have met you," Deke told her, sending a subtle contact into her mind that made her jump with an answering surge of desire.

Rattled, Nitsa nodded. When he shifted his eyes from hers she breathed deeply, feeling as if now she could move. It wasn't until she put a few wagons between them that she was able to recover fully from the encounter. In a moment she had gone to her family's wagon and collected towels, soap, and a change of clothes, before heading through the darkness beyond the torches towards the lake edge.

Deke rose from his place on the log.

"Where are you going?" Melak asked him.

"Nature calls," he replied.

"Please, stay within the perimeter tonight, chief."

"Don't worry," Deke assured him. "Most I'm going to do is have a swim in the lake. I'm feeling pretty dirty."

"Want me to come with you?" Melak's eyes were worried.

"No," Deke said. "Unless you want to hold my prick for me while I piss...?"

"I'll pass." Melak grinned.

Deke returned the grin and sauntered casually away from the light, certain by the look on Tim's face at least that he wasn't fooling anyone. His grin broadened as he approached the lake and hid behind a tree looking towards the water. He saw Nitsa drop her clothes until she stood nude in the starlight: tall, high-breasted, with a dancer's grace and suppleness he found truly marvelous to behold. It would be easy to desire such a woman, and the fact was, she did

292

make his prick stand up and take notice. But he had no intention of pursuing her that way, his attraction to her notwithstanding. No, he had another plan in mind, and when she was standing ankle deep in the water he walked out from behind the tree towards her pile of clothing on the shore and began to remove his own clothes.

She heard him when he let his weapons belt fall with a clink on the ground and turned, startled, her hands going to cover her nakedness. "What are you doing here, m'lord?"

"I was hoping you'd share your soap with me," he replied, slipping out of his vest and unbuttoning his pants.

She watched him disrobe and lowered her hands to her sides, realizing he already had seen everything there was to see. "You're a bold fellow," she said, trying to assert her age.

He pulled off his boots and socks, then dropped his pants, untying and stepping out of his underwear a moment later. "Aye," he agreed, walking into the water, relieved when his partial erection was submerged away from her interested gaze. He sighed with pleasure as he ducked under. It had been three weeks since his last full immersion in water.

Nitsa meanwhile had waded out deeper and was using the soap, aware of his eyes on her glistening body. She knew her father would like it if she cultivated a relationship with the young Wolfson heir, and truth be told, as she looked at him she realized he was hardly comparable to other boys his age. His assurance, the way his men leaped to obey him; these were qualities she would associate with a man.

He swam easily near her and she admired his lithe, relaxed strokes. "Are you finished with that?" he asked, gesturing to the soap. "I'd be indebted forever if you'd let me borrow it."

She handed it to him, amused by his hyperbole.

"So, Nitsa," he said while he washed himself thoroughly from head to toe, then repeated the entire process twice. "Do you enjoy traveling around entertaining people?"

She shrugged and settled in the water, her long hair spreading out on the surface. "It's a living," she said.

"You dance too well not to enjoy it," he told her.

"I like dancing," she replied. "But the traveling, living out of a wagon... Well, your folk move around, too, so you understand."

"Aye, we're nomads at heart still, though we don't roam the way we used to in my grandfather's day." He finished with the soap and offered it back but she pointed to the shore and he tossed the bar accurately towards her clothes before returning to the water near her. "Have you ever thought of settling down, living with someone?"

Nitsa's eyebrows went up. "I've thought of it," she said.

"I recommend it," he said, floating on his back.

She turned questioning eyes on him.

"Did you know that my mother died this past winter?" he asked, surprising her with the apparent change of subject.

"No, we hadn't heard. I'm sorry, m'lord. You and your father must be devastated."

"Mmm," Deke agreed. "He's been pretty lonely, I think."

"It's hard," Nitsa said with an understanding nod. "But a man as attractive as he is and in his position...I would think there are many women who'd be happy to keep him company."

"My mother was unique," Deke said. "It would take someone very special to tempt him right now."

The young woman looked at him penetratingly, starting to get a glimmer of what was in his mind. "You are a bold devil," she said. "And here I thought you were interested in me for yourself!"

"I am attracted to you," he admitted. "But I'm in love with someone else, or I'd certainly try to win your favor."

"I don't know what to say to you, m'lord!" Nitsa stared at him.

"Aye, probably I'm overstepping my bounds," Deke agreed.

"What did you have in mind?" Nitsa decided to hear him out. It wasn't every day a girl received such a bizarre proposition.

"You said you thought my father was attractive to women. Does that include you?" Deke studied her aura to gauge her response.

"Are you asking if I could love him, m'lord?"

"Aye," he affirmed.

Nitsa was silent for a few seconds. "I have to think about that one," she said. "For a girl like me ever to have considered Barr Wolfson in that way might be presumptuous, don't you think?"

"Why?" Deke asked. "You're beautiful, talented..."

"But he's the chieftain!" she said, astonished that he would need it explained.

"So?" Deke met her eyes. "He's always had an interest in beautiful, talented women." He paused. "Perhaps you feel he's too old for you?"

"Old? No, that wasn't what I was thinking at all." She studied him. "How do you know he'd want me?"

"A man would have to be dead not to want you, and even then, you probably could make him rise from his own ashes!" Deke smiled, his admiration sincere.

294

"I'm not a courtesan, m'lord," Nitsa said.

"I hope you didn't think I was suggesting you were," Deke told her. "I'm probably not handling this very well."

"What arrangement were you thinking of, then?"

"I was hoping you'd return with us to Spring Camp and consent to meet my father, just meet him, no obligation, no strings attached. If you and he don't get along, well, no harm done. I'll see to it you're escorted back to your folk. If you do..."

"Yes? If I do?"

"You tell me. What arrangement would you like?"

Nitsa thought about it. "My own tent, for a start. And official status."

"The tent is no problem. Official status? That would be up to him, I'm afraid. But I think if you were to play your cards right, you could have whatever you wanted."

"What if he were to grow tired of me? I would have to have some sort of security for the future." She stopped, staring at him. "I can't believe I'm even discussing this seriously!"

"Aye, it's a crazy conversation," he said. "But interesting, eh?"

She looked at him, then threw her head back and laughed for a long time. "You're quite the matchmaker!"

"It never would have occurred to me except for you being who you are." He smiled, enjoying her laughter and understanding it. The touch he maintained with her aura assured him of her honesty, and he realized he liked her direct, practical approach. At least she hadn't screamed with outrage at his suggestion. "I'd be willing to guarantee you whatever financial security you require for your lifetime," he told her. "In writing, if you like."

"So I would be his courtesan, then."

"No. This stipend, shall we say, wouldn't be a payment so much as a means of easing your anxieties about the future. It seems to me an artist would be glad for freedom from survival worries."

"Oh, you are a crafty devil, m'lord, to use that as a barter coin with someone like me!"

"I make the offer not out of craft or guile, Nitsa, believe me. I love my father very much, and I want him to be happy."

"What makes you think I can make him so?"

Deke thought of the various answers he could give, then decided on the truth. She had been honest with him and it seemed only fair to return the courtesy. "I just have a feeling about it," he said. "And I also have a feeling that he could do the same for you. When my feelings about something are this strong, I know I have to try and listen to them."

Nitsa's eyes were considering. She had heard the talk after last year's Spring Festival, how Deke Wolfson had spelled his uncle that night, how though young, he was by some reputed to command the forces of darkness. The story of his manhood ritual and relationship with wolves was known throughout the Wolfson domains. As Nitsa looked at him, she saw no sign that he trafficked with demons or other fell powers. What she did see was someone who was accustomed to getting his own way, but she also sensed that in this particular instance his motives were pure.

"Would you mind if I gave you my answer tomorrow?" she asked. "I feel I should discuss this with my family."

"By all means," Deke said. "I understand completely."

"Thank you," she told him. She started to wade from the lake and he followed, wishing the water had been colder. He dressed quickly, keeping his back to her.

When they were fully clothed, he stood in front of her, smiling down into her intelligent, dark eyes. "Thanks for listening seriously."

She nodded. "You're welcome," she said, not knowing what else to say, her thoughts whirling with confusion. As she looked up at him, she wished he wanted her for his own concubine.

He smiled and shrugged, knowing that if things were different, he would have taken her on the spot. She was incredibly beautiful, but more than that, there was a quality to her mind much like his own people's, and he realized that the Carillo family probably possessed the esper sense for the same reasons the Wolf People did: living in such close proximity to the ruins, even spending much of their lives traveling those dust-and-ash-covered wastelands, had shaped into new configurations the genes of those who hadn't perished directly from generational exposure to gamma radiation, and these new traits had been passed successfully to their offspring.

He sighed and said as she started to walk off, "Good night, Nitsa." The wistfulness of his tone made her stop and turn around.

She saw the desire in his eyes and wondered if she should take advantage of it. She had no doubt she could seduce him. He was so young and eager it would be the work of only a minute to make him willing.

"No," he whispered. "Please, don't try. You're right, you probably could do it, but I would hate myself and you forever, and I don't want that. I want us to be friends."

Nitsa stared in shock, wondering how he had known what she was thinking. Then she nodded, admiring his devotion to whomever it was he loved. "Aye," she said, "I'd like that, m'lord. You'll have my answer in the morning. Good night to you." She gave him a smile and left him standing by the lake.

"Ruins," Deke muttered, exhaling the breath he hadn't realized he was holding. He knew he had come very close to accepting her invitation. If she had touched him, he would have been finished. With a wry grin, he walked through a stand of trees, heading back towards the wagons and his bedroll.

"What's the matter?" Tim asked in a whisper when he returned. "She turn you down?"

"Go to sleep," Deke told him, laughing.

"She didn't turn you down?" Tim shook his head. "Andara'll kill you."

"We'll see," he answered. "You should know I'd never do anything to hurt Andara."

"So you didn't do anything. What a shame. Brother, sometimes I worry about you."

Deke laughed again. "Why?"

"It's not normal to be faithful when such a fantastic woman is available for a little fun."

"A little fun is all it would be compared to what it is with Andara."

Mastra spoke up from nearby. "Why?" he asked, trying not to sound too interested.

"Because no woman could give me what she does," Deke answered. "The intensity of her emotions, her feelings for me...I value these things beyond description. Should I risk losing her love by taking a woman who knows nothing about me, doesn't really care about me, is only interested in my role as heir to the chieftaincy, or at best, a quick screw?"

"Brother, what's wrong with a quick screw?" Tim rested his head on his hands. "You know none of us'd ever tell."

"She'd find out, if not from you, then from me. I can't hide anything from her. And I don't want to become like that poor bastard in the joke everyone keeps telling me, whose prick was spelled by his jilted witch woman lover!"

Tim and Mastra laughed.

"There's more to it," he said seriously when they stopped laughing. "I love Andara. There may come a day when I feel differently, but for now and the forseeable future, no, there's no chance I'd risk it for a quick hump with a stranger."

"She's that good a lay?" Mastra asked, not paying attention to what he was saying.

There was an abrupt silence, then Deke said very softly, "If you ever speak disrespectfully about Andara again, I'll challenge you. Do you hear me? I'll challenge you so fast your head will spin."

Mastra was taken aback by the menace in his tone. "Sorry," he said quickly. "It just came out. I didn't mean any harm."

Deke nodded, controlling the anger that had welled up like magma. "Good," he said. "Apology accepted." He turned away and pulled his blanket over himself. "Goodnight," he said to his friends. Minutes later they knew from his regular breathing that he was asleep.

"Ruins, Mastra," Tim whispered to him. "Are you crazy?"

"Aye," Mastra said. "I must be." He shook his head.

"That was so stupid! Didn't you hear what he did to Gant Murdock?"

"I know he killed him."

"He didn't just kill him, he cut off his head with a dull blade. What do you think he might do to you if he found out how you really feel?"

"What are you talking about?" Mastra whispered, glancing anxiously at Deke where he slept a little distance away.

"If I can see it, he can see it. Just be careful, all right? Find some other girl to get interested in."

"It's not like I have a lot of control over it," Mastra said miserably.

"Then get control," Tim told him. "Screw a courtesan, use your hand, whatever...but stay away from her. You're my friend, Mastra. I'd hate to see you dead over something stupid."

"You're probably right," Mastra agreed, though a stubborn part of him wasn't so sure Deke could beat him. At least, not if Deke was forced to fight fair, without magic or whatever he had used on Gant Murdock at the festival. He sighed, realizing how foolish he was being. Even if he could beat Deke in a fight, merely participating would make him outcast. For a moment he was filled with resentment, quivering with the strength of it. Then, as he calmed down, he told himself he had overstepped concerning Andara, and knew if his and Deke's positions were reversed, he would have reacted the same way. This awareness helped him relax, and soon he dropped off to sleep.

Tim looked back and forth in the fading firelight at his two friends. He had overheard his father talking to Barr Wolfson some months back, and knew who was Mastra's real father. He was sorry he knew, for it put stress on his friendship with both of them. It would never occur to him to tell either Deke or Mastra the truth, because if the chieftain had wanted anyone else to know, he would have said something. With his wife dead, the only reason he wasn't acknowledging Mastra legitimately had to concern Deke, and the last thing Tim wanted was to get in the middle of that triangle.

He turned on his back and gazed at the sky, picking out the constellations easily.

He wondered what would happen if Deke or Mastra found out. He wondered if Mastra would be able to stand it. Mastra had waited his whole life to know his father; his reaction might be explosive. As for Deke, Tim thought surely he would be happy to know Mastra was his brother, though if Mastra ever proved a challenge to him, his position, or most especially, Andara, Tim had no doubt he'd protect his interests ruthlessly.

What a mess, Tim decided, closing his eyes. Life was such a mess sometimes he couldn't believe it. Soon he dozed off, leaving his worries to float away on the gentle breeze now wafting from across the lake, bringing the scent of water plants and greenery to his nostrils.

The night passed without incident. In the morning after the soldiers had prepared breakfast and while they gathered their gear, Nitsa and Johnny Carillo approached Deke.

"Can I have a word with you, m'lord?" Johnny asked.

Deke nodded and walked with them towards the lake shore, resisting the urge to probe their minds. He smiled at Nitsa, thinking she looked even more beautiful in the sunlight, her long-legged stride an unspoken invitation difficult to resist.

"Nitsa told me your proposition," Johnny began, when they were well out of earshot of the campsite. "And I have a few questions."

"I'm listening," Deke replied, his expression attentive.

"It's of the utmost importance to me that my daughter be treated with the sensitivity and respect she deserves," he began. "She's told me she would like to go with you. She feels at the very least this would be an interesting experience which could only enhance her work as an artist. Also, she feels compassion for your father, as do we all." Johnny looked at his hands, then met Deke's eyes firmly. "But it is you, m'lord, who has made this offer, and I will hold you to your honor in terms of fulfilling it as promised."

Deke nodded. "We can put it in writing if that'll make you more comfortable."

"The honor of a Wolfson is beyond reproach," said Johnny. "Your hand on it will be all I require, m'lord, as long as we are completely clear."

"Then this is my offer and I'm willing to make it in front of whatever witness you wish: that Nitsa accompany me to Spring Camp, where I'll introduce her to my father. Whatever happens or doesn't happen after that is up to them. I feel a reasonable amount of time should be given, say a month or two, before we decide the experiment has failed. If it does, I will personally make sure Nitsa returns to you.

"If the experiment succeeds, then she'll receive a lifetime stipend plus horse and tent, though I'm sure under those circumstances my father will supply those things." Deke waited.

Nitsa and her father exchanged glances.

"In that case," Johnny said, putting out his hand, "I agree."

Deke took his hand and shook it. "Good." He turned to Nitsa. "Can you be ready to leave this morning?"

"I think so," she replied.

"You can ride one of our pack animals, if that's all right."

"That'll be fine," she told him, beginning to feel butterflies in her stomach now that the decision was made.

Sensing her disquiet, Deke smiled reassuringly. "It'll be all right," he said. "My father is extremely soft-hearted where women are concerned."

She smiled gratefully at him, then she and her father left to return to their wagons. He looked after them, then gazed around at the lake and its environs, thinking what a pretty spot this was. For a moment he thought he saw movement across the water on the far shore, and sent his awareness out in a rush. Aye, someone was there, and he zeroed in his thoughts like a sniper taking aim until he *saw* the camouflage-clad man crouching motionlessly in the ruins. Without his esper sense, Deke never would have spotted him, and now he studied the man with a sense as unlike sight as day was unlike night, yet it was linked to seeing because it translated for him as a clairvoyant inner vision that played itself out across his consciousness.

Seconds later he *saw* the mask covering the man's face and realized the fellow was a scout, keeping the Wolf riders under surveillance. The masked ones' lands must be nearby, Deke told himself. It occurred to him he would be well-served to come back this way accompanied by a stronger force. He didn't know why, but in the same way he had told Nitsa he had a feeling about her and his father, he was having another right now, and this one told him these scarred warriors were hiding a priceless secret that would change his people's lives forever.

He reached into his pocket and withdrew the steel cylinder, turning it in the sunlight. It was important, and this knowledge also was part of the premonition moving with the force of revelation through him. He spread his awareness like a spider's web and watched the scout, trying to get a sense of who he was, what was in his mind. Moments later he made contact with the man's thoughts, and was surprised by the churning emotions at work there, crude, harsh emotions with a viciousness and ruthless determination that was disturbing, particularly if it was typical among his people.

With a sigh, Deke rejoined his men, telling Willie what he had *seen*. Willie nodded, then went off to warn the soldiers to be extra vigilant. Deke warned the Carillo family to do the same, inviting them to travel with the soldiers until they were in safer territories. This the entertainers were glad to do, grateful for the protection.

By mid-morning everyone was ready and the caravan of wagons moved off while Wolf soldiers rode nearby forming a defensive screen of sharp-eyed riflemen who scanned the ruins tirelessly.

Nitsa had chosen to ride an unloaded pack mule rather than her family's wagon so she could converse with Deke. He had instructed his men to treat her with delicacy, and the riders were glad to comply. They had heard through the soldier grapevine that the beautiful dancer was coming home to be introduced to their chieftain, and were happy to be part of the surprise.

In dazzling sunlight, they moved without haste through the ruins, he and Nitsa chatting idly, occasionally joined by Tim or Willie. Mastra was quiet this morning, and Deke went out of his way to be warm to him, wanting his friend to know he was holding no grudge. After a while Mastra responded to his obvious effort to smooth things out and before long found himself telling Nitsa all about how to dismantle a tent and pack it for travel, and what enormous undertakings the winter and spring migrations of the People were, getting more difficult each year as everyone got richer and accumulated more possessions.

Deke listened with only part of his mind. His thoughts were reaching ahead to Spring Camp and Andara. With a grin, he imagined what she'd say about the present he was bringing his father. His grin got wider as he imagined Barr's face when he realized why Nitsa was there.

Aye, he thought, it was good to be homeward bound. As they rode through a patch of stark, tumbled ruins recognizable as an ancient highway system, he could feel at the edge of his awareness the presence of the masked scout following well behind the soldiers, making certain the armed men were heading away from his people's lands and back to the east.

Deke's grin turned predatory. Soon, he thought, withdrawing his awareness. Soon we'll find out what you scarred horrors are made of and what secret you're keeping so close you'll attack a force ten times your strength to preserve it.

The riders moved off through the dirt desert, and clouds of dust raised by their passage raced away behind them, making spectral shadows across the surface of the ruins.

CHAPTER FOURTEEN

The relationship between healer and warrior is superficially obvious; after all, the healer must clean up the mess warriors leave behind, and for most dedicated to the preservation of human life, the deliberate infliction of injury is true abomination, inexcusable in every way. At least, so we believe here in Beori.

It seemed curious to me, therefore, that a witch woman, whose connection with her patients is so much more empathic and complex, would be enamored of a lover whose purpose was to extend by violence his people's holdings in the world. Though I understood the issues of childhood friendship, common upbringing, status, even sexual attraction, for a long time I was unable to answer this incongruity satisfactorily for myself.

When I challenged the General on this point, he nodded agreement, surprising me.

"Aye, you're absolutely right. But I always regarded Andara's love as the greatest single miracle in my life, and never wanted to question it too deeply for fear she might wake up one morning and simply end it, for all the reasons you mentioned, as well as a plethora of others we've no need to go into now."

My interest was piqued, but it was clear he intended saying nothing further on the subject, and so I dropped it, at least for the moment.

— Ourn Rohlvaag; Collected Journals; City of Life, A.D. 3109

Andara was examining a badly twisted ankle on an eight-year-old when she heard the shouts outside announcing that riders were coming in. She wrapped the injury in a supportive bandage and handed the little girl a cookie, saying to her mother, "Try and keep her off it for a couple days. Nothing's torn but it is sprained." With a smile to the child, Andara helped her off the table and watched her limp away. She looked at herself in the wall mirror and pushed her hair back. Deciding she looked presentable, she went into the empty waiting area to talk to her assistants. "Unless we get an emergency, let's call it a day."

"Aye, m'lady," the women agreed, smiling. They, too, had heard the commotion outside and could see her barely restrained excitement.

Moments later Andara was through the door and heading for the main thoroughfare where she knew the riders would pass on their way through the city. Before long children ran by shouting and whooping, followed by the dusty band of men and horses. People moved out of the way of the soldiers, pressing in crowds around her. In an instant she spotted Deke and her face lit up with happiness until her gaze fell on the unfamiliar woman riding a little behind him on a pack mule. As Andara took in the woman's extraordinary beauty, a dart of jealousy stabbed her, and she had to struggle to keep her expression composed.

Deke found her in the crowd and waved joyously, wanting to jump off Micmac and grab her, but instead beckoned her to him. She approached slowly and he immediately perceived her disquiet.

"Come up," he said, taking his foot from the stirrup. She accepted his proffered hand and he lifted her to the saddle before him. Opening his thoughts, he invited her to see the surprise he had planned for his father, as well as how much he had missed her.

When she understood, she wound her arms around his neck and pulled his face to hers.

In the tumult of the homecoming, Micmac had continued moving along with the other riders until they came to Barr Wolfson's tent. The returning soldiers began to grin with anticipation, for many wagers had been made concerning how their chieftain would react to the spectacular dancer.

Deke dismounted, taking Andara with him. He stretched his saddlesore muscles, then, holding her hand in his, walked to the door of his father's tent. A moment later the flap was thrown aside and Barr ducked out. His eyes brightened when he saw Deke, and he grabbed him in a bear hug.

"So, my son, what have you brought your old father back from the ruins?" Barr grinned, relieved everyone had returned safely.

"Not what we planned, Father, I'm sorry to say. Just a few pathetic trifles barely worth enough to cover the expense of this trip. But I did bring back one pearl of great price," Deke said, unable to keep his eyes from sparkling with repressed excitement.

Barr noticed the young woman gracefully sitting her mule just behind Micmac. His eyes widened inadvertently, taking in her striking good looks. When she smiled at him, he swallowed, instantly understanding what Deke was up to.

"This is Nitsa Carillo, Father," Deke said, giving Andara's hand a squeeze. "Nitsa, my father."

"How do you do, m'lord," Nitsa said, her gaze sweeping his features boldly.

"It's my pleasure," the chieftain said in his deep voice, unable to take his eyes off her. "Your name is familiar," he went on. "Johnny Carillo must be your father, eh?"

"Aye, m'lord," Nitsa replied, thinking that grief and loneliness had left their marks on his face but if anything, this only made him more accessible, more human. "It's good of you to remember."

"Great musician," Barr told her. "Only a dolt could forget." He studied her curiously. She had the habit many beautiful women shared of keeping her face turned slightly away that one might more easily look at her while she maintained a somewhat flirtatious sidelong eye contact. "That pack saddle doesn't look very comfortable," he said. "Wouldn't you like to get down?"

"I thought you'd never ask," she said, and slid off.

Barr's eyes followed her. "Deke, what arrangements have you made for this lady's lodging?"

"I thought that would be better left for you to decide," Deke said innocently, feeling Andara's fingernails digging into his palm.

Barr's eyebrows went up. "I see," he said, and smiled at Nitsa. She smiled back with warmth the chieftain felt to his toes. "Perhaps you'll join me for dinner," he suggested, and she felt the magnetism of his personality as he put his gaze on her.

"I'd like that," she replied.

"Good," he said. "I'll arrange for servants to show you to guest quarters. Whatever you need, ask and they'll take care of it."

"Thank you, m'lord. You're very kind."

Barr signaled to his personal servant and spoke to him briefly. The man nodded, then went off to make preparations. A few moments later two serving women arrived to take Nitsa to her tent. Barr called after them as they started away, carrying some of the dancer's belongings. "Will eight o'clock give you enough time?" he asked, his eyes following the young woman's long-legged stride with unabashed interest.

"Aye, m'lord. More than enough."

"I'll have servants call for you," he said.

She nodded, smiling once more, her teeth white and even against her suntanned complexion, before going off with the women.

Barr turned to his son, noting the humor and mischief on his face, becoming aware of the nudges and grins among the soldiers. Willie O'Dale's eyes caught his and the chieftain saw his friend's mirth. He laughed and said, "Deke, a word with you, if I may? Inside?"

"Aye, Father," Deke said, hardly able to keep from laughing himself. He was delighted with the way Barr had responded to the young dancer, and spoke briefly to Melak, asking him to see to Micmac and make sure his weapons and saddlebags were brought to his tent. Then, his arm around Andara, he joined his father.

"You young wretch," Barr said to Deke when they were inside. He glanced at Andara who smiled to see the amused light in the chieftain's eyes.

Deke chuckled affectionately. "So you like her. She is beautiful, isn't she?"

"Aye, son, she is that. But what made you think to bring her back?"

Deke shrugged. "Your health is extremely important to me, Father."

Barr stared at him, then began to laugh again. "Will you and Andara join us for supper?"

Deke glanced at Andara and felt her touch his thoughts. "I think not, if you'll forgive us."

"You've planned this well, haven't you?" Barr said.

"No plan," Deke said. "Karma."

Andara chuckled and gave Deke's arm a subtle tug, putting a desire-filled image in his mind that made his pulse increase.

"Aye," Barr nodded. "Karma with a little Deke Wolfson twist."

Deke's eyes twinkled as he gazed fondly at his father. Then, more seriously, "There is something I'd like to discuss with you," he said. "But it can wait until tomorrow. Maybe we could talk then?"

"Aye, son." Barr's expression was bemused and Deke smiled again, sensing his father's distraction.

Deke moved towards the door. "Not too early, if that's all right with you."

Barr smiled, seeing Andara's thinly disguised impatience, picking up Deke's eagerness as well. "How about dinner tomorrow night?" he said. "I know Hawk'll be glad to see you, too."

"That's good. I'd like him to hear what I have to say."

Nodding, Barr waved them towards the door.

They were barely inside their tent when Andara turned to him, threw her arms around his neck, and locked her fingers in his hair. Her lips found his and he held her tightly, his hands slipping under her shirt to touch the warm flesh of her back.

"God, I've missed you," he said when she let him speak. Her hands were all over him and he groaned when they went between his legs.

"That woman," Andara said, her breathing ragged as she fondled him through his pants. "I thought you brought her for yourself."

Deke kissed her throat, then moved his mouth to her ear. "Don't you know you're all the woman I want?" He closed his eyes as her fingers moved behind his scrotum to caress him exquisitely. Kissing her mouth tenderly, he took a step back, still holding her in his arms.

She looked at him with fiery eyes. He took a few deep breaths and touched her cheek with his fingertips. "Hang on," he said, stepping back further. Her expression was questioning and she ran her fingers across his bare chest under his leather vest, brushing his tumescent nipples. "Wait a second," and he reached into the inner pocket of his vest. "I have something for you."

She rubbed the back of her hand against his prominent erection. "Mm," she said deeply. "I can feel that you do."

Deke grinned. "Close your eyes." When she complied, he pulled the jeweled necklace from his pocket, holding it spread in the palm of his hand to display its unusual beauty. "You can open them now," he told her.

"It's fantastic," she said, her fingers touching the stones in disbelief.

"Like you," he replied. "Turn around."

Andara turned, moving her hair so he could fasten the latch. She felt his warm breath on her nape and went to look in the mirror, opening her shirt to better view the necklace against her skin. "I can't get over it," she said, admiring the beautiful gems as the light took them. "Thank you."

"I like that Nitsa made you jealous," Deke whispered, bending a little to circle her ear delicately with the tip of his tongue.

She looked in the mirror at his eyes reflecting brightly above her head, surprised anew at how tall he had gotten in the last few months. "Why, for ruins' sake?" She stepped back, feeling his hands slip around her hips and draw her more firmly against him.

"It makes me feel how much you love me," he said, filled with yearning. She opened her mind to him as he did the same. They sighed at the comfort and familiarity of the contact and touched one another's thoughts more intimately. Deke began to move his hands over her, slipping them inside her blouse.

For a long while they stood together, their awarenesses interlocked. The room's details grew unimportant around them; its contents blurred. They could feel their heartbeats synchronize, their breath pump air together; their nervous systems resonating until Deke thought this was how it would be if they were one soul split into two halves.

Andara heard this thought and turned in his arms. They kissed, their lips clinging and releasing lovingly, their hands continuing to touch everywhere they could reach.

Before long they began to unfasten one another's clothing, dropping everything in a heap around their feet. He drew her down on the rugs and a second later had his arm behind her knee, opening her. Andara's breathing quickened and he looked into her eyes, letting her anticipation grow, touching her thoughts in new ways he had imagined during the lonely nights out in the ruins.

"I love you, Andara," he said, kissing each of her thighs in turn.

"I know," she replied with a sharp inhalation as he put his lips on hers and caressed her thoughts more insistently. "God, yes…I know."

Afterwards, they lay quietly, their minds spinning lazily in concert.

"The only thing I like about leaving you is the coming home," he said, his tone relaxed. Andara kissed him, thinking how much his voice sounded like his father's. She stroked his face affectionately, happier than she'd been in weeks. When he was gone he left a vacuum in her life nothing else could fill.

"That's the only part I like, too," she replied, her voice tender.

"This next trip, would you like to come?" He looked into her eyes and kissed her mouth searchingly, and she thought he must have been reading her mind.

"Will that be all right?"

"Of course. If I say we need a healer along, so we do." He smiled. "Besides, it might even be the truth. We're going against people who could be very tough fighters. I'd feel better knowing you're along in case we take any casualties."

Her fingers went to the scar on his flank and she nodded, disquieted. "Let's get up."

"I didn't mean to spoil the mood," he said as she moved away and rose.

She looked down at him where he lounged on top of their pile of discarded clothes. "You didn't. What would you like for supper?" she asked, dodging as he grabbed for her leg.

"You," he said, on his feet so effortlessly she thought it was like magic. Pulling her into his arms again, he kissed her until she stopped struggling against him. "Then again," he said huskily, "Maybe we could have a bath."

"When did you have your last one?" She inhaled his odor, enjoying the sharpness of his fresh sweat.

"Couple days," he said, remembering his swim in the lake with Nitsa but pushing that thought from his mind now. He studied Andara's naked body, observing the changes it had undergone since the previous summer. She was taller, her legs longer, her hips and buttocks more curvaceous. Her breasts were fuller, the nipples achingly lovely, inviting his kisses.

"Last time you came home you were pretty horrible," she reminded him, her eyes closing momentarily with pleasure.

"I didn't notice it stopped you then, either."

She made a face. "I'll call the servants," and she walked into the bedroom to find a wrap. He followed and stretched out on top of the bed luxuriously.

"Where're the wolves?" he asked.

"Running somewhere or another," Andara replied. She went through the hangings and stuck her head out the front flap, calling for the servants whose tents, now that Deke lived near his father, were conveniently nearby. When she had gotten them started with the bath, she went into the kitchen and searched the cold closet, quickly cutting four thick slices of bread and smearing them with seeded mustard. She layered pieces of pot roast and made two big sandwiches, bringing them and a jug of cold ale into the bedroom. "I thought a snack might be good," she said, joining him on the bed, sitting cross-legged nearby.

He sat up and accepted a sandwich. Glancing at the clock on the nightstand, he saw it was nearly seven-thirty and smiled. Andara saw his smile and raised her eyebrows. "Soon Father and Nitsa will be having dinner," he told her. "I wonder how it'll go."

"I'm sure they'll manage the ins and outs of the situation," she said with humor.

Deke laughed. "So soon? The first night?"

"There was plenty of chemistry between them," she replied. "And your father is no amateur."

"No." He was pensive while he ate his sandwich and washed it down with a long pull from the jug. Andara knew he was remembering his mother and gave his arm a rub. She finished her sandwich and took the plates back to the kitchen.

The tub meanwhile had been filled and she called to him as she gathered soap, shampoo, and a toothbrush.

A few minutes later they settled into the water, laughing. They soaped and shampooed one another, their hands a little too busy for simple bathing, each trying to gain an advantage in what quickly escalated to a slippery wrestling match with many low blows given and received. Their chortles of merriment and occasional excited exclamations could be heard outside by the servants who lounged in the warm evening air after their meal. The two women and one middle-aged man exchanged amused glances, and when the sounds of the mock struggle changed to rhythmic grunts and slapping, sloshing water, they began to smile. Before long they heard Andara's voice rising as she urged him on and soon his voice joined hers. For several minutes the sounds increased in volume and frequency while passers by stopped to listen, grinning broadly. There was a triumphant final shout as all the noises except for surging water came to an abrupt halt. The passers by shook their heads and continued on their way while the servants laughed softly among themselves. The middle-aged man held up his fingers and said quietly, "Two."

In the front room of his tent, Barr examined the table laid with his finest silver and crockery. His personal cook had prepared the meal and he was sure it would be superb. He had bathed earlier and trimmed his beard, dressing in a cotton shirt and lightweight canvas trousers, with soft moosehide moc-

309

casins on his feet. He spent a minute staring at himself in the mirror to see how he really felt about all this. There were no surprises in the deep, midnight blue gaze reflecting back at him, only, he was relieved to note, eager interest and anticipation.

At precisely eight o'clock there was a rattle at the door and Nitsa was shown in by servants who then discreetly departed. Barr greeted her warmly, taking her hands while he looked her over. Now that she had bathed and dressed she was even more beautiful, the simple, knit dress she had chosen clinging provocatively to every rippling curve, and he thought she was like a panther: all grace, balance, and feline presence.

"Thank you for coming," he said. "Would you like something to drink?"

"What do you suggest, m'lord?" Nitsa asked, her tone low and melodious.

Barr thought about it and went to the cold closet where he removed a ceramic jug. He collected two crystal goblets from the table and filled them, handing one to Nitsa. He took the other and touched it to hers with a quiet, musical clink.

"What shall we drink to?" Nitsa studied him, drawn to the quality of power restrained which radiated from him.

"To the pursuit of happiness," Barr said without hesitation, smiling into her brown eyes.

She nodded, liking his words.

They drank, and Nitsa's eyes widened. The drink was the paz for which the Wolf clan was famous: grain alcohol, fruit juices, and psilocybin mushrooms. The chieftain's choice of beverage spoke volumes to the young woman, and she looked more closely at him. Another man might have been showing signs of nervousness by now, but she could see nothing of the sort about Barr Wolfson. He was relaxed, unhurried, as if he knew the conclusion towards which he traveled was certain and foregone. This complete lack of urgency was strikingly sensual, and she wondered if he knew it and had cultivated this manner on purpose. But as she watched she decided that little about the man was tacked on for effect; he was a natural force too compelling for artifice or insincerity. When his eyes moved across her she felt as if he had touched her, and with a swift intake of breath, she remembered what his son had done to her by the lake.

"Please," he said, his voice a caress in itself, "Sit." He gestured to the soft, leather couch in the living area and she seated herself, looking around the tent curiously. The floors were thickly carpeted in wool rugs with complex woven patterns that set off the richly toned leather furniture. Throw pillows

310

made tasteful accents here and there, and the walls were covered in a mixture of tapestries and paintings representing both ancient and modern styles. There were sculptures on pedestals, an assortment of stringed musical instruments, and an array of books more impressive than any Nitsa had seen before.

Gesturing to the musical instruments, she asked, "Do you play, m'lord?"

"I dabble," Barr replied, sitting down and turning to face her, his elbow on the back of the couch. She noticed the broad swell of his chest and shoulders through his shirt, the way his muscles rolled beneath his tanned skin like powerful, living machines, and a quick thrill went through her.

"Will you play for me?" Her eyes were questioning.

"Perhaps another time," he replied, watching her.

"Do you mind if I...?"

"Please, I'd enjoy that," he told her.

She sipped her drink and set it down on the low table in front of the couch. In a moment she selected a guitar and brought it back. As she strummed the instrument she realized how perfect its tone was, how warmly melodious. Only someone who truly understood music would own such a guitar, she decided. Her fingers picked out bits and pieces of tunes while she examined him covertly. He must play often, for the strings were precisely in true.

"What would you like to hear?" she asked, her voice pitched lower than before. His appreciation for music stirred her emotions, and unexpectedly, she remembered what the young Wolfson had said to her, about having a feeling his father could make her happy.

"You decide," he said, feeling her increased receptivity. He smiled, realizing how much he was enjoying himself, how he had missed this delicate interplay only possible with a woman of refined sensibility.

She studied him for a moment, trying to divine his mood, and chose an ancient love song of such loneliness and tragic yearning that he was held transfixed. The purity of her rich contralto was matched by the skillful accompaniment of her playing, and he stared at her, almost holding his breath.

When the song ended, they sat quietly for a moment until Barr impulsively took her hand from the strings and brought her fingers to his lips, just brushing her skin before he released her. "You're an artist," he said softly, "As well as being beautiful. How fortunate I am to be able to listen."

Nitsa colored slightly. When he touched her she felt the flow of his vital energy leap into her flesh and she looked into his eyes, her own tumultuous.

"Did your father teach you?" Barr went on, draining his cup and handing hers over the guitar. She drank deeply to cover her nervousness.

"Aye, m'lord, when I was a little girl. After my mother died, he was everything to me, father, mother, teacher..." Her voice trailed off reminiscently. "I used to practice while we traveled."

Barr rose and retrieved the jug, refilling their cups, returning to sit a little nearer. Now he was within easy arm's reach, and she felt her breathing quicken. He didn't touch her, simply sat gazing, beginning to feel the effects of the psychedelic liquor on his senses. "Play something else," he said, and she felt the deep rumble of his tone viscerally.

She played a spritely song of ribald humor and off-color puns that quickly had him laughing helplessly, followed by a syncopated rhythm number seething with such implicit sexuality that he soon stopped laughing. She felt his eyes devour hers and when she finished the song she swayed towards him, caught by the flicker of desire in their dark depths.

"Let's have dinner," he suggested, removing the guitar from her unresisting fingers and returning it to its place with the other instruments. He could see the effects of the psilocybin in her eyes. Her pupils were dilated; he felt he could look through them to see all her feelings and most vulnerable thoughts, and was surprised by how this moved him. He took her hand and escorted her to the table, holding her chair until she was seated. He retrieved their goblets and the liquor and took his seat. Gesturing towards the bell which stood near her hand, he indicated she should ring it. She did, and moments later the servants appeared and began serving dinner.

The first course was smoked trout on a bed of fresh lettuce with sliced, baby radishes and crisp, pea pods. The trout was dressed with a sharp, sweet vinaigrette flavored with honey and mustard, and Nitsa smiled with pleasure.

"Delicious," she said. "Your chef should be congratulated."

"You can," he told her, "After the meal. Like all good cooks he likes to be appreciated." Barr ate hungrily, having skipped lunch and eaten only a bite at breakfast.

The servants brought a basket of hot, crusty rolls with butter, also a carafe of cool, pale wine. Moments later a platter of gorgeously presented game birds was set on the table, each stuffed with different combinations of fruits, nuts, and breads. Two different vegetables were brought, sautéed baby ferns and young asparagus with mushrooms, both swimming in butter and herbs. There were new red potatoes, incredibly tender and sweet. At Barr's hand signal, the servants withdrew.

"Allow me to serve you," he said. "We have grouse, game hens, and guinea fowl. All are excellent, but my personal favorites are the game hens."

"I'll trust your judgement, m'lord," Nitsa said, overwhelmed by the sumptuousness of the meal.

Barr selected a plump hen and put it on her plate, then added vegetables and potatoes. He handed it back and unstoppered the carafe, pouring wine. In a moment he had filled his own plate and was sitting again.

A breeze came through the open window flaps and door, bringing the scent of flowers to mingle with the tantalizing odors of superb cookery. They ate as if starving, talking occasionally between mouthfuls, but mainly concentrating on their food. They were just finishing and Barr was starting to pour another glass of wine for her when she froze, cocking her head to one side.

"What is that?" she asked, puzzled.

Barr listened, then continued pouring the wine. "That's my son and his woman," he said. "They're always glad to see one another when he comes home."

Nitsa also listened to the excited cries that traveled on the night air through the open windows and door. There wasn't much privacy in a tent community, she noted for future reference, particularly in warm weather. She smiled as she heard Andara's voice shouting, "Oh, you dog! There...aye!" and laughed aloud as Deke's deeper tones merged with hers.

Barr's humorous glance met hers and though they tried to ignore the climbing racket of erotic moans and pleas, it was impossible. Deke's tent was no more than thirty yards from his father's, and this spring his noisy reunions with Andara had become the subject of considerable amusement in the neighborhood. The amusement was friendly, for everyone was fond of both young people, and understood their ardent love affair completely.

"Lucky girl," Nitsa murmured.

"Aye," Barr agreed. As the sounds of love-making reached a frantic crescendo and silence fell, he looked into her openly titillated eyes and said, "Three."

"Three?"

He laughed softly and took her hand, bringing the palm to his lips. His beard tickled her skin as he kissed her. "Aye, so far."

She felt a shiver of pleasure at his touch.

"It's a little game," he explained. His mouth moved up her wrist to the inside of her elbow where his tongue lightly flicked her and she jumped with surprise. "Aye," he went on, aware of her surge of feeling by the increased pulse rate beneath his lips. "It's early yet; I'm sure they'll go for four or five."

"Oh," she said a little breathlessly, understanding.

He gave her elbow a final kiss and released her. He rang the bell once more and the servants cleared the table and brought dessert: a raspberry trifle layered with brandy-soaked apple cake, raspberry custard, and fresh raspberries topped off with whipped cream.

Nitsa closed her eyes with the depth of her enjoyment, trying to remember if she had ever tasted anything so wonderful.

Barr watched the way she savored each mouthful, taking pleasure in that enjoyment. There was something about a woman who appreciated good food that made him sure she would like all of life's sensual gratifications.

When at last the meal was finished and Nitsa had gotten her chance to compliment the chef, Barr took her by the arm and said, "It's a beautiful evening. Would you like to go for a walk?"

"Aye," she replied. "That would be lovely."

Barr stood aside while she ducked through the door, then followed. Outside, the night air was like warm breath on his skin and he caught a whiff of honeysuckle and mountain laurel.

They strolled comfortably, passing Deke and Andara's tent where now all that could be heard was indistinct conversation, occasional laughter, and the click of backgammon dice. Nitsa glanced at Barr's profile, seeing the combination of strength and sensitivity, admiring the proud set of his features. There was a regal aura to his bearing, a quality that made her think of ancient kings and pagan warriors. She slipped her arm through his, moving closer, surprised by the depth of her attraction. Her experience with men was limited to those boys she had grown up and experimented with during adolescence as well as the occasional encounter with another musician or artist. She had thought she was in love once, but the young man proved a total ass and the relationship ended in three months. She had discovered that although her physical beauty was good for attracting men it more often than not turned out to be a handicap, for most of the men she entertained had no interest in any part of her beyond her looks. Any man who might be interested in more generally was too intimidated by her appearance even to try.

Barr took her through some of his city, showing her places where one could go for a special meal or inebriant, for music or dancing, or to watch a play. He promised to take her through Merchant's Row so she might do some shopping for the kinds of items only available in the People's capital. After a while he led her out of the vast sprawl of tents across a spectacular meadow illuminated by the three-quarter moon. He explained that this was where festivals were held, and indeed, Nitsa could remember the last time she had been here as if it were yesterday. In her mind's eye she saw the multitudes of people, the mountains of food, the spectacular entertainments and fireworks, as well as the duel between young Deke Wolfson and that awful uncle of his.

Soon they were at the edge of the field beneath a spreading, old oak, and here Barr came to a halt. He looked up at the branches and rustling leaves, taken by the beauty of the evening and his companion. In a moment he turned his gaze to Nitsa and she felt the full force of his personality in his eyes. "This tree was here when my grandfather was a boy," he said quietly, holding her transfixed with the unconscious intensity of his regard. "It's said that if lovers begin their loving here, it will last through all their lifetimes."

"Do you believe that's true?" She was having difficulty breathing and swallowed hard.

He took her by the arms and drew her near. "Why don't we find out?" he said, and tilted her face up. Then he was kissing her, his lips parting hers, his embrace tightening as he put his arms around her. The kiss went on for a long time until finally he moved away slightly to let her breathe.

Nitsa put her arms around him and pressed herself to his powerful body, her head swimming. When he bent her back and ran his lips down her throat to her breasts she closed her eyes rapturously and relaxed into his grip. His mouth found hers again in a kiss both slow and insistent and soon his hands began to touch her, lightly at first, then more specifically. She could feel his rising passion, yet still his lips were so leisurely she could hardly believe it. Somehow they were on the ground and he was unfastening her clothing and his while his mouth traveled across every patch of her flesh as it was revealed. Before long she heard herself moaning incoherently as he touched and kissed her in more ways and places, with more consummate skill and knowledge, than she had ever experienced.

Overhead, the moon climbed through the star-strewn sky, casting their shadows against the cool meadow grass. As the sounds of the nocturnal world enveloped them, he took her again and again, each time inspiring bliss so piercing, she knew he would own her soul from this night forward.

In the late part of the morning Andara awakened quietly and disentangled herself from Deke's sleeping embrace. She laughed with total happiness as her gaze fell on the backgammon board, where the doubling cube stood at eight.

After using the chamber pot and washing she dressed in a sleeveless shirt which she tied up on her midriff and a pair of Deke's recently outgrown pants she had cut off into shorts. Slipping her feet into her favorite sandals, she stepped outside into sunshine that already was heating the day. She examined her potted herbs and several tubs of flowers which decorated the front of the tent fragrantly, deciding they could use water. As she turned to get some she happened to look towards the chieftain's tent and saw Nitsa emerge to admire the morning.

Andara approached the young woman, struck once again by her grace and beauty, noticing that if anything, she looked even more stunning this morning. Extending her hand and smiling, she said, "Good morning, I don't think we've been introduced properly. I'm Andara Farflight."

Nitsa shook her hand and said, "Nitsa Carillo." She made an apologetic gesture. "I'm afraid I was so nervous when we got here yesterday I wasn't paying attention to much else." Her eyes took in the girl's extraordinary radiance and self-possession and she thought she had never seen anyone lovelier. So this was young Deke Wolfson's paramour. Nitsa couldn't keep from smiling as she remembered the sounds of enthusiastic love-making which had continued on and off until dawn.

"I hope you enjoyed dinner?" Andara's eyes were mischievous. "Barr sets quite a table."

"Indeed," Nitsa agreed. "I can't recall a better meal." She sensed the girl's curiosity and was amused by her polite effort to control it. She motioned towards Andara's flower pots. "What are you growing?"

"Cooking herbs, mostly," Andara told her, leading her over to have a closer look. "A few pansies and petunias. I don't have time for more, unfortunately."

Nitsa nodded, remembering that Barr had told her Andara was a witch woman; and though young, was already showing her skill and gift for healing.

"So," Andara asked, "Have you decided to stay with us?"

Nitsa nodded and smiled again. "I hope we can be friends," she said.

"Me, too," Andara agreed, liking the young woman, admiring her courage in being able to leave her past behind and take a gamble on the future. She gestured to the chieftain's tent. "Is he still sleeping?"

"Aye," Nitsa said. She pointed to Andara's tent. "Him, too?"

"Like a dead man."

The two looked at one another, then burst into laughter.

"There is something I'd like to talk to you about," Nitsa said more seriously, "In your capacity as healer."

"Yes?"

"It's about preventing pregnancy," Nitsa confided.

"What are you using now?" Andara asked.

"Luck, mostly," admitted the young woman.

"Luck isn't very reliable," Andara said dryly.

"No," Nitsa agreed. "What do you use?"

"There are herbs I take in tea or food," Andara told her. "They aren't foolproof. Nothing is."

"What about a sheath?" Nitsa almost blushed.

"They work, unless they come off." Andara was matter-of-fact. "But Deke and I...well, we think they're less than romantic. He says they're about as much fun as wearing clothes in the bath."

Nitsa laughed. "Probably most men feel the same."

"I'll be happy to give you a supply of herbs and instructions on their use."

"Thank you," Nitsa said. "I can't tell you how you've relieved my mind."

Andara nodded. "Is there anything else you need, anything I can get for you?"

Nitsa shook her head. "The servants are so attentive I'm almost embarrassed," she said. "They bring everything before I even ask."

Andara heard a chorus of wolf howls and said, "Oh, ruins, brace yourself!"

Nitsa looked at her without comprehension until a moment later she saw a pack of wolves bounding towards them at top speed. They were young, she observed just before they smashed into her en masse in a flying tangle of wagging tails, flailing paws, and wildly licking tongues.

Andara put stern images of wolves behaving themselves in the pups' minds but it was minutes before they calmed down, and then only because Hopi laid among them fiercely, disciplining the more rambunctious ones by grabbing their muzzles and squeezing until they collapsed on their backs in submission. The largest puppy was a male with a black muzzle, and he seemed the least impressed by his mother's aggression. He kept clear of her flashing teeth and after a moment, turned and trotted off to Barr's tent, where he nosed the flap aside and went in.

"Goodness," Nitsa said when the hubbub had subsided. She looked at Hopi who came to inspect the newcomer. "What beautiful animals."

"Aye, but what a pain these pups are getting to be," Andara said, rubbing her stomach where one of the young wolves had caught her with a claw. "With Deke gone so much..."

"I'd heard he tamed a wolf pack," Nitsa said.

"Aye," Andara told her. "And Hopi stayed with him."

"It's said he can perform feats of magic."

Andara looked at Nitsa. "Some people call it that," she said. "But it isn't really, you know."

Nitsa was thoughtful. "What is it, then?"

"Deke's an adept." Andara's eyes were penetrating. "Some people find the notion of a male adept, or brujo, frightening. Brujos have been known to give in to the temptation of using their abilities to gather power."

"And Deke?"

"Power resides in him naturally," Andara said proudly. "His mother, who was my patron, called it sensitivity. And in some ways, that describes it best, for it's more than a learned technique; it's an emotional quality extending into all aspects of his personality. Surely you've sensed some of this about him, and that's why you're asking me these questions."

Nitsa met Andara's eyes. "It would be impossible not to sense how unusual he is."

"There are varying degrees of sensitivity, just as in anything else. You probably know people who can play and sing, but most of them don't approach your artistry." Andara gave a gracious nod. "We heard you last night," she explained.

"Thank you," Nitsa said. "I practice a lot."

"So do the best adepts. Deke is the strongest I've ever heard of, and he's still young. When he's fully mature..." Andara shrugged.

"How fascinating," Nitsa said. "My family has a tradition of fortune-telling and tarot, as well as astrology and psychic readings, but most of them use trickery and sleight of hand to make the fortunes come out right. Nothing like what a witch woman can do."

There came the sound of Barr's deep laughter from his tent and both young women looked in that direction. "I guess he's awake now," Andara said. "Lakota is a lively pup."

"I'll see if I can rescue him," Nitsa said, smiling to hear the chieftain's good-natured cursing as he greeted the puppy.

"See you later," Andara said, then added impulsively, "I'm so glad you're here, Nitsa."

"Thank you," she replied. "I'm glad to be here." She gazed around in a pleased fashion, happy to have met Andara and to have had such a strong feeling of connection with her. She could sense how intelligent and inquisitive the girl was, how focused and insightful.

What a surprising adventure this was turning out to be, she thought. First, an overwhelming night of seduction by the most powerful man in their world, an event in and of itself beyond her wildest dreams a few short days ago. To think such a man wanted her seemed incredible. Even more remarkable was how he had made her feel; she tingled merely thinking about him. And now a new friend as well. With a joyous little wave, she went back to the chieftain's tent and ducked inside, disappearing from view.

Andara watched her go, then looked down at the wolves milling about her legs. She put an image in Hopi's mind of Deke sleeping, making it clear the wolves couldn't come inside until later. Hopi actually sighed as she sent back an affirmative image.

A moment later Andara got a pitcher of water which she poured in her

318

flower pots. When finished, she went to the kitchen, filled two bowls with granola sprinkled with fresh strawberries, added milk and a little honey, and brought them into the bedroom.

Deke was sprawled on his back with the quilt thrown mostly off him.

"Deke, sweetheart," she called. She saw him smile at the endearment and open his eyes.

"Hi," he said, stretching.

"I brought breakfast," she told him.

He sat up and yawned widely. "One minute," he said, and rose to find the chamber pot. When he was finished, he returned and sat down. "Come back to bed with me," he invited.

Andara kicked off her sandals and sat next to him, handing him a bowl of cereal and taking the other for herself. "When did you plan to go after those people you were telling me about yesterday? I need to make arrangements with my assistants to re-schedule anything important."

"Soon, no more than a couple days," he replied, crunching through a cluster of rolled oats.

Andara nodded, her mind working. "How long will we be gone?"

He shrugged. "A week, ten days, that would be my guess. Unless these people have defenses better than anything we've ever seen, it shouldn't take long. Their weapons aren't much to speak of." He set his spoon down and took her hand, bringing it to his lips where he gave it a loud kiss. "Interesting combination," he said with a grin. "Battle and breakfast."

Andara smiled and changed the subject. "I met Nitsa this morning."

His eyes showed his interest. "How did dinner go? Were you able to get anything out of her?"

"From what I could see, everything went well," she said, her eyes dancing. "Your father slept late this morning, too."

He laughed. "Did she look happy?"

"Very," she assured him. "She looked like a woman in love."

"My father always has that effect on women," Deke said.

"Like father, like son," she murmured.

"I don't affect women that way," Deke told her.

Andara laughed at his modesty. "You must not be paying very close attention."

"We'll never know, I suppose," he said. "I never intend to give anyone else the chance."

She looked at him thoughtfully. "I would understand if someday you had to try it," she said. "As long as you didn't fall in love with anyone else. And as long as you didn't humiliate me."

"You mean if I was discreet." Deke looked at her, surprised by her words.

"Someday," she said. "Not now."

He grinned. "As jealous as you were of Nitsa...?"

"You're a man," she said with a shrug. "Don't you think I know what soldiers do?"

Now he was even more surprised. "How could you know?"

"Ruins, you're naïve," she said, kissing him lovingly. "I treat soldiers all the time for sex diseases."

"Oh." He was speechless at her frankness.

"But if you ever bring me home one of those diseases," she said with a fierce grin, "I promise you, I'll cut this off!" She grabbed for his penis, making cutting motions with her fingers.

He covered himself with his empty bowl. "Ruins, I think you mean it!" He laughed a little queasily.

"I do," she said, putting her bowl on the nightstand and slipping down to lie alongside him. Her arm stole across his chest and he pulled her head to his shoulder, kissing her forehead.

"What about you?" he asked. "Are you ever curious to try it with someone else?"

"I'm curious," she said. "But I'm sure he'd pale to insignificance beside you. So why bother?"

"That's exactly how I feel about it." He touched her thoughts lightly.

"I know Nitsa was interested in you," Andara told him.

"How could you know that?"

"Witch women know everything," she said mysteriously, her eyes filled with laughter. "Thank the ruins your father is an accomplished man with the ladies, or I'd be fighting her off you with a stick!"

"How could you know that about him?" He chuckled.

"Oh, please...you are joking, aren't you?" Andara chuckled with him. "Any female can feel it the moment she meets him."

"Should I be jealous?" He looked into her eyes.

Her eyes became several shades greener and she took his empty cereal bowl away and put it with hers on the nightstand. "You have nothing to worry about in that area," she said, and caressed him, her breathing changing as he grew erect in her hand.

"I don't know," he joked, turning to face her, his fingers slipping up through the leg of her shorts to touch her. "Maybe a firecracker like you needs a whole squadron of lovers." He kissed her mouth while she unbuttoned the shorts and wriggled out of them.

"You are a whole squadron of lovers," she whispered, before opening her legs and moving against him, ending further conversation.

CHAPTER FIFTEEN

*During one conversation on the subject of making war, we discussed
the various qualities that go into making a superior leader. My argument was
that a leader must be wiser, braver, more persistent and determined, more creative... In short, I postulated, a great military leader had to be better than those
he commanded.*

*The General thought about what I said for no more than a second
before responding, "The only thing any leader needs is followers. To obtain
these, he has to be more ruthless, brutal, and swift in dealing out retribution to
his enemies than they ever could dream of being."*

*"Such a person would not inspire much confidence in my heart," I
told him.*

*"On the contrary," the General said, with a gleam in his eye. "Such a
person already has."*

— Ourn Rohlvaag; Collected Journals; City of Life, A.D. 3109

T he soldiers moved through the ruins at an easy pace, with scouts
ranging in all directions for several miles. Each scout carried a small
mirror, and every so often a flashing signal could be seen as they sent coded
messages back and forth.

Deke rode at the front of the first column of his regular two hundred.
Following these men were two further columns of equal size. Each soldier was
heavily armed, and there were scores of pack animals bearing ammunition,
supplies, and mortars. Melak was in his accustomed spot to the rear and side
of Micmac, his rifle loose in his hand. Andara was on Romeo to Deke's right,
and beyond her rode Willie. Tim and Mastra were with the rest of their manhood group just behind.

Every so often Deke glanced at Andara, hardly able to believe she was
there. She gazed at everything eagerly, thrilled to be riding into the deep ruins.
He could feel her excitement when he touched her thoughts, and was happy to
share an experience that was so integral a part of himself.

They had departed Spring Camp after only two days of preparation,
leaving in the cool of the early morning. Now the sun was nearly vertical and
the memory of the pre-dawn chill was fading.

Deke smiled, thinking about his father and Nitsa, pleased at the apparent success of his experiment. At dinner the other night it had been obvious the
two were finding joy in one another, and he had remarked to Andara later that
his father looked fifteen years younger. He reached out to catch her hand,
Sending her an affection-filled image that made her color with pleasure.

Behind them, Tim and Mastra saw the gesture and exchanged glances. They were surprised Deke had brought Andara, but accepted without question his statement concerning the possible need for a healer.

The night they had arrived home from their last trip, Tim had taken Mastra to the courtesan district, where they had gone from tent to tent while Mastra looked the women over and turned down all offers. It wasn't until they got to a higher priced, more elegant place that Mastra had shown interest. They had been sitting in the outer room which led to several luxurious bedrooms where customers were entertained, when the madam who ran this particular establishment brought out her women for the boys to peruse.

Tim had joked with the woman whom he knew fairly well while Mastra looked at a particular courtesan and licked his lips. He had turned to the madam and said, "This one."

The madam had nodded and said, "You pay her in advance, understand?"

"Aye," Mastra had said hoarsely, unable to tear his eyes away from the young woman.

The madam had gestured and she had risen gracefully, taking Mastra's hand, leading him towards one of the back rooms. Tim had watched them go, his smile fading as he looked at the courtesan's dark hair and hazel eyes. She wasn't a perfect replica; no woman could be as beautiful or spirited, but the resemblance had been enough to be obvious and unsettling. Stupid, Tim had thought. Very stupid to pick a courtesan who looked so much like Andara Farflight.

The soldiers followed a route west that closely paralleled the one taken home only a few days previously. Deke had scouts probing an area on his map indicating the territory the Carillo family had told him was controlled by his intended prey. His scouts would criss-cross it thoroughly, searching until every detail was known.

"Willie," Deke said. "Warn the men to watch for rats."

"Rats?" Willie asked with disgust, and everyone within earshot made faces.

"Aye," Deke told him. "That last fort we hit...the leader said the territory to the west is loaded with them."

"I hate rats, chief," Melak said. "I really do."

Andara was curious. "Are you talking about cave rats?"

Deke nodded.

"Is it true what they say about them?" she continued.

"Everything is true," Tim answered. "And worse besides."

"You know how to use a pistol, don't you?" Deke asked.

"Of course," she said.

"I'll get you one when we camp," he said. "Keep it with you all the time."

"But if it's true they swarm like hornets..."

"It's not for the rats," Deke said soberly, and took her hand again.

"You're joking," she said, shaken.

"No. Make sure you don't wander anywhere. As large a force as ours isn't vulnerable, but if you're caught alone..." He shrugged. "You'd never have time to use your dagger."

"I understand," she said. "But there are a few things a girl needs privacy for."

"We'll give you a tent," Willie told her. "You can do what you have to in there."

Andara nodded, her mind working. She'd heard stories about cave rats but never had seen any. Generally they were found only in deep ruins, living in ancient, buried wreckage or buildings. As rats went, they weren't large, but their esper capability and packing instincts more than made up for lack of size. Communities of rats were known to number in the thousands. They were intelligent, savage carnivores who lured prey within reach of their hidden holes, lulling any likely meal into a false sense of security before attacking en masse and eating it alive.

"The worst thing about them," Tim said, "Is that sometimes it's hard to tell where they might be hiding. There are old basements and underground cavities that are invisible from the surface. Like all rodents they can squeeze through openings you might not notice or think of as entryways into rat cities."

"So how do you avoid them?"

"We're pretty good at that," Willie reassured her, and glanced at his son reprovingly, knowing Tim's proclivity for accentuating gruesome details.

Tim grinned. "Don't worry, Andara, we won't let any rats nibble on you...at least, none that you don't want." His grin widened as he winked at Deke.

She laughed, her cheerfulness restored.

They rode steadily through the ruins, and every so often riders cantered up to report to Deke, letting him know at regular intervals that so far no one had taken an interest in their progress. This information pleased him and he opened his mind, allowing his awareness to spread its sensory net to encompass a roughly circular area several miles in diameter, seeking the energy emanations associated with sentient creatures. In particular he was looking for his wolves, hoping they were ranging in the local vicinity. Their presence gave him a feeling of security far greater than that supplied by his soldiers. He Sent a more powerful subliminal call out across the wasteland, knowing if they were nearby they would hear and respond.

Before long he heard them in his mind, and with a quick series of images made it clear he would appreciate their continued awareness of any dangers or opportunities in the hot, dust desert surrounding the horsemen. There was a chorus of affirmative signals inside his head and he smiled, maintaining only a whisper of psychic connection to monitor their movements.

He felt Andara in his thoughts and opened his mind further that she might experience the expanded perceptions he took for granted in himself but for which he knew her own esper capability didn't allow. Their talents were different and yet complementary. The more they practiced, the more accomplished they became, able to enhance one another's abilities when needed. In the same way she had helped him *see* his mother's energy at the funeral, he was able to help her project her mind in what essentially was a vast and ongoing Sending. Their connection was made stronger by physical contact, strongest of all when they were joined in the act of love, though simple palm to palm handholding could boost their potential to a much more vivid intensity.

Deke had noticed that when connected to Andara, he could spread his awareness farther, that her participation made him more powerful. He felt like a better person altogether when she was in his mind, as if she brought a degree of unselfishness to what he honestly acknowleged was his own basically self-centered personality. She made him want to be kinder, more compassionate, if that would win her approval and respect. She made him want to be the kind of person his mother had raised him to be, and which he rarely was any more.

Andara felt his downturn of mood and caressed his fingers subtly, trying to distract him. She loved the sensation of expanded awareness she experienced with him, loved the feeling of god-like omniscience, as if her mind was rising up to a soaring perspective that allowed total consciousness of the environment with no loss of detail.

Don't be sad, her caress said, and he turned towards her, drawing his thoughts in to focus them on her.

I'm not sad, he told her, and put his mind through his physical senses once more. Andara released his hand and gave him a look that let him know he wasn't fooling her, but that she respected his privacy.

Mastra watched them surreptitiously, aware of a hidden communication but unable to hear it. He sighed, his eyes following Andara as they always did while apparently focused on something else.

He had gone back to the courtesan every night they were home, knowing he was torturing himself with his counterfeit lover but incapable of stopping. That first night he had convinced himself she was Andara's twin sister, and it wasn't until after they'd had sex that he was able to see she really didn't look much like Andara beyond the most superficial resemblance. The experience itself had been satisfactory on a physical level; the girl had been skilled and gently guided him past his first awkward, fumbling efforts until success was achieved. Thereafter, once he had gotten the hang of things, he managed very well, especially when he pretended it really was Andara he was lying with, and not a paid substitute.

But now, riding a little behind and to the side of her, he could see that she was as unlike Andara as ragweed was unlike a rose. He didn't know how he was going to stand being in such close proximity to her, or how he was going to bear it if she and Deke made love. As it was he thanked his lucky stars for whatever intuition had made him put up his tent in an entirely different section of the city from theirs, for word of their uninhibited coupling had spread through his manhood group with the typical adolescent glee one might expect from that bunch.

Mastra tore his eyes away from watching her hips sway back and forth as Romeo walked along, and forced himself to look at the ruins. With luck, her presence on these expeditions would be limited to this trip, and he could put her out of his mind at least while soldiering.

When the day was waning the riders made camp in a patch of desert basically clear of rubble and debris, where the ground was a combination of sand and dust compacted enough that any cavity would have been filled in centuries ago. They set elaborate perimeter defenses anyway, tripwires that would trigger explosives to discourage the most determined rats or other predators, especially the two-legged variety.

Double guards were posted while Tim helped Andara put up a small tent. He teased her about her need for privacy, trying without success to convince her that the men could be trusted not to peek. She chuckled steadily while he ran on, appreciating his efforts to distract her from any worries she might be feeling.

Soon Deke joined them and he, too, laughed at the little tent surrounded by the bedrolls of six hundred bloodthirsty fighters who spoke so politely to Andara and were fiercely solicitous of her welfare.

"Will you share it with me?" she whispered, looking about to make sure no one was listening.

"The men'll hate me if I do," he told her.

"I'll hate you if you don't," she said, laughing.

"I wouldn't dare leave you alone with all these randy bastards, anyway," he said, tossing his bedroll through the low tent flap. He added after a humorous pause, "They'd never be safe."

"Very funny," she said.

He threw his head back and laughed with such unfettered enjoyment at his own wit that she blushed furiously and hit his forearm with her fist, hard.

Willie approached, wiping sweat from his forehead with a small cloth. "Everything's secure, chief," he said to Deke. "Which shift do you want?"

"I'll take the first one," Deke replied. "Make sure everyone gets supper." He looked at Andara. "Sorry to say supper's just biscuits, jerky, and dried fruit."

"I'll manage," she said.

"Good. I'll see you in a couple hours, then." He kissed her and started away, saying, "Tim? A word with you?"

Tim followed him. "Aye?"

"Will you keep an eye out for her until I get done?"

"No problem," Tim agreed readily.

"Where's Mastra?" Deke asked next, and Tim felt his stomach contract at the question.

"I think he was setting up the tripwires."

"I wanted to talk to you about him," Deke said, glancing around to make sure they weren't overheard.

Tim raised his eyebrows.

"Aye, something's eating him. I don't expect you to betray any confidences, but is he all right? Feeling well?" Deke's expression was worried, and Tim felt a surge of affection for his friend.

"He's healthy enough," he said. "But you know how he feels about having no father."

Deke ran a hand through his hair, pushing it off his face. "I may have to solve that mystery for him one day," he said thoughtfully.

"Do you think you can?" Tim asked as casually as he could.

Deke shrugged. "Someone must know who his real father is, or was."

"You think he's dead?"

"Why else wouldn't he acknowledge Mastra? He left a hefty inheritance for Mastra and his mother to live on...probably he's dead."

"What if he isn't? Maybe his privacy should be respected?"

Deke's expression grew hard. "Any man who wouldn't acknowledge someone as good and decent as Mastra is a son of a bitch."

"Maybe he has an overpoweringly good reason," Tim said.

Deke looked at his friend, his eyes penetrating. "Do you know something you're not telling me?"

Tim shrugged. "I've never been much for gossip," he replied. "That's why you trust me."

"Aye," Deke said with a little laugh, and gripped Tim's shoulder. "You're probably right, it's not my business."

Tim gave him a pat on the arm. "I'd better get back to Andara," he said. "I won't have much time alone with her if I stand here with you," and his grey eyes were warm, appreciating that trust his friend had in him beyond words.

Deke laughed again. "Be careful," he warned. "She's a handful."

"I like the sound of that," Tim said, his expression comical.

"I'll bet you do," Deke said, grinning as he walked away to collect his weapons from Micmac's saddle.

Tim exhaled, watching Deke's back disappear into the crowds of soldiers, Melak appearing out of nowhere to accompany him as usual. Thank the ruins for Deke's honor, he thought. Were he not so honorable, Tim was sure he'd have had the secret from him in an instant. He turned and headed back to the tent, putting a grin on his face for Andara's benefit, one which became genuine as she smiled beautifully and asked if he would eat his rations with her.

In two hours the darkness was almost full and stars began to shine overhead. In the east, the moon hugged the horizon, swelling slowly, nearly at full. As it rose it cast a yellow glow across the ruins, creating a vista both supernatural and surrealistic. Enthralled, Deke hurried off his guard shift and back to Andara's tent, drawing her outside to enjoy the unusual evening.

They stood quietly among the soldiers who also were watching the moonrise, hypnotized by the stark beauty of the broken landscape. He put his arms around her and gave her forehead a little kiss.

"This would be romantic as hell if we weren't surrounded by six hundred soldiers," he whispered into her ear.

"Behave yourself," she murmured. "You're not allowed to embarrass me in front of your men."

"Don't you think they know what we do?"

"That's not the point." She smiled at him.

"I know," he said, squeezing her affectionately, smiling with her. The soldiers nearby smiled as well, the pair's happiness contagious.

Soon the moon had risen high enough to lose its unusual color, and the soldiers began to find their bedrolls. Deke and Andara crawled into their tent and dropped the flaps. It wasn't very roomy, but it did give privacy of a sort. He unrolled their blankets, putting them together into one bed, and pulled off his boots. Unstrapping his body daggers from the insides of his forearms and the outsides of his calves, he laid them and his weapons belt alongside the blankets. His rifle was propped near at hand and he quickly lay down, watching Andara arrange her belongings in the streaming moonlight which illuminated their tent through the unfastened flaps.

She pushed a covered metal chamber pot against the far wall beyond their feet and took off her boots, lying down beside him. He put his arm around her and she moved against him, glad to use him as a pillow.

"This is less than comfortable," she said, wriggling away from a stone under her hip.

"Aye, we should have brought you a cot," he agreed.

"Undressing isn't done?"

He smiled. "I don't like to now that I'm in command."

Her hand slipped under his waistband.

"I thought you didn't want me to embarrass you," he said.

"We could be quiet," she murmured, unbuttoning his pants.

Deke caught her hand and kissed it, laughing aloud. "I'm sure I can," he teased. "But you!"

She put her hand back in his pants and caressed him while he bit his lips to keep from making a sound. "Let's try," she whispered.

"This is probably unwise," he told her, pulling her against him, unfastening her pants and sliding them down with her underwear. "Anyone could call me."

"I know," she said, freeing her legs. "That's what makes it so exciting."

"Aye," he whispered when they were joined, "But that's just a detail. You're always what makes it so exciting," and he kissed her. In the moonlight his eyes shone like sapphires, mesmerizing her. Soon she had to bite his shoulder to keep from crying out and he buried his face in her hair, their pleasure made more intense by the need to remain silent.

Afterwards, as their breathing returned to normal, Andara gently kissed the place she had bitten while he curled against her, and pulled the blanket over them. "Do you think anyone heard us?" she asked, moving her lips against his ear.

"Probably they all did," he replied the same way, holding her lovingly. "Poor bastards."

She chuckled. "Do you have any idea how much I love you?" she asked, her warm breath sending shivers through him.

"Aye, if it's as much as I love you," he replied, his grip tightening.

"I'm so glad you brought me," she said, kissing his cheek.

"So am I," he told her. "Let's try and get some sleep," he suggested. "We have another two or three days of riding at least, and it's a lot easier if you're well rested."

"Aye, chief," she agreed, already drowsing as she felt his arms enfold her securely.

Sunup found them on the move again. Today when Deke Sent his awareness across the ruins he began to have the uncanny sensation they were being watched, but by what or whom he couldn't imagine. His esper sense scoured through every dip and crack in the countryside, looking for camouflage-clad masked men, finding none. Still he was uneasy, and every so often he cantered off, Melak at his side, to speak to one or another of the scouts. No one had seen anything but he warned them to be extra-vigilant nonetheless.

In a way what he was feeling reminded him of his manhood test, when he was under surveillance by the ruins tiger. There was the feeling of being observed in every essential detail by a disturbingly non-human intelligence and he felt as if he was itching beneath his skin.

"Do you feel that?" Tim asked Mastra, the hairs on his scalp stirring with the strength of his discomfort.

"Like an itch I can't scratch," Mastra agreed. "Deke feels it, too," he said, gesturing to where their friend rode, visibly restless.

"We all feel it," Andara commented, overhearing their conversation. "What is it?"

"At least a few different things," Deke said, beginning to sort through the contradictory sensory information. "Rats, first of all," he said. "Lots of 'em. We're riding through at least two separate colonies, both scared as hell of each other or maybe they'd be after us."

Andara shuddered.

"They're having a mental rat war, and we happened into the crossfire."

"Are we in any danger?" she asked.

"No," Deke said, and a satisfied look came over his face. He signaled to the boys of his manhood group. "Look, fellows," he said pointing to the right where a collapsed building half-buried under the dirt lay at an angle. "There's a colony over there. And to the other side, see?" He pointed to another half-buried structure. "That's the second one. Let's get 'em."

The boys grinned, pulling an assortment of grenades and pipe bombs from their saddlebags.

"What are you going to do?" Andara asked.

"Blow 'em to hell," Deke grinned.

"Why not just leave them alone?"

"Cave rats are a pestilence," Willie said. "We always kill them when we can. You never know when you might have to come back this way on foot."

Meanwhile the boys had released the hairtriggers on their explosives and tossed at least a dozen towards the wrecked buildings. Watching them, Andara could almost believe they were playing ball, so casual were their motions.

A few seconds later both buildings blew up, and the soldiers smiled happily as they felt the rat-induced itching snap off.

"Still something there," Deke said, casting his awareness outward, "But I'm damned if I can figure out what it is. Doesn't feel warm-blooded at all."

"What does it feel like?" Andara asked, touching his mind with her own.

Look for yourself, he told her inside her thoughts, and opened himself to her fully, that she might get a better idea of what he was sensing.

I can't see, she thought, and then made a little sound of dismay. She broke off the contact abruptly, grabbing Deke's hand and forcing him to do the same.

"What is it?" he asked, shocked by her sudden pallor. "What did you *see*?" He was about to Send his awareness out again but she sensed the upsurge of his energy and quickly went into his thoughts to stop him.

No, she told him. *Not now, stay focused here.*

What is it? he demanded. *Tell me.*

Do you remember that night after your mother's funeral...? Andara's eyes were frightened.

He steadied her with a gentle contact. *How can you be sure?*

Because, she responded in his innermost thoughts, replaying the emotion she had sensed now and the one from the night in the blizzard. *They're the same, exact.*

Where is it coming from? Can you tell?

No, she replied. *I only know the essence is the same.*

Why don't you want me to look closer? His eyes were locked on hers.

When you Send yourself out in that way you become visible to...whatever it is. I don't know if it's looking for you specifically, or just anything like you that puts out a certain type of energy.

If that's true, it should sense me all the time, he responded.

It senses you if its awareness is turned in your direction, she told him. *If you also happen to be outside yourself at that moment...* She shivered.

It is looking for me. Darkness rose through his psyche like a rushing storm.

You can't know that for sure. She tried to comfort him.

I do know, he replied. *I've always known.*

Their eyes met: hers worried, his despairing, and they put themselves through their physical senses once more, wondering if there was any way to tell the others what they had perceived at the periphery of Deke's consciousness.

Willie gave an involuntary shiver. "Feels like demons are around."

Deke's eyes opened wider in surprise and he stared at Willie. "*That's* what demons feel like?" he asked, his expression intent.

"Aye," Melak nodded. "I've felt 'em only a couple times, but you're right. Feels the same."

Mastra spoke up. "What interest would demons have in a party as large as ours?"

"A demon doesn't have to be interested to affect you," Willie told him. "They're like skunks that way; they stink even if they're not spraying you specifically."

"Look!"

All eyes followed Tim's pointing finger.

Skittering like a crazed top over the surface of the dust, a tiny whirlwind spun along parallel to their march, pausing every so often before continuing. Occasionally it moved nearer, then withdrew, almost as if it was taunting the soldiers, or, Deke thought, fascinated, watching them. He could feel the draining effect of the thing and immediately understood that the reason humans felt awful in the presence of demons was because demons drew energy from people, sucking at their essence the way mosquitos sucked blood, but with greater effect. Flicking a glance at Andara, he Sent a part of himself out towards the whirlwind, and instantly it seemed to grow agitated, frantic. With a final puff of dust it spun away towards the southwest, moving quickly. In seconds it disappeared completely.

"Not the same," he said aloud to Andara. "Similar, but weaker. Far weaker."

"Same essence, though," she murmured. "There's a connection here, Deke."

He nodded. "Aye," he said thoughtfully. Then louder, to the others, "Where do they come from? Does anyone know?"

"Does it matter? They're here, that's the important thing." Willie studied him, wondering what he was thinking.

"It would be good to know," Deke said. "There's no mention of anything like demons in any book I ever read from before the war. They must be relatively new to the Earth."

"How are you going to find out anything like that?" Willie asked.

"I don't know." His expression was grim. "But I will."

They rode for a while without conversation, everyone busy with his own thoughts.

At midday scouts reported a pair of esper tigers in the vicinity but otherwise nothing to threaten them. Throughout the afternoon, while the sun beat

333

with torrid strength on their shoulders, they continued westward through ruins that were becoming noticeably greener. Everyone was sweating in the heat and soon Andara tied her hair back and put on a hat. She had to relieve herself and wished she could simply hop off her horse, turn her back, and do it standing up the way the men did.

She put her discomfort aside and examined the terrain over which they traveled. Shrubs and small plants sprouted from the rocky soil, and an hour later, stunted trees began to appear, standing forlornly in the arid ground, waiting, she thought, for the rain.

By late afternoon the scattered bits of ancient rubble and debris were practically hidden by tall grass which now grew fairly thickly. Not far ahead Andara could see the reflection of sunlight from a small lake surrounded by dense vegetation and a copse of trees. Scouts rode the perimeter to its far side, sending back flashes of coded light which Deke and Willie noted before exchanging pleased nods.

"Are we camping here?" she asked Tim.

"Aye," he replied. "The horses need water. We'll head west again tomorrow."

They saw Deke stand in his stirrups, whistle to the riders near the rear of the last column, and wave his hand overhead in quick circles. Almost immediately two score of them split away from the main group and fanned out to circle through the area. She could see them looking at every detail of the ground and underbrush, checking for danger.

Soon the riders sent back all clear signals, and the soldiers approached the lake, setting up their campsite with the usual assortment of trip wires and booby traps around the periphery. Once again Tim helped Andara erect her tent, and the men chuckled as she snatched up a chamber pot and rushed inside.

Deke spoke briefly to Melak and ordered double guards. He didn't need to remind them of the scout who had dogged their steps for a full day after leaving this place the last time. Then he went with Mastra to collect fresh canteens of water as well as dried rations for himself and Andara.

He studied Mastra obliquely, trying to get a sense of his friend's mood. Superficially, Mastra seemed fine. He even joked about his experience at the courtesan district, bragging that once he had figured out how to do it, he had done it until his prick was sore. Deke laughed and suggested he use a lubricant, which led to a fairly graphic comparison on the virtues of various kinds. Soon Mastra was laughing so hard he was doubled over, clutching his canteen and dinner to keep from dropping them.

"How'd you learn about these things?" he wheezed, trying to catch his breath.

"My mother was a witch, don't forget," Deke said with humor. "She kept everything you can imagine in her apothecary, and often prescribed one or the other for people who needed them. When I started to do myself, you know," and he made the universally understood gesture, "I probably tried every oily or slippery substance she had. The time I got one with menthol and camphor by accident I thought my prick would burn up."

Mastra wiped his eyes, still hysterical.

"Now I know which ones to use," Deke grinned, glad to see him laugh. "I'm sure Andara can give you whatever you need."

Mastra looked at him, wondering how his friend could imagine he would discuss such a matter with Andara. But then, Deke always had been natural and relaxed about these things, probably because he had been raised by two parents. Children growing up in tents soon learned everything they needed to know about sex, if not by direct visual observation, then by indirect auditory means. "Maybe you could get something for me," Mastra suggested.

Instantly understanding, Deke nodded. "Sure," he said. "I'd be glad to. But probably your lady friend has whatever you need."

They reached the little tent where Tim and Andara sat outside joking, watching the soldiers care for horses, collect their dinner rations, and roll out their blankets on the ground.

Deke squatted beside her and handed her a full canteen and plate heaped with jerky, fruit, and biscuits. He began to eat ravenously from his own plate, taking several bites before speaking. "If you want to bathe, after supper would be the time. I don't know when we'll next be near clean water, so I recommend it."

"Won't all these soldiers be wanting to do the same?" she asked, smiling at Tim and Mastra.

Deke shrugged. "When you're ready, I'll order everyone to turn their backs,. Not that any soldier is that obedient," he added, his eyes twinkling.

Andara laughed. "I will bathe," she said with spirit. "And the hell with everyone. If they want to watch, I hope it'll be worth it."

"It will be," Deke, Mastra, and Tim answered simultaneously, bursting into laughter.

After they finished eating, Deke ordered the men away from the lake so Andara could have her bath. He sat on the shore watching, enjoying her graceful motions in the water. For a minute he spread his awareness over the wilderness, seeking any sense of the scarred warriors, but felt nothing amiss. Reaching into his pocket, he withdrew the steel cylinder he had carried with him all these miles, and rotated it between his fingers, wondering again what it was and why the masked raider had kept it.

His intuition told him the Wolf riders would be coming into the scarred ones' territory the following day, and he focused his thoughts, making sure he hadn't forgotten anything which could tip the balance. With a nod to himself, satisfied that every preparation that could be made had been made, he dropped his clothes and swam out to join Andara. He knew they were being guarded discreetly but didn't mention it to her. No order he could give would make Melak do anything else. When they were done, they emerged from the water together and dressed, walking hand in hand back to their tent.

"Are you standing a shift tonight?" she asked him, her eyes shining in the moonlight.

"Aye," he said. "Midnight to two. I'll try not to wake you."

"Don't worry about it," she said, as they crawled into the tent together and dropped the flaps.

Tonight Andara was exhausted, her muscles sore from so many hours in the saddle. She loosened her clothing and took off her boots, nestling against him with a yawn. He put his arms around her and kissed her cheek. In seconds he was asleep, snoring lightly, his limbs relaxing against hers. She caressed his hair gently, amazed as always at his ability to drop off so quickly. Sighing, she slipped her hand under his vest to touch his skin, and soon she, too, was sleeping.

He awakened a few minutes before midnight. The moon had traveled halfway across the sky, and everything was quiet. He strapped on his weapons, slung a bandolier of ammunition over one shoulder and picked up his rifle. Without waking Andara, he emerged from the tent and went towards the western perimeter to relieve Tim, who was glad to see him. "Anything to report?

"Nothing specific," Tim replied. "But I got that feeling again."

"Rats?" Deke put his awareness into the darkness beyond the perimeter, searching meticulously for any psychic whiff of danger. There was none and he said, "Seems all right now."

"Not rats," Tim said. "Demons."

"When?" Deke asked.

"A half hour or so ago. What do you make of it, Deke?" Tim's voice was worried. "In all these trips, we've never had demons fool with us; why now when we're three times stronger?"

"I don't know," Deke replied. "But the one we saw earlier didn't seem interested in tangling with us."

Tim shook his head. "Watch well, brother. My guts are doing a dance tonight, and they're rarely wrong."

Deke nodded agreement.

In a moment Tim was gone. Deke sensed the presence of other soldiers in the darkness around him as the next watch came on duty, but soon the changeover was complete and the men faced silently into the night from sheltered spots behind rocks or trees. Leaning his shoulder against a tree trunk, Deke stared outward beyond the perimeter. After a time he heard wolf howls float across the lake and knew the pack was hunting on the far shore tonight. Glad for their proximity, he sent an image of wolves greeting wolves in their direction. Soon he was rewarded by their responses, and as he established a connection with them he became aware that there was someone else hunting the far shore, someone entirely too interested in his people.

He identified the intruder as one of the scarfaces, perhaps even the same who had trailed them previously, recognizable by his cruel and ruthless mindset. Left alive, he might well lead them to his home, but he'd certainly have time to give warning.

He made a small sound, drawing the attention of the soldiers nearby. "We're being watched," he told them. "I'm going to take care of the fellow. Don't do anything to make him nervous."

Seconds later he had penetrated the perimeter and was moving silently around the lake, his awareness focused on the man who watched the campsite but was unaware of the danger stalking him with sinister purpose.

Swiftly he rippled through the shadows, leaving no more trace of his passage than a ghost. No one except another adept would have seen him, and Deke knew from his mental contact with this fellow that he was no adept.

When he reached the man he stood behind him for several moments, studying every detail of his being. Once he was sure he knew everything he could get without betraying his presence, he struck rapidly, his right hand driving a dagger under the base of the skull, severing the spinal cord. The man was dead before he hit the ground, and Deke searched him thoroughly, ripping the mask off to confirm the facial scarring, taking his haversack to look through later. He turned the pockets out and froze as his fingers touched something metallic. He removed the object and examined it in the moonlight, his fingers already having told him what it was. Stainless steel reflected the light, and there on the end of the cylinder were the two stiff, wire probes, identical to the one he already carried with him.

Exhaling slowly, Deke crouched over the body and wiped his blade on the man's shirt. Thoughtfully, he returned the knife to its sheath. He picked up the man's rifle, putting it over his shoulder with his own. Then, as silently as he had come, he departed.

When he returned to camp the watch was changing again. After he and the other soldiers were relieved they walked away together and when one looked at him questioningly, he drew his finger across his throat. The man nodded.

On his way back to Andara's tent, Deke stopped by Willie's bedroll.

"What?" Willie asked before his eyes were open.

Deke displayed the haversack and cylinder, explaining what had happened. Willie gripped his shoulder approvingly. "Good work."

Deke opened the sack and dumped the contents on the ground. A water bottle made from a strange material bounced twice before Willie caught it.

"Look at this," he said in wonder. There was a rectangular box made from the same material that held unfamiliar food items. There was a box of cartridges for the rifle Deke had carried away, along with a few garments.

"Here's the interesting thing," Deke said, holding up the cylinder. He reached into his pocket and withdrew the other one. They were identical in every way, even including the scrape marks near the prongs. "Two men, each carrying one. Is it a ritual item? A totem of some kind?"

Willie shrugged. "Beats me. But it's a good thing you killed the bastard. He would have given warning for sure."

"Aye," Deke said, putting all the objects except the cylinders back in the haversack. "Hang onto this," he told Willie, handing it over. "I'd like to know more about these things."

With a nod, Willie said, "Better get some rest, Deke. I've been thinking all night that tomorrow's the day. Now you've killed that scout, I'm even more sure of it."

"Aye," Deke agreed. "See you in the morning, Willie."

In a minute Deke was stripping off his weapons, removing his boots, and lying down beside Andara. She half-awakened as she felt him put his arms around her and smiled sleepily, murmuring, "Everything all right?"

"Everything's fine," he told her. "Go back to sleep."

She felt something wet on her hand where she had laid it on his leg. "What's this?" she said, opening her eyes to look at her fingers in the moonlight. "Ruins!" She wiped her fingers vigorously on his trousers. "It's blood! Are you hurt?"

"No," he said. "Don't worry."

"How'd you get blood on you?" Her tone made it clear she wasn't going to sleep until he explained. With a sigh, he did so. "You mean you just killed someone?"

"Aye," he said.

"Take those pants off," she said. "No telling what's in that man's bloodstream!"

"Ugh," he said, sitting up to skin out of his trousers. He put the two cylinders alongside his daggers then drew the blanket over himself and drank from his canteen. When he lay down again Andara pressed herself against him and put her arm across his torso.

"You could have been killed," she whispered.

"Not likely," he said, stroking her comfortingly.

"Why didn't you just shoot him?" she asked as she touched his thoughts and got a picture of what he had done.

"Too much noise. A gunshot at night really carries."

Andara digested this. "Will you be able to sleep?"

"Why not?" He was surprised by her question.

She shrugged. "I might have trouble sleeping right after putting a dagger in someone's skull."

"Would you have trouble sleeping after completing a surgery?"

"What's that got to do with it?"

"Well, you've been trained to do that. I've been trained to do what I do. It's not so different."

"You don't think there's a difference between taking a life and saving one?"

"Of course there's a difference...but you know what I mean."

"I do," she said. "Do you?"

"Do you think I'm amoral?" he asked, and she heard his smile.

"I don't know what to think about that part of you," she said. "I don't understand it."

"That's what you always say," Deke told her, and she saw his white-toothed grin in the moonlight. "But we both know better. I bet if you weren't so tired right now you'd be frantic to make love."

"You really are offensive sometimes, Deke," she said, but he felt her smile against his chest.

"I'm frantic to make love, too," he whispered into her ear and put his hand between her legs. "But let's try and get some sleep. Tomorrow's another day."

"Aye," she said, her hand moving to touch him the same way. "So it is."

At dawn they were riding again, skirting the lake and then heading due west, away from the rising sun.

Before long they had left the greenery of the oasis behind and were deep in a desert of dust, pulverized stone, and ancient ash. Here the ruins were considerably more flattened with fewer upthrust steel beams or recognizable structures. Everything was bare, featureless, and at noon Willie took a sextant reading of the sun and marked their position on his chart.

Sometime in the midafternoon when the heat was at its worst and the brilliance of the sun nearly intolerable, the riders once again began to feel the nagging psychic itch made by hungry cave rats. Scouts sent flashing signals indicating routes around the colonies of vicious pests, and Deke led them south of west in order to avoid the danger. His eyes scanned the countryside tirelessly, seeking sign of the scarfaces' community, wondering why in such a flat landscape it wasn't becoming visible. He was certain he was in the right area, everything jibed on his map, but he couldn't get so much as a glimpse either with his eyes or his esper sense.

All he got was the subliminal whirr of rat colonies and every so often Andara caught his gaze, sensing his disquiet. His nervous system was wound so tight he practically vibrated with energy, and she wondered what his sensitivity was telling him.

He heard her question inside his thoughts and opened his mind to her. *It's telling me exactly nothing.*

She caught the accompanying nuance which told how strange this was. *What will you do?*

He shrugged tensely, rivulets of sweat running down his bare arms into the leather straps of his body daggers, darkening them. Andara shivered, having the unpleasant thought that blood would do the same; she could almost *see* his blood dripping while she watched. With a surge of fear, she knew she was having a precognitive vision of an upcoming event, and by the urgency with which she felt it, she knew it would be soon.

Don't worry, he told her. *It'll be all right.*

She shook her head stubbornly, trying to fight her anxiety.

You're not sensing my blood, he thought, *but theirs.*

Wrong, wrong, wrong, she insisted.

Is the wound mortal? he asked, and she paused, calming as she thought about it.

Probably not, she responded after a moment, relief flooding her. She took his hand and held it as they rode, grateful for his cool question which had forced her to analyze logically instead of reacting emotionally.

Good, he replied, stirred by her protectiveness, wishing the world would drop away long enough for him to embrace her.

They rode through an area of more densely packed ruins, the horses picking their way around tumbled chunks of concrete and half-buried, twisted heaps of disintegrated metal that Deke knew were skeletons from ancient vehicles, self-propelled and fast.

The sun was beginning to near the horizon when they came into an area of even more concrete, most of it sand and dust covered, but some bare to the sky. Here and there were long, flat, rectangular slabs at least two feet thick, with rust-covered vertical girders alongside them. Deke counted four in the immediate area, and another four approximately two hundred yards distant. What caught his eye was that none of these slabs showed any of the signs of weathering common to concrete in the ruins. He pointed this out to Willie who nodded and said,

"Maybe made differently...but this looks like a good place to camp, Chief. I don't see any rat-sign anywhere, and the country's so open we'd see any scarfaces approaching from miles off."

Deke nodded. "Funny," he said, "I thought we'd find them today."

"Me, too," WIllie said.

"Is it possible the Carillos got the location wrong?" Deke continued. "It seems hard to believe people so mobile wouldn't know where they are."

"Let's give it another day before we decide about that," Willie suggest-ed.

"They can't be far," Deke said quietly, almost to himself. "Their scouts are on foot." He tossed his hair out of his eyes with a nervous jerk, wondering why he felt so edgy.

They searched the vicinity meticulously and found no sign of rats or other dangers, and the soldiers set up the perimeter defenses. This evening, Deke helped Andara erect their tent, and they went together to the mess ser-geant to get their supper, joining Mastra, Tim, and Melak on top of one of the rectangular slabs to eat it. A hot breeze blew across the ruins, ruffling every-one's hair, and they watched quietly as the sun fired the horizon with red and orange tipped with gold.

After eating, Deke arranged with Willie to take the last watch of the night, between four and six a.m. He was still feeling uneasy and when Andara tried to draw him towards the tent, said, "I'll be there in a second. I want to have a look around."

She nodded, knowing there was no point in arguing. Besides, his para-noia was beginning to get to her as well, and she looked behind her every so often, feeling as if something was about to sneak up on her.

Deke walked the camp perimeter, speaking to the soldiers on guard duty, warning them to be extra-vigilant. He felt Melak at his shoulder.

"Aye, chief, everyone feels it," the sergeant told him. "Battle soon, I'm thinking."

"Me, too," Deke said. "I feel like we're being watched, but I can't see anyone."

"These damn ruins are haunted, sure," Melak agreed.

Deke nodded. "I'm going to try to sleep a little, if I can."

Melak smiled and left him at the tent.

Andara looked up as he crawled through the flaps. "Everything all right?"

"Seems to be," he said without conviction.

"What's bothering you?" She took his hand and held it between hers, kneeling with him on the blankets.

"I don't know," he said. "Something feels wrong."

"In what way?" She ran her hand lightly up his arm across the leather straps of his body dagger to his shoulder. He began to take off his weapons and laid them alongside the blankets.

"I feel I'm missing something obvious," he said in a low tone, his eyes on hers, watching them turn from hazel to grey to green as she touched him under his vest. He swallowed when she put his hand on her breast. "This is probably proof we're mad," he whispered.

"Aye," she agreed, reaching for the buttons of his pants, her respiration accelerating as he touched her thoughts tantalizingly and drew her closer.

Then his lips were on hers in a slow, sensual kiss that emptied her mind of thought. In another moment he had her pants unfastened and was helping her out of them before removing his own. She slipped off the leather vest, wanting his flesh against hers. He peeled back her shirt and tossed it aside, his lips finding her nipples.

"Your men," she whispered when he spread her legs and slid down her body.

"What about them?" he muttered, giving her kisses so exquisite she began to tremble uncontrollably.

"They'll see," she said, waving vaguely to the moon-glow illuminating their tent through the walls.

"I don't care," he told her. Soon he was too aroused to wait any longer, and moved until he was over her. She was more than ready and welcomed him when he plunged joyously. They both groaned, then buried their faces against the nearest skin they could find to muffle their cries. She put her legs around his waist and they moved together in long, slow strokes. Eventually he lifted her legs and put them over his shoulders, whispering, "Is this all right?"

"Aye," she breathed as he penetrated her to her limit. She struggled to stay silent but his every thrust drove a grunt from her that try as she might she couldn't suppress. He grunted also, a deep, gutteral sound that quickly whipped her to a higher level of excitement. He released her legs to wrap them around him in a more intimate embrace and kissed her as she hooked them behind his thighs, her hands gripping his buttocks marvelously.

Before long, they were moving faster, and he felt her begin to go. He went with her, his muscles straining with the arcing pleasure of it.

"Ah," he murmured after a while, spent.

She ran her hands up and down his back lovingly, depleted by the strength of her orgasm. Finally, "I know they heard us that time," she whispered in his ear.

"No doubt about it," he said, and pulled her more comfortably against him.

"I'm going to be so embarrassed in the morning," she told him.

"Why? It would only be embarrassing if you didn't enjoy yourself," and he kissed her ear. "At least for me." He laughed with complete happiness. "Terrible to be known as the commander who couldn't satisfy his woman."

Andara giggled, then began to laugh out loud. "Not a reputation you have to worry about, Commander," she finally managed. He laughed again and groped for his clothing. She caught his hands and said, "Don't dress on my account."

"It would be wise," he replied. "Especially with the way I've been feeling." He pulled on his underwear and trousers, and reluctantly she did the same.

"You were going to explain that," she reminded him.

He put his arms around her and she pulled his head to her breast, her fingers in his hair. "Something just feels wrong," he told her, and she could feel the tension return to his body.

She touched his mind with her own. "Why not try to get some rest," she suggested, caressing him soothingly.

He nodded and kissed her before shutting his eyes. "Goodnight, sweet Andara," he whispered, certain he would never sleep tonight, but hoping she would.

Her arms went around him. "Goodnight, sweetest heart," she answered, drifting off.

When he was sure she was sleeping, he carefully extricated himself from her grasp and re-strapped his daggers to his arms and legs, slipped his feet into his socks and boots, put his arm through his bandolier and the strap of his automatic rifle. He lay down and smiled slightly as she moved against him, her arm going across his bare chest and her lips brushing his skin in her sleep. He studied her face as he often did, adoring her, his fingers delicately smoothing strands of hair away from where they had tangled in her long eyelashes. Putting his arm around her, he concentrated on her even breathing, using it to center himself, meditating within the silences between breaths. His awareness picked up the presence of his wolves in the vicinity, and he relaxed as he sent them a greeting image which was returned. He felt himself doze and gave himself over to the sleep he had been certain wouldn't come, until after a time he was snoring gently and knew nothing more.

Outside, Mastra stared at the tent from his bedroll nearby, still unable to look away from what the bright moonlight had shown him in every vivid detail, albeit in silhouette. At the height he had realized he wasn't the only one watching when he heard someone say admiringly, "Take a lesson, boys, that's what I call screwing!" and there had been a low murmur of laughter as several others expressed agreement.

From his own blankets, Tim saw where Mastra's eyes were focused and said quietly, "Go to sleep, brother."

"Who can sleep with that going on," Mastra whispered.

"They're finished now. Come on, get some rest. Who knows when we'll have to be alert."

"Aye," Mastra agreed, his feelings stirred by the unexpected shadow show. "I can't believe they did that."

"Don't be stupid," Tim told him. "Of course they would."

"With everyone watching?"

Tim shrugged. "I'm sure they weren't paying attention to us."

"Ruins," Mastra said under his breath. "Did you see the way she moved?"

"Shut up," Tim said, turning away. "They're in love. Live with it."

Mastra lay on his back, remembering everything, every sound she had made, the way his friend had ridden her so expertly, and felt tears come to his eyes. He had no words to describe the heartbreak that filled him, and didn't try to find any. He simply lay quietly, clenching his teeth with loneliness and despair, praying for the strength to endure what couldn't be changed.

After a while, when there were no further sounds from the tent, he finally relaxed and went to sleep.

In the hour after midnight the soldiers were jarred awake by the sound of someone screaming. Deke jumped to his feet, weapons ready, said to Andara's worried look, "Back as quick as I can," and was out the tent flaps in an instant. He grabbed a soldier by the arm and said, "What's going on?"

The man shrugged and they listened for a second to the ghastly shrieks.

"Take a dozen men and guard this tent," Deke said.

The soldier nodded and a second later Deke took off across the camp, seeking the source of the screams. He felt Melak at his shoulder, saw Tim and Mastra racing behind.

When they reached the perimeter, the guards on duty were staring transfixed at a seething mass of rats where they ripped and tore at a frantically struggling figure.

"Who is it?" Deke asked, raising his rifle to his shoulder.

"One of ours," said a guard.

A second later the sound of his shot rang out and the tortured figure fell. The horde of rats dragged the body away into the ruins, feeding as they went.

"Why didn't anyone shoot him sooner?" Mastra asked, repulsed.

"Noise," Deke answered for the guards. "They were ordered to fire only at the enemy."

No sooner had he finished speaking then there was a roar of gunfire, and the perimeter erupted with the sound of explosives.

Camouflage-clad masked men leaped out of the darkness, firing at the Wolf soldiers with their single-shot weapons. Deke shouted to his men to return fire, running with Melak to where the attackers were swarming. He quickly killed two, saw Melak take another pair. Before long the attack wavered, then broke off.

Willie pounded across a patch of concrete. "You all right?" he panted, his face streaked with sweat and dirt.

"We're fine," Deke said, watching the raiders take off into the ruins. "Damned rats distracted us, otherwise we'd have gotten all those bastards."

"How'd they get past the perimeter?" Willie wanted to know.

"They blew it over there," Tim told him, pointing.

"Is everyone accounted for? Who was that who got swarmed by rats? And what was he doing outside?" Deke glanced at the faces of the men clustering protectively around him.

"I'll find out," Willie said.

There was a shout from across camp and Deke jogged over in response. One of the boys from his manhood group drew him towards the tent. He walked slowly, his belly twisting with fear. The bodies of a dozen men lay where they had fallen, defending the tent. Five times that number of dead scarfaces were heaped helter-skelter in the dust among them. In a rush Deke tore open the flaps and looked inside, his eyes taking in the signs of a struggle. Andara's dagger reflected the moonlight where it lay on the empty blankets. He stared in disbelief, then picked it up in nerveless fingers.

"Andara," he whispered, anguished.

He backed out and stood up. "They've taken her," he told the men who guarded him. He looked at their shocked faces, hardly able to think, forcing himself not to panic. "The attack at the other end of camp was a diversion," he said, his eyes beginning to darken with rage. "So how'd they get down to this end? Willie, check to see the perimeter's sound."

O'Dale nodded and took off.

Deke stalked around the tent looking for any sign, any track, that might give a clue to where the scarfaced warriors had taken her. There was nothing; the ground was a confused mass of footprints too chaotic to decipher.

He breathed deeply, then in an abrupt upsurge of energy, Sent his awareness out to scour the ruins around the camp. Nothing moved, even the rats had finished their grisly meal and departed for their nest. He searched carefully for a minute or two, wondering where the fleeing raiders had gone. No sign of them remained, and he drew his awareness back to himself, trying to understand what was going on. He fought his grief and rage, forcing himself to think clearly, knowing Andara's life depended on him making the right decisions and making them swiftly.

"Tim," he said, keeping his voice steady with an effort. "Find out if anyone saw anything."

Tim nodded, clapped him on the shoulder, then went to question the soldiers.

"What are you going to do?" Mastra demanded, his anxiety mounting. He stared at Deke, saw the control his friend maintained. In the face of that self-discipline he reined in his emotions, realizing by the acute concentration on Deke's face that he was using his sensitivity to comb the area.

Deke closed his eyes, sending a distress call out to the wolf pack, calling them towards him. They responded inside his thoughts with images of themselves racing under the moon as they covered the intervening ruins between them. He spoke to Melak. "Tell the soldiers to open the perimeter."

"But, chief..."

"Do it!" Deke's expression brooked no argument, and Melak leaped to obey.

The soldiers watched their young commander close his eyes again, and in moments they heard the wolves howling as they approached.

When Deke opened his eyes, it was clear to Mastra that he was in an altered state of consciousness. "Anyone who fires at a wolf is dead," he said, and fixed an otherworldly stare on his friend. Unsettled, Mastra nodded and passed the word along.

A breath of wind stirred Deke's hair as he concentrated, gathering energy, focusing it inward, pulling it out of the living environment around him. The wind increased and a flash of heat lightning strobed the sky, while in the distance there was the sound of thunder. He spread his palms and extended his arms, turning in a complete circle as he called on his spirit guides to aid him. The lightning flickered again, and the bounding shapes of wolves appeared out of the darkness, following precisely the path he indicated by esper vision so they would pass safely through the open perimeter.

The soldiers muttered and stepped back as the Alpha approached Deke, thrusting his huge muzzle into his hand and leaning against him. The other wolves crowded around, their emotional radiations expressing concern as they caught the strong, adrenaline whiff coming off his body.

Deke reached into the tent and withdrew one of Andara's boots which had been left behind, giving it to the wolves to smell. He put a search image in their minds, one showing wolves following a scent trail, and instantly the Alpha yipped at him, indicating Deke should follow.

The wolf barely put his nose to the ground, instead air-scenting, sniffing deeply and seeking the emotional vibration also attached to the boot. He ran approximately thirty yards until he came to one of the rectangular concrete slabs. Here he stopped, whining nervously, putting his nose to the edge of the concrete on one of the short sides. He looked expectantly at Deke who approached with a puzzled expression. Putting an interrogative into the wolf's mind, he tried to imagine what the Alpha was trying to tell him and realized the wolf was saying the trail led here.

Deke examined the slab, crawling around the edges, trying to get his fingers underneath. He felt a metal track against his nails, and dug frantically along one side, trying to peer beneath it.

"Help me, boys!" he shouted to the soldiers who watched in amazement. "The goddamned thing is on tracks! The bastards are underground, they've been right here under us all the time!"

Tim put his weight against the slab with Deke. "They've been watching us, then...there must be peepholes everywhere!"

"Aye," Deke said grimly, straining at the concrete. He cursed viciously at it. "Move, damn you," he gritted, pushing with all his strength.

Tim put his hand on Deke's shoulder. "We'll never move it," he said. "There must be a trick to it."

Deke looked into Tim's eyes, taking comfort from the steadiness he saw there. "You're right," he agreed. He stood up and began to scan the area again, stopping when his gaze came to one of the metal girders standing upright in the concrete near the slab. He tapped the girder, running his fingers over it. In a second he felt a seam with tiny hinges along the top, and he saw how a cover swung up, opening the top four inches.

His fingers fought the cover briefly, then it popped up and he held it open. A chill passed down his spine and he looked up for a second. All soldiers not on perimeter duty had gathered nearby and were watching him and the wolves who milled around him. The sky flashed with intensifying lightning and the wind drove sand and dust against their skin. There was a deep rumble of thunder as if the world was expressing his anger and outrage. He thought

347

about what Tim had said about peepholes and glanced around, wondering if they were being observed right now. Then he shrugged to himself, realizing he didn't care. He examined the open post again, making certain of what he had seen, and reached into his pocket, withdrawing one of the steel cylinders. While his men watched incredulously, he inserted the two rigid wire prongs into the corresponding openings in the post and turned his hand. The lock rotated with the cylinder, and suddenly, in a silence absolute except for the soughing of the sand and the sound of the rising storm, the concrete slab slid back.

Deke felt in his pocket to be sure he had the other cylinder. He looked at Willie, his face all sharp angles in its severity, his blue eyes more focused than his mentor had ever seen them. "I'm going down," he said. "I'll take volunteers only."

"No!" Willie grabbed his arm. "No, you can't do it! You have no way of knowing if she's even alive down there. Besides, it's obviously a trap, they're just waiting for us to come after her..."

"That is completely irrelevent," Deke told him, freeing his arm with a jerk. "It doesn't matter if not a single man follows me. I'm still going."

"Don't be a fool, Deke! Would you step into something without ever knowing if you could get out again?" Willie's eyes were intent.

Deke had a chilling sense of déjà vu, remembered Andara asking him the same question when they had discussed opening portals the previous summer in his mother's tent. "She needs me," he gritted stubbornly. "She's not dead. Don't hinder me, Willie."

Willie stared at him, feeling the implied threat but filled with fear for his former student.

Deke made sure his rifle was loaded and checked the pistol at his belt. He drew his machete from its sheath and turned for the shadowed concrete stairway. Resolutely he stepped down, fighting what probably was the greatest fear for any tent-dwelling nomad, what had always been his own most overpowering terror: the fear of the trap, of walls closing in and burying him alive. Breathing deeply, he took a step downward, his awareness spreading ahead of him into the darkness.

Without hesitation Melak, Tim, and Mastra followed, the other boys from his manhood group right behind. Deke felt them at his back and was filled with a surge of gratitude. He turned to Willie.

"Give us some time to distract them," he said. "Then come down with the others. There are lots of these slabs around. Probably many are entryways. I suggest you swarm down several simultaneously, but that'll be up to you." He paused. "If you think the danger's too great, don't risk yourself."

Soldiers began to call out, shouting that they were ready, would happily follow him into that hellhole and the ruins take the consequences.

Willie stared at him, unable to believe that last fling at his manhood, and Deke felt a momentary pang at his callous manipulation of his friend. Then he forgot about it. Time was passing, and he stretched out with his consciousness, sending his awareness into the ground ahead of him, seeking Andara's energy in what felt like a giant warren filled with strange, scarred, human rats. He knew Willie was right: Andara was the bait, but it didn't matter. He was frantic at the thought of her in the hands of people with mentalities like those he had probed, who might do ruins knew what.

They counted forty steps going down. At the bottom they found themselves in a small room with a door at one end. There was a wall panel which opened, revealing another two prong socket. Deke pulled out his second cylinder and inserted it, giving it a quick twist as he had the other. The door opened and he removed the cylinder, putting it back in his pocket. Gesturing Melak and his manhood group to follow, he moved swiftly through the doorway, glanced up a long, shadowy corridor which led straight ahead for thirty or forty yards before connecting with another running at right angles to the first. There were doors to either side, all closed. Feeble light came from widely-spaced glass globes on the ceiling.

A door opened and a bizarrely scarred female started out. When she saw the heavily armed band of youths she tried to jerk the door shut, but Mastra reacted quickly and jammed his foot in the way, grabbing the hysterical woman by the arm and covering her mouth with his hand to stifle her shrieks. The boys looked at her curiously, amazed by the pattern of burnt scar tissue on every inch of her skin surface: face, arms, legs, everywhere they looked. One of the boys unfastened her shirt and she was scarred even under her clothing. The pattern was a complex basket weave, lines of scars criss-crossing everywhere.

"Ruins," another boy said, touching her mutilated breasts. "Looks like she was stuck in a giant waffle iron!"

"There's your answer, Melak," Tim said. "These women wear burn scars after all."

"Different from the men, though," Deke commented, gesturing for the boys to stop touching her so personally. She gave him a grateful look and then he went into her mind, searching for an image of Andara, or any useful information. There was nothing, and he looked away from her, withdrawing his thoughts and sending them out again in search.

"What do you want to do with her, chief?" Melak asked.

"We'll leave her bound and gagged."

"Killing is better," Melak said.

"No," Deke said sharply. "We don't harm women or children unless they fire on us, understand?"

"Aye, chief." Melak was composed, trusting Deke's judgment in this as in all things.

Throughout this conversation the woman's eyes were mutely anxious, flicking rapidly from one face to the next. She felt drawn to the tall, blue-eyed youth whom the others looked to for orders, and was glad he was there. Without his presence, she thought these others might have done something unspeakable to her, then killed her as the more mature man wanted to do.

"Let's go." Deke was chafing to get moving again.

Two boys meanwhile had gone into the room from which she'd emerged and pronounced the area clear. Mastra hurried her inside, bound her with material torn from a bedsheet, and secured her to the bed. Moments later he rejoined the group who had reached the end of the corridor where a second one crossed it.

Deke's esper capacity swelled as he sought for any echo from Andara's mind, any clue to tell him which way she had been taken. He thought he caught a wisp of something to his left, and started in that direction, the others following. Two of the boys covered their rear, their rifles sweeping the semi-darkened hallway nervously.

Another door opened in front of him, and three armed men emerged, their unmasked faces showing little discernible emotion. Their mouths dropped open: ghastly slices of darkened, decayed teeth amidst the horrific scarring. Deke's machete flashed, and one head rolled, while another man's intestines spilled like a sack of tripe on his back stroke. The third turned to run, but before he got five steps a dagger flew at his back, dropping him. Deke turned to look at Tim who had thrown the blade, and nodded acknowledgement.

As they passed the bodies, Tim bent and retrieved his knife, wiping it on the man's shirt, jamming it back into its sheath.

They spread out down the corridor, and at each door they passed, Deke sent a part of his awareness to seek for Andara. There was no sign of her and he was beginning to get wild. The passageway seemed to stretch forever, and he was sure they had covered half a mile by the time they came to a circular spot from which further passages radiated in all directions. Deke halted, gnawing his lips worriedly, feeling the whole place pressing on his mind, as if the weight of the earth over his head was exerting its strain on him. Which way?

He called to her, using his sensitivity to make a Sending, certain that if conscious she should hear it, but got no response.

Again he spread his awareness, turning in a complete circle, trying to remain centered enough to use his senses to their utmost but fighting through so much panic he wasn't sure he could trust his responses. Here, under the ground, he felt hemmed in, claustrophobic. It was necessary to put himself down all these corridors simultaneously, and this produced a confused, surrealistic vision of events. He set his jaw, concentrating, drawing energy out of the air itself. The lights flickered and his friends looked uneasily at him and one another. Finally, not completely certain, but having nothing else to go on, he again started down a corridor to the left, thinking he had caught a tiny whiff of Andara's scent in his nostrils and following it like one of his wolves.

This corridor ran straight for a hundred yards, then branched into three. Deke practically snarled, and once again the lights flickered, dimming noticeably for several long seconds. This brought people out of their doors to investigate. They gaped at the grim band of intruders while with a flick of his head Deke signaled to Mastra to grab an unarmed man and put a knife to his throat. Deke put his face directly in front of the man's scarred visage and the man cried out at the rushing energy that poured into his skull. He felt his mind ransacked like a room torn apart in search, and strained to provide the information demanded, desperate to escape the brilliance of the blue eyes which held him. When the youth turned his gaze away, the man fell limply to the floor, unconscious.

"Nothing," Deke muttered. "None of them know anything. Someone's got to know..." He put his gaze on the people who stared from their doorways, some of whom were beginning to run for help or, perhaps, weapons. "Take out all the men," he said to Melak.

"Aye," Melak said and indicated for Mastra to come with him. Moments later the sound of gunfire told the others what was happening in each room. They finished quickly and rejoined the group, Mastra visibly shaken, Melak matter-of-fact as always.

Deke chose the center of the three branching corridors, and now he was running. There were no rooms in this hallway, and it continued in a fairly straight line for more than a thousand feet, slanting down. At the end was a doorway with the usual cylinder mechanism, and Deke jammed the prongs into the socket, turning it. The door slid back, and they were in a hail of whizzing bullets.

"Down!" he shouted. They dove for the floor, aiming their automatic weapons at the dozen or so men who had to pause to reload. After a deafening burst of fire, the last of the scarfaces fell in a heap. "Anyone hurt?" he asked, eyeing his friends with concern.

One of the boys had caught a graze along the side of his head but insisted he was fine. Otherwise, every bullet had missed its mark.

Stepping over the pile of dead bodies, Deke continued down the corridor, his friends following. After several hundred feet and many twisting turns, he saw a place where one of the scarfaces sat behind a low counter, looking through a strange tube sticking down through the ceiling. The tube had hand-holds permitting it to be turned this way and that.

The man hadn't seen them. Gesturing for quiet, Deke ran up silently behind him and put the machete blade to his throat. At the same moment he entered the man's mind, and abruptly there was information he could use, for this man indeed had seen the party which had kidnaped the young woman, and he knew why it had been done and what was planned for her. Ruthlessly, Deke sifted the man's thoughts, and when he was certain he knew everything, cut his throat, tossing the body aside carelessly.

Mastra stared, flabbergasted by the easy way his friend killed these people, as if their lives meant nothing in the greater scheme of Deke's life. He himself was sick from what he and Melak had done, and wondered if he ever would be able to kill the way Deke, Melak, even Tim, could.

Deke sprinted ahead of the others, the information he had gotten from the dead man filling him with such dread as he never had experienced, not even when his mother was murdered. He continued to draw energy from the environment as the Old Man had taught him, tapping every natural and unnatural source provided down here. There was some kind of ancient, electrical generator in the community; this he knew from the whisper of his spirit guides in his inner ear, and he opened himself to that level of perception more completely, hoping to gain specific knowledge of Andara's location.

The corridor turned a corner and he looked ahead to a stretch where cross-corridors and turnoffs occurred every fifty feet on both sides. He heard a commotion coming from one of those turnoffs, and withdrew behind the corner, waiting until the others caught up to him. Raising his finger to his lips, he used battle language to indicate danger ahead, and they leveled their rifles.

The commotion was coming closer, and when Deke judged the moment was correct, he leaped around the corner. He dove across the smooth floor, his rifle spitting, providing cover for those who came after. Tim and Mastra followed, skidding at different angles, while Melak and the other boys charged straight ahead into the mass of scrambling, screaming, masked warriors who had been caught completely unawares. After a frenzied fusillade of bullets, all but one of the scarfaces lay dead or dying, and Deke jumped up to grab the survivor by the front of his shirt, putting his machete point under the man's chin.

"Where were you going?" he demanded, his eyes fiery, his blood-spattered expression savage. The man moaned with terror. "Eh?" The machete broke skin as Deke pressed it harder.

"'e 'ere told there 'ere intruders in the outer 'assage," he croaked, his words distorted by the mutilation of his burned lips.

"The girl you took from above," Deke said, his teeth baring unconsciously.

The scarface shrugged, then screamed as Deke entered his thoughts with total disregard for the integrity of the man's mind. He felt the psyche tear like rotten cloth.

"Where is she?" He Sent a surge of pain into the masked warrior, making him gibber and shake madly. His grip on the man's mind strengthened and he quickly squeezed his thoughts until every one lay naked and quivering before his pressuring awareness. There was nothing useful to be found, and with an inarticulate sound of disappointment and despair, he slashed once, quickly, and allowed the body to fall.

He paced slowly along the corridor, forced to pause at each turnoff to Send himself partway into it, seeking traces of Andara's psychic echo. There were none yet, and he clenched his fists around his weapons, his desperation filling him with near-madness. It was taking too long, too much time to find her. At once he became certain she was dead, and that was the reason she didn't respond to his repeated calls. He struggled to contain his emotions and wiped a flood of tears from his face, smearing them across the blood splashed on his cheeks. He felt the others move closer, lending silent support as they exchanged glances with one another, overwhelmed by the grief and pain radiating from his skin surface.

Halfway down the corridor he finally felt something, an echo, and he touched a place on the wall with questing fingertips, sensing that Andara's hand had grabbed there during a frantic struggle when her captors had bundled her on their shoulders as they passed this way not long since. He closed his eyes and once again drew energy from what his guides now explained was an electrical system created with a creaking, pre-War nuclear plant and which would provide him with the power necessary to fuel his esper sense at its highest levels. The energy wasn't as potent as what he could utilize from the natural world, but it worked, and at the moment, that was all that mattered.

The lights buzzed and snapped with a peculiar electronic whine, and when one of the little globes unexpectedly exploded, sending glass flying to the concrete floor with a tinkling splash, Deke stopped pulling energy. He jogged swiftly to the end of the corridor where a heavy steel door blocked the passage. Laying his palm flat on it, he turned to his friends and in hand signals told them there were many men on the other side, more than they'd encountered so far. Tim loosened two pipe grenades from his carrying sack and half-smiled grimly. Deke nodded, and with a series of quick gestures, indicated what he wanted to do.

A moment later he turned the cylinder in its socket and the door began to slide open. Tim quickly tossed the grenades through while Deke turned the cylinder in the opposite direction. The boys flattened against the wall where most of the door remained to block the concussion. Flames and debris roared down the corridor past them, and as soon as the blast died back, Deke was squeezing through the opening into the badly damaged hallway, coughing in the acrid smoke. Wires hung crazily from the ceiling along with sheets of metal sheathing. Beyond, there were no lights for hundreds of feet, and Deke reached out with his sensitivity, probing for danger. All he felt was the pressure that seemed to beat on the top of his head constantly in this place.

Soon he heard Tim say in an openly irritated voice, "Where are our soldiers? Shouldn't they be along by now?"

"They may be here already," Deke said, "Behind us, maybe even somewhere ahead if they came in through other openings. I've been thinking that's why the resistance we've encountered is so minimal. We may not be considered the major threat."

"That's good," Mastra said grimly. "They can provide the diversion until we find Andara."

"Aye." Deke nodded approvingly.

When they came into the light again, they took a right turn past a door marked "Authorized Personnel Only." Deke felt drawn to look behind this door but knew Andara wasn't inside, and there was no time to waste on sidetracks.

"By the ruins," Melak muttered as they trotted down another endless corridor beneath the flickering lights, "Doesn't this place ever stop?"

"What I'm worried about is how we're going to find our way out," one of the boys said.

"That'll be easy," Mastra told him. "We'll just backtrack the dead bodies."

"If they've hurt Andara, I'll give them dead bodies," Deke said in a low voice, his tone betraying the strain he was under. "I'll bury them all like rats in their stinking rat city." He stopped, his head tilted to one side. "Listen," he told them.

Muffled by distance and intervening ground, they heard the thump and rumble of heavy explosives, and exchanged looks of grim pleasure. Just as he was about to start moving again, he felt a disturbance in the flow of his mind, a growing awareness like a sympathetic vibration that resonated with greater and greater strength as he focused on it, until abruptly his entire being was suffused with it. He heard the rising cry for help inside his head gain in volume until it was all he could hear or feel, until his senses were overwhelmed by it, and involuntarily, a matching cry was torn from his own throat.

"Andara!" he shouted, fear like a fist in his chest.

His friends stared at him, startled.

Without another word, he broke into a sprint. As they pounded down the corridor after him, it seemed to them that they, too, could hear the desperate scream of terror and agony that had burst from Andara's mind, as she called with futile hope for Deke to find her.

From her place on the vertical restraint system where the masked horrors had shackled her, Andara lifted her head defiantly and stared at the leader of the band of fifteen who had survived the raid to kidnap her.

Since that awful moment when the sneak attack had taken place, she had been fully confident Deke would come after her. She didn't know how he would manage this, because she herself had been shocked when the warriors opened one of the slabs and carried her down, bound hand and foot and gagged with a filthy rag she still could taste, even though it long since had been removed from her mouth. But she believed he would come for her nevertheless, that he would work out the solution. To believe anything else was impossible even to consider.

The leader's eyes were on her, as were the eyes of his men. He ripped off his mask and stuck it in a pocket of his pants. His men did the same, and Andara wished they would put the masks back on. She'd never seen such hideous scarring, and that it was obviously deliberate turned her stomach.

"Look at her," the leader said through his damaged mouth, his scarred lips stretching in a grimace she knew he meant as a smile. "So 'erfect...such 'eauty. I 'ant her 'efore 'e 'ark her."

"You know the law," another man said, but his eyes devoured her with open lechery.

"Yes," the leader said. "'Ut the law doesn't say she has to 'e con'lete-ly 'arked, just 'egun." He grimaced again. "We'll 'ut the first un so'e'lace out of the 'ay, so I don't have to see it. I al'ays 'anted an un'arked fe'ale, and I'll have this un. The rest of you can have her 'hen I finish."

There was an eager mutter from the scarred men and Andara was filled with anxiety. She could imagine what "arking" was from looking at them, and her anxiety grew as she imagined her face destroyed as theirs were.

The leader saw her fear and laughed. "Don't 'orry, gorgeous un," he said. "This 'ark is only for 'ales. 'E do it differently on your sex." He approached and put his hand on her breast, squeezing and fondling it while she struggled. She spat at him, her eyes green-slitted with fury and hatred, wishing her esper ability was fully mature so she could spell this filthy piece of manure with a *glamour* that would make his soul depart his body.

The leader laughed and wiped the saliva from his face. "Hot little 'itch, isn't she?" he said to his men who laughed with him. "'E'll see how nasty she fights after a good 'arking."

With an abrupt motion, he ripped her shirt open and fondled her again while she concentrated on his mind. She found the place she wanted, and immediately his lust diminished while his eyes grew surprised. She almost laughed to hear the thoughts in his head as he wondered why he no longer was getting pleasure from touching her. Angry now, he clenched his fist and struck her viciously across the face. His knuckles left an angry red mark on her cheekbone as her head whipped to the side with the impact. She clamped her jaw shut to keep from crying out, unwilling to give this repulsive creature the satisfaction.

"Let's do it," he said to his men, and they nodded agreement.

In a moment they had removed a strange piece of apparatus from a cabinet, a long-handled device with a cable attached to one end and iron shaped in a rounded cross-hatch pattern at the other. "This is 'hat 'e use for fe'ales," the leader said and stuck the unattached end of the cable into a hole in the wall. The iron began to heat until it glowed redly.

Andara struggled wildly against her bonds. The men laughed at her desperate attempts to free herself until the leader signaled to one of them who drew a sharp knife from a belt sheath. With a quick motion, he cut the remains of her shirt away, then did the same for her pants and undergarments.

The leader approached her, holding the iron where she could see it.

"According to our law, 'efore 'e can take a girl like you, who's so fresh and such a 'eauty, 'e first have to 'ark you, and 'ake you un of us. 'Ut the 'arking takes 'onths to con'lete, and I don't intend to 'ait that long," he said, and once again his mouth stretched horribly.

Andara's breath came rapidly and she felt blood drip down her arms where the wrist shackles had cut into her flesh. Her ankles were similarly bloodied from her frantic struggles. She watched as the hot metal came nearer, a tiny wisp of smoke rising from the end.

"'hat 'art of her 'ill you 'ark?" asked one of the men, his avid gaze raking Andara's naked body as his tongue passed over his mutilated lips.

"'Aybe 'ore than un s'ot," the leader said, a strange, excited light in his eyes as he ran his left hand over her, groping her thighs and belly before grabbing roughly at her breasts and pinching her nipples hard. Laughing, he pressed the hot iron to the outside of her left thigh, the skin sizzling under the burning metal.

Andara let out an agonized scream, her body arching as she tried to get away from the indescribable pain. She felt her consciousness rising up out of herself and squeezed her eyes shut, calling to Deke with every fiber of her being. She fought the hopeless realization that he wasn't coming, that he'd never find her. Tears overflowed her eyes as the torture continued, and she flailed against her restraints helplessly. Grief joined her searing agony when she thought she might never see him again, or if she did, she would be so dreadfully disfigured he wouldn't want her.

Finally the leader pulled the iron away from her flesh, and, grinning horribly, circled her like a hungry buzzard, trying to decide where next to brand her.

A second later, he pressed the iron to the inside of her right forearm, holding her still with his left hand, his scarred face before hers while she jerked and fought furiously and the men laughed with pleasure to see her naked vulnerability.

When he removed the iron she hung limply, panting, her hair in her face. The leader handed the iron to one of the others and said with obvious satisfaction,

"Now, the law has 'een taken care of," and unfastened his pants eagerly, drawing out his erect penis and moving until he was between her legs.

Andara lifted her head and looked him in the eye with such deadly hatred that for a moment he hesitated.

"Fuck you," she rasped out, her voice hoarse from screaming.

"No, gorgeous, fuck *you*." He shoved her knees apart with a brutal motion.

Abruptly, there was a splintering crash of metal, and the door to the room exploded inward. The scarred men grabbed for their rifles, but before anyone could fire, a whirling, tumbling blur shot across the room moving too fast to see clearly. A machete blade flashed and men began dying, the screams and confusion of the living mingling with the shouts of those whose lives were ending. Blood spurted everywhere and scarred warriors fired frantically at the barely-seen figure wreaking violent havoc among them. The lights dimmed and flickered insanely; there was the stench of ozone in the air. The leader reached for his weapon but something held him frozen, unable to move. He watched in mounting terror while the chaos of struggling bodies simplified and their numbers rapidly dwindled. By the time Melak and the boys of the manhood group burst into the room, the scarred warriors lay dead or dying, their blood flooding the floor.

Deke's eyes roved across the carnage. The level of energy powering his consciousness gradually returned to something approaching normal and he became fully visible as he emerged from between moments. His gaze stopped on the scarred leader who stood alone, his uncircumcised penis flopping out of his pants. He rose from the man he had just decapitated, the bloody machete alive with threat in his right hand, and padded over, looking for all the world like a stalking wolf, using the point of his blade to push the man to one side.

"Hold him," he said to Melak, his eyes on Andara, the rage in them briefly covered by his relief that she was alive. He quickly unshackled her hands and ankles, catching her in his arms as she collapsed against him.

"Tim, give me your shirt," he said without turning, tears of pity blurring his vision as he kissed her hair and murmured comfortingly.

Tim peeled it off and handed it over. Deke put it around her shoulders and got her arms through the sleeves, buttoning it up the front.

She looked at him, shocked to see him there, unable to process what she had seen happen. "Deke," she said wonderingly, touching his face as he put his arms around her and hugged her tenderly.

"It's all right," he said, his voice rough with emotion. He examined the burns on her arm and leg, saw they were serious but could wait. He checked the wounds at her wrists and ankles, afraid the veins were cut, and was relieved to see the bleeding had slowed. "Did he... Did they..." His voice trailed off, hardly knowing how to ask her.

"No." She shivered hard while he stroked her lovingly. "How...?" she asked, making a weak gesture towards the bodies strewn across the floor.

His gaze followed hers and he shrugged. As he did, he felt pain in his left shoulder and looked at himself. A bullet had gone through the flesh and come out the other side, leaving two ugly wounds from which blood seeped, dripping into the straps of his body dagger. He'd never even felt it hit him.

"You're hurt," Andara said, and touched him.

"I'll live," he said.

Melak stood quietly, his eyes and those of the boys near him wide with amazement. Obviously all these men were dead, and just as obviously Deke was responsible, but they couldn't imagine how it had happened.

"What do you want to do with him, m'lord?" he asked, indicating his prisoner, his tone reflecting respect so complete that for a moment Deke was nonplused.

After a second, he turned to Andara. "It's up to you," he said. "I'll kill him any way you like."

"Give me your gun," she said, her eyes narrowing.

Deke opened his holster and removed his .45. He chambered a shell, then handed it to her, grip first. She drew herself upright and walked over to where the scarred leader was being held by Melak and another boy. She stopped in front of him and thumbed the safety off the pistol.

"You *hurt* me," she said in a low tone expressing her total outrage. She pointed the gun at his face and saw him swallow. With an abrupt gesture, she dropped the barrel between his legs and jerked the trigger.

Stunned, Melak and the boy let go of the man who fell to the floor screaming and holding himself while blood pumped out of him in surges.

Andara stood over him watching his wild contortions. After an interminable minute during which the boys grimaced involuntarily to see the scarred leader twist across the concrete, she pointed the pistol at his face and pulled the trigger once more. The man jumped, then lay still.

Andara handed the gun to Deke and looked up at him, her eyes beginning to blur with tears. He holstered the pistol and said, "Do you think you can walk? We have to get out of here, find Willie."

She nodded and leaned against him, her face against his bare chest, the bandolier cool on her ear. He wrapped his arm around her shoulders and looked at the others. Melak nodded at his unspoken request and slipped outside, looking up and down the corridor for danger. There was none, and he gestured to those in the room that all was clear. Deke helped Andara through the shattered door, making sure she didn't cut her bare feet on any shards. The others followed, surrounding them protectively.

"Which way, m'lord?" Melak asked.

"Back the way we came," Deke replied. "There's something I want to look at before we leave."

Melak's eyes were questioning.

"Aye," Deke said, "There's something these people are protecting, and I want to know what."

"Maybe just this place...what a boon to be hidden so well."

"It's more than that. There are riches here, boys, beyond our wildest dreams. I can feel it."

Tim grinned. "What kind of riches, brother?"

"I don't know...something important, something that's going to change our lives." His tone held both wonder and prophecy.

Andara put her arm around his waist, fighting exhaustion. All she wanted was to lie in a soft bed with comforting poultices on her burns and opium tea to soothe her nerves and pain.

"Are you all right?" he asked, sensing her weakness. There was a shocky pallor about her features, and abruptly he handed his rifle to Tim and swept her into his arms.

"I don't know; I suddenly got so dizzy," she said faintly.

"Just relax, I'll be your legs," he said with reassuring gentleness.

Mastra saw the loving look, the near worship, shining out of Andara's eyes as she gazed at Deke; saw his eyes meet hers with the same expression in them, and sighed, realizing how trivial was his crush in the face of their commitment. He knew that without Deke to lead him down here, he never would have had the courage to rescue Andara. He would have heeded Willie's advice and left her rather than take on a whole community with only one experienced warrior and a handful of untried boys at his back. He knew now that Andara had made the right choice when she picked Deke, and though this knowledge hurt, becoming aware of it also made him feel free from the foolish jealousy and resentment he had been harboring these last six months. Looking at his friend, he found himself filled with esteem he could think of only one way to express.

"What are your orders, my lord?" he asked.

Deke looked up in surprise at the unexpected honorific, then nodded, accepting it. "Clear the corridors," he said quietly. "Make sure we're unimpeded."

Mastra clapped his hand to the hilt of his machete. "Aye," he said, and gestured to two of the boys from the group to accompany him.

The others followed more slowly, Melak and Tim flanking Deke and Andara, the other boys fanning out to guard their backs and the immediate way ahead.

Andara put her good arm around Deke's neck and opened her thoughts to him. He did the same, and she was permeated with the joy he felt to be holding her securely in his arms, his profound gratitude that she was alive. She rested her head against his hard bicep where it was flexed under her, knowing in her heart that what he had done was adept magic of the highest order. Only a sorcerer could have found her in this rat maze of corridors and doors, only a brujo could have splintered steel the way Deke had, and only the most powerful warrior-adept could have drawn the necessary energy from the air to accomplish these things and vanquish his enemies.

She kissed his wounded shoulder and he smiled at her, hearing her voice inside his thoughts as she thanked him again and again for coming after her.

Twenty minutes later Deke told them to stop, and he lowered Andara to her feet, stretching his stiffened arm muscles and wincing at the pain in his shoulder. They stood before the door that said "Authorized Personnel Only." Almost lazily he Sent his awareness through the heavy steel, sensing enormous space beyond it, as well as many scarfaced warriors.

For a second he considered carefully, then Sent his thoughts out to find Mastra and the other two boys. When he located them in the corridors not far away, for the first time he consciously put a command into Mastra's mind. He saw his friend's reaction, saw him and the two boys turn and begin to trot back. In a minute the three rounded a corner and approached him questioningly.

"Everything's clear ahead," Mastra said. "We didn't see a soul, man or woman."

"Strange," Deke said. "They must be fighting our men." His eyes were worried but he put his concern aside. "We're going in here," he said, gesturing to the door. "There may be something we don't want to damage inside, so be very accurate." He looked at Andara. "I want you to stay with me, all right? Can you manage?"

"Give me a weapon," she said. "I'll manage."

He grinned, overflowing with pride in her. "You're some real fire-cracker, you know that?" He took his pistol from its holster and handed it to her. Reaching into the back of his belt, he withdrew a flat dagger which he also gave over.

Her fingers caressed the familiar blade and she looked into his eyes, saying, "You kept it with you all this time..." She brushed at the tears rolling down her cheeks. "Sorry I'm being such a sap," she said to everyone, trying to smile.

They protested and were very understanding, which made her even more emotional.

"Please stay behind me," Deke said, touching her cheek, drying her tears with his fingers.

"All right," she said, snapping a bullet into the chamber of her pistol. Her stance became more aggressive.

"Here we go," he said, readying his rifle. "I'm going left, boys, the rest of you scatter and roll, hear?"

"Aye," they chorused, eager now to see what was behind this "Authorized Personnel Only" door.

Deke jammed his cylinder against the door's socket and turned it. As the door drew aside, he pocketed the cylinder once more. A moment later, he ducked through, running bent over, with Andara on his heels. The others leaped after and he watched them scatter across an expanse of concrete floor towards what looked like an altar of some kind. There were no traditional religious accoutrements, only hexagonal panels containing decorative metal.

Two masked warriors shouted a warning and opened fire at the rolling, dodging figures swarming towards them. A minute later Melak's shot took one of the warriors through the throat and Deke's caught the second in the eye.

A ceremony was in progress, one involving flares of sparking light and weird, sizzling noises. At least twenty masked men were gathered in a circle around this bizarre light show, chanting unintelligibly in a dull monotone.

361

When they heard the gunfire, they leaped up, grabbed rifles, and turned to do battle. A young boy sat strapped to a chair, wispy tendrils of smoke rising from a patch of destroyed skin on his forehead. Another man held an unfamiliar device across his knees, which he was using to perform the scarring. He dropped it with a clatter and reached for his rifle.

Automatic weapon fire rang out and in seconds the masked warriors began to fall, some before they even got off a shot.

"Keep me one alive!" Deke called and waved to Melak who acknowledged the order and leaped after a scarface who swung his empty rifle at the charging Wolf soldier, then turned and ran. Melak drew a dagger from his forearm sheath and tossed it underhand into the back of the warrior's thigh, hamstringing him. With a scream of pain, the man went down, and an instant later Melak withdrew his dagger and hauled him up by the collar.

A scarface raised his rifle directly behind Deke, and Melak yelled, 'Behind you! Look out!"

Deke spun but before he could fire, a shot rang out and the masked man crumpled. Andara lowered her pistol and met his eyes. "Thanks," he said, exhaling in relief, sure he had been about to catch one that time.

In the meantime the others had dispatched the remaining scarfaces and Deke took the .45 from Andara's hand. He put his arm around her and together they walked towards the man Melak was holding under guard. "What is all this?" he asked, gesturing to the altar.

The man said nothing, merely glared sullenly.

"All right," Deke said, his eyes measuring. "I see you want to make this difficult." He turned to the boy who watched him fearfully. "Don't worry, we won't hurt you. You've been hurt too much already." He examined the mark on the boy's forehead and others on his chin, nose, and cheek.

His gaze fell to the device on the floor, and Andara felt his hand grow clammy as he clutched her reflexively. His face was pale and he stared at the thing disbelievingly. He handed his rifle to her, knelt, and picked it up.

Closing his eyes momentarily, he cast his mind back to the last time he had seen such a thing, remembering his dream on the edge of disaster, beside the plain of shattered glass. As then, he saw himself fully mature with a strange rifle slung over his shoulder. His hands moved across this device he recognised as a weapon of extraordinary power.

He opened his eyes and looked at the altar. Now he knew why it had seemed so odd; it was made from interlocking panels, each of which held a weapon exactly like this one. There were hundreds, even a thousand. As he gazed at them incredulously, he understood the significance of his discovery immediately, and what it would mean for the way his people waged war.

Swallowing hard, he eyed the scarface with the cut hamstring. "How does it work?" he asked softly. "Don't make me experiment by pointing it at you and pressing buttons."

"Two 'ays," the man said, surrendering before the blue eyes boring into his soul. "Like you see, it can cut or 'elt or 'urn. Rotate that energy 'ack there, and it 'ecomes a disru'tor."

"A what?" Melak asked, not understanding.

"A disru'tor," the man said impatiently. "It causes 'olecular disru'-tion."

"Molecular disruption," Deke said, getting it. "Is that right?"

"Yes," the man said reluctantly.

"Why don't you use them as weapons?"

The man's expression was horrified. "Never! It's for'idden."

"How are they powered?"

The man shrugged. "Don't know," he said. "'E have used this sa'e un for centuries."

"Centuries," Andara said in wonder, putting her hand on Deke's arm.

"Those on the wall?" Deke jerked his head at the altar.

The man was scandalized. "They have never 'een used," he said. "'Ut of course they 'ork."

"Let's find out," Deke said. "Mastra, Tim, get a couple. We'll give 'em a go."

"Aye, chief," Tim said, tossing his rifle to Mastra and pulling a disrup-tor free from its panel with a clang. He pulled down a second one and returned to the group. Mastra laid the rifles on the floor, then both boys held the weapons ready, pointed at a bare patch of wall.

"Now," Deke said, spinning the power pack on the one he held and pointing it with them.

With ear-splitting whines the three weapons fired almost simultane-ously and an instant later the entire wall was gone. A heap of something like ash was all that remained.

"Ruins!" Deke muttered. "That was steel and concrete!"

"Aye," the others agreed, exchanging awed glances.

Elation rose in their minds.

"We're going to need to transport them home somehow," Deke said.

"We have enough pack animals for the job if each man carries one on his horse," Mastra said.

"Let's find Willie and see how our men are doing," Deke decided. "Meantime, we'll arm ourselves with these."

"No!" the scarface shouted, struggling against Melak's grip. "You can't!"

Deke looked contemptuously at the man. "Are you going to stop me?"

The man subsided, frightened by the expression in the tall youth's eyes.

"Bind him," Deke ordered.

Melak complied, tearing strips from the man's clothing to do so.

Then the others took disruptors from the wall and Deke handed one to Andara while he took a fresh one for himself, uncertain what the power charge would be after centuries of burning faces.

"Awkward to hold," she said, balancing the ungainly weapon in both hands.

"Aye, it needs a strap," Deke agreed. "Time enough for that. Are you all right? Can you walk?"

She nodded.

"Watch for broken glass," he warned, and led the way out of the altar room.

For thirty minutes they backtracked their way through the corridors. They saw no one, and without further incident, reached the outer stairwell which they climbed wearily, emerging into the open air and the deafening roar of soldiers.

Willie came through the crowding men and stopped in front of Deke, glancing quickly at his son and the others, nodding as he saw Andara. He met Deke's eyes and said, "Everything's secure, m'lord. Prisoners are under guard over there." He pointed, then fell silent, unsure what to say.

"Thanks, Willie," Deke said with a tired smile, and handed him a disruptor. "Have a look at this. There's a mother lode of these down there."

"What is it?" Willie asked in astonishment, turning the weapon in his hands.

Deke told him.

"By the ruins," Willie said in amazement. Again he met Deke's eyes, obviously wanting to speak, but not knowing how to begin.

"It's all right, Willie," Deke said quietly, and took Andara's hand in his. "You understand I had to go."

"Aye, m'lord," Willie said, his respect enormous.

"I'll draw you a map of the corridors so you can find the altar room. Meanwhile, have someone bring me a container of clean water and Andara's medical bag from her saddle. Also some food would be good."

"Aye, m'lord." Willie gazed at Deke, saw the crushing exhaustion, the wounds in his shoulder. For the first time he saw him as he truly was, a man in essence if not years, a consummate warrior with the powers of a sorcerer-adept.

He looked at the boys of Deke's manhood group, at Andara and all these Wolf soldiers, saw their loyalty and commitment to their youthful commander. Willie knew his own time was passing, and as he assessed objectively this young man who someday would rule over all the People, he knew the future would be in safe hands, for Deke would stop at nothing to protect and hold what was his. With great affection, the older man touched his shoulder and said, "You should get this seen to, m'lord."

Deke nodded. "Andara and I'll see to one another."

"Your father will be proud," Willie told him.

"Thanks," Deke replied.

With a last lingering look, Willie went off to see to the food and medical supplies.

"Better get yourselves something to eat and catch some rest," Deke said to Melak and the others. "Tomorrow I'll decide what to do with all these scarred folk and then we can head home."

"Can we vaporize some rat cities on the way?" Tim asked with a wicked grin, already in love with his new weapon.

"As many as you like," Deke said, returning the grin.

"I'll bring you water and fresh clothes," Mastra said to Deke and Andara.

"Thanks," Deke replied, taking the disruptor from Andara's hands and putting his arm around her shoulders. She put her arm around his waist and leaned tiredly against him. Together they walked to the little tent surrounded by the soldiers' bedrolls. The dead bodies had been removed and prepared for cremation at the opposite end of camp and everything looked familiar and even cozy to the exhausted pair. They crawled through the flaps and sat on the blankets looking at one another.

Soon Mastra arrived with a bucket of water and several clean cloths as well as fresh clothing from both their saddlebags. A moment later Tim showed up with Andara's medical bag, a sack full of food, paper, pen and ink.

"Do you need anything?" Tim asked. "Any help?"

"No, thanks," Deke said as Andara's fingers twined through his hair and he quickly sketched a map of the tunnels which he handed to Tim. "Please give this to your father."

"No problem," Tim replied.

"Any other orders tonight?" Mastra wanted to know.

"Just get some rest," Deke told them. Then, "There is something else."

"Aye?" they asked.

"Thank you," Deke said, his heart in his eyes. "I can never thank either of you enough."

"Aye," Andara agreed, her green gaze flooding once more with tears. Both boys were embarrassed by the open show of emotion.

"It was nothing," Mastra finally said.

"He lies," Tim said with a grin. "It was something! And you know what? I'm ready to go again, any time! This was a hell of an adventure, brother."

Deke smiled tiredly.

"We'll let you get squared away," Tim said, jabbing Mastra with his elbow. The two rose from the tent doorway and walked off.

Deke dipped Andara a cup of water from the bucket, watched as she drank deeply, then refilled it for himself. He drank thirstily as she examined his shoulder. "It's too dark in here for me to see," she said. "And I should check your men who need it..."

"If there were any serious injuries, Willie would have said something," he said, sticking his head outside and calling for a soldier to bring a lantern. A minute later the man handed them a small kerosene lamp. Andara thanked him, quickly igniting the wick with Deke's flint and steel.

She looked at his shoulder, touching it with her fingers. He caught her hand and turned it palm up to look at the burn on her forearm. His eyes filled as he kissed her palm and she felt her spirit scalded by his tears. He reached for her leg and she extended it so he could examine the burn on her thigh. Dipping one of the clean cloths in the cool water, he carefully laid it over the burn and Andara sighed to feel the heat diminish somewhat. He dipped another cloth and put it on her arm, unable to stop his tears as he imagined her terror and loneliness in that place beneath the earth. With yet another cloth he began to clean the wounds on her wrists and ankles while she passively allowed him to minister to her, knowing he felt responsible for what had happened.

"It wasn't your fault," she said. "There was no way for you to know."

He looked up at her, his eyes filled with sadness and empathy. "I know that," he said. "I was just thinking how frightened you must have been, and how I can't stand to think of anything scaring or harming you."

"I *was* frightened," she admitted. "I was afraid that..." She paused, unable to continue.

"What?" he asked.

"I was afraid if they hurt me you wouldn't want me any more," she whispered.

"Oh, Andara," he said, and put his arms around her. "How could you ever believe I wouldn't want you?"

"If they had done what they were about to do...."

"It wouldn't have mattered," he told her. "Any more than these mat-

366

ter," and he touched the compresses on her burns compassionately. "They would have been the same thing, wounds gotten in battle. You should wear such wounds proudly, because they're medals of honor." He kissed her softly and said, "Your courage ravishes me, don't you know that?"

Tears were falling from her eyes and she took his face between her hands, kissing him until he felt as if her whole soul was pouring through him.

"No one else would have come for me," she said, weeping hard, her voice choking as she tried to speak. "No one else would have even tried to save me from those dirty bastards."

He rocked her, helpless before her emotion, murmuring softly and stroking her hair. "Shh," he soothed. "It's all right. Soon we'll be home again with your father and mine, and Nitsa and the wolves, and with this incredible arsenal of weapons..."

She stopped weeping and raised her tear-stained face to his. "And then you'll be off again, won't you? With all these weapons, you'll be invincible."

Deke's expression was troubled as he looked at her. "Do you really want me to stay home, Andara? Will you still love me if I'm underfoot all the time, itching for the ruins?"

Aye! she wanted to shout. "You love it out here, don't you?" she asked instead, studying him thoughtfully through the prisms made by her tears.

"Aye, I do. I never thought I would; mostly the ruins are so barren and desolate, but this year...they speak to something in me. I don't know why, but I'm claustrophobic if I'm not roaming a good part of the time."

"You've always looked for adventure, Deke. It's your way."

"Do you mind?"

She began to clean the bullet holes in his shoulder, using her sensitivity to check what she couldn't see with her eyes. "These are flesh wounds," she said. "You were lucky."

"You aren't answering my question," he chided.

"I wouldn't change a single thing about you," she told him.

"I'm glad," he said and kissed her. "Nor I, you."

"Please, hold me," she said, her eyes luminous in the lantern light.

He saw her need and kissed her. The kiss deepened and they opened themselves to one another, their thoughts intertwining. "I love you, Andara," he told her huskily, filled with emotion. "I always have loved you, always will love you. Nothing will ever change the way I feel about you. Nothing will ever make me stop loving you."

"I love you, too," she whispered, "More than my life, more than my father's life." She gave herself up to his kisses, so glad to feel his hands and mouth on her that tears began to flow once again. He touched her mind inti-

367

mately, and she felt him seeking the place where the pain from her wounds was registering. In a moment he found it, and the pain was gone.

He drew her down beside him on the blankets and unbuttoned her shirt while she unfastened the straps on his forearm knives. In a minute he kicked off his boots, peeled off his socks, and unstrapped his leg knives which he tossed into a corner. His pants and underwear followed and he lay beside her with a sigh. Every muscle was ringing with pain and fatigue but he gingerly put his wounded arm under her, turning to face her so she could lie with the burn on her thigh facing the air. He moved closer and put his knee between her legs. She put her injured one over his hip and reached to caress him as he did the same for her, all the while looking into one another's eyes. Touching her breasts gently, he kissed her mouth, moving as slowly as in a dream.

When she was ready he moved against her and she shifted slightly, easing his way. In a moment the connection was made and they sighed with emotion, their tears mingling as they kissed. They pressed together and he wrapped his arms around her. Her hands were in his hair and she was kissing him when she felt his body relax against hers and his head drop back onto the blankets.

"Deke." Her voice was worried. "Are you all right?"

"Aye," he said, unable to move, completely played out. His whole body was limp and aching. "I'm sorry," he murmured.

"No matter," she said tenderly, stroking his hair, holding him even tighter.

"Are you sure?" he asked, wanting to please her but too weary and drained to do more than caress her drowsily.

"Aye," she replied. "I think I'll sleep." She brushed his cheek with her lips.

"Goodnight," he whispered, and pulled a blanket over them, draping it so her burned thigh was left uncovered. His hand moved unconsciously to her hair and he kissed her lightly.

In moments they both slept, remaining connected within and without their dreams.

Shortly afterwards the sun inched over the horizon and the soldiers began their day in silence, careful not to disturb Deke or Andara, or their friends who lay insensibly on their bedrolls.

Willie organized the removal of the weapons from the altar room, then released the prisoners to return to their underground warren. He wasn't sure what Deke would want to do about this place, but for now the inhabitants were beaten, their tunnels wrecked, and he felt certain they no longer would be a threat to anyone in the area. Half their male population had been killed in the battle when the Wolf soldiers had invaded their hole in the ground the way

Deke had suggested, attacking from a dozen entrances simultaneously. Even though the scarfaces had been waiting for them, the Wolf attack had been so overpowering, their weapons superiority so pronounced, and the men so fired up by the kidnaping, that the masked warriors quickly were subdued.

Willie shook his head, unable to understand why these people didn't use their disruptor weapons on intruders. But who could understand anything about people who had spent all these centuries living underground and performing ritual mutilations on their children?

Sighing, Willie made sure everything was ready for whenever Deke gave the order to depart. Then, tired from his busy night's activities, he stretched out on his bedroll and was soon asleep. Before long he was joined by all those soldiers not standing guard duty.

The sun climbed higher into the cloudless sky, heating the day. A short distance away a tiny dust devil spun slowly, casting its draining pall over the brilliant glitter of pulverized glass and dusty ash. The little whirlwind seemed to hover deliberately as if scrutinizing the Wolf soldiers, then, as the perimeter guards pointed and took notice, it skated away towards the west, into the deep ruins.

At noon Deke awakened, baking in the little tent, his skin drenched in sweat. He sat up cautiously, his body feeling as if it had been pummeled, and rubbed the sleep out of his eyes. He looked at the angry burn on Andara's thigh and the darkened bruise on her cheekbone, and his lips tightened. Gently. he replaced the wet compress on her leg and turned her right arm to put one there as well. She stirred as he rummaged in her medical bag, looking for antiseptic to put on her wrists and ankles.

"It's hot," she murmured, her eyes still closed.

"Very," he answered, dabbing her raw flesh with lotion which stung enough to bring her to full consciousness. When she winced he raised her hand to his lips, saying, "I'm sorry, but these need to be tended before we go."

"You have wonderful hands," she told him. "You'd have made a good healer."

He looked at his large, square hands, flexing them, and she knew what he was thinking as if he had spoken aloud. "No," she said quietly. "These are not the hands of a murderer." She kissed each in turn.

"You'd be the only one who thinks not." He clenched them into fists.

Calmly she unfolded his fingers and put her hands in his. "These are the hands of my dearest love, and I would take offense at anyone who thought or said differently." Her eyes were serious as she watched his face become incredibly emotional.

There was a sound outside the tent and Willie's voice said, "Sorry to bother you, m'lord, but are you going to want to travel today?"

Deke struggled to get himself under control. "Aye," he managed. "Please make everything ready, Willie."

"Of course," the older man said. "What do you want to do about this place?"

"I want to blow it up," he said, and saw the shock on Andara's face.

"What?" Willie wasn't sure he had heard correctly.

"Aye," Deke affirmed, "I want to blow the place up, but I won't." He breathed deeply a few times. "There are still secrets to discover here, lucky for these miserable bastards."

Andara sighed with relief, her features relaxing.

"We'll leave a hundred men to search the place thoroughly, then send back artisans to see if they can figure out what makes everything work."

"Good thinking," Willie agreed, and Andara heard the relief in his voice as well.

"I'll be out in a few minutes," Deke said.

"Take your time. It'll take a while to get organized." Willie walked off to select the garrison force.

When he was gone, Deke continued to work on Andara's abraded wrists, wrapping them in clean bandages, then moved down to her ankles. He kissed the inside of her calf before applying the stinging antibiotic, and soon, satisfied the wounds were clean and uninfected, he wrapped them as well.

"What should we do about these?" he asked, gesturing to her burns.

"Light coverings only," she said. "There's some ointment in my bag that should help. I'll have to be careful not to get the sun on them."

He handed her the bag and she found the ointment which he applied with care.

"Are you all right?" he asked in a low tone.

She knew he wasn't talking about her injuries. "Aye," she said. "I think so. Would you really have destroyed this place if there was nothing left to find?"

He sighed, wrapping the burns lightly after placing single layers of bandages on each. When he was finished, he put everything away in her bag and held her hands in his.

She watched him think about what she had asked, understanding it was a complicated question for him right now.

"I want to bury them alive for what they did to you," he said eventually. "I can't describe how much a part of me wants to see them obliterated." He paused. "But even though I want to kill them, I probably only would destroy

370

this place. I may still do that when I know everything about it."

"What about the people?" Andara held her breath.

"Relocation," he said quietly. "Give some of the young ones a chance to live a real life under the sky."

"Is that a choice you can make for them?" she asked.

He shrugged painfully, his shoulder hurting him. "It's a choice the victor always gets to make," he replied. "If we were beaten, someone else would make that choice for us."

"Does that make it right?"

"Probably not," he admitted. "But these people...they must be mentally deranged to do what they do to themselves."

"And you want to heal them, is that it?"

Deke smiled with rueful self-awareness as her questions forced him to evaluate his behavior in a moral sense. "I only want to conquer them," he said, "And take whatever they have that would be useful to us. Except for the children and women, I'd just as soon consign all these scarfaces to the flames."

"They didn't kill me," she pointed out.

"They were going to," he said grimly.

"Rape isn't terminal," she told him.

His eyes met hers. "You said you know what soldiers do on campaigns. I've heard of women being raped to death. Fifteen men might have been enough to do it."

Andara shivered though the tent was sweltering.

His arms went around her in a stranglehold and he buried his face against her neck. "Just their intent to do it is enough."

"Those fifteen already paid," she said, holding him.

"They were acting under orders," he said in a muffled voice. "I hold the whole goddamned community responsible, and I'll have to think about what they can do to make amends."

"Please, be careful," she whispered. "You hold such power over their lives."

He moved away slightly and took her face in his hands. "What do you want me to do?"

"I think I'd like it if they really could be healed," she told him.

He stared into her eyes.

"Aye. They have souls, too. Maybe the Universe has given you the gifts it has so you can do more than conquer your enemies."

"You want me to convert them as well, is that it?" he asked. "But I'm not interested in their souls. Their souls are their own affair. If they once had behaved decently...they've had chance after chance to make friendly contact, not only with us, but other people as well, and each time they've chosen blind attack."

"All the more reason to enlighten them," she replied.

"All the more reason to destroy them. They can gain enlightenment in another life, when they've learned the lessons from this one; when they've learned that actions have consequences."

"And you'll be their teacher?"

"Aye," he said, and for a moment she saw the darkness shifting behind his eyes. "I'll always be their teacher."

Andara shivered again and held him tight. He returned her embrace, kissing her lightly.

"Let's get dressed," he said after a minute.

"All right," she agreed.

When they had pulled on their clothes and gathered their belongings, they crawled out of the tent together.

"You're upset with me," he said when they stood in the harsh sunlight.

"No," she replied. "I don't understand you. But I will," she added, and looked up at his face with a smile. "I just need a little more time."

He smiled back at her. "We have all the time in the world," he said, his love for her shining from his eyes.

Soon those soldiers remaining behind to ransack the underground community waved farewell to the riders heading back to Spring Camp. Several disruptors were left with them in case of emergencies. Deke knew that a few men armed with the new weapons would be the equivalent of divisions.

He reined Micmac closer to where Andara rode on Romeo, pulling alongside until their stirrups bumped and their legs touched. She turned to smile at him, remembering the first time that had happened, and thinking that his most casual touch had the power to give her goosebumps. His eyes met hers and she knew he was remembering the same thing when he reached out and took her hand, weaving his fingers through hers.

The afternoon lengthened their shadows as they rode across the dust and crushed debris. Occasionally Tim led the other boys of his manhood group on a gleeful rat hunt in the surrounding ruins, happily vaporizing several communities of the pests lying in their path.

That evening they picked a quiet place to camp and the night passed without incident. At dawn they were on their way again, and by midday reached the oasis where they stopped to make camp early on the lakeshore. While the soldiers secured the perimeter, Deke and Andara swam and bathed their wounds thoroughly. Afterwards, they dressed in the last of their clean clothes and sat under a tree in the shade while the men took their turns in the lake and their cheerful jokes and curses filled the air.

Deke sat with a small basin of water between his knees and made lather with soap and a brush which he rubbed all over his face. Using a straight razor with edge freshly stropped, he peered into the little mirror he held in his left hand and carefully scraped at the red-gold bristles that weekly seemed to sprout more densely on his skin. Andara observed with an enigmatic expression, thinking that soon he would be fully mature, and wondering what it would be like to make love to him when he was. He looked up and saw her watchful gaze, touching her thoughts with curiosity. He caught the tail end of her musing and smiled.

"It'll be the same," he told her, stretching his neck to work under his chin. "Except better."

Startled, she laughed aloud. "Why better?"

"Because it gets better every time. In another few years, it'll be so good we'll never do anything else. I'll give up soldiering, you'll give up being a witch, and all we'll do is make love from sunup to sunup."

Chuckling earthily, she squeezed his thigh. "I can't wait."

He jumped at her touch and nicked himself with the blade. "Ouch," he said, dabbing at the blood.

"I'm sorry," she said contritely, squeezing him again more intimately.

"You have to let me finish," he said, his eyes growing warm. "I haven't shaved in a week."

"Let me," she said, taking the razor from him and setting the mirror and basin on the grass. She straddled his lap, then sat down while he rested his hands on her hips and raised his eyebrows. She turned his face to one side and carefully began to shave his cheek, the tip of her tongue clutched between her teeth as she concentrated. He wiggled a little under her and moved his hands to her buttocks, squeezing them through the taut material of her pants.

"Hold still," she told him.

"You're not making it easy," he said, very aware of her warm body. He shifted again, his pants feeling entirely too tight. "What'll the men think?" he wondered aloud as she deliberately pressed against him and worked with the razor on his beard. "There's something dangerous about this," he said a little nervously as the slick sharpness of the blade slid along his skin at the same moment she rubbed herself on him.

"Don't move," she said, her breathing languid.

"You're going to make me go right here," he groaned suddenly, his eyes glazing.

"In your pants?" She was amused.

"Aye, you hussy," he said, trying to look around her and see if anyone was watching them.

She turned his face the other way and began shaving that side. "What a shame," she said, moving on him again, even more suggestively.

He put his hands under her shirt on her breasts, watching her face change as the balance of power shifted. She stopped shaving him for a second and drew a deep breath. "Am I distracting you?" he asked with a playful grin.

"Let me finish or you'll look like a billy goat."

"Not much of a threat under the circumstances," he said, his fingertips brushing her nipples until they were erect and plainly visible through her shirt. Her breathing quickened. "You'd better hurry," he told her.

"Aye," she agreed, finishing his cheek and working on his chin and upper lip. In a minute she was done and wiped away the excess soap with her hand, admiring her work. She caressed him and said, "Now you feel the way you did the first time you kissed me."

"I was hard then, too," he said, and kissed her mouth.

"Were you? I didn't know."

"Aye," and he stood up with her, setting her on her feet. "But I hid it under a towel." He grinned. "I'm sure your father knew."

"No wonder he worked so hard to keep us from being alone together," she laughed.

He laughed with her. "Do you suppose everyone'll know what we're up to if we go into our tent?"

"I think they've known all along." She brushed her hair away from her face.

"I think so, too. But it wasn't broad daylight."

"True, but Melak is probably prowling around somewhere just out of sight, so we can't do it here."

"Sometimes he's too devoted," Deke chuckled.

Andara dumped the basin into the grass and handed it and the shaving kit to him. "Let's at least move the tent into the shade so we can pretend to be napping."

"Good idea," he said, holding the basin in front of him as they walked. Andara noticed this and began to laugh again. He saw where her eyes were and grinned. "Until we began making love, I spent half my time carrying things this way," he told her. "More."

"Is that normal?" she asked.

"Oh, aye," he replied.

"You mean all the boys walk around that way?"

"Books, towels, plates, you name it, we use 'em."

"Thank goodness that doesn't happen to girls."

374

"Have you looked at the front of your shirt lately?" he asked with a comical expression.

She looked down and quickly folded her arms across her chest.

Now both were laughing. In a few moments they reached their tent, dragged it away to a shady area nearby, and tumbled inside. Their laughter was still plainly audible as Mastra and Tim walked over, planning to join them for lunch. The two boys stopped outside and listened for a few seconds as the laughter changed to passionate murmurs and grunts of pleasure.

"Do you think they ever get enough?" Mastra wondered.

"What're you going to be doing when we get home?" Tim asked with a grin.

"Same thing you are," Mastra replied, grinning back. "But next time, let's try a different place. I'm ready for a little variety."

Tim's grin broadened. "I know a place where the women actually like it," he confided. "Of course, it's more expensive, but these women tell you the truth so it's possible to learn something."

"That's good," said Mastra. "I'd like to be able to make a girl do that," and he jerked his head towards the tent where Andara could be heard crying out excitedly.

"Aye, it feels better when the woman is enjoying herself," Tim agreed. "Much better."

"Then he's probably in paradise right now," Mastra said with a laugh. "Now I know what everyone's been talking about."

"You don't know the half of it," Tim told him. "Let's leave; I can't stand it any longer. I'm getting stiff just listening to them."

"Aye," Mastra said as they walked off. "Now, tell me about this new place...."

In the morning before they departed, Deke led Andara back to the lake for a quick swim. They splashed happily for a while, then she approached him and examined his shoulder.

"This looks better already," she told him. "You heal quickly."

"It's you," he told her. "You heal me quickly."

She put her arms around him and he caressed her under the water where no guard could see. "I can't wait to get home," she murmured, his touch making her dizzy.

"Don't you like it here? It's so pretty."

"I want to be alone with you, really alone."

"Oh? And here I thought you were getting used to an audience."

She put her hand on him. "Now you won't be able to come out of the water," she said a moment later.

"Oh, you are a wench," he said as she turned him loose and walked out of the lake. He watched as she dressed, then sat down on the grassy shore. "This could take a while," he told her.

"I'm not going anywhere," she said, her eyes laughing at him.

"To leave your lover in this condition..." He smiled, glad to see her happiness. "Well, it smacks of torture."

"Aye," she agreed.

"I might have to take care of this myself," he said.

"You wouldn't do that here, would you?"

"Watch me," he said.

"How did you get so crude?" she asked, her gaze heating up at the idea.

"Come back in here," he begged. "Or at least give me my pants."

She took pity on him and walked to the water's edge, tossing him his underwear. He waded out and put them on, then grabbed her, pulling her tight against his body.

"When we get home," she said, smiling as he kissed her, "I may take you up on that."

"On what?" he asked, his breath warm in her ear.

"Watching you," she answered with a little gasp as he put her hand between his legs.

"I'm willing, under one condition," he said.

"What condition?" She moved away a little and looked at him.

"That you let me watch you, too."

Her eyes were very green. "I've never done that before," she said.

"Aye, I know."

She kissed his lips again. "Let's ride fast today," she said.

He nodded, and kissed her once more. Then he released her and pulled on his pants while she admired his lithe muscularity and naturally graceful movements, repressing her desire to touch him again.

Soon the riders were heading east away from the oasis. The sun rose higher, hotter, and brighter until it seemed to fill the sky. Occasionally one of the boys in Deke's manhood group cantered away to destroy a cave rat nest, but otherwise the day passed without incident.

They camped that night in the ruins, setting up perimeter defenses by sunset. When the darkness was complete, Deke walked with Andara to the periphery and they gazed out together, looking at the stars, listening to the small sounds of night creatures rustling through the sand and dirt. They put their arms around each other and Deke opened his mind to her, spreading his awareness across the vast, tumbled wreckage from another age, now layered over with dust. He heard the howls of his wolves coming nearer, and impulsively, as their thoughts made contact with his, lifted Andara in his arms, centered himself, and passed like a wraith through the perimeter. He moved easily until they were out of sight of the guards, then set her on her feet. Her aura permeated his and their eyes met. They undressed, leaving only their boots on. Deke rebuckled his weapons belt around his waist and seconds later, the wolves bounded out of the darkness, surrounding them in a heaving, joyous mob of furry bodies.

Andara stood transfixed, watching the Alpha thrust his muzzle into Deke's hand while he scratched and petted the huge wolf affectionately. In a moment the Alpha walked to her, sniffed her thoroughly, and licked her fingers. She looked at Deke, her eyes showing her wonder, then, as the wolves filled their minds with images of them running beneath the slowly turning stars, she heard their clear thought inviting her to join them.

Deke caught her hand and instantly her awareness joined with his to perceive the world as only adepts could, completely, filled with detail and nuance invisible to physical eyes. Together they saw the energy glowing from everything around them, the colorful emanations from the wolves, the light that leapt from their flesh where their hands met. Immersed in the mythic presence of the past that had defined them and the mysterious present which sustained them, they felt their connection to the Earth and Universe as a vital bonding that dwarfed them even as it filled them with exaltation.

This night, in ruins with which Deke was familiar, they ran with the wolves for hours, stopping when Andara got tired, continuing while the moon rose and colored the desert silver.

In the hour before dawn when the emerging light changed the rich shadings of night to the sharper edges of morning, they reluctantly returned to their clothing and dressed. Andara put images of joy and thanks into the minds of the pack, and they bumped her affectionately before surrounding Deke and exchanging fast and esoteric thoughts with him until she lost the thread. She could see the regret on his face as he stroked the Alpha's head and gazed into his eyes. Finally, catching the farewell images of wolves returning to their den site, Andara watched as the pack disappeared from view, their yips and howls retreating into the ruins.

Once again Deke took her in his arms, crossed the perimeter without a soul seeing them, and carried her to their tent.

There, suffused with the aesthetic beauty of their experience, they made love in silence, with only the smooth sounds of their bodies moving against one another and their deep breathing audible on the morning air.

When the sun was up and the soldiers began to make preparations to leave, they came outside and ate breakfast with the others, slowly beginning to return to normal consciousness.

Soon they were mounted again, riding beneath the strengthening sun, with scouts sending their flickering messages back and forth, reassuring the columns that all was well.

Now Deke became filled with the anticipation of their homecoming. Eagerly, he scanned the ruins, his eyes noting the landmarks that told him how close they were getting. When they passed beneath the ghostly, rusting skeleton of an ancient highway system, he actually fidgeted with excitement.

By late afternoon they had left the ruins behind and were riding through rolling grassland criss-crossed by small streams. Shortly thereafter, they could see the sentinels wave to them as they passed in towards the picturesque sprawl of their tent city, and home.

Half an hour later the riders made their noisy way along the main thoroughfare of Spring Camp while children and dogs ran yelling and barking alongside, and the People of the Wolf crowded to welcome them.

Deke rode directly to his father's tent, and when Barr and Nitsa emerged through the flap, sprang down from Micmac's back. He reached up to catch Andara as she jumped down from Romeo, and holding her hand, approached his father.

Barr grabbed him in his usual bear hug, and Deke grinned, returning the embrace, for the first time lifting his father off the ground with the strength of it. Then he gave Nitsa a hug while Barr did the same for Andara. Hawk appeared and kissed Andara happily, while around them people greeted their returning men.

When the immediate furor died down a little, Barr smiled at his son, his eyes taking in the shoulder wounds. He saw the bruise on Andara's face, the bandages on her wrists and arm, and wondered what had happened. He noticed there were fewer soldiers returning than had departed, but said nothing, certain Deke would explain in time.

Then he spotted the strange object slung over Deke's uninjured shoulder by a leather strap.

"So, my son," he said, as was his wont, "What have you brought your old father back from the ruins?"

Deke looked out across the men, women, and children who had gathered, and his eyes touched those of his soldiers, particularly Mastra, Tim, and Melak. He unslung the disruptor, and put it in Barr's hands.

"The world, Papa," he said softly. Then, with greater firmness, his arms going around Andara, "I've brought you the world."

END OF BOOK ONE

To be continued

Acknowledgments

Thanks to Carlos Casteneda, and his work "The Teachings of Don Juan," for his invaluable information about Native American sorcery, and the brujo *way of knowledge.*

Thanks as well to Sy Levy for his beautiful backcover blurb.

Special thanks to all my friends, family, and spirit guides whose constant support and encouragement made *Ruin* possible.

The Author

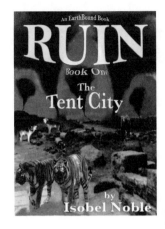

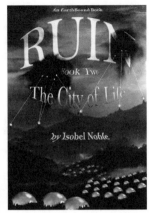

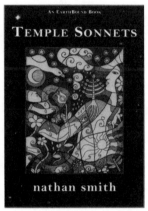

ORDER FORM

RUIN: The Tent City $16.66 ea.
No. of copies_____   Total enclosed $_____

RUIN: The City of Life $28.00 ea.
No. of copies_____   Total enclosed $_____

Temple Sonnets $12.00 ea.
No. of copies_____   Total enclosed $_____

**Send to: EARTHBOUND BOOKS   **Check or Money Order Only
          P.O. Box 549   **Add $8.00 for S & H
          North Egremont, MA 01252

Name:_____ Tel.# _____
Street:_____ Apt.# _____
City, State, Zip:_____, _____ _____